New York Times bestseller
A Read with Jenna book club pick as featured on *Today*
A *New York Times* Editors' Choice
A *New York Times* Group Text pick
A LibraryReads pick
A 2022 Most Anticipated Book:

Glamour • *W Magazine* • *Essence* • *Parade* • PopSugar • Fortune.com • The Everygirl • *Town & Country* • *Good Housekeeping* • BookBub • *Marie Claire* • Goodreads • *Vulture* • *BookRiot* • *Bustle*

"*Black Cake* is a delectable read. Wilkerson's scenes unfold as quick-paced vignettes, immersing readers into the minds and environments of the characters. . . . The novel allows for a full reflection on how one's self-identity can change in an instant. Wilkerson's intent is clear: We are left to think about the things we inherit from our ancestors—physical traits, mental and emotional strife, even cultural attachments, like a beloved recipe that has the power to bring us home, if only in our minds." —*The Washington Post*

"A sprawling, vibrant, second-chance-celebrating debut. Wilkerson approaches her plot like a mad chef, grabbing ingredients from all over the world, slicing and dicing with abandon, tossing characters and palm fronds and a few drops of rum into a pot and letting it all come to a simmer. She isn't measuring, she's eyeballing, as confident cooks do." —*The New York Times*

"A delicious debut." —*People*

"[A] ravishing debut novel . . . [the] juxtaposition of contrasting emotions—humor and devastation, glee and fear, and more—is characteristic of Wilkerson's novelistic style, and one reason it is so affecting." —*Oprah Daily*

"*Black Cake* is a character-driven, multigenerational story that's meant to be savored, just like a piece of Eleanor's cake. It's thought-provoking and poignant."
—*Time*

"There's much more to recommend here, including weighty themes about race, identity and protecting the environment, as well as the power of family recipes to convey love without words, but the fun is in the reading. *Black Cake* is a satisfying literary meal, heralding the arrival of a new novelist to watch."
—*Associated Press*

"A thrilling debut novel about sibling ties and hidden family history."
—*Glamour*

"As delicious as the titular dessert."
—*W Magazine*

"A stellar first-time entry from a talented new writer that's full of food, surfing and rich patois."
—*BET*

"Crafted with delicate intention and textured with a blend of perspectives."
—*Vulture*

"Wilkerson explores the nuances of racial identity and betrayal in a powerful novel."
—*British Vogue*

"Wilkerson's debut brings together two estranged siblings after the death of their mother, Eleanor. . . . This engrossing read is highly recommended."
—*Library Journal*, starred review

"A beautifully poignant debut novel . . . Wilkerson uses one Caribbean American family's extraordinary tale to probe universal issues of identity and how the lives we live and the choices we make leave 'a trail of potential consequences' that pass down through generations. Memorable, fully developed characters ground a story that spans decades and continents." —*Booklist*, starred review

"Wilkerson debuts with a shining family saga that stretches from the 1960s Caribbean to present-day Southern California. . . . Readers will adore this highly accomplished effort from a talented new writer."
—*Publishers Weekly*, starred review

"Fans of family dramas by Ann Patchett, Brit Bennett and Karen Joy Fowler should take note. *Black Cake* marks the launch of a writer to watch, one who masterfully plumbs the unexpected depths of the human heart." —*BookPage*, starred review

"Wilkerson is clearly an author to watch. There is plenty to savor in this ambitious and accomplished debut." —*Kirkus Reviews*

"Exquisite and expansive, *Black Cake* took a hold of me from the first page and didn't let go. This is a novel about the formation and reformation of a family, and the many people, places, and events that can shape our inheritances without our knowing. A gripping, poignant debut from an important, new voice. How lucky we are to read Charmaine Wilkerson."
—Naima Coster, *New York Times* bestselling author of *What's Mine and Yours*

"*Black Cake* is a beautiful, deeply resonant story of children trying to understand the mother they have lost. Charmaine Wilkerson transports you across the decades and the globe accompanied by complex, wonderfully drawn characters. She has managed to tell a story that is as meaningful as it is delicious. At turns delightfully juicy and then stunningly wise, *Black Cake* is a winner."
—Taylor Jenkins Reid, *New York Times* bestselling author of *Malibu Rising*

"I was instantly taken in by this multigenerational tale of identity, family, and the lifelong push and pull of home. This novel has a tremendous heart at its center, and I felt its beat on every page. . . . What an extraordinary debut."

—Mary Beth Keane, *New York Times* bestselling
author of *Ask Again, Yes*

"*Black Cake* has all the ingredients of the tastiest stories: secrets, romance, danger, and a cast of characters so real you want to scream at them one moment and hug them the next. I felt nearly breathless while reading Eleanor's truth—as if I were right there in the room with Byron and Benny, wholly immersed in their mother's tragedies and triumphs."

—Dawnie Walton, author of *The Final Revival of Opal & Nev*

"So beautifully written, I'm struggling to believe it's a debut. The cake is the glue that holds all the layers together and the scenes are so well drawn I could almost taste the cake, feel the warm sea on my skin. My heart broke and was put back together. Bravo."

—Nikki May, author of *Wahala*

"With fantasy-like sensual detail, Wilkerson slips through time and place to explore the emotional weight of family traditions passed down through generations to heirs challenged to find their own emotional truths."
—Lucy Sanna, author of *The Cherry Harvest*

BLACK CAKE

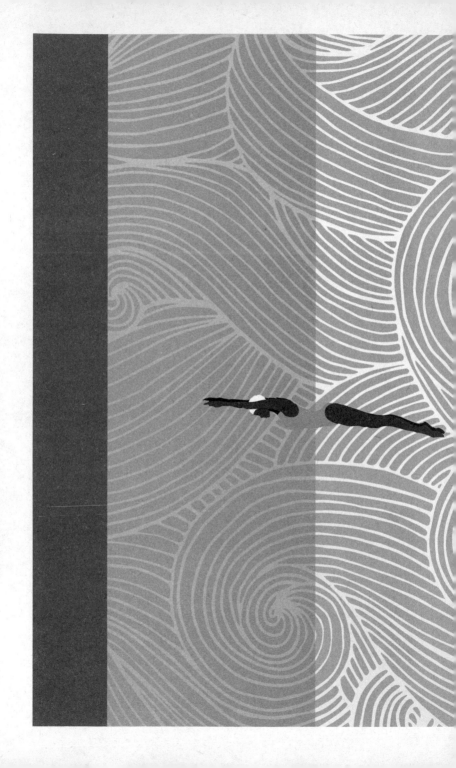

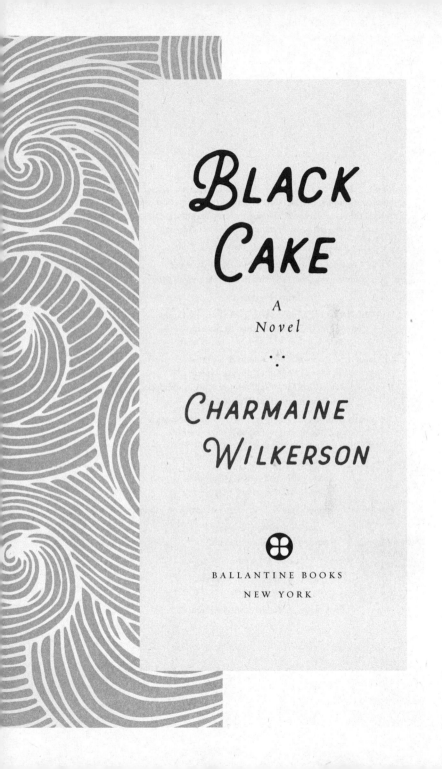

Black Cake

A
Novel

∴

Charmaine Wilkerson

BALLANTINE BOOKS
NEW YORK

2022 Ballantine Books Trade Paperback Edition

Copyright © 2022 by Charmaine Wilkerson
Book club guide copyright © 2022 by Penguin Random House LLC

All rights reserved.

Published in the United States by Ballantine Books, an imprint of Random House, a division of Penguin Random House LLC, New York.

BALLANTINE is a registered trademark and the colophon is a trademark of Penguin Random House LLC.

RANDOM HOUSE BOOK CLUB and colophon are trademarks of Penguin Random House LLC.

Originally published in hardcover in the United States by Ballantine Books, an imprint of Random House, a division of Penguin Random House LLC, in 2022.

ISBN 978-0-593-35835-1
Ebook ISBN 978-0-593-35834-4
Target ISBN 978-0-593-59450-6

Printed in the United States of America on acid-free paper

randomhousebooks.com
randomhousebookclub.com

2 4 6 8 9 7 5 3 1

*Title-page and part-title art assembled
from iStock images*

Book design by Barbara M. Bachman

For my parents.

All four of them.

BLACK CAKE

PROLOGUE

*T*HEN

—

1965

—

H E SHOULD HAVE KNOWN IT WOULD COME TO THIS. HE SHOULD have known the day that *hak gwai* wife of his ran away from home. Should have known the day he saw his daughter swimming in the bay as a storm bore down on her. Should have known when his parents dragged him to this island and changed their names. He stood at the water's edge, now, watching the waves crash white against the rocks, waiting for his daughter's body to wash ashore.

A policeman beckoned to him. The policeman was a girl. He'd never seen one of those before. She was holding a fluff of white fabric, his daughter's wedding dress, smeared with black cake and lilac icing. She must have dropped the cake on herself as she jumped up from the table. He remembered a clattering of plates, the splintering of glass on the tile floor, someone crying out. When he looked toward his daughter, she was gone and her satin-covered shoes lay strewn on the lawn outside like tiny capsized boats.

PART ONE

∵

Now

—

2018

—

S HE'S HERE.

Byron hears the elevator doors peel open. His first instinct is to rush toward his sister and embrace her. But when Benny leans in to hug him, Byron pushes her away, then turns to knock on the door to the attorney's office. He feels Benny put a hand on his arm. He shakes it free. Benny stands there, her mouth open, but says nothing. And what right does she have to say *anything*? Byron hasn't seen Benny in eight years. And now, their ma is gone for good.

What does Benny expect? She took a family argument and turned it into a cold war. Never mind all that talk about societal rejection and discrimination and *whatnot*. It seems to Byron that whatever kind of problem you have in this world, you can find someone to show you understanding. And times are changing. There's even been a study in the news recently about people like Benny.

People like Benny.

The study says it can be a lonely road for people like her. But she won't be getting any sympathy from Byron, no. Benedetta Bennett gave up that luxury years ago when she turned her back on her family, even though she claims it was the other way around. At least she showed up this time. Six years ago, Byron and his mother sat in the church across from his father's coffin up in L.A. County, waiting for

Benny to arrive, but no Benny. Later, Byron thought he saw his sister skirting the burial grounds in the back of a car. She'd be there any minute, he thought. But, still, no Benny. Only a text from her later, saying *I'm sorry*. Then silence. For months at a time. Then years.

As each year went by, he was less certain that Benny had been there that day or that he'd ever had a sister to begin with.

That he'd ever had a chubby, squiggle-headed baby girl following him around the house.

That she'd ever cheered him on at the national meets.

That he'd ever heard her voice sailing across the auditorium as he closed his hand around his doctoral diploma.

That he'd ever *not* felt the way he does right now. Orphaned and pissed as hell.

Benny

—

HER MOTHER'S ATTORNEY OPENS THE DOOR AND BENNY LOOKS past him, half expecting to see her ma sitting in the room. But it's only Benny and Byron now, and Byron won't even look at her.

The lawyer is saying something about a message from their mother but Benny can't concentrate, she's still looking at Byron, at the bits of gray in his hair that didn't use to be there. What's with the pushing, anyway? The man is forty-five years old, not ten. In all these years, her big brother has never shoved her, never hit her, not even when she was little and tended to pounce and bite like a puppy.

Benny's first memory of Byron: They are sitting on the couch, she is settled under her brother's arm, and Byron is reciting adventure stories to her from a book. His feet can already touch the floor. Byron stops to fluff Benny's hair with his fingers, to pull on her earlobes, to pinch her nostrils shut, to tickle her until she is breathless with laughter, until she is dying of happiness.

The Message

—

THEIR MOTHER HAS LEFT THEM A MESSAGE, THE LAWYER SAYS. The lawyer's name is Mr. Mitch. He's talking to Byron and Benny as though he's known them all their lives, though Byron can only recall meeting him one other time, when his ma needed help getting around town after her accident last winter, the one his friend Cable insisted wasn't an accident. Byron walked his mother up to Mr. Mitch's office, then went back outside to wait for her in the car. He was sitting there watching some kids skateboard down the broad, buff-toned sidewalks between one high-end chain store and the next, when a police officer rapped on his side window.

This kind of thing had happened to Byron so often over the course of his adult life that sometimes he forgot to be nervous. But most times, whenever he was approached or pulled over by an officer, he slid down into that space between one heartbeat and the next where he could hear his blood crashing through his body, a waterfall carrying centuries of history with it, threatening to wipe out the ground on which he stood. His research, his books and social media following, the speaking engagements, the scholarship he wanted to fund, all of it, could be gone in a split second of misunderstanding.

Only later, after the officer had opened the trunk of his patrol car and come back with a copy of Byron's latest book (*Could he have an autograph?*), did it occur to Byron that a grown man of any color, sitting alone in a car watching pre-adolescents skateboard up and down the sidewalk, could elicit a reasonable degree of suspicion. All right, he could see that, it wasn't always about him being a black man. Though, mostly, it was.

"Let me just warn you," Mr. Mitch is saying now. "About your mother. You need to be prepared."

Prepared?

Prepared for what? Their mother is already gone.

His ma.

He doesn't see how anything after that is going to make much of a difference.

B and B

—

THERE'S AN ENTIRE FILE BOX LABELED *ESTATE OF ELEANOR BENNETT*. Mr. Mitch pulls out a brown paper envelope with their mother's handwriting on it and puts it on the desk in front of Byron. Benny shifts her seat closer to Byron's and leans in to look. Byron removes his hand but leaves the packet where Benny can see it. Their ma has addressed the envelope to *B and B*, the moniker she liked to use whenever she wrote or spoke to them together.

B-and-B notes were usually pinned to the fridge door with a magnet. *B and B, there's some rice and peas on the stove. B and B, I hope you left your sandy shoes at the door. B and B, I love my new earrings, thank you!*

Ma only called them Byron or Benny when she was speaking with one sibling or the other, and she only called Benny *Benedetta* when she was upset.

Benedetta, what about this report card? Benedetta, don't talk to your father that way. Benedetta, I need to talk to you.

Benedetta, please come home.

Their mother left a letter, Mr. Mitch says, but most of their mother's last message is contained in an audio file that took her more than eight hours, over four days, to record.

"Go ahead," Mr. Mitch says, nodding at the packet.

Byron cuts open the envelope and shakes out its contents, a USB drive and a handwritten note. He reads the note out loud. It's so typically *Ma*.

B and B, there's a small black cake in the freezer for you. Don't throw it out.

Black cake. Byron catches himself smiling. Ma and Dad used to share a slice of cake every year to mark their anniversary. It wasn't the original wedding cake, they said, not anymore. Ma would make a new one every five years or so, one layer only, and put it in the freezer. Still, she insisted that any black cake, steeped as it was in rum and port, could have lasted the full length of their marriage.

I want you to sit down together and share the cake when the time is right. You'll know when.

Benny covers her mouth with one hand.

Love, Ma.

Benny starts to cry.

Benny

——

BENNY HASN'T CRIED IN YEARS. AT LEAST, SHE HADN'T, UNTIL last week, after being fired from her afternoon gig back in New York. At first, she thought her boss was being crabby because he'd seen Benny thumbing her smartphone while taking customer calls. There was a rule against that sort of thing, but there was a message from her mother. Four words that she just couldn't shake out of her head.

Actually, the message had been in her voicemail for a month already, but just then, Benny had been looking at her cellphone, wondering what to do. She hadn't really spoken to her mother in years. Not talking to your own ma for that long took a certain kind of gall, Benny knew. But so did not standing by your own daughter when she'd needed you most.

For years, it had been easier for Benny simply to stay away, to not respond to the rare message from back home, to steel herself against every birthday and holiday away from her family, to tell herself that this was a form of self-care. In her weaker moments, she'd plug in the old digital photo frame that she kept under some sketchbooks in a desk drawer and watch as a series of smiling faces that she'd thought would always be part of her life popped onto the screen, one after the other, then off again.

One of Benny's favorite pics showed her with Byron and Dad, arms linked and dressed in black tie for some event, the kind of fundraiser or tribute or gathering of lawyers at which her father had often taken the lectern. The resemblance between the three of them was striking, even to Benny, who had grown up with this fact. And from the identical light in their eyes, you could tell who had been taking the photograph. Her ma.

Benny's boss was raising his voice at her now.

"You weren't doing your job," he said.

Benny slipped her phone into the pocket of her cardigan.

"Your job is to read from the goddamned script. Your job is not to volunteer social commentary on the durability of consumer electronics!"

Oh, that. Not the phone.

By the time Benny figured out what her supervisor was talking about, she was out of a job.

Benny was still dry-eyed when she walked out of the call center with the only personal items she'd kept in her shared cubicle: a coffee mug with stained, fractured insides and a fringy-looking plant. What kind of plant it was, Benny could not recall, but it had never let her down. Nothing seemed to deter it, not a lack of water, not fluorescent lighting, not the plastic-smelling office air, not her supervisor's noxious language. Every once in a while, she would lift the plant's tiny stems with her fingertips and wipe the dust from its fronds with a damp cloth, just so.

It was fifteen minutes before Benny realized that she had taken the wrong bus. She got off at the next stop and found herself standing in front of an old coffee shop with fake-pine garlands and fake-velvet bows on its doors. She hadn't realized this kind of place still existed in the city. At the sight of the spray-on-imitation-frost lettering spelling out *Happy Holidays* across the plate-glass window, at the thought of yet another year without having a coffee shop of her own to run (though with less kitsch), at the sight of a young father inside the café kneeling down to button his child into a puffy, lilac-colored jacket and tucking her dark hair into the lilac fur-lined hood, Benny burst into tears. Benny had never liked lilac.

The Recipe

Recording

M R. MITCH TAKES THE MEMORY STICK WITH ELEANOR Bennett's recording and inserts it into his desktop computer. Eleanor's children lean forward in their seats when they hear her voice. Mr. Mitch wills himself to keep a placid face, breathes deep and slow. This is not personal, this is professional. Families need their attorneys to stay unruffled.

B and B, Mr. Mitch is recording this for me. My hand is not so steady anymore and I have a lot to say. I wanted to talk to you both in person but, at this point, I'm not sure I'll get to see you two together again.

Benny and Byron both shift in their seats.

You are stubborn children, but you are good children.

Mr. Mitch keeps his eyes focused on the notepad on his desk, but he can still feel the air shifting in the room. A stiffening of backs, a squaring of shoulders.

B and B, promise me you'll try to get along. You can't afford to lose each other.

Benny stands up. *Here we go.* Mr. Mitch pauses the recording.

"I don't need to hear this," Benny says.

Mr. Mitch nods. Waits a moment. "It's what your mother wanted," he says.

"Can't you make me a copy of the file?" Benny says. "Make me a copy. I'll take it back to New York."

"Your mother expressly requested that you listen to this together, all the way through, in my presence. But you know, we don't have to stay in the office. If you prefer, we could stop now and I could bring the recording to your mother's house at a later time. Would you like that?"

"No," Byron says. "I want to hear this now." Benny scowls at Byron, but he doesn't look at her.

"Your mother was very specific," Mr. Mitch says. "We need to listen to this together, so I'm happy to continue this when both of you can make yourselves available." He opens an agenda on his desk. "I could come by the house late this afternoon or tomorrow morning."

"I don't see how it's going to make a difference to Ma now, anyway," Benny says. Still standing, she looks down at Mr. Mitch with steady eyes but her voice wobbles on the word *Ma*.

"I think it will make a difference to you and your brother," Mr. Mitch says. "There are things your mother wanted you to hear right away, things you need to know."

Benny lowers her head, stays there for a minute, huffs out a breath. "Better this afternoon," she says. "I'll be leaving town right after the funeral." Benny looks at Byron one more time but he keeps his eyes fixed on the desk. She walks out of the room without saying goodbye, her blondish Afro puff quivering as she stomps across the waiting room, pulls the door open, and steps into the darkened hallway.

Mr. Mitch hears the faint chime of the elevator down the hall and Byron stands up.

"Well, I guess I'll see you later," Byron says. "Thank you."

Mr. Mitch gets up to shake his hand. Byron's phone buzzes and by the time he reaches the door, his cellphone is already clapped to his ear. There must have been a time, Mr. Mitch thinks, when Byron was just a kid, trawling the beach, more interested in putting a conch shell to his ear than anything like a phone.

"My son listens to the sea for a living, can you imagine?" Eleanor said to Mr. Mitch one day, back in the days when her husband Bert was still alive and they were at some lawyers' event together.

"It's actually a job!" Bert quipped. They had a good chuckle together over that one. Eleanor and Bert had a way of doing that, being funny together.

Maybe, when all this was over, Mr. Mitch could ask Byron about his latest project, about how the institute he works for is helping to map the seafloor. The oceans are a challenge, Mr. Mitch thinks. And what about a person's life? How do you make a map of that? The borders people draw between themselves. The scars left along the ground of one's heart. What will Byron have to say about that, once he and his sister have heard their mother's message?

Homecoming

—

BENNY LETS HERSELF INTO HER MOTHER'S HOUSE THROUGH the back door and stands in the kitchen, listening. She hears her mother's voice, hears her own laughter, smells clove in the air, but sees only a dishcloth folded over a chair, two prescription pill bottles sitting on a counter. There's no sign of Byron. She walks into the living room. It is silky with light, even at this hour. Her dad's armchair is still there, the blue fabric nubby in spots where Bert Bennett once sat. The last time Benny saw him, he stood up from that chair, turned his back on her, and walked out of the room.

Hard to believe it was eight years ago.

Benny had been trying to explain herself. She'd sat down next to her father, though not without great embarrassment. After all, who wanted to have a talk with their parents about sex? Though this wasn't only about the sex, that was the whole point. Benny had taken way too long to get around to this conversation and it had cost her, big-time.

Benny remembers running her hand back and forth over the crushed-velvet sofa that day, murmuring a compliment. Her mother had kept the seat encased in a plastic covering all those years that Benny and Byron were growing up and long after that. It was the first time that Benny had seen the sofa this way. She couldn't get over the feel of it, how it could be so soft and ridgy at the same time.

"We just woke up one morning and realized we're not going to live forever," her mother said, touching the sofa. "It's time we enjoyed it."

Benny smiled and petted her end of the seat like a stuffed toy. The sofa was still an ugly thing to look at, its brassy fibers glinting in the light, but just the feel of it under Benny's fingers helped to calm her nerves as her father began to raise his voice.

When she was little, Ma and Dad used to tell her that she could be anything she wanted to be. But as she grew into a young woman, they began to say things like *We made sacrifices so that you could have the best*. Meaning, the best was what they envisioned for Benny, not what she wanted for herself. Meaning, the best was something that, apparently, Benny was not. Letting go of a scholarship at a prestigious university was not. Taking cooking and art classes instead was not. Working precarious jobs with the hope of opening a café was not. And Benny's love life? That, most certainly, was not.

Benny walks over to the sofa now and sits down next to her father's empty chair, placing a hand on the armrest. She leans in and sniffs at the tweedy upholstery, searching for a hint of the hair oil that her father used to use, that green, old-style stuff that could fuel a pickup truck. Benny would give anything now to have her parents here, sitting in their favorite chairs, even if it meant they might still have trouble understanding her.

Benny finds herself smiling, now, thinking of a different time in this room. Her mother, perching her rear on the arm of this sofa, watching MTV with teenaged Benny and her friends while Benny kept hoping Ma would remember she had grown-up things to do and scoot. Ma had always seemed different from the mothers of other kids. Super athletic, a bit of a math wiz, and yes, a fan of music videos. The whole music thing was something that Benny, in her thirteenth year, had found somewhat embarrassing. It seemed Ma was always doing things her way. Except when it came to Benny's dad.

Benny's phone is pinging. It's Steve. He's left a voice message. He's heard the news. So sorry, he says, though he never knew her ma. He's thinking, maybe they should get together, when Benny gets back to the East Coast. Steve's voice is low and soft, and Benny feels the old stirring of the skin along her shins, just as she did the last time he called.

Benny and Steve. They've gone back and forth like this for years, now. Every time, Benny promises herself it'll be the last. She never calls him back. But each time, there has come a moment when she's finally answered Steve's phone calls, when Steve has made her laugh, when she's agreed to meet him.

Steve's laughter, Steve's voice, Steve's touch. Years ago, these things had helped to pull Benny out of the muck of her breakup with Joanie. She had followed Joanie all the way to New York from Arizona, though later she was forced to admit that Joanie had never given her a reason to think that they would get back together. So there Benny was, a few months later, staring down at her boots in the music section of a bookstore in Midtown, when Steve came up to her.

Steve wiggled his fingers in front of Benny's face and she looked up to see this gorgeous block of a man with a broad smile, pointing to his headphones, eyebrows raised, then pointing to the console where she was plugged in. Benny smiled and nodded. Steve plugged his head-phones into the jack near hers and, at the sound of the music, he nodded his head and laughed silently.

By the time they stepped out into the slushy streets together, Benny had begun to feel that maybe she was still made of all of those things that Joanie once saw in her and that maybe someone else could see them, too. It would be a while before Benny would realize that Steve, her music-loving, yacht-sailing new lover, could make her feel as threatened as he could make her feel desired.

Byron

——

THERE ARE THINGS TO DO, THINGS TO DISCUSS, BYRON KNOWS this, but he doesn't feel like dealing with his sister right now. The funeral arrangements are set. Byron took care of them while waiting for Benny to fly out to California, and everything else can wait. Byron sits out on the deck at his place, scarf up to his chin, watching the waves. He will stay here as long as he can before going back to his mother's house.

After all those times he's felt Benny's absence, she's finally back, but instead of relief, what he feels most is resentment. If things had gone differently between them, Benny would be sitting with him right now. She'd probably be drawing something in one of those sketch pads of hers. He still has that goofy surfing sketch she did of him, wiping out big-time, legs every which way. But Byron has been bitter for so long that it even kept him from calling Benny about their mother's illness until it was too late. He'd intended to call her before this happened, he really had, he knew they were running out of time. He just didn't realize how quickly.

Last Friday, Byron walked into the house and sensed right away, before he reached the other side of the kitchen, that his mother was gone. He found her just beyond the kitchen, on the hallway floor. It could happen that way, the doctor said later, the kind of sudden episode that might claim someone's life unexpectedly. It could happen to a person when their body was struggling against something fierce. Ma had still been able to get up on her own most days, wash her face, pour herself a glass of water, though with trembling hands, turn on some music or the television, until the effort of it sent her straight back to the sofa.

As Byron took his mother's head and shoulders in his arms and held her cool face against his chest, he thought of Benny, wondered how he would tell her, felt a new grief over the loss that Benny, too, would soon feel. He couldn't get the words out, at first.

"Benny, Benny," was all he could say when she picked up the phone. Byron stopped, his throat tight. He could hear noise in the background. Music and chatter and plates. Restaurant sounds. And then Benny, saying, "Byron? Byron?"

"Benny, I . . ."

But Benny had already understood.

"Oh, no, Byron!"

Then Byron got off the phone after breaking the news to her and began to think of all the other phone calls he would need to make, the arrangements, the sense of his mother being gone, the memories of his father's passing, the awareness of all those miles and years between Benny and the rest of them, and he felt the resentment toward his sister flooding back.

Dammit, Benny.

As he drives up to his mother's house now, he sees a rental car in the driveway.

Benny.

Byron walks through the kitchen door, kicks off his shoes, and stands still in his socks, listening. Silence. He walks down the hallway, peers through the window into the backyard, looks into Benny's old room, but no Benny.

Of course.

He continues down to his parents' room. There she is, lying in the middle of the bed, wrapped in the comforter like a giant egg roll, snoring lightly. She used to do that when she was little, pounce on the bed between Ma and Dad, peel the cover off Dad and roll. *A Benny roll!*

Dad would yell every time, as if she didn't do the same thing every single Sunday morning. Benny used to have this way of making everyone giggle, of making a person feel light. But it hasn't been that way for a long time.

There's that feeling again. A mean feeling. Byron wants to rush over to the bed and shake Benny awake. Then the next second, he just feels sad. His phone buzzes. He looks down. There's a reminder. Mr. Mitch is on his way.

Mr. Mitch

—

WHEN MR. MITCH GETS TO THE HOUSE, BENEDETTA SHAKES his hand and takes his jacket. Byron brings out cups of coffee and biscuits from the kitchen and unplugs his mother's telephone line. Eleanor's children still aren't talking to each other, but now the daughter doesn't seem as edgy. Mr. Mitch is still struck by how much Eleanor's children resemble their father, one the color of mahogany, the other the color of wet straw, both looking a bit like stubborn toddlers at the moment, their beautiful heads held high, their mouths turned down at the sides.

Benedetta folds her six-foot-tall frame into the couch and hugs a large cushion to her middle. Again, like a child. He wouldn't have expected that of such a regal-looking woman. Byron leans forward from where he is sitting, his elbows resting on his knees. Mr. Mitch opens his laptop and calls up the audio file. They really have no idea, do they? They think this is all about them. He clicks play.

Byron

—

THE SOUND OF HIS MOTHER'S VOICE SPLITS HIM DOWN THE middle.

B and B, my children.

The sound of her voice.

Please forgive me for not telling you any of this before. Things were different when I was your age. Things were different for women, especially if you were from the islands.

Byron's parents always said *the islands* as if they were the only ones in the world. There are roughly two thousand islands in the world's oceans and that's not counting the millions of other bits of land surrounded by seas and other bodies of water.

Byron hears his mother stopping to catch her breath and clenches his fists. *B and B, I wanted to sit down with you and explain some things but I'm running out of time and I can't go without letting you know how all of this happened.*

"How all of *what* happened?" Benny says. Mr. Mitch taps the keyboard on his laptop, pauses the audio recording.

Byron shakes his head. Nothing has ever happened to them, nothing at all. And that's saying a whole lot for a black family in America. Before their parents died, their only real family drama was Benny, freaking out Ma and Dad because she'd insisted on filling them in on the details of her love life. Couldn't she just have brought home her girlfriend that year and let that settle into their parents' heads a bit?

Then, if she'd ended up dating some guy another year, she could have explained the switch. A slow reveal. Their parents could have handled that. They would have adjusted, eventually.

But, no, Benny was Benny. Always needing attention, always needing approval, ever since college. She was no longer the easygoing baby sister she used to be. Benny had become this person who didn't leave room for dialogue. Either you were with her or you were against her. If Byron had behaved that way, if Byron had walked away every time someone hadn't agreed with him, hadn't accepted him right away, hadn't treated him fairly, where would he be today?

Not that Byron can really complain. He loves his work, he was born to be an ocean scientist. He's damn good at it, too, even if he's been passed over for the director's position at the institute. He's much better paid than he would be as director, anyway, thanks to his public appearances and books and film consulting. More than three times better paid, actually, but he likes to keep that between himself and the tax man.

Byron didn't set out to be the African American social media darling of ocean sciences, but he's going to get as much mileage out of it as he can. He's just put in for the director's position again, even though he knows his colleague Marc is hoping to get it, too.

Chances are, Byron thinks, he will hear the same old reasoning from the founders. That the center needs Byron *out there* as its ambassador, that Byron has brought unprecedented attention to the institute's work, that he's helped it to get more funding and greater say-so in international meetings than it would have mustered otherwise.

The last time around, Byron countered that line of argument by putting on his best team-player smile and saying he could do an even better job from the operations office, while helping the center to sharpen its way of doing things. He walked out of that uncomfortable conversation with a slight swagger to his step, just to show how much he was taking their decision in stride.

So, one more try. If the institute still won't grant him greater say in their organizational affairs, then he'll continue to find other ways to build his influence. It was Byron who was called to speak on television about the underwater volcano in Indonesia. Byron who was asked to give that paper at the Stockholm meeting. Byron who was called by the Japanese about the seabed-mapping project. He's been photographed with two presidents and was recently held up by the current one as a shining example of the American Dream, realized. It was at about that time that his girlfriend told him he was full of himself and broke off their relationship.

"This is not the kind of example I would want my children to follow," Lynette shouted at Byron that last night. It was the meanest thing a woman could say to a man, really. He didn't even know that Lynette had ever thought about children.

Lynette just didn't get it. If you were invited to the White House, you simply went, no matter who was sitting in the Oval Office. Here was another opportunity to advocate for things that mattered. To speak out against cuts in research funding, to push for broader access to quality science education. Here was another chance for a black man to be at the table with the decision makers, instead of flinching from abuse. Instead of standing outside yet another closed door.

But Lynette didn't agree. Lynette didn't seem to understand what he had to go through to be seen and heard in this world. Though his mother had understood.

"What are you willing to do?" his mother once asked him when he'd made a comment about taking flak from some of the guys in high school. "Are you doing something wrong, Byron? Do you think you're a bad person for getting a perfect score on that test? For being recognized for your work? Are you going to let someone else's view of who you should be, and what you should do, hold you back? Do you think those boys are really your friends?" His mother's eyes took on that glint that he saw whenever she stood at the edge of the sea.

"So, what are you willing to do?" she said. "Who are you willing to let go of?"

Anyway, Byron hadn't meant to let go of Lynette. She was the one who had done the letting go. Had it been up to him, he'd still be holding on to her right now. But she had made her decision and Byron wasn't the type to grovel. That was another thing Lynette didn't understand. What Byron could not allow himself to do.

Strange, how things have turned out with Lynette. It had never been Byron's style to date the people he worked with. For years, he'd managed to stick to this rule. He knew a lot of guys who didn't worry about those things, but workplace dynamics and harassment issues aside, he just didn't like to go there. And, yeah, it could get lonely.

All that time spent working on calculations and having meetings and writing papers and, in the early days, the ship expeditions, carrying out deep-water mapping for weeks at a time. Then later, the books and public appearances. Airport lounges and hotel rooms. Where was a guy like him supposed to make a connection that went beyond a one-night thing?

Cable, Byron's self-appointed advisor in all things, swore by Internet dating. Well, sure, that's how Cable had met his wife. Cable was lucky that way. But where was Byron supposed to find the time to sift through all those descriptions and set up all those encounters with new people? Byron met new people all the time, that wasn't the issue.

Then along came Lynette.

"Sorry," Benny is saying now, and Byron's thoughts come back to the room. "Sorry, Mr. Mitch," she says, again, waving a hand, "we can keep going." Mr. Mitch clicks on the audio file.

You children need to know about your family, about where we come from, about how I really met your father. You two need to know about your sister.

Byron and Benny look at each other, mouths open.

B and B, I know, this is a shock. Just bear with me for a moment and let me explain.

Byron and Benny look at Mr. Mitch now and simultaneously mouth the same word.

Sister?

Sister

——

SISTER? WHAT DOES THIS MEAN? WHAT HAPPENED TO HER? She and Byron are both talking at once, asking the same questions in different ways, asking, in essence, *How could this be?*

Mr. Mitch is shaking his head, insisting that Benny and Byron listen to the entire recording first, as their mother requested. He juts his chin toward his laptop. Benny looks at her brother's face, his large, dark eyes, so much like Daddy's, so much like her own, and thinks back to all those moments with her brother, running along the beach together, making faces at each other across the dinner table, Benny sitting bowed over her math homework with Byron next to her, talking her through the exercises. All those times, they were missing a sister?

How is it possible they didn't know this? Benny's ma and dad had been married forever and Benny's dad once told her that he and Ma had hoped for more babies, but there had been only Byron, at first. Then Benny came along years later, surprising her parents and delighting them with her chunky little body and her goofy smile.

"We could see that you had your ma's smile from the very start, just like your brother," Benny's dad told her, pinching her chin. Her mouth was the only thing that Benny's father hadn't passed down to her. That, and her pale skin.

Benny had always thought of her parents as being made for each other. Her parents would have had a lot in common, both being from the Caribbean, both orphaned, both having immigrated to Britain before moving to the United States together. But it might not have mattered, it was love at first sight, they'd always said that, and some people were meant to find each other, no matter what.

"Your mother thought I was so good-looking," Dad used to joke, "that she fainted on the spot." Everyone had heard the story. One day in London, Bert Bennett saw Eleanor Douglas drop to the ground and went over to help her and, as they say, the rest is history. Sometimes, when Daddy told that story, he would lean in and tap Ma on the nose with his own, just like that. A nose kiss. Does anyone ever fall in love that way anymore? Without hesitation, without terror? Or is everyone else like Benny?

And does every couple keep secrets this big from their own children?

THEN

∴

B *and B, I know, I need to explain why you never knew any of this. But it won't make any sense if I don't start at the beginning. This isn't only about your sister. There are other people involved, so just bear with me. Everything goes back to the island and what happened there more than fifty years ago. The first thing you need to know about is a girl named Covey.*

Covey was born in a town that bordered on the sea, a deep, rolling, blue thing that paled to turquoise as it neared the land. And the bigger Covey got, the harder it was for her to stay away from the water. When she was little, her father used to stand her on his shoulders in the swimming pool and launch her into the deep end. But it was her mother who taught her how to ride the waves, and this is what determined her fate.

Now, I know you may be thinking of those nice, Caribbean beaches with calm waters where you can look down and see the fish swimming around your ankles. Yes, they had those, too, but where Covey grew up, it was surfing country and there were beaches where, if you didn't know how to handle yourself, the waves would pull you under. Her mother's favorite spot was like that. It was no place for a child, that's what Covey's father used to say, but her mummy took her there anyway. So Covey grew up strong. And she would need that strength when things began to fall apart.

Covey

—

EVEN TOWARD THE END, THERE WAS SOMETHING ABOUT THAT moment that always made the women laugh.

Twist, twist, twist.

These were Covey's favorite days, when she was done with school and could kick off her saddle shoes and sit in the kitchen with the women, the radio dial turned up to calypso and rockabilly, the aroma rushing to their heads as they twisted open the jar of fruits soaking in rum and port. The grassy breeze mixing with salt air, slipping through the louvers to cool their sweaty necks. The whispered gossip, the pips of laughter.

Covey's mother and Pearl, the family helper, had a small but popular cake business going. Most people they knew had common-law marriages, Covey's own parents included, but a formal arrangement was more respected, and someone with money was always planning a wedding. On such occasions, a black cake was indispensable. And that's where Mummy and Pearl came in.

Mummy always laughed when she was making black cake. And there was always some point at which she would not be able to resist the pull of the music on the radio.

"Come, Pearl," she would say, but Pearl was not much into the dancing. Pearl would give that closed-mouth smile of hers and bob her head to the music while Mummy raised a batter-covered spatula in the air and waved it to the beat, stepping toward Covey and then skipping back and grabbing Covey's hand. *Cuh-vee, Cuh-vee, Cuh-vee,* she would sing to the music. She would pull Covey into a kind of shuffle, giving off a smell of granulated sugar and butter and hair pomade as the two of them spun into the dining room and toward the living room.

Pearl liked to act stern-like with Mummy. "Miss Mathilda," she would say, sounding more like she was scolding Covey than talking to her employer. "These cakes are not going to *mek* themselves, you know?"

There was a time, when Covey was little, when Mummy used to dance with Pa out in the backyard. It was always on a night when the power had gone out and they had lined up candles in glass jars along the edge of the patio and taken the transistor radio outside. Mummy would step in close and run her hands up and down Pa's back. At some point, Mummy and Pa would each take one of Covey's hands and dance with her. Sometimes Pa would lift Covey up into his arms and dip her this way and that and Mummy would laugh.

In those last months before she disappeared, Mummy rarely laughed at all. Her face would grow still whenever Covey's pa passed by. It was one of those grown-up things that Covey would not understand until much later. Like the weight of Mummy's kiss in the middle of the night.

Covey felt the kiss in her sleep. Then another. Then a hand along her hairline. A hint of rose perfume and her mother's salty-forehead scent. Then it was daylight, Sunday morning. Her mother must have let her sleep late. She waited. No Mummy. She got up and went to the kitchen. No Mummy.

Twelve hours later, no Mummy. Pearl left supper, as usual. Pa came home tipsy, as usual.

Two days later, no Mummy. The police came to the house, nodding as her pa talked. Yes, they said, they'd see what they could do.

One week later, Pa took Covey's hand in his and wiped the tears from her face. He said her ma would be back soon, she'd see. Pa was tipsier than usual. Pearl hugged Covey extra tight.

One month later, no Mummy.

One year later.

Five years later.

Pa spent more time than ever at the cockfights. He kept a bottle behind a carton at one of his shops, Covey had seen it. Pearl still gave Covey a hug before leaving for home. Covey still woke up in the middle of the night, sniffing at the air for the scent of roses and salt.

Lin

—

IT TOOK SIX YEARS FOR JOHNNY "LIN" LYNCOOK TO ADMIT TO himself that his woman would not be coming back home, not even for their daughter. He sat in the backyard with a bottle of beer, watching a lizard snap-snap at insects too small to be seen, thinking about what a struggle it had been to keep things going, with or without Mathilda. It had always been a struggle for Lin, as for his parents before him, and for all those countrymen who had crossed the oceans in previous generations.

His *ba* liked to tell his boys the story of how some of their people took their degrading start in the Americas and turned it on its head. Back in 1854, he told them, some of the men working on the Panama railroad got so sick they vomited a blackish bile and their eyes turned yellow. Many of the Chinese laborers who'd been brought over to work on the railroad project demanded to be sent away to a safer place. Some of them ended up on the island. Already weakened by hard labor and illness, few of them would survive for long. One of those who did make it went on to open a wholesale supply store, setting a precedent that encouraged other Chinese immigrants to do the same.

And then came the Lin family. A new century, a window of opportunity. Or so they'd hoped. Lin's father came over from Guangzhou as a cook and somewhere in there, his documents started listing him as *Lyncook*. He worked off his contract, sent for his wife and their young son, Jian, soon to be called Johnny, and joined the ranks of the local shop owners. When he finally opened that first store, he put a sign above the shop, *Lin's Dry Goods & Sundries,* and folks soon took to calling him Mister Lin and his eldest son simply Lin. Later, there would be another store and other sons with English names. But getting to that point turned out to be a hard path to follow.

Fish tea. That was all they'd had to eat, most days, when Lin was still a pickney. Lin's mother would make the broth with a fish head and serve it with a bit of scallion and a Scotch bonnet pepper for as many days as she could. It was years before Lin realized that other families on the island made the broth with actual pieces of fish meat, with green bananas, and maybe even shrimps. By that time, his parents could afford other things. The family's shops were finally making a profit. His father would cure pork and hang slabs of it on hooks around the veranda and the boys would sit in the yard and watch the pieces twisting in the breeze.

But that was later.

In the early years, only Lin's arithmetic lessons kept his mind off his stomach. Teachers said the boy had a gift. But Lin already sensed that it wasn't enough to be good with numbers, you had to be willing to defy their logic to succeed in this world. You had to be willing to take a chance. Even as a boy, he could watch the men play Sue Fah and guess at the odds. In high school, he started betting on horses. Then he discovered the cockfights and held his first fistful of dollars. Breathed in the smell of paper money mixed with dust and blood. Breathed in his first real chance at a future.

Lin learned that you could improve the odds of winning by keeping tabs on how a man bred his birds, on which supplements he gave them. The extra cash helped to modernize his father's stores, helped his parents to buy a house with tamarind and breadfruit trees. It was a good thing, too. In all, Mamma Lin had given birth to four boys but there were only two of them left after the tuberculosis, and only Lin had remained in town.

Lin had always been loyal to his family. This was the way he'd been raised. When the betting brought in good money, he always gave something extra to his brothers' widows and children. And when Covey was born, he hired a helper, Pearl, the best cook in the parish, because that was what Covey's mother wanted. But then the money stopped coming in.

In time, the breeders of gamecocks found steroids that could plump up a bird, but they also made an animal harder to handle, especially when it was fitted with blades. One owner up in the next parish died after his own bird slashed through his arm. No one even saw when it happened, only saw the life flying out of the man's wrist in a spray of red.

Lin had been counting on that bird to win big. Instead, the slashing incident triggered a long losing streak, during which time Lin's woman grew louder, more argumentative, then quieter, then altogether silent. One day, she simply disappeared, leaving behind a brief note and their twelve-year-old daughter, who kept trailing Lin around the house, gazing up at him with her mother's round eyes.

Lin suspected Mathilda had left him under the influence of all that *Rasta-black-power-independence* business that was going on in the streets, though she used to complain because Lin wouldn't give her a formal marriage. That, and because he kept going to the cockfights.

"You don't like the betting?" Lin asked her one time. "Where do you think I get the money to keep the shops going? Half of our customers are buying on credit, which they will never pay off, by the way. Am I supposed to let them go without? And where do you think this house came from? You *tink all dat money fall out a de sky?*" The woman's face took on that vexed look she used whenever Lin spoke patois around their daughter.

No, Mathilda had never appreciated her good fortune. Some of the merchants had wives on the far side of the ocean or women on the other side of town, but not Lin. Still, she was the kind of woman a man tried to tolerate. All that skin billowing out of the top of her shirt. The way she would march their daughter straight into the waves without hesitation, aggravating Lin and exciting him at the same time.

In the tired but hopeful years after the end of World War II, a lot of the fellows who came back to the island after serving in the Royal Air Force and such would talk of nothing but going back to Britain. Some of the Chinese lads from the capital were leaving the island for Florida. But Lin didn't want to immigrate again, he wanted to improve his lot right where he was. Mathilda, two years younger than Lin, said she liked his attitude. When they were alone, she would run her hand over the top of his head and say that she liked that funny hair of his, black and straight and coarse as a brush.

Lin could have married someone else. Lin's mother had been fussing with him to take up with the "right sort" of girl, one of the new ones who had come over from China. Someone who would know the proper way to clean the house for the Chinese New Year. Someone who would know how to prepare the small envelopes of Fung Bow for the children. Someone who knew what to cook for good luck, whose presence would make the family proud when important people came to visit for the holiday feast.

And he knew that Mathilda would not have sat idling for long. All she had to do to find someone who was better off was to train her eyes on some hotel owner farther up the coast or even one of those movie stars who had managed to get rich despite lounging on the beach half the time. But then Mathilda told him she was pregnant and he understood that this was what he wanted. To live with Mathilda and their child.

Love was a mystifying thing and the way it could corrode, doubly so. Yes, Lin needed to accept the fact that it was just him and his daughter now. They had been abandoned.

Within three years, Covey's shoulders and chest had puffed up and she was taller and swimming faster than any girl and most boys in the parish. Her eyes took on an edge that Lin recognized as his own. This girl was like him. It wasn't just a matter of talent. She wasn't just having fun. She was driven to win.

Covey kept winning, but Lin kept losing. The funny thing was, Lin knew better. He knew better than to gamble without taking a break. He knew better than to spend all that cash on liquor. Lin never forgot a number, had entire armies of them in his head, but he couldn't for the life of him remember the date on which he stopped being able to stop himself.

At some point, Lin began to think, again, about the men who had moved away. He considered selling what was left of his belongings and going back to China.

"What China?" his one remaining brother said. "*Yu belong to dis island now.* What China?"

Then there was Covey. Lin knew he couldn't take her with him, not with her mother's brown face and long nose and her English talking. Probably, he hadn't said more than a word or two to Covey in Hakka since she was still in nappies. She would never find herself a husband over there. *Cho!* He was wasting his time, he knew, fretting over a girl-child who was already getting fresh with him. Talking back in that modern way, instead of doing as she was told. He suspected that Covey was already a lost cause. Still, he stayed.

The Bay

—

UNTIL THE BAY BECAME FAMOUS, THEY HAD IT ALL TO THEM-selves.

Pull, pull, pull.

No self-respecting islander would go out there on a weekday without a boat or surfboard, only Covey and her friend Bunny.

Pull, pull, pull.

From time to time, the movie stars and writers who kept homes farther up the coast would come by with their glamorous friends and stretch out on the sand, but most afternoons, the beach was deserted when the girls arrived.

Pull, pull, pull.

On Sundays, Covey and Bunny behaved like the other fifteen-year-old girls, strolling along the shore in their matching two-piece swimsuits, poking sticks into beached jellyfish, burying each other up to their necks in sand, eating fresh snapper and cassava cakes cooked on an open fire by Fishie and his wife, and washing off their fingers in the breakers afterward.

Fishie was an institution around there. He'd been selling lunches made with his freshly caught fish since Covey's and Bunny's own fathers had been young boys. He'd seen Bunny's father go to war for Britain and come back across the oceans to raise his two children, unlike some of the others who'd turned right around and gone back to England or Wales or what-have-you. He'd seen Covey's pa grow from a *skinny likkle ting,* as he'd told Covey more than once with a chuckle, to a *skinny big ting.* And now, these boys were men, holding court around Fishie with bottles in their hands and arguing about the island's independence from British rule.

Some weekends, when Covey's pa wasn't full of drink, he would drive the girls and their friends up the coast to the falls. They'd run under the cascade, yelping from the cold rush of the water. *Look at me, Pa!* Covey would shout. *Look at me!* It was a good day when she could get him to throw back his head in laughter and slap the side of his thigh. It was a good day when she could feel that she was still more important to Pa than a bunch of smelly roosters fighting to the death.

Then on weekdays, Covey and Bunny would pull on their swim caps and Covey would revert to her truest self.

Covey was in the water at the swim club when she first saw Bunny. Covey had been treading water, going over the lines of a passage she'd memorized to recite at school. Just then, Pa's friend Uncle Leonard walked in with his daughter, Bunny.

Uncle Leonard let go of the girl's arm and gave her a slight shove toward the instructor. *Just concentrate, Bunny,* he said, then walked away as Bunny took a few awkward steps forward. Covey had never seen her before, they went to different primary schools, but she had seen Uncle Leonard pull up to the house in his white van to pick up Pa. Back then, Mummy was still around and she'd heard Mummy kiss her teeth and mumble under her breath every time he and Pa drove off to the cockfights.

At the pool, Bunny did everything the instructor said with a worried look on her moon-shaped face. She didn't have any of the basics but she caught on fast. Then one day, Bunny's mother came to watch and she smiled. Covey and the other kids looked over at one another in surprise. Bunny had the brightest smile that any of them had ever seen on a girl. Not even Covey's mother had teeth like that. As time went by, Covey saw that, apart from the smile, Bunny had something else. Once she started swimming, she never seemed to get tired.

Bunny started walking back with Covey to Covey's house after swim club. The two of them would sit side by side at the table in the kitchen, legs swinging, tummies growling, as they waited for Pearl to slip them a piece of fried breadfruit or a hot, chewy dumpling while preparing the evening's supper. If there was still some daylight left, they would run into the backyard to catch lizards and climb the enormous old almond tree, until Mummy called to them to come down.

Then Covey told Bunny she wanted to start training in the bay.

"But why?" Bunny said. "We have the pool."

"You'll see," Covey said, and looked in the direction of the coast.

"But is it safe?"

Covey hesitated, but she could tell, from the gleam in Bunny's eyes, that she didn't really need to answer.

Their longest swims took place when their fathers were gone to the cockfights. Covey and Bunny would beg rides from the neighbor boys and head farther down the coast. While their fathers were wiping flecks of blood from their dollar bills, the girls were already on the sand, kicking off their shoes and stepping out of their dresses and plunging head-first into the sapphire waves.

With Bunny, Covey no longer felt like an only child. She felt as though she'd found a sister on land and in the water. Covey was the faster swimmer of the two girls but Bunny could go forever, and she could navigate the straightest line in open water of all the swimmers Covey knew. If Covey moved like a dolphin, then Bunny was like one of those giant turtles you heard about that were capable of crossing the world without losing their way.

People liked to tease Covey about the swimming. She was like lightning, some of them said. But with Bunny, they often grew quiet. Word had gotten around town. Bunny was the stuff of reverence. Bunny was a *duppy conqueror*. But then they turned sixteen and things began to change. People started calling them *young ladies*. Covey knew what some people thought about young ladies. That they ought to have more *respect* for the sea and what it could do. That they ought to stop courting danger by going out into the bay.

"It's not natural," her pa said. When Covey was still small, Covey's father placed a couple of fortunate bets and told her he would use the money to enroll her in the swim club. Pa kept paying the fees even when he said there was nothing left for other expenses and, over the years, Covey made good on his investment by lining her bedroom shelf with swimming medals. Then Covey decided it wasn't enough.

Because her pa was wrong, there was nothing more natural for Covey than swimming in the sea. And as long as she had Bunny, Covey felt that she could keep doing what she loved best.

"The harbor race," Covey said to Bunny. "Let's do it. Let's see if we can get sponsorship to go to the capital."

"The harbor race?" Bunny said. "You know I don't like to race."

"But we could win."

"No, *you* could win, Covey."

"But you could finish in the top three, I'm sure of it. It's a good, long swim, the kind you like. Plus, some of those big-time racers from the other islands wouldn't have the courage to come here."

Their island was one of the smaller countries on Earth, but it had one of the world's largest natural harbors. There were always rumors going around of what might be lurking in its waters.

Everyone on the island had a shark story. Sharks that left nothing but a man's torso to wash ashore. Sharks that lunged when someone threw a dead dog off a cliff. Sharks seen circling a sandbar off the southern coast. But in her entire life, Covey had never seen so much as a shark fin in the water. Barracudas, yes. But she wondered if shark sightings weren't like ghost stories, tales that you didn't quite believe, but that left you feeling afraid all the same.

Covey would convince Bunny to enter that harbor race, she was sure of it.

"They would have boats tracking us, right?" Bunny asked.

"Right," Covey said. "Listen, I'll admit I get a little nervous, thinking about it. But we swim out here, so why can't we swim there? Are you thinking you might not want to go?"

Bunny shook her head.

"Then don't think about it, just come with me."

Covey couldn't imagine not going. Couldn't imagine not feeling the froth bubble away from her skin as her arm came out of the water, the blue-green world below growing black with depth, the bright sky above, and even the salt burning her mouth. She dreamed of being invited to compete abroad. She knew it was unlikely, but it could be her ticket away from this island. Because, yes, Covey intended to leave this town someday, even if her mother never came back to get her.

"But your pa," Bunny said. "What if he doesn't agree?"

"I'll think about that later," Covey said.

Three afternoons a week, Covey pulled through the waves, pulled through her fear of sharks, pulled against lactic acid, and breathed in gulps of her future as a champion. Three afternoons a week, Bunny smeared grease on her face, pulled through the jellyfish stings, and studied a map of the island's big harbor. Because wherever Covey went, Bunny wanted to follow.

Covey and Gibbs

—

IN THOSE DAYS, THERE WERE BOYS WHO WOULD HACK INTO THE hulls of discarded fishing boats, shape them into flat boards, and ride the waves. Some of them went body boarding and surfing on pieces of refrigerator foam. They'd trim the polyurethane and laminate it with resin and fiberglass. They would laugh as they jumped off their boards and ran back to the sand. By the time factory-made surfboards came to Covey's hometown, she was ready to try her luck at the sport.

Covey turned out to be a natural. She didn't have a surfboard of her own, but Gibbs Grant did. Covey had just turned sixteen when Gibbs joined the swim club. He was one of the older boys, but fairly new in town. His family had moved to be near relatives after a mining company bought his father's land. Covey had heard about the Grant boy but when she first saw him step out of the changing room and into the pool area, she was sure that their paths had never crossed. She was certain of it because she would have noticed if they had.

Covey had reached that age where the boys had stopped pulling at her hair. She had reached that stage where boys whispered as she walked by, hissed at her from cars, stood too close to her at parties, embarrassed her, repelled her, and sometimes, made her daydream. But none of them had done what this new boy did when he walked into the club that day.

As Gibbs moved toward the border of the pool, Covey took one look at him and felt as if this boy, looking right back at her with those eyes of his, had just shot out his arm and given her a push, sending her falling, falling, falling backward into the deep end.

Later, he said, "I see why dem call you Dolphin."

"Oh, yes?" Covey said.

"You're fast."

She shrugged and looked down at her feet. As usual, her toes were puckered from all that time in the water. She pretended to find this interesting.

"The boys say you've been swimming out in the bay."

"Yeah, Bunny and I."

"Just you two?"

"Mostly just us, but not always."

"You think I could come out there and swim with you sometime?"

"If you're good enough," Covey said, smiling up at him.

"I'm good enough," Gibbs said, grinning.

Gibbs joined them in the bay the very next week. One day he brought a surfboard. Covey wanted to try it immediately but Bunny scrunched up her nose. It was this interest in surfing that gave Gibbs and Covey their first excuse to see each other without their swim club friends, or their schoolmates, or the inquisitive eyes of their parents.

The first time Covey and Gibbs followed a path down through the brush and into the cove where the surfers went, they found a trio of Rasta men on the beach. The oldest of them waded into the water and the next thing Covey knew, he was up on the board, a thing to behold, his graying dreads flying as he came up the face of a wave and cut back in the other direction.

When it was Covey's turn to use Gibbs's board, the men stared openly at her, following her as she crossed the narrow band of sand, pushed her way into the breakers, and hoisted her trunk onto the board. For the rest of her life, Covey would remember the feeling that came over her the first time she stood up on the surfboard. She would remember hearing Gibbs whoop before she fell and wondering if the elation of that moment was only from the surfing or if it was from knowing, too, that Gibbs was there, watching her.

Covey would remember, too, her sense of satisfaction when, the next time they saw the surfing Rastas, the older men merely dipped their chins in greeting, then carried on with what they were doing.

Covey hadn't said anything to Bunny about going surfing with Gibbs. She would have to say something eventually and Bunny would say *Oh, yes?* and smile, but Covey knew that Bunny would be jealous. She sensed it from the way Bunny eyed Gibbs whenever she thought Covey wasn't looking. She knew from the way Bunny touched Covey's face as she helped Covey adjust her swim cap, from the way she rested her head in Covey's lap when they lolled on the beach after swimming, waiting for the sun to bake their suits dry. She didn't want Bunny to feel bad. Bunny was her best friend. For Covey, this meant everything. But for Bunny, it wasn't quite enough.

"Boss!" Gibbs shouted when Covey came running out of the waves after standing up that first time.

"You have a true talent, Dolphin Girl," Gibbs said later, as they sat on a towel with a pineapple that Gibbs had bought from a higgler woman.

"Oh, what are you doing?" Covey said.

"What?" said Gibbs. He was holding the pineapple on his thigh with one hand and digging into the side of the fruit with a knife.

"You trying to kill that pineapple? What are you cutting it that way for? Here, pass that to me." Covey took the pineapple and set it, crown up, on the towel. "And you say you come from the country? I don't believe it."

"Well, it's just a penknife, it's not big enough."

"Which is your first problem right there."

"What? Am I supposed to be roaming the coast with a big old knife, just in case I run into a pineapple?"

Covey kissed her teeth, and then they both laughed and Gibbs let himself fall back on the sand. Covey tried not to stare at his trunk, gleaming in the sun. She held the pineapple in place and began to shave off the skin, bit by bit, exposing the yellow flesh covered with dark eyes. Then she cut diagonally into the side of the fruit, digging out the spots, one or two at a time. With Gibbs's small knife, it was going to take a while. And Covey was glad.

"So," Gibbs said. "What are you going to do when you finish school? You want to teach swimming like Bunny?"

"Well, first, I want to win that harbor race and, yes, I want to keep swimming. But I want to go to university. See if maybe I can go to England. Maybe I could do something with numbers. I'm good with numbers, like my pa."

Covey saw a look pass over Gibbs's face. She could imagine what he was thinking. What most people thought about her father. "And you?" Covey asked.

"I'm definitely going to London next year. I'm going to study law," Gibbs said. Covey felt her heart thudding. They could both end up in Britain.

"Law?" Covey said. "You mean, like criminals and such?"

"I was thinking more of people's rights. You know, people whose rights are denied. Like my family's."

"Why, what happened?"

"My father. He had a farm, you know this. But it was taken away. That's why we had to move."

"I thought some big company bought your father's land?"

"That's what they called it, anyhow. It's not like he had a choice. They paid what they wanted to pay. Then they made us all move. The whole village."

Covey looked at Gibbs silently. She didn't know that such a thing could happen.

Gibbs took a chunk of pineapple from Covey.

"If you go to London, do you think you would come back?"

"Not *if* I go, *when*."

Each time they met alone, Gibbs insisted that leaving the island was the key to his future. The rest, he'd have to see. At some point, he stopped talking about his future only, and started talking about a life together with Covey.

We, he started saying. *We*.

Gibbs, who had shoulders as broad and brown as a guango tree.

Gibbs, whose arms around Covey's waist burned her with a warmth that ran down through her middle.

Covey's father had forbidden her to stay out with boys alone, but Covey and Gibbs kept finding excuses. The swim club, the debate team, and in the summer, the recitals to practice for Independence Day. They lived in a town surrounded by quiet coves and lush tree cover. It was easy enough for a pair of teenagers to find places to steal time together and, like each generation before them, they were emboldened by adolescent love.

Covey and Gibbs, holding hands down by the breakers.

Covey and Gibbs, kissing in the hollow of a sea cave.

Covey and Gibbs, clinging and probing and whispering promises.

Lin

—

THINGS HADN'T BEEN EASY WITH COVEY. THAT SHE WAS A girl-child was bad enough. That she had grown to inherit her mother's eyes and bust and teeth had become a problem. The local men were already taking notice of her looks, not to mention the wife of one of Lin's suppliers who, everyone knew, was *that way*. But the worst part of it all was the disrespect his daughter had begun to show him.

When Covey was old enough to understand that her mother wouldn't be coming home, she started acting up, started getting home late from school. Lately, she'd been telling Lin that she was studying with a friend after class, or training extra hours at the swim club, but he could see that the girl had been up to something. She would walk into the house with that look on her face and Lin knew that there had to be a boy. But Covey denied it.

One afternoon, Lin ran out of patience and grabbed Covey by the hair. That was when he realized what had been going on.

"What is this?" Lin said.

Covey's ponytail was stiff with salt. She'd been swimming in the sea after school again. Lin had forbidden it and, still, his fool of a daughter had been going out there in the afternoons. And lying to him about it.

"Are you mad?" Lin said. "Haven't we talked about this before? Do you know what can happen to you if you go out there alone?"

"Nothing is going to happen to me," Covey said, picking up a mango and running the point of a paring knife along its skin.

"And right you are, Coventina. Nothing is going to happen to you because you will not be going out there again."

Covey cut her eyes at him and turned away. Back in Lin's day, a girl would never have given her own father an insolent look of that sort. Nowadays, there was all manner of loose behavior going around. The previous week, Covey had sewn herself a new skirt, or Lin should say, a new strip of cloth, halfway up her backside. All the girls were wearing them, Covey had said. Lin put a stop to that business right away, made her let out the hem. But this was what the world was coming to.

"Anyway, you can't stop me," Covey said, slicing a piece of mango away from the seed and swallowing it whole.

That was it. Lin pulled his belt out of his trousers, brandished the leather strap, and taught Covey a lesson. Or so he hoped. Covey was fearless. And a fearless girl, without a mother or husband to keep her in check, was a dangerous thing.

Storm

———

I N SEPTEMBER 1963, THE CREW OF A JETLINER FLYING FROM Portugal to Surinam noticed an area of significant disturbance off the west coast of Africa. This was followed by reports from ships traveling east of the Lesser Antilles. By the time the first advisory for Hurricane Flora was issued to the general public, the storm was moving in on Trinidad and Tobago and beginning its deadly march up through the Caribbean.

Back then, no one in Covey's town knew that a hurricane was coming until it was almost fully upon them, though islanders knew that this was the season for big storms. Merely being sideswiped by a tropical storm was enough to destroy crops, knock out communications, and claim lives.

On Saturday, October 5, 1963, three teenagers were swimming across Long Bay, while two others followed them in a small boat. None of them wanted to admit to the others how worried they were. The tropical storm had come in faster than they'd expected and the boat had already capsized once.

Two miles inland, Lin was herding chickens into the garage. The chicken coop was already buckling in the wind and Covey was nowhere to be seen. The schools were closed and the roads were filling with muddy water. Lin had told the girl to get back from Bunny's house by lunchtime. The phone rang. It was Bunny's father, Leonard.

"Lin, we have too much water up our way. Could you drive Bunny to the halfway corner? I'll come and get her on foot."

"Bunny?" Lin said. "Bunny isn't here. She's not at home?"

"No. I thought she and Covey were with you," Leonard said.

"Oh, shit."

"Oh, Christ Almighty."

Lin picked up Leonard at the halfway corner and they headed toward the shore. Thankfully, most roads were empty. Stores and such had been shut in anticipation of the storm, but the flooding slowed them down.

"What if they're not there?" Lin said, as they pulled parallel to the sand.

"Where else would they be?" Leonard said. "That daughter of yours . . ."

"Daughter of *mine*? What about Bunny?"

"Bunny goes where Covey goes. You know the influence Covey has over her."

Lin kept his mouth shut. There were things that one father avoided saying to another, things that could ruin a friendship.

Lin spotted a cooler and shoes on the sand, clothes of various colors blowing about. He and Leonard ran down to the water, already soaked to the skin. Lin peered through sheets of rain and saw a canoe being buffeted by the waves. Three swimmers were in the water ahead of the boat, flicking their arms through the spray. He recognized Covey's yellow swim cap.

Lin switched on his torch and signaled to the group. There was nothing else that Lin could do at this point, just hold his breath. This was the worst trick that nature could play on you, really, to make you a father, to fill your chest with that kind of fear for a child. He and Leonard shouted as a high wave capsized the boat and scattered everyone.

After the wave retreated, Lin counted five heads. There was Covey, with her yellow cap, trying to grab hold of the canoe. They had almost reached the shore but if they didn't move fast, the next big wave would turn that boat into a missile.

Thank goodness she was a powerful girl, that Covey. The sight of his daughter's legs emerging from the water filled Lin with pride and a sense of relief so strong it stung his eyes and nose. Then came the fury. At sixteen, Covey was already as tall as he was but Lin grabbed her by the arm like a pickney and pulled her toward the car.

"Go on, get in," Lin said. He looked over his shoulder at the Grant boy, the oldest of the group. Way too handsome for his own good.

"You, Gibbs Grant," Lin said, "you should know better."

"Yes, sir," Gibbs said, and lowered his head. The way Covey was looking at that boy made Lin's stomach burn.

"Yes, sir?" Lin said. "Yes, *sir*? That is all you have to say for yourself? You are the eldest one here, you should have taken responsibility."

"No, Pa," Covey shouted, "I was the one who said we should come here."

"You, young lady, be quiet."

Gibbs looked over at Covey, then back at Lin, head high. "You are right, Mister Lin, I take full responsibility." And in that instant, Lin saw it all, in the set of Gibbs's neck and shoulders, in the gleam of his large eyes, saw everything that a boy like this could become to his daughter. Bloody hell, he thought.

That weekend, Hurricane Flora caused twelve million dollars in damage and killed a dozen people on the island. Covey was forbidden to see Gibbs, and she and Bunny were grounded for a month, swim club included. But Covey was already in love with Gibbs, and Bunny was already in love with Covey, and they were too young, still, to imagine that anything could keep them away from one another for very long.

Burning

—

Ayear after the big storm, Covey was pulled out of her sleep by the sound of someone banging on the front door of the house and shouting *Lin! Lin!* She stepped out into the hallway in time to see her father shoving his feet into his sandals and dashing through the door.

Covey followed her pa outside as he hurried down the driveway, brushing past the bougainvillea and out into the street. At the end of the road lay the small cluster of businesses that included one of his stores. In the daytime, Covey would have been able to see the intersection in the distance, but now there was only an orange glow against the night sky.

"Go home, Covey!" her father said when he saw her. "Go on, and lock the doors behind you." The thought of locking the doors to their home came as a shock. It was something that Covey, at seventeen, had never done. Not even with the political business farther up the coast, the killings the previous year. There had never been any need.

"But, Pa," Covey said, coughing. A hint of smoke scraped at her throat. Her father put his hands on her shoulders and turned her around.

"Don't talk back to me," he said, "just go on. And look at you. In your night clothes, no less. Go cover yourself up."

Covey ran back to the house, keeping her arms folded over her pajama top to cover the bounce of her breasts. Before leaving, she'd seen enough to understand that her father's stores were probably burning along with other businesses on that stretch of road. Just as Covey turned into her front yard, two women passed her on the street. One of them was saying that a *chiney* shopkeeper had roughed up one of his workers, that's why somebody had set fire to the shops.

"The woman asked for her wages and 'im *mash up her face,*" she said.

The other woman kissed her teeth.

Chiney? They didn't mean Covey's father, did they? Most of the stores in the parish were owned by Chinese islanders, so Covey supposed it could have been any one of them. But not her pa. Everyone knew her father was prone to the gambling and drinking. But beating up an employee? That didn't sound like Johnny "Lin" Lyncook. Her pa? Her father had pulled a belt strap on her once but he hadn't actually hit her. He'd seemed so certain that the menace of it would be enough. His bark had always been greater than his bite.

As Covey reached the house, she saw Gibbs and his father running toward the fire. Gibbs hurried across the street to her.

"Gibbs!" his father yelled, pointing at the fire. Gibbs's father had opened a shop with his wife's cousin and he looked worried.

"I'm sorry, my father . . . ," Gibbs said.

"I know, I know."

"Can you meet me tomorrow?" Gibbs said. "Try to meet me. The usual place."

Covey nodded, tears building up in her eyes as she opened the gate to her house. But she didn't have to wait until the next day. An hour later, Gibbs was back, rapping a stone against the gate until Covey looked out the window and ran out to let him in. Holding hands, they ran through the side garden to the back of the house.

"You mustn't let my father see you."

"I don't think your father is coming back anytime soon, Covey."

Covey felt her body go heavy. She rested her head on Gibbs's shoulder. "And your dad?"

"He's all right, the store's all right, he's just helping out."

They fell silent, kissing and touching until she pushed him away. "You'd better go before someone sees us."

"You're right," Gibbs said, leaning into her one more time, then pulling away.

After that, Covey was alone in the house until after dawn, waiting and worrying. Lately, Covey had spent most of her time steering clear of her father, dreaming of the day when she and Gibbs could get away from the island together, but on this night, she only wanted to see her pa walk through the front door. Her mother had left, but her father had stayed. Her grandparents had passed on, her uncle and aunts and cousins had moved away, but her pa was still there. That selfish, bad-tempered, narrow-minded man was all that remained of her family.

In the light of day, some of the men from the neighborhood helped Covey's father and the other merchants pick through the mess. Four shops had caught fire, in all, including one of her pa's two stores. No one knew who had set the blaze. Or, at least, no one was saying. They all came back to her father's backyard, shirts and Bermudas covered in soot, her father walking with one foot bare and a broken sandal in his hand. Covey ran to the washroom to wipe away her tears.

The men rinsed their hands and faces with water from the garden hose and settled into chairs, or perched themselves on the veranda steps. Pearl and Covey brought them glasses of ice water and plates of chicken and rice and peas, the scents of coconut milk and garlic mingling with the distant smell of burnt wood and metal. Covey's father was muttering to another shopkeeper about the man who had reportedly beaten up his employee.

"Is not the first time him rough up somebody," her pa said. *"Dat man only causing trouble for the lot of us."* Covey's mummy would have glared at her pa for slipping into patois that way, but Covey's mummy hadn't been home in five years.

Hadn't telephoned.

Hadn't written a letter.

Hadn't come back for Covey.

"And this won't be the end of it, either, Lin," the other shopkeeper said.

Covey wanted to hear more, but Pearl called her into the house. If you wanted to know what was going on around town, you either hung around the men in the backyard or, once your body had sprouted points and curves and you were no longer permitted to linger, you sought out the women in the kitchen, especially on laundry days. There was usually a lull in the afternoon after school, when the white clothes had been laid out on the patio to bleach in the sun and Pearl had time for a piece of fruit and a chat with other helpers from up the way.

Like everyone in town, Covey had heard complaints about Chinese merchants who didn't pay their employees their due or who had made advances toward the women. But they weren't the only ones doling out mistreatment. Covey knew this because the women had always passed stories of such difficulties among themselves. This was the kind of thing that happened to them or to someone they knew all the time, wherever they worked, or shopped, or went to school. No difference if they were dealing with *chiney* or *blacka* or *dundus*.

Pearl said the human being was born to be a *ginnal* and it was a rare person who didn't take advantage of a weaker one, or pretend to be the friend of a stronger one just to reap the benefits. But even Pearl said Covey's father wasn't a real rat, not like some of those others. Take Little Man Henry and all his badness, for instance. Little Man, Pearl said, had taken his delinquent behavior well beyond the limits of their parish.

According to Pearl, it was common knowledge that Little Man was *tekkin'* money from the politicians to help stir up violence on the west end of the island. But that was not the worst of it. Little Man was capable of murder. More than one unlucky soul who had benefited from Little Man's so-called generosity had turned up dead after failing to pay him back. Others had limped home, all mashed up and not telling.

"Where money is involved," Pearl said, "not everything from above is a blessing."

The word was, Pearl said, that the woman whose body had been found farther up the coast a while back was a *gyal* from another town who had refused Little Man's advances. Of all the Little Man gossip, this was the story that sent a thick vein of dread running through Covey. That a man would cause so much hurt to someone who had done so little. It was said his brother was no better. It was said that the Henrys both profited from and caused the misfortune of others all too willingly.

Perhaps Covey or Pearl should have imagined that soon, Little Man would be getting himself involved in Johnny Lyncook's affairs. But they didn't.

It would be a while before Covey realized that the fire had marked the beginning of the end. The pullback before the wave of her father's debts engulfed them both. Most of the goods in her pa's store were lost. The rest was too smoky to be sold. On the day after the blaze, she overheard Pearl telling the helper from next door that she didn't think Mister Lin should have to be ruined because of someone else's bad deeds. Mister Lin, Pearl said, was perfectly capable of ruining things for himself.

Lin

—

WHO WAS A MAN, LIN WONDERED, IF HE NO LONGER HAD a place to call home?

Lin knew people still saw him as a foreigner, even after he'd gone to school in the same town, run a business here, taken a wife here, and raised a child here. Even after he'd lost his brothers to the TB, like so many others. Lin, too, had always thought of himself as a foreigner, even as he slammed down his domino tiles on the table in the backyard, even as he spat out a local cuss word, and even as he sat on the veranda sucking on a Bombay mango from the tree that his father had planted with his own two hands.

But all that changed on the night that he watched his store burning up, on the night that someone set fire to one of the businesses where he had worked since he was a pickney, on the night that he found himself fretting for the safety of his daughter in the town where she had been born. On the night that Lin, out of cash and nearly out of things to barter, finally admitted to himself that he was in over his head.

On that particular night, all the names that people had called him under their breath, all the looks of disapproval they'd once given him as his motherless, brown child followed him around town, clinging with one hand to the hem of his shirt, came back now to slice him across the chest like the tip of a cutlass. And he saw that he was not a foreigner at all, that this was his only home, that he had no other place to go. He may have come here as little Lin Jian from Guangzhou but he had spent more time as Johnny "Lin" Lyncook from Portland parish, sixty-odd miles from the capital city and a lifetime away from China. He could no longer be one without the other.

Had his *ba* been wrong to insist on being called by his Chinese surname and encourage the same for Johnny? Had he been wrong to speak to his sons in Hakka in public? Had Lin been wrong in going to the cemetery on Gah San every spring to sweep the tombs of his lost brothers and, later, his parents? Would it have changed anything?

No matter now. The blame that people were laying at Lin's feet for the misdeeds of another man who happened to look like him was about to bring him down, not because he had anything to do with them but because of his own mistakes. Lin would not be able to recover from this fire because his own vices had already put him too far into debt.

Lin looked down at his feet. They were still stained with soot. He turned on the garden hose and ran the water between his toes. He looked up at the kitchen window, listened to Covey chatting with Pearl inside, the clack-clack of plates being washed and sorted. Just as Lin was coming to accept that what he had here was all that mattered, he saw that he was on the verge of losing it all.

Now

—

A Piece
of Home

—

WHO ARE ALL THESE PEOPLE BENNY'S MOTHER IS TALKING about? What do they have to do with her ma? And what about the sister she mentioned? It's still not clear to Benny what happened. And Benny isn't even sure she wants to know. She feels panicky. She feels like everything is slipping away. She just wants her ma, the way she used to be.

Benny tells the men she has to go to the bathroom but instead, she heads farther down the hallway to the room where she grew up and digs into the contents of her wheelie bag.

There.

She unrolls an old university sweatshirt she inherited years ago from her brother and takes out a measuring cup, a cloudy-looking piece of plastic that is older than she is. It goes back to the days when Ma was a young bride, newly arrived in America. Ounces and cups on one side, milliliters on the other.

"Take this," her mother said as Benny was packing for her move to college. She pressed the cup into Benny's tote bag and patted the bag. "This way you'll have a little piece of home with you, wherever you go." After that, Benny never did pack a suitcase without slipping the old cup in among her clothes, a little reminder of all those days spent together in the kitchen with her ma.

Benny's nose was barely level with the kitchen counter when her mother first showed her how to make a black cake. Ma reached down and pulled a huge jar out of a lower cupboard. One of her tricks was to soak the dried fruits in rum and port all year round, not just a few weeks before.

"This is island food," Ma said. "This is your heritage."

While the batter was in the oven, her mother hoisted Benny onto a dark green stool. She told Benny that the seat was the color of the trees that grew straight out of the water where she had grown up. Benny imagined a wide, dark sea pierced by tall trees, like the redwoods that her parents had taken her and Byron to see farther up the California coast. She imagined them standing firm like massive sentinels, as tall waves washed past their trunks.

"One day, you'll see," her mother told her.

Benny grew up thinking that her mother and father would take her and Byron to the island someday, but they never did. It was years before Benny realized that the towering water trees she'd imagined were actually mangroves, low, verdant clumps of life rooted in those intertidal zones where fresh water mixed with seawater, where the roots were both hardy and vulnerable, where both sea and land creatures made their homes. Where nothing was any one thing but, rather, a little bit of everything. Kind of like Benny.

Her ma had been using the same measuring cup for twenty years or so when her dad took Benny and Byron to a department store to find a replacement. They ended up choosing a bigger one made out of thick glass.

"For her black cake," their father said, raising the cup as if in a toast.

"Oooh!" their mother said when she opened the package. She left the gleaming new cup on the kitchen counter and used it almost every day, only never for the black cake. When baking time came around, she would burrow into a bottom cupboard and fish out the old plastic thing, closing off the kitchen to everyone but Benny as she measured and mixed.

Even after Benny grew up and moved out, Christmastime baking with Ma remained an annual ritual. She would come back each winter for the blacking of the sugar, the rubbing of the butter, the sifting-in of the breadcrumbs. And each time, she brought the old measuring cup with her. Whenever her ma saw it, she would wrap her arms around Benny and kiss her on the neck, *mwah-mwah-mwah.*

Then came the big rift with her parents, that disastrous Thanksgiving Day, two years before her dad died, and Benny stopped visiting altogether. But by then, Benny had already evolved into a person who could smell the weather in a handful of flour and taste the earth in a spoon of cane sugar, and this is what had led her to take culinary classes. That, and dropping out of college. Which, Benny sees now, was what had started it all.

Benny's decision to leave her elite university, years earlier, had caused the first tear in the fabric of their family home. The fissure had widened with her parents' growing disappointment in her. They were irritated enough when she went to Italy to take the cooking courses but when she came back to the United States and moved to Arizona for art school, even her brother looked perplexed. The three people Benny loved most in this world no longer made any attempt to hide their doubts in her.

For Benny, the move made sense. Maybe it was the time she'd spent in the pastry-making classes, working with her hands and exploring the use of color and texture. Maybe it was being steeped for one year in the visual stimulation of an Italian city, the mustard- and salmon-colored façades, the marble fountains, slick with water, the faces, the language. Benny only knew that she had come back to the States wanting to do more with her painting. She sensed that some combination of food and art in her life would help to ground her.

Benny didn't want to work in a kitchen full time so much as she wanted to be surrounded by beauty and comforting things and decent people. She wanted to sit alone in her own café, before the first customers arrived, and work in her sketchbook, looking up through a glass window to see the morning sky turn metallic blue, then white gold. She wanted to use the café to teach children about culture through cooking. She wanted to do things her own way and have it work out all right. Benny wanted to have a safe space and a life that would always be under her control.

But Benny was Bert and Eleanor Bennett's child and this was not the Bennett way. If you were a Bennett, you were expected to finish college, go on to graduate school, find a *real* profession, and do everything else in your free time. If you were born to Bert and Eleanor, you banked on your university degrees, you built your influence, you accumulated wealth, you quashed all vulnerability.

In short, you became Byron Bennett.

Benny turns the measuring cup over and over in her hands. The plastic has cracks here and there from repeated drops and house moves, plus the hot liquids that Benny's mother had warned her never to pour into the cup, but which she'd done anyway.

Benny, plunking butter into the measuring cup and melting it in the microwave.

Benny, drinking mulled wine out of the measuring cup, sitting alone at a table set for two.

Benny, eating soup out of the measuring cup, the bruises on her face and neck aching with each spoonful.

Benny, sipping tea from the cup, feeling that her own brother had turned his back on her.

Benny hugs the cup to her middle now and runs a finger back and forth across the remains of the manufacturer's label. In nearly fifty years, it has never fully disintegrated. Her mother's hand would have touched that fuzzy gum every time she measured out a cup of flour or rice or beans or oil, every time she used it to cook for a birthday party, a holiday dinner, a fundraiser. She wondered, could there still be a bit of Ma's DNA on this cup? Could her mother, perhaps, not be fully gone from this earth? Scientists have found DNA in ice dating back hundreds of thousands of years.

Benny pulls her smartphone out of her jeans pocket and dials up her voicemail. For the umpteenth time, she listens to her mother's message from the month before.

Those four words: *Benedetta, please come home.* She lowers her head, swallows hard, hears the soft tap of a teardrop in the measuring cup.

Homesickness

—

BENNY HEARS BYRON CALLING TO HER FROM THE OTHER
end of the hallway, but she ignores him. She's not ready to go back to
hearing her mother's story. She needs to think. Benny looks around at
the turquoise-colored walls of the room where she slept almost every
night until she was seventeen. Her parents painted it this color because
she'd insisted on it. She smiles at the memory. Why didn't she come
back to California sooner?

Benny could have seen her mother a month ago, even a week ago,
but she didn't realize that her mother was ill. And, of course, Byron,
dammit, didn't call until it was too late. So Benny had hesitated, hoping
that this would be the month she'd secure financing from a bank for her
business plan. Hoping to go home to Ma and Byron with something to
show for all that time she'd spent away. Hoping to prove that she had
been right all along to follow her own path, instead of the one that her
parents would have chosen for her.

While Benny's mother stood leaning against her kitchen counter in
California, a blood clot quietly inching its way up from her pelvis to
her lungs, Benny was still back in New York, getting fired from her
afternoon job and boarding the wrong bus and finding herself standing
in front of the kind of coffee shop that she wanted to have for herself.
The café, with its too-early Christmas decorations, stood next to a
small bookshop in a neighborhood that hadn't yet had the stuffing gen-
trified out of it.

Inside, Benny found comfort in the sound of a thick, enameled cup as it settled into the saucer in front of her, the shriek and crunch of the coffee grinder, the smell of bacon grease settling into the weave of her woolen cape. Benny didn't eat meat but even she had to admit that there was something about the smell of bacon that could take the edge off a feeling of homesickness.

This coffee shop reminded her of the old place back in California that she and her brother used to go to with their father when they were kids. There was a spigot and a bucket in the parking lot where Dad would let them soap up the car, rinse it off, then leave it to dry in the sun while they went inside to eat things that you found only in such places. It was well before Benny moved away to college, then to Europe, then Arizona, then New York. Years before she ever imagined not getting along with her dad.

Her dad had been gone for six years now, and Benny was nearly thirty-seven years old, still working a jumble of jobs and still unable to convince a bank to lend her the money to open her own café. But just as a person could feel the breeze switch directions and pick up speed, Benny could sense that her life was about to change. She'd been saving money, she was doing better emotionally than the year before, and she wanted to make one more attempt before giving up altogether on her business idea. Especially since she had no idea what to do otherwise.

This café she'd stumbled upon in New York was going out of business. There was a sign on the front door. If she could manage to pay the lease on a place like this, she'd put in lounge chairs and coffee tables with phone- and laptop-friendly electrical outlets. She would keep the lighting soft and the colors warm but declutter the central space. She would offer a super-short menu and only one signature dessert per season. Her winter dessert would be her mother's black cake.

Benny needed to find more work right away. She'd made a mess of things, getting fired, and yet she was still feeling somewhat righteous because she'd refused to lie to a client. It wasn't that Benny didn't know how to stick to a call center script, as her supervisor had suggested. It was that she understood that one of the things that made you human was your willingness to deviate from the script. The problem was, scripts were like battles. You had to choose when to go with them and when not to. And you had to be prepared to live with the consequences.

Benny had responded to the customer call with the standard "My name is Sondra, how can I help you today?" You never gave your real name at that company. You adopted a moniker that was easy to pronounce, even better if it was just different enough to seem authentic, as in Sondra with an *aw* sound as opposed to Sandra with an *ah*. Benny had become practiced at that sort of thing, making people feel comfortable. The script helped, with a list of appropriate greetings and a checklist of things to ask for. Error code, serial number, *just a moment, please,* et cetera, et cetera.

Benny informed the customer that it was surely a problem with the printer head, which was not removable, though she was sorry to say that the particular printer in the customer's possession was no longer under warranty. It was not worth it, Benny said, to seek assistance, since a consultation alone, without repair, would cost the customer more than half of what it would cost to purchase a new product.

"And to think that I've hardly used the thing," the customer said.

"That, ma'am, is the problem," Benny said. "This particular technology is not advisable for people who are not going to be using their printers every day, or at least on a regular basis." At this point in the call, Benny was still following the recommended language.

"But no one told me this when I bought it," the customer said. "Apart from the fact that I'm now forced to buy a new printer after only two years, it seems like a real waste of materials. Aren't we supposed to be reducing the trash we produce?"

"Yes, ma'am, I am in complete agreement with you," Benny said.

It was the next statement that got Benny fired, according to her boss, who happened to be walking down the aisle behind her cubicle and overheard her.

"Alas," said Benny, "we are living in a dumping ground for electronics, from printers to computers to mobile phones that fall apart, or that we are encouraged to replace with newer models that are marketed as being more desirable, and this, ma'am, is one of the main reasons for the environmental degradation that our planet is experiencing today."

Benny did not forget to ask, "Is there anything else I can do for you today?" but it didn't really help her case, though she remained convinced that the customer had gone away feeling relatively satisfied, because sometimes all we really want is for somebody to acknowledge that we were right all along.

At least the supervisor fired Benny in person. Back when Benny was still seeing Joanie, poor Joanie only learned she'd been laid off one morning when the electronic key card to her office building failed to open the door to the staff entrance. Benny was deeply offended on Joanie's behalf. She'd even gone to Joanie's former workplace to tell the manager what she thought, before being escorted off the property by a security guard. But this episode only added to the resentment that Joanie had been feeling. About the job, about her boss's lack of respect. About Benny's failure to tell her parents about her and Joanie. Again.

Maybe, Benny thought, she could supplement her income by selling more of her drawings. She hadn't tried to sell the others, she'd simply been offered ridiculous sums of money for them by people who had seen her sketching to pass the time in cafés and airports and, once, in a laundromat. She had replicated the laundromat work on heavier paper with a toothier surface, mounted it, and earned enough to pay an entire month's rent.

Benny had felt like a bit of a fraud at first, but then she got to thinking. She had studied drawing, hadn't she? And if she could be paid to dress up in an animal costume, which she did on weekends at the mall, then why couldn't she accept good money for her artwork? She hadn't really tried before this only because she hadn't thought it possible.

Benny pulled out her sketchbook and placed it on the café table. Drawing, like baking, usually cleared her head, but she kept thinking about how this diner reminded her of her dad and, by extension, her ma. By the time she was ready to head back to her apartment, she had come to a decision. She would go home this winter, no matter what. It was time. It had been a month since her mother had left that voice message on her cellphone.

Benedetta, please come home.

Maybe her ma was ready to apologize. Maybe Benny was ready to hear her out. Plus, her ma had sounded tired. Her ma had never been one to sound tired. Yes, it was definitely time.

Benny's phone was ringing. Her brother's number. Her brother never called. All of a sudden, everyone was getting in touch.

Leaning against the wall of her old bedroom now, letting the cool seep through the back of her sweater, Benny can't get away from the feeling that maybe, just maybe, she'll step out into the hallway and find her mother there, or see her father pop his head into the room and narrow his eyes at the color of the walls, the way he used to. That, maybe, all this can be undone.

Byron

BYRON'S PHONE IS VIBRATING ALONG THE KITCHEN COUNTER, its screen flashing, *one-two, one-two,* like lightning strikes in a wall of clouds. Byron feels like the phone. Agitated. Where the hell is Benny, anyway?

"Sorry, just a second," he says to Mr. Mitch. He gets up to turn off the phone when he recognizes the number.

Lynette.

It's been three months since they last talked. She must have heard about his ma.

Byron had wiped Lynette's number from his list of contacts on the night she'd walked out on him. He'd punched delete with a sense of satisfaction, as though she might feel the defiance in his gesture throbbing across the airwaves, as though it might lead her to regret her hasty exit. It was only later that he realized that when Lynette slammed the door shut, she had already emptied her side of the bedroom closet, had already stuffed her computer and toothbrush into a bag, had already left the earrings he'd given her the previous month on the desk in his studio.

Byron hadn't noticed any of this at first, he'd only seen Lynette's arms waving around, her face turning wet, as they argued. She'd been doing that a lot, lately. Crying, yelling, bugging him about plans for the future. Who talked about The Future nowadays? Byron didn't like that kind of pressure. Did it mean nothing to her, at all, that they were already living together? Didn't it count that he had offered to mentor her nephew Jackson? Why was it that nothing Byron did ever seemed to be enough?

Officially, Byron hadn't gotten together with Lynette until after the documentary project they'd been working on together had ended. Still, he knew the moment he first saw her that he'd have to try. He knew that's what he was doing during filming breaks when they took to chatting together while they picked out sandwiches and fruit cups from the catering table. He knew that's what he was doing when he invited the director and the entire crew for a barbecue at his place. He knew it was what he was doing as he watched Lynette step out onto the deck of his house, saw her lips part slowly at the view, watched her shoulders rise with the sea air.

It would be too obvious to say that he couldn't resist her fluffy crown of hair, or the slopes of her body, or the sight of her deep-brown fingers with their tiny, burgundy-painted nails buzzing over the keyboard of her laptop, or the quiet way she moved through the clamor of a production set. Lynette managed to inhabit space in a way that was different from other people and Byron wanted to be there with her.

In the end, Lynette was so critical of Byron, and yet she'd started out drawn to everything about him. Back then, she didn't seem to mind his status, his expertise, the house within view of the Pacific. Then things got serious between them and she suddenly expected him to separate out who he was from what he had to do in life.

Lynette, who wouldn't have met Byron if he hadn't been the host of that documentary.

Lynette, who he suspects would never have looked at him otherwise.

Lynette, whose neck smelled like nutmeg and who slammed the door when she left him for good.

And now, for the first time in three months, his phone is lighting up with Lynette's number. Maybe it's not about his ma, at all. Maybe Lynette needs something from him. Calling about Ma would be a way in. His friend Cable would tell him he's being a jerk for thinking about

Lynette that way. Cable would say that of course Lynette was calling about his ma. And Cable wouldn't mince words if he believed otherwise.

Byron will call Lynette later. Or maybe he won't call. She's the one who walked out on the relationship. He feels that old burn just below his sternum. He's pissed that Lynette should still get to him this way. He looks one more time at the flashing screen on his smartphone, then taps reject to silence the call.

Byron and Benny

———

BYRON WANTS TO FINISH LISTENING TO HIS MOTHER'S RECORDING, but Benny is off and wandering around the house. Benny, who always used to say that she needed to go to the bathroom when she really just wanted to take off and do something else. Sure enough, Byron finds Benny in her old bedroom, wearing an ancient college sweatshirt and hugging something small to her chest.

Benny looks at him, her face all knotted up. He knows what she's thinking.

"Who is she, Byron?" Benny says.

Byron shakes his head. "I have no idea," he says. "This is the first I've ever heard anything about us having a sister."

"I don't mean this *sister* person. I mean Covey. Who in the world was she?" Benny's shoulders slump. "What did she have to do with our mother? They must have known each other, with all those things they had in common. The island, the sea, the black cake. Don't you think?"

"I don't know what to think."

"This is taking too long. Let's just go and make Mr. Mitch tell us right now."

"No, you heard what he said, he's not going to tell us. Let's just go back and listen."

Benny nods. She has that cloudy-looking face of little Benny at age six and, once again, Byron must resist the urge to hug her. He needs to remember that this is not his baby sister anymore. This is a woman he hasn't seen in eight years, who didn't come to their own father's funeral, who wasn't there for their mother's seventieth birthday, and with whom he's exchanged only a handful of words in all that time. Apparently, no one is who they used to be. Not his sister and not even his own mother.

Byron holds out a set of keys.

"What's this?" Benny says.

"I had to change the locks on the front door. This is your set."

"But I never come in the front door."

"Well, we have a front door, so just take the keys."

Benny puts out her hand. "What happened? Burglary?"

Byron shakes his head. "Earthquake. Shifted the doorframe."

"Oh, yeah, now I remember."

"You do?" Byron says, the sarcasm making his upper lip curl. "What do you mean, you remember, Benny? You weren't even here. And, by the way, you didn't bother to call, did you, to see if we were all right?"

"I didn't have to. Ma let me know."

"Ma? You talked to Ma?"

"No, not really. Ma would leave messages once in a while."

"You were in contact with Ma? All this time? I thought you weren't talking to each other."

"I told you, once in a while she'd leave a message. Birthdays, holidays, you know. Then the earthquake."

"But you never came to see her."

Benny shakes her head. "She never told me to come and see her. She never even asked me to call her back. I did call the house a couple of times, but she didn't answer. I wrote her a letter, not long ago, and she left me a short message. She didn't say she was sick." Benny opens her mouth to say something else, then stops, shakes her head.

"She was on some heavy-duty meds the last few months. Of course she wanted to see you. She was just very hurt, you know?"

"Ma? She was hurt? And what about me? I was the one who was rejected by my own parents."

"They did not reject you, Benny. They were upset because you walked out on them."

"They were not upset because I walked out on them. They were already upset and we both know why."

"And you made it worse. You walked out on them in the middle of a holiday, and you never even called to apologize. You didn't give them a chance. And I was pretty upset, too, Benny. No, wait, correct that. I was pissed off at you. I'm still pissed off at you. And what about the funeral, Benny? When I called you that time, you said you would come."

"I did come to the funeral, Byron. I came all the way to California, I went to the cemetery, it's just that. . . ."

"What are you saying? You were here? You know, I thought I saw you, but then I said to myself, *No, Byron, you're imagining things.* But I wasn't. You mean to tell me, you came all the way out here and then you had the nerve to just leave us on our own?"

"You weren't exactly on your own, Byron. There were a lot of people there."

"And that's your excuse? That with all those people around, you didn't need to be there?"

"No, that's not what I'm saying, it's just that I couldn't . . ."

"Couldn't what, Benny? Couldn't *what*? Couldn't get out of the damn car for your own father's funeral? Couldn't get out of the car for Ma and me? And then all I get is a text message saying *I'm sorry*?"

"It's not that simple, Byron."

"No, it's not that *complicated*."

Byron turns and walks out of the room, but not before seeing what Benny is holding. It's their mother's old plastic measuring cup. He turns back and pulls the cup away from her.

"No, Byron!" Benny cries as she follows him down the hallway. "Byron!" Now she's pulling at his sweater with one hand, trying to grab the cup with the other.

"Don't do that," Byron says, batting Benny away from his sweater. "That's cashmere."

"That's cashmere?" Benny says. "That's *cashmere*? Are you kidding me, Byron?"

"This is ridiculous," Byron says, shoving the cup back into Benny's hand. "There. Does that make you feel better? Does it make you feel like a good little daughter, keeping that cup for the memories? Where the fuck were you all these years, Benny?"

"You don't really want to know, do you, Byron? You don't really want to hear anything from me. You just want to remind me that you're Byron Bennett, the perfect son, admired and accepted by everyone. Well, you know something? You're not so perfect. And no one gets to have any feelings until you decide they have feelings."

Byron is stunned. Is that what she thinks? Is that what Benny really thinks of him?

"Why didn't you call me sooner, huh, Byron? If Ma was so sick?"

"Why didn't *I* call *you* sooner? Are you even listening to yourself? Do you know what Ma would say if she heard this?"

Byron turns and walks off down the hallway, muttering, "This is not the Bennett way." Then he winces. He sounds so much like Dad.

Benny shouts at his back. "Wrong, Byron. This has always been the Bennett way. No missteps allowed, no room for comprehension, no room for dissension."

Byron stops, stands still, but doesn't look back.

"I used to think it was because we were black, you know?" Benny says. "That our parents wanted us to achieve, that we had to work twice as hard, be beyond reproach, that sort of thing. But now I get it. We had to be perfect to make up for the fact that our family was built on a colossal lie."

When Byron finally reaches the living room, Mr. Mitch isn't there. Byron hears the water running in the guest bathroom. He doesn't know that Mr. Mitch is simply leaning against the dusty pink wall in there, eyes closed, pretending not to have heard all the shouting.

Lost

——

CHARLES MITCH HAS SEEN WORSE. SIBLINGS WHO DON'T care about each other. Relatives who are only looking for what they can inherit. He can see that Byron and Benny aren't like that but this is turning out to be a struggle, anyway. They've lost their mother and they can't seem to find their way back to each other. Yes, Eleanor warned him that it might be like this, worse yet because Byron and Benny used to be inseparable.

∵

BENNY'S WORLD USED TO BEGIN AND END WITH HER BROTHER. When did he become this person? Or had he always been this way? Byron has accused Benny of not being there for her family. But what about Benny? Has it ever occurred to Byron, so accustomed to being cheered on by the whole world, that someone needed to be there for Benny, too?

∵

BYRON DOESN'T KNOW WHAT TO DO ABOUT BENNY. THEY haven't said a civil word to each other since she arrived. It's like she's hostile one minute and needy the next. But this is not a new thing, Benny making a bigger deal of things than she needs to. It's been this way for a long time now, ever since Benny dropped out of college. Yep, that's really where it started.

How to Become a College Dropout

———

Benny, at the school of her parents' dreams.

Benny, seventeen, at the top of her class.

Benny, getting the side-eye at the black student union.

Benny, not black enough. Benny, not white enough.

Benny, not straight enough. Benny, not gay enough.

Benny, alone on a Saturday night.

Benny, in bed with bruises all over.

Benny, signing papers in Administration.

Benny, walking down the marble staircase.

Benny, nineteen, a college dropout.

What You Don't Say

—

I N HER THIRD YEAR AT COLLEGE, BENNY WAS CORNERED IN THE dorms by two girls who had seen Benny getting flirty with one of the guys from the African American fraternity. They called her a traitor. One of them pushed her into her room and when Benny caught her foot on the metal leg of her bed and fell, she kicked Benny in the face.

It was the surprise of what was happening that caused Benny to stay there on the ground, more than any of the blows landed by her schoolmate. She was, after all, six feet tall, and though she'd never loved the surfing and swimming as much as her parents and Byron, she'd done a bit of sport all the same, she'd grown up pretty strong.

In the end, it was all soft-tissue damage; the bruises would heal in time. But there was a deeper hurt that drove Benny away from the school. These were girls who she'd thought would have supported her for her differences, not lashed out at her. The one who kicked her while she lay on the ground had once danced with her at the student pub, then leaned her against a dark wall that smelled like beer and sneakers and kissed her. They had both smiled, then headed back to the dance floor.

This is the kind of thing a person doesn't say. That these were senior-year students who'd initially made her glad to be on campus. That instead of closing ranks around Benny, they'd closed her out. That as the one girl kicked Benny where she lay, the other didn't say *stop*. But Benny would never report them. She refused to give anyone the chance to look her up and down the way people sometimes did and say, *You see?*

From then on, with each move, first back home to California, then Italy, then Arizona, Benny yearned consistently for one thing more than any other, a life that felt emotionally unremarkable. A life that felt safe.

Arizona had seemed like a good place to start once Benny had decided to go to art school. She would get as far away as she could from the feel of the northeastern university that she'd left behind. She would study something that interested her, not her parents. She would take that time to figure out exactly how to move forward, how to find her place in the working world.

Benny was energized by the broad, seemingly barren expanses that, seen from up close, were popping with life. The furred leaves of the velvet mesquite. The blue-green bark and yellow flowers of the blue palo verde. The bristly javelinas, the splotchy Gila monsters, the baby rattlesnakes that flicked their tiny tails to warn of the potency already pooled within.

Arizona had a good art program that Benny could afford and Benny had grades that could get her into the school, almost no questions asked. And that was how Benny met Joanie. At the time, Joanie was a graduate assistant in ceramics. She had a sharp jaw and wavy ponytail that pulled at Benny the first time she saw her walking down a corridor with clay-splattered coveralls.

Then Benny saw the blue vase. It was nearing the end of the first term and some of the students had gone over to Joanie's townhouse for drinks and snacks. The poured-cement floor in Joanie's living room was cool and bare. The only carpeting in the central space was a claret-colored rug hanging on one of the walls and below it, on the floor, was a row of Joanie's ceramic pieces. The partygoers were clustered together in front of an enormous blue vase.

To say the vase was blue was about as imprecise as calling a person interesting, but everyone agreed that it was, at the very least, bluish. Benny sat staring at the waist-high object for what felt like an hour, pulling her gaze up from the mostly emerald lower border, through its rich celestial middle, to the pale aquamarine splash at the top, the flecks of gold and amber near the upper edge, and finally, part of the lip and bulge of the vase, which had been left uncolored, the natural, reddish tone of the pottery exposed. Benny contemplated the vase, then looked over at Joanie. And Joanie smiled back at her in that way that Benny would come to know.

Four years into their relationship, Benny still hadn't told her family about Joanie, and this had become a problem. Joanie was ten years older, *been there, done that*, plus they were living in the twenty-first century, for Pete's sake, she said. Benny tried to make it up to her. She filled Joanie's kitchen, decidedly nicer than her own, with spices and sautés. She sent emails around to promote Joanie's exhibits. She waited every Friday night for Joanie outside the office where Joanie worked part time, so they could grab a pizza together.

But Joanie was the kind of person who appeared not to mind the slights of others, until finally they had crossed some invisible line. And now, it was Benny's turn to find out what that could mean.

As another winter of holiday plans approached, Joanie told Benny that Benny had been doing too much for her, suffocating her, when all Joanie had ever asked her for was one thing. Benny rushed over to Joanie's place. As soon as Joanie let her inside, Benny saw that the blue vase and a couple of the other pieces were gone, leaving empty spaces along the floor. It was then that Benny noticed the wall rug, rolled up and bound with plastic ties, the cardboard cartons lined up near the kitchen counter. Joanie told Benny she had decided to move to New York to take a teaching job, she'd be leaving before Thanksgiving. And just like that, it was the end of Benny and Joanie.

But only for now, Benny told herself, as she sped away from Joanie's house, hands tight on the steering wheel. Only for now, she told herself the following week, as she drove home to California, eye on the speedometer, trying to stay under ninety miles an hour.

The
Bennetts

———

THANKSGIVING DAY, 2010, RIGHT HERE IN THIS HOUSE. WHEN
Benny's father finally grasped what Benny had been trying to say about
her love life, he raised his voice. And Dad was not the voice-raising
kind. She tried to interject but her dad kept talking over her. Then he
stood up.

"I don't see how you can manage to live a decent life with this kind
of confusion," Bert said.

"Decent?" Benny said. "Are you saying I am not decent?"

"Don't you raise your voice at me, young lady," Bert said.

"Daddy, you are the one who is shouting at me. You are the one
who asked me if I was dating someone. You are the one who said, why
don't I bring someone home? I was just trying to explain that it might
be a *him* or it might be a *her*."

"So your mother and I are supposed to be okay with you sleeping
around?"

"I am not sleeping around, Daddy. I've been with the same woman
for four years. I've only dated a couple of people, ever. But that's not
the point. . . ."

"The point is, you're not even sure what you want."

"Yes, I am sure, Daddy. This is who I am. I'm Benny."

There was a look in her parents' eyes that she had never seen before. Everything went quiet, like that second before a pot of water
comes to a boil. She looked over at Byron but he was just sitting there,

looking at the floor. He wasn't going to help her, was he? Benny had feared it would come to this. She breathed in and out slowly, letting the hurt of what she was thinking run through her until she heard herself saying it.

"It's you who aren't sure, Daddy." Benny worked hard to keep the quiver out of her voice. "It's you who aren't sure if you love me anymore." At which point her father turned away from her and stalked out of the room, her mother following after him, saying, "Bert, Bert." Benny hadn't intended to spend Thanksgiving Day all alone, but she didn't see how she could stay, what with her dad saying she was *indecent,* and her mother wet-eyed and trailing after her father, and a bunch of people on their way over to the house for dinner.

The Bennetts usually entered and exited by the back door of their family home, the one that led directly into the kitchen, but instead of crossing through the house as usual, Benny headed straight for the front door. It took a couple of tries to get the door to open, its tendency to stick being one of the reasons why they'd always preferred the back entrance. When Benny finally tugged it open, she went through without saying a word.

She left the door open. She figured her brother would follow her out, but he didn't. When she got home, she checked her messages, thinking Byron would have called her, would have grumbled, *What the heck were you thinking?* But he hadn't. At least the long drive back to Arizona had its advantages. By the time she turned onto her street late that night, the holiday was over, and she was not the only person on the block to be seen trudging up the walkway, turning a key in the lock, and switching on the lights in an empty unit.

Benny tried to take comfort in the fact that lots of people didn't celebrate Thanksgiving.

The problem was, that wasn't how Benny had been raised. This was a time of year when Benny's family gathered together with friends and took time to be grateful. It was the being together that counted and Benny had just been excluded from it all.

In the weeks that followed, the landline at home would ring and the caller ID panel would light up with the word *Private* and Benny would punch the button to answer, but no one would speak. Benny would tell herself that it was her mother calling, because it wouldn't have been her father. Sometimes, after a pause, a telemarketer would greet her in that buoyant tone that a person tended to use when bracing themselves for rejection.

Benny was always polite when she said no to the telemarketers because she understood that they were just trying to earn a living, they were just trying to get through the week, they were just hoping for a sign of acceptance.

Hoping for acceptance. Benny knew a thing or two about that.

She started sorting through her things that very night. What to take with her to New York, what to donate. There was that charity group that sent around a truck that made you feel better about having to part with stuff. You could tell yourself you were doing something good for someone. When Benny moved to New York soon after, hoping that, in time, Joanie would forgive her, she didn't even bother to send her new address to her folks. They had her cellphone number, anyway, and they hadn't used it in a while, now, not since she'd texted them to say that she'd be spending the Christmas holidays elsewhere.

Byron on
the Tube

———

I N THE YEARS AFTER HER MOVE TO NEW YORK, BENNY'S BROTHER became so popular that she could see him every day, if she wanted to, on the television news, on a late-night talk show, on her laptop. Lately, Benny has been keeping a link on her smartphone that takes her to a documentary where a camera crew is following Byron around. TV Byron feels much more accessible right now than that other Byron who is out in the living room with Mr. Mitch.

TV Byron tells an interviewer that most of the world's oceans remain uncharted, that information about the depth and shape of the seafloor could be used in so many things. Tsunami forecasting. Pollution control. The mining of materials for the electronics that people use every day. Everything we need to know about our past and our future is here, Byron tells the camera, pointing at a screen showing remote-sensing images. And everything that we can learn about who we are as human beings and what we are willing to do will be tested by this kind of technology.

Robots under the sea are helping scientists to carry out a major mapping project, but Byron says having more information will be an enormous test of international good faith. With every new technological development, knowledge has to be shared. Accords must be developed and respected. Otherwise, there is a risk, he says, that human greed will be the dominant force, just as it has been on land.

"What if I had a vegetable garden at home," he says, "and every time I wanted something like corn or tomatoes for dinner, I'd pull up all the plants by their roots or chop down an entire fruit tree just to have, say, a few apples? Well, you would say that makes no sense, right?"

Byron points now to a full-screen image of an idyllic seascape. "We need to be more careful with our underwater resources because that, out there, is the biggest garden we have on Earth. It may look infinite, but it's not. We need to go easy on the seabed, we need to allow it to flourish."

All the things that had initially threatened to work against Byron as a young scholar in ocean sciences have ended up turning him into a media darling. He talks about things like sonar technology, topography, and hydrothermal vents in ways that folks can understand. He looks like a fashion model for a high-end outerwear company. And, of course, he's black.

There was a golden moment there, at about the time that Byron completed his PhD, when ethnic minorities were being encouraged more than ever to go for STEM degrees, though they didn't always land the jobs with the best potential for professional growth. Byron had a very specific idea of what he wanted to do with his training. He kept knocking on doors and when, finally, one of those doors swung open at a newly formed foundation, wouldn't you know it, he told Benny back then, he walked right through the reception area and into his dream job.

Byron grabbed the ball and ran with it and social media took him the rest of the way. Hashtags frequently seen alongside #ByronBennett include #ocean #science #underwater #tides #tsunami #globalwarming #environment #geohazards #oil #gas #pipeline #minerals #mining #defense #AfricanAmerican #sciencestud and #bachelors.

By tracking Byron online, Benny could pretend, at times, that it wasn't true that they hadn't seen each other in years, or hadn't spoken in ages. She could allow herself to forget that she no longer had the kind of brother who would pick up the phone just to say hello, who would want to know how she was doing. Who might have gotten on a plane, banged on her front door, and pulled her into a bear hug had Benny called him in the middle of the night to say *I need help*.

She knows that part of this is her fault. But she's here now, isn't she? Still, it feels like Benny could yell at the top of her lungs and Byron, just down the hallway, wouldn't hear her. Or he'd choose not to.

Byron

—

BYRON AND MR. MITCH ARE SLOUCHED ON THE LIVING ROOM furniture, scrolling through their respective smartphones and waiting for Benny to come back into the room. Byron is pretending he hasn't just had a huge argument with his sister, and Mr. Mitch is pretending he hasn't just heard it.

Byron's phone rings and he sees it's Lynette again. This time, he answers.

"Lynette, how are you?"

"No, how are *you*? I'm so sorry about your mom, Byron."

Weird, this super-polite conversation after three months of radio silence between them, after the way they left each other. No, correct that. After the way Lynette left Byron. But now that he hears her voice, he's glad she's made the effort. His ma really did like her. Lynette says she'll be at the funeral service tomorrow.

"Maybe we could talk, afterward?" Lynette says. "Could we do that? Sit down somewhere together?"

"Sure, if you want," Byron says.

"Yes," says Lynette. "I do. Actually, there's something I've been meaning to talk to you about."

Oh, there we go. So she does need something from him, after all.

Lynette, Lynette, Lynette.

It used to be easy to talk to her. But that was the old Lynette, before they'd fought and she walked out on him. Byron wishes he had someone like the old Lynette to talk to right now. He'd tell her about his mother's recording, about the black cake tucked away in the freezer. The old Lynette would laugh at the cake. She would say, *That's just like your mom, Byron*. And she would have Byron chuckling, too, right now, despite this cavern of loss in his rib cage.

His mother and her black cake was what had gotten Benny into baking to begin with. He didn't see why his parents were so surprised when she started talking about wanting to go to Europe to take culinary classes. Though, sure, they were all pretty stunned when, sometime before that, Benny quit college and refused to talk about it.

"It just didn't feel right," was all she would say. "I need to try a different way."

"Give her some time," Byron said to his parents. When Benny said something about the diaspora of food and the recipes that intrigued her, Byron picked up on this. He suggested Benny go back to college and do something related, like a major in anthropology. But Benny just shook her head no. Then off she went, and when she came back, she decided to study art. How the heck was Benny going to support herself, Byron wanted to know.

There was a time when Benny would have debated the idea with him, at least, but something had shifted in her, something had gone brittle. She only seemed like she was still his kid sister when she was in the kitchen with Ma.

His mother used to say she would make a black cake for Byron and Benny when each of them got married, but neither of them had. Ma's cake was a work of art, Byron had to admit. That moist, loamy mouthful, the tang of spirits behind the nose. But Byron had never shared his parents' emotional attachment to the recipe. *Tradition*, his ma used to say. But whose tradition, exactly? Black cake was essentially a plum pudding handed down to the Caribbeans by colonizers from a cold country. Why claim the recipes of the exploiters as your own?

Tradition? How about coconut gizzada? How about mango ice cream? How about jerk pork, rice and peas, Scotch bonnet peppers, coconut milk, yellow plantains, and all those flavors that Byron had come to enjoy, thanks to his mother's cooking? Now, that was what he called island food. But no, these had never been enough for his ma. More than any other recipe, it was the black cake that brought that creamy tone to his mother's voice. That shine to her eye.

When Dad died, Ma buried what was left of their anniversary black cake with him, but she still kept a jar of the fruits soaking in rum and port in the lower kitchen cupboard. There was always Christmas to think of. She used to wait to make black cake every winter with Benny, even after Benny had moved out to live on her own. But after Benny walked out on them that Thanksgiving Day, Ma never made the cake again. Or so Byron had thought.

Now he knows that his mother did make at least one other cake.

Distance

—

THE PENDULUM HAS SWUNG. AFTER A FEW TENSE HOURS, BYRON and Benny are now being extremely polite to each other, their earlier hostility doused by the strain of hearing their mother's story.

"Do you know this guy?" Byron says to Benny, flicking his chopsticks toward the television screen. "Ma was really into him." They are watching images of a Frenchman who's been forced to abandon his swim across the Pacific due to bad weather.

"Yeah, I've read about him," Benny says. "She was into all of that stuff."

Benny and Mr. Mitch are nodding. They have ordered Thai takeout, having stopped listening to Ma's recording after the umpteenth knock on the door by neighbors who'd seen the lights on. Earlier, Byron took one look at the grief casseroles in the fridge that visitors had brought over and decided that he just couldn't go there. For the first time all day, he and Benny were in agreement on something.

"It's the thought that counts," Benny said, as they stood side by side, eyeing the long, rectangular dishes with their sauce-topped contents. "The fact that they went to the trouble to make these and bring them over, that's what really matters, right?"

Byron nodded.

"And we appreciate that, don't we?"

"We do," Byron said. "Let's serve them tomorrow after the funeral." Byron started scrolling through the numbers on his smartphone for the name of his mother's favorite takeout. But now, as they sit around the kitchen table, they're all stabbing at their dishes without actually eating anything.

It's too late in the evening now for anyone else to come by the house. After this break, they've agreed, no cellphones, until they get further along in their mother's recording. There's no way they'll hear the entire thing before the funeral tomorrow, though. They're just too tired. Strange, Byron thinks, how it can be hard to keep your eyes open at a time like this, even when the most important person in your life is gone, even when you hear your mother's voice telling you that much of what you grew up believing about your family was a lie.

It really is a pity about that Frenchman. Byron had been following his swim, too, especially the science aspect, the collection of samples, the campaign to improve ocean health. But his mother was into the pure challenge of it, man versus water. Ma had been tracking the swim on the Web every day. You would have thought that she was the one in the escort boat, marking the direction, keeping an eye out for sharks, handing out bananas. Byron could almost feel her heart rate ticking *up, up, up,* as she looked at the screen.

For sure, his mother would have been watching, too, for news of the American who is fixing to land his mini-submarine on five of the deepest points of the seafloor. That series of expeditions will be sending information to ocean-mapping scientists like Byron. But Ma would not have been as impressed by this project. It was the direct interaction between the human body and the elements that always had fascinated her most.

He was intrigued by the look on his mother's face as she peered at the French guy's website, the same look she'd get whenever she stood at the breakers looking out over the sea. Is that what he looked like, Byron wondered, right before he slammed his board down on the water? It was his mother who had taught him how to surf, how to find his center, how to look ahead for that window of opportunity. It was his mother who had taught him how to focus his hunger, how to be one with himself.

And it was his father who had shown Byron what a man could look like once he had accomplished all of that. Byron's parents were exceptional people. He doesn't think he'll ever feel as bold as his mother was or as secure in his actions as his father.

Now they're interviewing other distance swimmers, including Etta Pringle, the *grande dame* of them all, the black woman who's done all the most famous crossings. Byron knows they should get back to listening to his mother's recording, but Etta Pringle has an accent just like his mother's. Very British-sounding kind of West Indian. Old-school. Last winter, when his mother's leg was broken after that so-called accident of hers, Byron took her to see Pringle speak at the convention center.

"Distance swimming is like a lot of things in life," Pringle told the audience that day. "There is no substitute for preparation, for training, for putting in the miles to build strength and endurance. But none of these elements really matter if you're not in the right frame of mind."

The marathon swimmer tapped the side of her head with a finger, then nodded as she looked around the room. She stopped and squinted when she saw Byron's mother. Yep, island people. They can spot each other a mile away. Satisfied that his mother was properly settled in, Byron slipped outside to take a work call. One thing led to another and by the time he was done, he'd missed the talk entirely.

When Byron walked back into the auditorium, he saw the speaker hugging his mother, laughing with her, then being ushered out of another exit at the far end of the hall by a small cadre of assistants. Only his mother and a few other stragglers remained in the lobby. She was stabbing at the floor with her crutches, moving quickly toward him.

"Was it good?" Byron asked.

"It was good," his mother said, her face pulled wide by a smile.

"What did she say?"

"She was happy that I'd come to the event."

Byron chuckled. "No, Ma, I meant, what did Etta Pringle say about the swimming? What did she say was the right frame of mind?"

"She said that you had to love the sea more than you feared it. You had to love the swimming so much that you would do anything to keep on going." His mother looked out the car window. "Just like life, you know?"

Byron is thinking, now, of the girls in his mother's audio recording. The swimmers. How, exactly, did Ma come to know them? What happened to them? And what was so terrible about those times that she had to wait until the very end of her life to tell her children the truth?

BEFORE COVEY'S MOTHER DISAPPEARED, SHE AND PEARL HAD amassed a long list of clients. Pearl's black cake was widely acknowledged to be the best in town, though it riled some people to admit it. As far as they were concerned, Pearl was too uppity for a domestic with skin as black as hers. Pearl had a perfect partner in Covey's mother, who could make icing flowers that were second to none. Again, some of the ladies from the town's upper crust felt awkward about this. Covey's mother had shown poor judgment by having a child with that Chinaman.

Covey had heard people saying these things because no one ever thought young children had ears. The teachers in the corridor at school. The shoppers at the market by the carrots and potatoes. She'd heard them say that Mathilda Brown was so beautiful to look at that she could have married up. At the very least, she could have done better than Johnny "Lin" Lyncook. That man was always off at the cockfights and they knew no good could come of it. It was a mystery to them how he remained so popular among some of the more decent fellows around town.

Still, there were more important considerations, such as the satisfaction of having a black cake worthy of applause wheeled into the reception hall at your daughter's wedding lunch. A cake that would be discussed for years to come. Covey's mother could turn sugar into delicately colored periwinkle blooms or, for the more daring brides, hibiscus flowers and orchids in bright reds, deep purples, and golden yellows. And Pearl could make a person close their eyes at merely the thought of her cakes.

Mathilda and Pearl pocketed and divided up their cake profits and gained a few well-placed admirers in the process, women with the right surnames and enough funds to get things done. Some of whom, over time, had come to understand the misfortunes that could befall a woman with fewer material resources.

One day, those alliances would come to bear fruit and change the course of Covey's life. But until then, Covey had no idea that her mummy would leave the island with the help of a former customer. She did not know that Pearl would remain in her father's employ, in part, to keep an eye on her. Covey was too young to understand what it meant to be a mother, what it must have taken for Mathilda to leave. She only knew that black cake meant sisterhood and a kitchen full of laughter.

Covey

—

I N THE SPRING OF 1965, COVEY'S LIFE VEERED ONTO THE PATH that would eventually connect her to Eleanor Bennett. The kitchen floor was littered with tamarind pods that day. They crackled underfoot as her father approached.

"Mmm, tamarind balls," her pa said, reaching into the bowl and pinching a bit of pulp as Covey kneaded it together with sugar. Pearl, described by some as the best cook in the parish, had taught Covey to mix in a touch of Scotch bonnet pepper and a few drops of rum before separating the pulp into balls, though Covey's favorite way of eating tamarind was still fresh out of the pod, scooped up off the dirt floor under the tree, cracked open, pulled away from the stringy bits and dipped right into a bowl of sugar before being popped fully into the mouth, the tartness of the fruit drawing her face tight.

Covey batted away her father's hand. As he laughed, she noted a solicitous tone to his voice, a tone that rode up her back and stiffened it into a wall of resistance. When Covey's father mentioned Clarence Henry, she knew it meant trouble.

"Little Man?" Covey said. "What business does that delinquent have coming to our house?"

"Clarence Henry," Lin said, insisting on using the man's formal name instead of the nickname he'd earned for his massive shoulders, "is coming around to see you."

"To see me? What for?"

"I think he's coming to court you."

Covey let out a sharp laugh. "*Court* me?" She didn't know which sounded more ludicrous, the idea that Little Man would be so genteel as to court anyone or the idea that she was expected to entertain a visit from a gangster and bully of a man who was nearly as old as her father. From what Covey had heard, Little Man wasn't the type of person who should be welcome in anyone's home, not even on a Sunday.

"Court me? *And what mek dat man tink . . . ?*"

"Patois!" That's all her father ever had to say to stop her from slipping into the dialect, which had always been off-limits to her.

She began again. "Where did that man get the idea that he could come around to court me, when you don't even think I'm old enough to go down to the beach with my friends?"

"I never said you couldn't go down to the beach, I said you shouldn't go swimming out in the blasted sea alone in the middle of a bloody hurricane." Swearing, on the other hand, was not off-limits to her father.

"It wasn't really a hurricane, Pa."

"No, of course not, just a deadly little storm."

"Plus, I wasn't on my own."

"I was there, too, remember? I saw how you *were not on your own*. I saw how you had to pull the so-called *safety boat* to safety. What a joke." Her father put his hands on his hips. "And, anyway, that is neither here nor there, young lady. Clarence Henry is coming around this afternoon, so you'd better go and get yourself cleaned up."

"Clarence Henry can come around to court *you*, Pa, I will not be here."

"Oh, yes, you will, Coventina." Her father raised his voice in that way he often did when he'd been at the drink, but there was a softness around the eyes, a kind of question. No, a kind of pleading that turned her skin cold.

"What did you do, Pa? What did you do?"

"Covey, just do this for your pa, won't you?" he said, more softly, now. "Just humor the man. It's Sunday. Let him come around and have a cool glass. I did some business with him and he expressed an interest in—"

Covey slammed her hand down on the kitchen counter next to the small tower of sweets that had been forming on a piece of parchment paper. A couple of tamarind balls tumbled off the counter onto the floor.

"You did business with Little Man?" she said. "What kind of *business*, Pa? Gambling business? You don't owe him money, do you?" Covey's father didn't respond, but the shift in his face made it clear enough. Covey turned and walked away, flattening an errant tamarind ball underfoot. She could see now why her mother had left her father. She just couldn't see how Mummy could have left her, too.

"Coventina!"

She didn't turn around when her father shouted her name, but she was trembling. She thought of Little Man's reputation as a ruthless moneylender, as someone whose threats could have deadly consequences. Covey's hands were still shaking as she pulled open the door of the wardrobe in her bedroom, as she tried to pull up the zipper of the dress she'd chosen.

Covey wanted to slip out of the house but if she did so, it could mean big trouble for her father. If she even said the wrong thing to Little Man, it could mean trouble. Later, she kept these thoughts firmly pinned to the front of her head as she showed Little Man Henry into the front room and he leaned back against the settee, closing his fingers around a tamarind ball.

"Delicious, Coventina," Little Man said, settling his gaze in the dip below her collarbone before sliding it down past her waist. "You're turning out to be quite an accomplished young lady, in addition to being very beautiful."

Coventina bit into a tamarind ball to camouflage the expression that she knew must be crossing her face right then. She thought of her mother, who surely would not have hidden her disdain. No, her mummy would have put her hands on her hips and cut her eyes so sharply at

Little Man that he would have stood up and slinked toward the front door, as her pa had on more than one occasion. But her mother was not here. Just when Covey needed her most.

Covey thought of the knives that Pearl kept in a lower drawer of the kitchen, the biggest, sharpest ones reserved for cleaving meat and stripping sugar cane. One day, she would regret not having kept one of those knives with her.

The Price

—

LIN WASN'T SURE AT WHAT POINT, EXACTLY, HIS DESTINY HAD put him on the path toward Little Man. He was already in trouble when the first rumblings of that anti-Chinese fuss caused the fire at one of his shops. When the cockfights weren't going so well, Lin had wagered goods from his store, figuring he'd win back the value, but his debts kept accumulating.

Things got worse when his woman left him and, still, he made sure their child never went without new school uniforms, which she outgrew at a nerve-racking pace. On this much Lin and Mathilda had always agreed. Covey was going to get a good education, never mind that she was a girl.

In the end, Lin's finances were so bad that he'd had to turn to Little Man Henry. Lin should have known better. He should have known it was only a matter of time before Little Man would come to extract his price. Because as far as Lin had been able to observe, that was what most men in this world were about, the price you were expected to pay. And the person who would suffer the most would be his daughter, the only thing of value that he had left. Because the day was fast approaching when Lin would have to ask himself, *What are you willing to do?*

Covey

—

THE WAILERS WERE ALL OVER THE RADIO THAT SPRING, AND A bit of dance music could go a long way to making Covey feel better, even in times like these. Pearl had left for the day and Covey turned up the radio and shuffled to the music, holding her hair off her neck to cool her damp skin. Her back was turned to the kitchen door when Little Man walked into the house.

Since the fire, her father had warned her more than once to lock the front door when she was on her own, but Little Man had used the back way. Pearl must have left the gate open on her way out. And Little Man walked in without so much as rapping on the doorjamb.

Little Man had been showing up every Sunday for several weeks now, and during that time, her father's fire-damaged shop had been fully refurbished. The connection between the two seemed evident to Covey. All the more alarming because her father hinted that Little Man was interested in what he called *a closer relationship* with Covey.

Whenever her pa raised the subject of Little Man, Covey would walk out of the room. Her pa would come to his senses, she thought, and surely, Little Man would come to realize that it was a preposterous idea to spend time with her. Yet here he was, all the same, walking unannounced into her family's kitchen at the height of a weekday afternoon, like he owned the place.

"The Wailers," Little Man said. "Good tune."

"My father is not here," Covey said.

"I know," Little Man said. "That's why I'm here." He stepped toward Covey. "Aren't you glad that I'm here?"

Covey held her breath. Little Man was now close enough for her to smell his too-sweet aftershave. Little Man was now close enough for her to feel his breath on her forehead.

"We could get to know each other a little better," Little Man said. He tried to kiss Covey but she turned her face to the side. When Little Man leaned in again, she pushed him away but this time, he grabbed her wrists and held them back against the wall, his grip so tight that she thought her bones might snap under the pressure. At school, Covey had learned about a kind of toad in Asia that could twist itself up and make itself look dead, to ward off its predators. She held still and focused her mind on that one thing now, the toad's red underbelly exposed, its fiery surface crisscrossed by black markings, its body filled with venom, just in case.

She kept her face turned to the side, her jaw tight, her eyes narrowed, trying to look fierce, but she was certain that Little Man could hear the pounding of her heart in her chest. It was a well-known secret that he had forced himself on girls before. She thought of the kitchen drawer with the knives. It was too far away to be of any use.

"So, you're a shy girl, are you? Or are you just pretending?" Little Man lowered his voice. "I wonder, are you this modest when you go down to the beach with that Grant boy?"

So this was what people meant when they said your blood ran cold. Covey didn't think anyone knew about her and Gibbs, except for Bunny and Pearl, who'd eventually found out. But Pearl once said that Little Man and his brother had people in every cove and village of the parish who owed them something. And when you owed something to someone dangerous, you were willing to spy for them. You might even be willing to hurt someone else, if it kept your own family from being harmed. The important thing was to keep the Henry brothers from taking note of you. But Little Man had already taken note of Gibbs. The mere sound of his name on Little Man's lips was enough for Covey to understand that Gibbs might be vulnerable.

"What yu doing wasting yu time wit dat boy, eh?" Little Man hissed,

releasing her wrists. He stepped back but hearing Gibbs's name had left Covey's legs so weak, she didn't dare to move.

"You think Gilbert Grant is going to help your father to get out of debt, Coventina? You think Gilbert Grant, more interested in university than going out and earning himself a decent living, could ever come up with the kind of money your father needs to keep someone from cutting him open with a cutlass?"

"My pa . . . ," Covey began.

"Your pa," Little Man said, "is a gambling man who couldn't even keep his woman at home. Couldn't even keep the titles to his stores. Did you know that, Coventina? Did you know those shops don't even belong to your pa anymore? Oh, no? Well, it's true. They belong to me. And if you don't want your father to lose this house and don't want to find yourself living in a shack, or worse, then you will watch your manners around me, young lady."

Little Man turned away and stalked out of the kitchen without another word. The next evening, when her father told her that Little Man had asked for her hand in marriage, Covey couldn't even muster her anger. She only whispered, "No, Pa, please, Pa." This was a strange, new feeling for Covey, this feeling that had stolen her voice.

She sat alone in her room for how long, she wasn't sure. She stepped outside and listened to the buzzes and clicks of the garden, to the sound of her father's snuffle spilling from his bedroom window. She breathed in the moisture that was starting to settle on the leaves, that was turning the ripened fruit to rot. She slapped away a bug, wiped away a tear. Everything was the same, but nothing was the same. She wanted to find Gibbs and tell him, but she knew she couldn't. Not now. Though he would hear about it soon enough.

The stunned feeling was starting to wear off. From below that came something that felt like thunder in the distance, like a howling wind coming off the sea, like a wild animal approaching. And now she was that animal, and she was unlatching the gate and running into the street, tears wetting her face, wetting her neck, wetting her shirt. She was running up the road, her voice coming out of her like a growl.

Covey and Gibbs

―――

COVEY DIDN'T KNOW HOW SHE WAS GOING TO TELL GIBBS about Little Man, but Gibbs had already heard. Covey was leaving school with Bunny the next day when she saw Gibbs hurrying toward her from across the road that ran between the high school and the bluffs.

"Is it true?" Gibbs said loudly.

"Shhh," Covey said, looking straight ahead and walking fast down the road.

"Well, is it true?" Gibbs said, lowering his voice. "Is it true what dem saying about you and Little Man?"

"Wait, wait," Covey said. They walked for a while with Bunny, both closed-mouthed, until Bunny finally said *likkle more* and kept going straight while Covey and Gibbs doubled back on a road that led down to the beach.

"When were you going to tell me about you and Little Man?"

"There is no *me and Little Man*, Gibbs, this is all my father's doing. They have this idea in their heads that I am supposed to marry Little Man, but of course I'm not going to marry him."

"If Little Man wants to marry someone, he will marry them."

"But it's ridiculous, don't you see? My pa will realize that soon enough. And Little Man? Can you imagine him, married? He'll forget about it, he's just showing what a big man he is, that he can get whatever he wants. I am not going to marry that man, Gibbs." Covey wrapped her arms around Gibbs. "But please," she said. "I need you to be calm for me. We need to let some time go by."

"Time? What time?" Gibbs said. "I'm leaving for England in two weeks. What is going to happen to you?"

Gibbs held Covey's face in both of his hands. This was not the life that Covey had imagined for herself only days earlier. Covey had hoped to follow Gibbs the following year once she'd worked out her school papers and sponsorship and a ticket for the transatlantic crossing. She had planned to move to England to be with Gibbs. She had planned to marry Gibbs, attend university like Gibbs. Have children with Gibbs.

"Covey, please, come with me now."

"What, to England? But I'm not ready."

"Then I'll wait for you. We'll go together."

Covey gasped. That wouldn't do. She needed to get Gibbs away from Little Man.

"No, you can't stay. Your studies . . ."

"There's no other way, can't you see?" Gibbs had said.

But Covey managed to convince Gibbs that she was right. Gibbs would leave and, Covey promised, she would make her plans for her own departure.

"Don't worry," Covey told him on their last day together, even though Covey herself was beginning to worry. They were treading water in their secret place, that stretch of coast where they went when they wanted to swim alone together. As Covey clung to Gibbs, as she felt his saltwater mouth on hers, she thought back to the way Little Man had pronounced Gibbs's name on the day that he had cornered her in the kitchen. He had said *Gilbert Grant* like a curse, like a warning, like an ultimatum.

Matrimony

—

MORE THAN FOUR THOUSAND YEARS AFTER THE FIRST marriages were recorded between men and women in Mesopotamia, plans were under way for a similar ceremony in August 1965 on the north coast of a small West Indian island. In keeping with tradition, Coventina Lyncook was to be bound to Clarence Henry, not only for Henry's personal benefit but also for the greater social good. In Covey's case, the wedding would result in the easing of the financial obligations that her father held toward Little Man.

Covey stood on a low stool in a dressmaker's shop in town, feeling the wedding dress being pinched here and there by pins, not fully believing that her marriage to Little Man Henry would really take place. Covey, who had been brought here by Little Man's mother, had chosen the ugliest dress she could find, a monstrosity of puffs and fluffs, hoping to consume as much of the woman's money and patience as possible.

Surely, Covey's father would figure out something. There had to be an alternative, she thought. In the meantime, she refused to speak to her pa. She eyed herself in the dressmaker's mirror and considered whether, in a worst-case scenario, one of the knives Pearl used in the kitchen could be concealed in the many folds of the wedding dress. If it came to that, would she have the courage to use it? What would she be willing to do?

And what would she do after that?

Covey kept believing that her father would work things out with

Little Man, that there would be a last-minute reprieve. Things would settle down, she and Bunny could do that harbor race, and Covey would travel to meet Gibbs the following year. But Little Man would have to back down first.

It wasn't until two days before the ceremony, when Pearl went to the hotel to start work on the wedding cake, that Covey's marriage to Little Man seemed inevitable. Covey, still ignorant of the delicate mechanics of having to work for a living, was furious with Pearl. How could she agree to make a cake for a wedding that was taking place against Covey's will? When Pearl came with Bunny to see Covey right before the ceremony, Covey couldn't look Pearl in the face. She merely turned her cheek to accept a kiss.

Bunny held Covey tight, rocking her from side to side, then walked her into the hallway where her father waited. As Covey's father lifted his bent arm to support her gloved hand, Covey felt her mind unhitch itself from her body and drift, just as it did during her longer swims, when she could see the stroke of her arms from above, the drift of the current, the distance from her destination.

In the wedding hall now, Covey floated above the rows of guests, their dark blazers and sculpted hats. She hovered above the circle of bare scalp at the center of Little Man's head, then streamed past the floral arrangements and through the plate-glass window, heading northeast toward the Atlantic Ocean, reaching out for Gibbs on the far, far side.

Then Little Man was pressing his mouth against Covey's lips and she tumbled back into her body. The guests were applauding. The rest was a blur. There was a lunch, a speech or two. Her father, looking slack faced, stood and raised a glass in the couple's direction, said a few words. Then Covey found herself standing in the center of the reception hall, watching Pearl's black cake being wheeled into the room from the hotel kitchen. Covey felt Little Man place his fingers at the side of her waist, and her heart squeezed itself into a tiny ball of steel.

Black Cake

—

WHAT HAPPENED NEXT HAD ALREADY BEEN SET IN MOTION two days before the wedding reception. On that Thursday, Pearl turned up the fire under the heavy-bottomed pot and opened a sack of cane sugar. She sank a measuring spoon deep into the well of brown crystals, releasing the smell of earth and molasses. It was the finest raw sugar produced on the island but it was about to be wasted, along with eight hours of labor, to make a wedding cake for what would be a sham of a marriage.

Sacrilegious.

In keeping with tradition, the bride and groom were meant to save a portion of the rum cake to mark their first anniversary. A few modern couples who'd married for love and owned electric freezers were now keeping pieces of their cakes for longer periods, slicing off a bit to celebrate each passing year. But this marriage, Pearl thought, would not be worthy of such an honor. For Pearl, Covey's wedding day would be a day of mourning and 1965 would be a year of bitter farewells.

Pearl had known Covey since she was born, when Covey's parents hired her through a friend. She had come to work for them on the north coast, taking time off only to have her two boys. Hard to believe that before coming here, Pearl had never left the capital city. She had grown up hearing of this area's famous lagoon, everyone had, but not even the prettiest southern beaches had prepared her for such beauty. That seemingly bottomless pool of water with its shifting colors. The beaches nearby with their aquamarine coves, ringed by thick vegetation. The sands that lit up at night with tiny, glowing creatures.

Pearl grew to love this part of the island, grew to love a local man, and grew to care for Coventina almost as much as her own children. And Covey's mother—Miss Mathilda, as she used to call her in front of other people—had given Pearl something that she hadn't been counting on. A friendship.

Pearl didn't blame Mathilda for running away from Covey's father. Their home had been filled with regrets. What she couldn't understand was how Mathilda could have stayed away from her own child for so long. She had promised to send for Covey, she had left money with Pearl to make the arrangements. *When the time comes,* Mathilda had said. But the time had never come.

Six years had passed since Covey's mother had left and Pearl had not heard from her for the last four. Covey didn't know this, of course. She'd never told Covey that they had been in contact after her mother's departure. And Pearl had decided that she would never let Covey know. She hated to think that something serious might have happened to Mathilda, but it was worse to imagine that Mathilda might have, for some reason, changed her mind.

Pearl had tried to make up for some of the maternal care that Covey was lacking, but she knew it wasn't the same. She made sure Covey kept herself clean and ate plenty of food. And before going home every afternoon, she would wrap her arms around Covey and give her a tight squeeze, even when the girl had grown taller than Pearl. But this whole wedding business had changed things between them.

At seventeen, Covey was all grown up, turning heads everywhere she went, though she didn't seem to notice. All she seemed to care about was the Grant boy and Bunny and the swimming. Always, the swimming. But Little Man had put a stop to all that. He came by the house almost every afternoon now, his voice all cheerful-like but eyes like stone.

Covey had a habit, when she was feeling low, of slinking into the kitchen, slumping onto the stool, and saying Pearl's name in the way that she had since she was little. *Peaaarrrl*. But as the day of the wedding approached, Pearl watched as Covey slipped away from her. She stopped coming into the kitchen. Only spoke when she was spoken to. This wounded Pearl's heart, though she could see why it was happening.

Earlier in the week, Covey had walked into the kitchen and found Pearl gathering supplies for the wedding cake.

"What is this?" Covey said, when she saw what Pearl was doing. Before Pearl could answer, Covey stalked out of the room and as quickly as that, their relationship had changed. Pearl understood that Covey felt betrayed. By Pearl, by her father, by people who should have been protecting her from such a fate. But how, exactly, could Pearl have done anything to stop this?

Baking could always soothe what ailed her. Pearl dropped spoonfuls of sugar into the pot and breathed in deeply. The scent took her back to the hot afternoons of her childhood, to the smell of fresh cane stalks being sliced open and stripped, to the sweet juices that slipped into her mouth as she chewed on the cane fiber, to the orange-blossomed shade of a ponciana tree. Pearl had shared this special treat with Covey when she was little, just as she later did with her own two boys.

Now Covey wanted Pearl to follow her to her new home, but the groom-to-be was against it. Little Man's undisguised hostility toward Pearl made it easier for her to decide on her next move. Right after the wedding, Pearl would leave the employ of Covey's father. She was always getting offers from important men's wives. But Pearl preferred to go to one of the resort villas up in the hills, where the wages would be good and the guests would never stay long enough for her to get mixed up in their lives.

Only one question remained. How could Pearl help Covey get free of Little Man?

That beast.

The sugar began to darken and smoke as Pearl stirred. When it was almost black, she took a small pot of boiling water and poured its contents onto the sugar, turning her face away as the mixture sizzled and splattered. She would add the blacking to the batter to darken it, but only after she had whipped the butter, added the eggs, flour, spices, and, finally, the mixture of fruits that had been soaking for weeks in dark rum and port. This cake would be a work of art.

As Pearl cracked the eggs and beat them into the batter, she wondered if there was a way to poison a portion of the cake without putting Covey or the wedding guests in danger. She had something she could use, something that would take effect quickly, something that she had shoved into the pocket of her apron on impulse. Pearl opened the jars of marinated fruit and let the alcohol tickle her nostrils. She poured and stirred and scraped and stirred again. By the time she had put the first couple of pans of batter in the oven, she was despondent. She was no longer certain of what to do.

Surely, few of the wedding guests would be sorry to see Little Man Henry go to the devil, but you couldn't attack such a powerful man without courting trouble. Even if Pearl were to come up with a way to poison only Little Man's piece of cake, there would be an obligatory show of indignation among the citizens and police, and the evidence would point straight to Pearl.

Pearl pulled the bottle of poison out of her pocket and turned it back and forth, studying the label. No, Pearl had no intention of ending up in prison. She couldn't do that to her children or to her late husband's memory. And she was no longer convinced that it would resolve Covey's problems. It would not be beyond Little Man's family to force Covey into a marriage with his brother, should Little Man meet a sudden demise. Pearl slipped the bottle back into her pocket.

She needed to think. Pearl knew how people saw her. Few people suspected a woman like Pearl of having the means or cunning to take care of certain things. There were advantages to being looked down upon by certain people. It was precisely for this reason that Pearl felt confident that she would find a way to help Covey. This train of thought calmed her nerves. That, and a few words of prayer to the Lord to deliver her from this fire.

On the morning of the wedding, Pearl topped the cake with a cluster of icing flowers, delicate periwinkles that would dazzle the guests and which would spell out a code that only Covey could decipher. Pearl had adjusted the coloring to give the flowers a lilac tone. The top tier of the cake, laden with the flowers, was the section that would go home with the bride and groom. Despite her distress, Covey would smile when she saw them, Pearl was sure of it. Covey had never liked lilac. Just like her mother before her. Covey would understand what Pearl was trying to say.

Pearl reached into her apron pocket for the small bottle that she'd been carrying around for three days and put it on the counter. She began to spoon more icing from a mixing bowl into the piping bag. Just then she heard a *psst* and turned to find Bunny looking in from the kitchen doorway. Pearl pushed the bottle behind the bowl and waved at Bunny to come in.

"Well, look at you," Pearl said.

Bunny spun around to show the pale swirl of the dress that she'd put on for Covey's wedding. She tipped her feet from side to side. Her shoes had been dyed to match. Then Bunny's smile disappeared. She walked over to Pearl, leaned against the kitchen counter, and hung her head.

"I know, Bunny, I know," Pearl said. She jutted her chin out toward the cake. "But look."

"It's lovely, Pearl," Bunny said, sounding on the verge of tears. Then she twisted up her face. "But the flowers, they're lilac colored."

"Yes, they are," Pearl said, nodding proudly.

"But Covey hates that color."

"Yes, she does," Pearl said. She put her hands on her hips and waited for Bunny to make the connection.

Finally, Bunny smiled and nodded slowly. She straightened up and reached into the mixing bowl, swiping a bit of icing from the side with her finger. Bunny licked at the icing then reached toward the bowl again.

"No, go on, now," Pearl said. "I still have to finish up. I'll see you out there."

"All right, later," Bunny said, wiping her hands on a dishrag.

"Walk good," Pearl said, as she crouched down and reached under the counter for more confectioner's sugar. When she stood up again, Bunny was already crossing the next room.

On the afternoon of the wedding, the black cake was wheeled into the reception hall under a veil of white lace. There was the traditional moment of silence as four attendees lifted the veil. The guests cheered and applauded Pearl's latest creation, but Covey just stood there, staring at the cake, her face blank. It was as if the girl wasn't even in the room. It took her a few moments before her face began to change. First, she looked confused, just as Bunny had. She looked up at Pearl and back at the cake, and then her face softened. Finally, Covey understood what she was looking at. It was small consolation, but it was something.

No one was more shocked than Pearl by the suddenness of what transpired soon after. At about four o'clock that afternoon, Clarence "Little Man" Henry, aged thirty-eight, ruthless moneylender and occasional murderer, stood up from the table where he and his new bride, Coventina "Dolphin" Lyncook, nearly eighteen, had been finishing their plates of rum cake, stumbled backward over his chair, and dropped dead on the white tile floor.

Pearl hurried across the room, trying to get to Covey. But when she reached the other side, Covey was gone.

Lin

——

"MISTER LYNCOOK?"

Lin looked up. He hadn't been called by his English surname in a long time. Most people still called him Lin, including the police officers who frequented his store. Only his woman and his schoolteachers had ever called him Johnny. But this evening, he was Mister Lyncook to everyone here. His daughter had gone missing and she was suspected of murder and the police were now deferring to protocol, including this young man who now approached him, followed by the police girl who, earlier, had gathered his daughter's wedding gown from the sand where it lay and handed it to Lin, gently, as if it might break.

"We're calling off the search for the night," the policeman said. Lin knew this officer. He was Bunny's older brother. Lin had gone to the cockfights with this man's father. He had watched this young man grow up. This boy used to call him Mister Lin. This boy used to be as narrow as a river reed.

Lin looked down at Covey's wedding dress, balled up in his arms. Lin had hoped that this would resolve everything, Covey's marriage to a wealthy man, but Covey had accused him of selling her to Little Man to pay off his debts. And now this. His daughter, running away in the only way she knew how, toward the sea.

"Couldn't you . . . ?" Lin began. "Isn't there . . . ?"

"I'm sorry, Mr. Lyncook," the policeman said. "Look at the sky." Lin narrowed his eyes at the darkening canopy, listened to the thudding force of the waves as a storm moved in. Not even Covey could survive out there alone for very long. He kept telling himself it was too late, but what if it wasn't? What if they were giving up too soon?

The policeman turned his back to the water and walked away, followed by Lin, who, dragging his shoes through the sand, head down, didn't see two of Little Man's thugs running toward him. Little Man Henry had been that powerful. His brother hadn't hesitated to order an attack on Lin, not even with police officers present. It was a widely known secret that the police tolerated most of the Henry family's illegal antics, anyway, helped along by strategically placed envelopes of cash. But this public ambush was going too far.

When the police pulled the thugs off Lin, he had only a couple of superficial cuts. But the officers didn't lock up the hoodlums, they merely chased them off and warned them not to repeat their actions. Which, of course, Lin fully expected them to do. Lin retrieved his daughter's wedding dress from the sand and shook it out. The rustling of the chiffon unleashed a faint scent of gardenia mixed with rum and sugar from the ceremonial cake. When her plate clattered to the floor, leaving a trail of cake and icing on her dress, Covey, like everyone else, must have been distracted by the bridegroom, who was on his feet, gagging and stumbling.

"She hated lilac," Lin said out loud.

"Sorry, sir?" said the officer.

Lin shook his head and bundled up the dress again. Covey hated lilac and Pearl knew it, and yet Pearl had put lilac icing on the girl's wedding cake. Lin looked back at the beach, now shrouded in twilight and storm clouds, and thought of where he'd seen Pearl earlier, standing just inland with a small group of onlookers near the pocked asphalt road that skirted the sand. They'd all been staring at the sea, leaning forward, as if willing it, like Lin, to send Covey back to them. But even Pearl had since abandoned her watch.

Pearl had spent more years with his daughter than the girl's own mother had. She probably knew more about that girl than Lin himself did. And she cared for his daughter, he was sure of it. Lin thought of Pearl standing by the beach road, wiping her eyes with the hem of her skirt, and a disturbing idea began to pick at the edges of his mind.

Bunny

—

BUNNY FELT A SPRAY OF SEAWATER ON HER FACE. NOT A GOOD sign, so far in from the breakers. She stood on the beach road with Pearl and the others, scanning the choppy waters of the bay for a sign of Covey. Bunny knew that even a strong swimmer could miscalculate. But even in her haste, Covey must have understood what kind of wind was blowing, what kind of sky was taking shape. Covey would know that she couldn't stay out there for very long.

And now Bunny tried to imagine her friend's calculations. How far along the coast could Covey get before having to come ashore again? The police would have thought of this too, of course, but they had already come back in. They'd already given up on Covey. They didn't understand Covey, or the currents, the way Bunny did.

It had been calmer the other day, during their last swim together. They had pulled easily through the warm water, then sat on the sand to dry in the sun, licking the salt off their lips, braiding each other's hair, saying nothing. There was nothing left to say, after their tearful discussions, after their *what-if*s. Bunny's heart had cracked a little every time Covey had whispered to her of her plans to follow Gibbs to England, but Bunny would have taken anything over this, this forced marriage to another man, this smothering of Covey's dreams.

Through the growing twilight, Bunny saw that the storm was coming in quickly. Covey would know this, but Bunny was no longer certain that Covey would have time to swim to safety without being cut up on the rocks, or forced out to sea. This was not about strength or speed. This was about being made of flesh and bone and blood. This was about having respect for the power of nature. And, just like that, Bunny understood what Covey might try to do.

Of course, Bunny thought. Of course. Bunny grabbed Pearl's hand and pulled her all the way to Covey's house.

Pearl

—

"SHE'S NOT DEAD," BUNNY TOLD PEARL. "I DON'T BELIEVE it."

Pearl looked at Bunny. She felt a softness in her heart for this girl. She had known her almost as long as she'd known Covey.

"Bunny," Pearl said.

"No," Bunny said, and the stubbornness in her voice brought Pearl close to tears. Bunny, like Covey, had turned into a young woman overnight. Bunny was still a little thing when she first ran into this kitchen with Covey to show Pearl her first swimming medal, waving the bronze-colored disk at Pearl and sending potatoes rolling off the counter and onto the floor. She still tended to trip and knock things over, that child, but she had grown as big and strong and beautiful as a tree.

Bunny's mother told Pearl that the clumsiness had begun with a fever. Sometimes, Bunny still got the aches and, when she was tired, she limped. The fever had left something in her, Bunny's mother said, but nothing that couldn't be managed if Bunny would only concentrate. The swimming had helped her to do that. Now at seventeen, Bunny towered over Pearl, her shoulders broad and square, a look of clarity in her eyes.

"Pearl, if anyone can survive out there, Covey can," Bunny said. But more than four hours had passed since Covey's disappearance and the last traces of peach had left the sky.

"That big race you were training for," Pearl said, "were you girls ready for it?"

"Almost, yes."

"And how many hours would it take to swim it? As long as she's been out there now?"

"No, less."

"So, how could she manage out there alone, and with a storm coming in?"

Bunny shook her head. "I don't think she could, Pearl. But that's my point, don't you see?" Bunny said, banging her elbow into a pot behind her and sending the cover clattering onto the counter. "I don't think she would even try."

Pearl put her hands on her hips and shifted her head to look at Bunny with her good eye. "What are you saying, Bunny?"

"There's a place we know," Bunny said. "Close to the shore. If she's there, she might be all right," Bunny says, her voice cracking.

Without another word, Pearl handed Bunny a battery-operated torch, a modern luxury from Mr. Lin's shop. She put a canvas ice bag on the kitchen table and stuffed it with a towel, dry clothes, and food. She left the room and came back with a small wooden box with bank notes inside. The box was the only item of value Covey's mother had ever had, a beautiful thing with carvings around the border of its lid. After Mathilda left, Covey used to sit on the edge of her parents' bed, holding the box and lifting the lid then letting it drop, lifting it then letting it drop, over and over again.

Pearl tore a strip from a sheet of brown paper and wrote down the name and address of someone who could be trusted. She was someone who could be trusted because, like Pearl, her value was largely unrecognized, except by certain influential women who had come to rely on her. She was someone whose name was never pronounced in the company of their husbands, whose presence they pretended to know nothing about.

As Pearl handed over the ice bag, Bunny knocked the flashlight into a bottle of oil, sending it toppling.

Concentrate, Bunny, Pearl thought.

"I'm so sorry, Pearl," Bunny said, grabbing the bottle of oil as it spilled its contents on the counter.

"Leave it," Pearl said, picking up a rag. "I'll do it." Pearl couldn't trust Bunny in this kitchen but she knew that she could trust her to get to Covey, if Covey was still alive. Bunny knew the coast as well as Covey did.

"You know I can't go with you, Bunny," Pearl said. "Little Man's people are all over the place. You'll have to go on your own. Just act normal-like, Bunny, and if you find her alive, don't stay with her, just leave her these things and go. And walk slow. Be quiet, don't trip on anything."

Pearl jabbed at the name written on the piece of paper. "You make sure Covey understands she's not to talk to anyone, except this person here. They will know what to do." She pushed Bunny toward the door now.

"And under no circumstances are you to come back here until after daylight, do you hear me?"

Covey

—

COVEY WAS CUT UP AND BLOODIED BY THE TIME SHE CRAWLED onto the sand, dressed only in the slip she'd worn under her wedding dress. First came the nausea. Then she blacked out. When she woke up, she was being pelted by rain. She burst into tears. What had she been thinking? Where could she go? Who could help her? She'd heard the voices coming off the beach that afternoon. Covey had run off. The police assumed that she had murdered Little Man. Her only advantage now was that everyone would think she was dead.

Covey had watched her father earlier, as she lifted her head above water behind the rocks where she'd been hiding. There was an opening in the stone where she could come up for air. Where she had let Gibbs kiss her more than once. Where she struggled on her own, grabbing at things that cut and stung, dropping below the water line when the search boat approached. The boat slowed but didn't enter the hollow. Everyone knew that no one could withstand the surf near the rocks for very long, that their body would be spit out of the space like a clump of uprooted seaweed.

Covey watched her father turn his gaze from the water, then lower his head and walk away. Holding Covey's wedding dress balled up in his arms, he stopped to look back, then walked, then stopped. When Covey came up for air again, she heard a shout. She saw two men knock her father to the ground, but Bunny's brother was there to pull them away. They must have been Little Man's men.

Her father bent down to pick up her dress again. He looked sorry. Pa.

Well, too late. He had no one to blame but himself. Johnny Lyncook should have thought twice before going to those cockfights, before going into debt, before selling her off like a sack of red peas. Yes, let them all believe that Covey was dead, Pa included. Her father had stolen her destiny from her, and now she was going to steal it back.

Covey started. There was someone in the dark. She held her breath.

"Covey!"

It was Bunny.

Of course!

Bunny was the only person who knew how well Covey knew the cave, except for Gibbs. But Gibbs was too far away now to be of any help.

"Don't stay until it's too late. If you change your mind," Gibbs had said, as Covey clutched at his shirt, weeping, that last day together, "send me a letter, come and find me." But she couldn't, not now. She couldn't even place a long-distance call. She was a fugitive from the law. If she had any chance of getting away, if she wanted to protect the people she cared for, she would have to close the door to everyone and everything she knew.

Bunny was standing over her with a flashlight, which she turned on, then promptly turned off. Dear, dear Bunny, with a towel and dry clothes, with water and food and money from Pearl. Bunny, with the address of someone who could be trusted. Bunny, who loved Covey enough to make sure that she would get away.

London

—

COVEY LOOKED OUT THE BUS WINDOW. SHE COULD SEE THE university coming up. She rang for the stop and stepped outside, her legs quivering. The campus was a sprawling thing of angles and columns and greenery. London could be funny that way. So much stone, then so much life. Covey found a bench across the way and sat down, scanning the crowds of people coming and going. She pulled her cardigan close around her body and watched all those faces, chatting, laughing, frowning. People she might have been, lives she might have led.

There were other brown-skinned people here, people who looked like students and even one who must have been a professor. Gray hair, corduroy jacket, an air of well-being. Still, she was sure, she would have no trouble spotting Gibbs. He would be taller and darker than most. And he would recognize Covey, she was sure of it, even with her ponytail cut off, even with her curls tucked under a hat, its brim pulled low. She let herself imagine that Gibbs would sense that she was here, that he would have felt her arrival like a current breaking over a reef, that he would be walking straight toward this bench where she sat, her heart hammering under her sweater.

Covey's arrival in England already seemed years ago, though it had only been the previous autumn. She recalled the dark ribbon of water that had separated her from the ship as she counted down the minutes to her escape from the island. She'd kept glancing over her shoulder as she followed the crowd of passengers up the ramp, but she needn't have worried. Everyone back home thought she was dead. They would never think to look for her here, on the far side of the island, on a ship that was bound for London and Liverpool.

The British Nationality Act 1948 granted citizens of the Commonwealth free entry into Britain. Covey had just turned eighteen in the fall of 1965 and was traveling under her mother's surname as a nanny to the children of someone who knew someone who knew Pearl. A family with the means to ensure a smooth transfer for Coventina Brown, despite the newer legislation that was now limiting migration from the islands.

In exchange for passage and forged documents, Covey had promised to work for her employer for at least one year. The family who had taken her on were not aware of the risks involved. They only thought they were helping the young relative of a friend of a friend to gain new opportunities overseas. And they were wealthy enough and light-skinned enough to be spared close questioning by the authorities. But Pearl's contact in the capital had reminded Covey of the danger of being caught, and of her responsibility to those who had gone out of their way to help her.

"Is not a hundred percent *conventional* what we doing for you, you know," Pearl's contact had said. Covey only knew her as Miss Eunice. She never did learn her full name, only that she was a midwife with a knowledge of traditional remedies who was consulted by women from all over the island on "questions of a female nature."

Miss Eunice reminded Covey that there were laws against forgery. There were laws against traveling under an assumed identity. There were laws against helping a murder suspect to escape. Trying to find Gibbs, trying to contact Pearl or Bunny, even socializing with the wrong people on the cruise ship, any one of these things could get her into trouble, along with anyone who had tried to help her or who had ever cared for her.

Miss Eunice's advice was explicit: "You never know who around you could be a *blabba mout*, right? Don't forget that you going to a place where the people dem not all black. You a woman from the islands and you need to behave better than dem."

Covey was to keep her hair and shoes tidy, keep her dresses at the knee or not too far above. She was to stay away from the dance halls and the concerts. She was to stay away from the street demonstrations. There were more and more protests in Britain, these days, by colored people tired of slumlike housing, tired of being hit with police clubs, tired of receiving training and then being turned away from jobs. She should avoid the big market where islanders liked to shop. She was to reduce the chances of running into someone from back home. Be discreet, Miss Eunice said. Keep safe, stay out of trouble.

In other words, Covey thought, be lonely.

But Covey understood. She needed to stay as far away from Little Man's family as possible. Stay out of sight, let time go by. Eventually, she might be able to resume her studies overseas. Eventually, she might be able to look for Gibbs. On the bad days, on the nights when she couldn't sleep, Covey thought of all the plans that she and Gibbs had made together. But she couldn't risk trying to contact him too soon; maybe one day. Maybe not.

Not being able to swim made everything more difficult to bear. Whenever she could, Covey would go out walking and the surprise of her surroundings helped to distract her. She had grown up seeing photographs and news films of London and thought she knew the city, but now she saw that she'd had no idea what it would be like. The traffic, the advertisements, the brick-walled shops. The living mannequins, young women, modeling clothing from inside a window. Office girls walking down the street in short-short skirts, even in winter. The lead-colored river slicing through the heart of it all, the smell of coal almost everywhere.

Once in a while, Covey would come across a block of crumbling buildings, piles of rubbish spilling onto the sidewalk, and people, white and brown, bracing themselves against the cold in a level of squalor that she had never seen in her hometown. It made her think of all those things that she could no longer enjoy. A warm, silky feeling to the air, a hint of ripening fruit, the sweet-salt smell of the Caribbean Sea. On some days, she missed even the tang of cow patties drying in the sun, the sound of flies buzzing around. It would take some time for Covey to get used to her new surroundings.

And time to get used to being stared at.

To being muttered at.

To being ignored altogether.

To being treated like a woman from the islands.

Living this way for months softened Covey's resolve to keep to herself. It wasn't long before she made the acquaintance of other young women like her, girls from the Caribbean who warmed to the sound of her familiar accent. There was a large house where people from various countries would gather to socialize and swap information, though, thankfully, no one from her own small town.

As Covey listened to their stories, she came to understand how fortunate she had been with the family that had hired her, with the boots and gloves they'd given her to shepherd her through that first damp, frigid season. Covey's employers gave her books to read from the family's library. Instead, other girls had struggled to find accommodations, had been turned away from doors with *Rooms to Let* signs out front, were paying much more for a room with a washbasin than the white girls at work.

Covey's employers talked to her as if she was someone because they were friends with a well-placed government man whose connections went all the way back to Pearl. The government man's wife knew Miss Eunice, and Miss Eunice, it turned out, was the former school friend of the wife of the wholesaler who sold supplies to Covey's father and other shopkeepers. None of the men had ever heard of Miss Eunice, but each of the women had turned to her for help at some point in their lives. And all of them had purchased or tasted Pearl's black cakes.

Unlike Covey, most of the island women she'd met planned to go back to the Caribbean as soon as they'd completed their studies or saved enough money to return, but the reality was, few would have the means to do so. Some would fall in love and still others would disappear, the rumor being that they may have gone off somewhere to have a child.

"And Judith?"

"Judith? Haven't seen her for a while."

Then silence, a nod, a few looks exchanged. They knew not to ask more than once.

Each of the women talked about their lives before England. Unable to tell the truth about her own past, Covey spoke, instead, of a childhood that she had invented. Without a chiney father, without a runaway mother. She painted a vague picture of growing up with a grandmother who had lived much longer than her own grannies had. She spoke of living in a rural part of the island that she'd never seen.

Some of the women had been recruited from the islands to study nursing.

"The National Health Service is always short on nurses, you know," one of them told Covey. "You should think about it. I could help you."

Soon, Covey was convinced. She would leave the nanny position to enroll in nursing school. She wasn't sure that this was the profession for her, she only knew that she would do whatever it took to move forward, to take control of her life. She thought of her father. Her father had lost control of his life and here Covey was, paying the price.

Covey had wanted to come to Britain, but not this way. The loneliness hit her hardest at bedtime. Sometimes, when she was too upset to read, she would sit on the edge of her bed and run her hand over the top of her wooden box, its ebony lid as smooth to the touch as a child's arm, its carved edges tickling her fingertips. She would lift the lid and let it fall shut, lift then shut, over and over again, thinking of her mother. Thinking of home.

All that Covey had left of the island was this box and whatever she could keep closed away in her head and heart. She tried not to think too much about whether she would ever see Pearl or Bunny or Gibbs again. She told herself that, sooner or later, things might change and she would be free to live her life again. But until then, her life was not only hers to live. Covey had ended up here not only because of her father's foolish ways and Little Man's cruelty. She was here, too, because of the kindness of others. She owed it to them to stay invisible.

But as the months went by, she found it harder to resist the awareness that Gibbs was out there somewhere, that they were back on the same piece of land. Sometimes Covey would say she was going to the cinema when instead, she rode the bus line up to the university where Gibbs was supposed to be studying, staring out the window as it pulled up in front of the old quadrangle and taking her seat on the bench to search for Gibbs among the students who followed the paths that led toward the green.

Covey came back to the campus several times, and on each occasion, she would scan the crowd for Gibbs. But she also dreaded the possibility of finding him. How could she see him and not call to him? How could she speak to him and not touch him?

True, Gibbs had told her to contact him, but when you came from a small island like theirs, everybody knew somebody. When you came from an island like theirs, you grew up hearing stories of big men around town, like Little Man, who could find other men to hurt the people who had crossed them, even on the far side of the ocean. How much was legend and how much was truth, Covey could not be sure. She only knew that she couldn't afford to find out.

A young man sat on the bench near Covey and opened a book. She wondered if he could hear the dry churning in her stomach. Finally, she stood up and crossed the street. A bus going back in the other direction came to a stop in front of her. She waited until everyone else had boarded, took one last look at the university green, then stepped into the bus, her hope folding itself up inside her.

Now

—

Mrs.
Bennett

—

B *and B, by now you've probably understood what I have been trying to tell you, that I am Coventina Lyncook, the girl who ended up living in England as Coventina Brown. Or, at least, I was. That was fifty years ago, another life. And yet everything is connected.*

I know, this must be a shock. I'm so sorry. But there is no one else who can explain all of this to you. I could have left it alone, not said anything, left you two to go on with your lives, but then what? You two have a sister. If I don't tell you the truth now, before I go, the three of you will be lost to each other forever. I spent so much of my life keeping this from you, but I owe this to you. I owe it to you to let you know about my past because this is your story, too.

Byron and Benny

———

MA IS GETTING UPSET, BYRON CAN HEAR IT IN HER VOICE. He looks over at Benny and sees that her eyes are shining. Do they want to take a break, Mr. Mitch asks. Byron nods. Byron needs to step away for a moment, he needs to think. Too many names, places, dates. Should he be writing all this down? No, that would feel too strange. He looks back at Mr. Mitch. Of course, Mr. Mitch. He will have taken notes.

What stays with Byron now: His mother was a runaway bride. His mother had another child. His mother may have been a murderer. Or was she? She doesn't say. But she doesn't say that she didn't kill that man, either, does she? How could Ma do this to them? How could she drop this bomb on them and then leave them to deal with it on their own? Byron turns to look at Benny again. She is watching him with those Benny eyes, her brows pulled together, and then just like that, her whole face goes smooth and she stands up, and Byron sees a touch of the Benny that he used to know.

Benny, the thoughtful one. Benny, and that gentle way she has of offering a cup of coffee or tea or a glass of water that makes it sound like an afterthought, like they're all just hanging out in the living room, chatting comfortably. Like this is just a friendly break, and not an excuse to stay away from that recording for just a bit longer, a way to step back from the confusion that it has unleashed in this house.

..

BENNY KNOWS THAT DOING KITCHEN THINGS WILL HELP TO CALM her. She moves slowly as she thinks about everything that she has heard. Did her mother kill that man? No, Benny doesn't believe it. She refuses to believe it. Her mother ran away because she saw an opportunity. But how is it possible that she and Byron lived with Ma all those years and couldn't tell that she was hiding something?

Benny throws out the used coffee filter, pulls a fresh one out of a box. She listens to the coffee grains falling from the scoop into the paper filter, breathes in the smell of the new coffee, pretends her mother is right there with her as Benny puts some cookies out on a plate. Her ma never called them cookies, always biscuits. Benny pulls open the spice drawer, just to see. She pokes at bottles of allspice, jerk seasoning, caraway, and tarragon. Seasons of the south and north. She walks over to the fridge in her socks and recalls the sound of her mother's slippers flapping across the floor.

Benny stands there in front of the refrigerator, letting the cool air fall on her toes, and thinks of the last cake her mother ever baked. She knows it's sitting in the freezer but she can't bear to look in there right now. Instead, she leans her forehead against the upper door of the fridge. *This is your heritage,* her mother used to say when they were making black cake, and Benny thought she knew what her mother meant. But she sees now that she didn't know the half of it.

There was a point, fairly recently, when it occurred to her that Ma would have been orphaned too young to learn how to make black cake in her own mother's kitchen. Benny reasoned that Ma must have learned how to make black cake from the nuns at the children's home. Was there such a thing? Nuns who made black cake? Like those sisters who made cheese? Like those monks who made chocolate?

Her mother's childhood stories had always been vague. Criss-crossed timelines, missing details. A lot of missing details. Benny had grown up with the feeling that there were things her mother had preferred not to say about her past. She'd grown up hearing that her parents' upbringing had not been as easy as hers, so she hadn't insisted on knowing more. Well, she finally has a chance, now, and the thought of it scares her. Benny feels like, the more she knows about her mother, the more of her she will lose.

Mrs.
Bennett

———

*S*ometimes, the stories we don't tell people about ourselves matter even more than the things we do say. I told you children that I'd grown up in an orphanage, but of course, I didn't. There's a reason for this. I had a friend in England who was raised by nuns in a different part of the island from where I grew up. When we met, I was still quite lonely, feeling separated from everyone I cared about, and not sure how, or if, I would ever see them again. Well, she just sort of took me over and filled up some of the empty spaces in my life. And I needed that. I wouldn't be here today if it weren't for her.

I'm sorry. Wait a moment. Can we just stop, please?

Yes, stop the recording.

I'm sorry, this is so hard.

PART
TWO

..

Then

Elly

ELLY'S FATHER WAS NOT COMING BACK, THE NUNS AT THE orphanage reminded her. Her father had gone to heaven to be with her mummy and now, there was a new family looking for a little girl. When the time came to get ready, the nuns kept calling for Elly, but Elly was not interested. Elly was busy digging cockle shells out of the backyard.

There was no sand in these parts, no seashore in sight, only yellow-brown earth. And yet there were seashells here, a million-billion beige and white and pinkish ones and, even at her age, Elly knew the shells were magic. She knew she was living in a land of miracles where anything could happen, where Pa might come back to get her. Maybe he could take her to heaven to be with him and Mummy, Elly had said, but the nuns told her it was way too soon for that, and she'd have to go live with another family first.

A cricket leapt out of the grass and clung to the top of Elly's knee before skipping off again. If only Elly could stay here until teatime, there might be cake from the ladies who brought things to the orphanage. Elly looked up for a moment, contemplating the aroma of cake, then pushed the stick farther into the dirt. She took a pinch of the earth, put it into her mouth, and chewed on it. She pretended not to notice Sister Mary coming to take her to the dormitory. She hung her head as Sister Mary reached out to take her hand.

"Keep still now," Sister Mary said, braiding Elly's hair. Elly's shoes had been shined and her tunic starched and ironed. Sister Mary smoothed Elly's shirt collar.

"Look at you," Sister Mary said. "Your father would have been proud." But Elly's father was right there, she wanted to tell Sister Mary. Elly could see him. She had watched him from behind the window more than once, his spirit soaring up among the trees in the shape of a butterfly, his wings glinting bright yellow and black. He would dip down to check on her, fluttering just beyond the glass.

"Oh, look, a swallowtail," Sister Mary said, pointing to the window, her eyes gleaming. Sister Mary had a cold. She kept wiping her nose with a handkerchief. Her eyes were red and wet. "Largest butterfly in the entire region, did you know that?" Sister Mary said. She touched Elly's cheek. Elly scrunched her mouth into a half smile and shook her head no.

"We don't see those around here much anymore," Sister Mary said, taking Elly's hand in hers and leading her toward the door. They walked down the corridor together as slowly as they could. Elly wanted to stay with Sister Mary but they'd already had a long talk about that. She thought of her swallowtail father and knew that even though Mother Superior didn't want her at the orphanage anymore, wherever she went, she would never be alone.

Needless to say, Mother Superior was furious, several months later, when Elly's new family un-adopted her. Elly hadn't known that such a thing could be done. Mother Superior told Elly that no one wanted a liar for a child. Elly had done a wicked thing, she said, telling those fibs about that man. But Elly knew she wasn't supposed to tell untruths and usually, she did not. Still, she had been sent back to live with the nuns and the only one who seemed happy was Sister Mary, who hugged Elly tight and brushed out her hair and said, "Go on, now, say your prayers and into bed. Lessons tomorrow, bright and early."

The next day, Sister Mary showed Elly a picture of a swallowtail that she had cut out of a newspaper and slipped it into Elly's exercise book, and Elly understood that she had come back home. The next day she ran back into the garden to dig.

In time, Elly came to learn that the island hadn't always been an island. There was a time when the Earth's eruptions and shifts had pushed the land under the sea, where layers of life and debris formed a mantle of limestone that one day would rise from the water. And now, here Elly was, thirty million years later, sinking her fingers into the warm dirt outside the children's home, listening to the hum of the world, and sensing, even then, that she could not live without the feel of it.

Elly wasn't sure how the shells had come to be in that particular place, Elly's place, between the guava and guinep trees and the cerasee bush. She only knew that she was most content when she could scoop them up and paint them with watercolors, or crush them into a pinkish grit, or feel for them in the pocket of her tunic. She tucked the best ones into the cardboard box where she kept the coins and a pretty old hair comb that she'd plucked from the dirt.

In the dormitory at night, Elly sometimes spent hours turning a shell over and over in her hands. Later, she would read enough to understand that these shells were not so much out of place as out of time. Elly's breasts were just beginning to bud when she finally realized that she and the shells had been meant to find one another. And this was her first understanding of her destiny.

Elly had been born to sift through the dirt, to look for her history and future by picking through fossils, rocks, and sediment. She might walk to her lessons with a clip in her hair and shoes on her feet and books in her arms, but she knew now that these were superficial things, that what she was at the core was not what other people gave her or called her or told her or denied her, that none of these had anything to do with her true place in the world.

The Bible said *for dust thou art* and now Elly saw what it really meant. She knew that she had been part of the world forever and always would be, and had nothing to fear, nothing at all. And she would do whatever it took to realize her dream. She would study the dirt and shells and rocks at the heart of the world, because that was her destiny.

The Gate

—

ON JUNE 7, 1692, THREE POWERFUL EARTHQUAKES STRUCK the island. The soil turned to putty and a large tsunami sucked the island's richest city, a famed haven for pirates, into the sea. Three thousand people were killed. Another two thousand died in an epidemic that followed.

In the spring of 1961, a group of orphans took turns dipping a small plastic bucket into the shallows at the marina. The girls were scooping up water full of tiny fish, waiting to begin a day trip to a minor island, when one of them cut her foot on the remains of a three-hundred-year-old gate. Regulars knew the gate was there below the surface, but these girls were from the interior. They had never been to the marina before and some had never even seen the sea up close.

Elly didn't know it then but when she sliced her foot open on that gate, she set her life on a new path. She ended up in the hospital with an infection and fever that, the sisters later claimed, nearly killed her. After the fever passed, Elly would watch each day as the morning nurse unwound a bandage from around Elly's foot, patted at the area ringing the cut with a piece of gauze doused in something that stung, and wrapped her foot again in clean cotton.

"Do you like being a nurse?" Elly asked one day.

"Why, yes," said the nurse. "It's a respectable profession for a young woman. And I get to help people." The nurse snipped at the bandage with a pair of scissors, then looked at Elly. "Do you think you would want to do this someday?" she asked.

Elly shrugged. "I want to go to Britain, to study," Elly said.

"Well, there's a great need for nurses in Britain," the nurse said. "And the government is recruiting our women to study there. You should think about it." Elly was already aware that the health service in Britain was sponsoring women from the Commonwealth to complete nursing certificates there in exchange for a minimum work commitment. She had heard it on the radio in the kitchen at the children's home. Going to nursing school could be her first step toward fulfilling her destiny. Elly emerged from her stay in the hospital with a plan.

She still had a couple of years to go before finishing secondary school, but now she knew what to do. She would study hard in high school and when the time came, she would travel across the ocean to take up nursing. She might find a job in a hospital or a doctor's office. And then she would apply to a university where she could study what she really wanted to do. There was a name for what Elly was destined to be, she had seen it in books. Elly was going to be a geologist.

Her timing was fortunate. In those days, the benefactors of the orphanage were still generous enough to fund her overseas passage. Her exam results were better than almost anyone's on the island and this was the kind of thing that made a sponsor proud. By the time she met Coventina Brown six years later in England, Elly was finishing her nursing studies and already in the midst of formulating a new plan.

Cake

———

"GO ON, ELLY," COVENTINA SAID.

Elly closed her eyes but could still see the light from the candles through her lids. She took a deep breath and blew. She was twenty-one years old. Not long ago, she was just a skinny pickney living in an orphanage thousands of miles away.

Elly at ten, always hungry, never sleeping.

Elly, walking barefoot on cool tiles in the dark.

Elly, praying for no scorpions in the hall.

Elly, at the kitchen door, searching for the tin.

Elly, breathing in the smell of rum-soaked fruit.

Elly, scooping cake crumbs out of the tin.

Licking her fingers, closing the lid.

Rushing toward her bed, praying for no nuns.

Now she had her very own cake. The birthday candles were for her. The applause and hugs were all for her. The girls who shared the kitchen in this London bedsit had been soaking the fruits for weeks and setting aside the eggs, just for her. Elly was still motherless, still fatherless, but not alone.

"Here," Coventina said, handing her a knife to cut the cake. Coventina had made the cake and Edwina had done the icing and Elly the Orphan was happy. She had found a new family in a chilly, damp city, an ocean away from her island home.

Elly didn't know when she would get back to the island. It might be years yet. She kept a picture of a butterfly tucked in a Bible that Sister Mary had given her. She kept a cardboard box with a letter from Sister Mary and some shells from the garden at the orphanage and the old hair comb and coins that she'd found while digging in the dirt. One day, she would go back and show Sister Mary her photograph of the girls from the nursing school. They were smart-looking and smiling and standing in a row as if they had always been together and always would be.

Covey
and Elly

—

WHEN COVEY FIRST MET ELEANOR DOUGLAS AT THE TEACHING
hospital, Eleanor said, "Call me Elly, like jelly, or belly!" She was such
a serious-looking *gyal* but she'd come out with things like that to make
Covey smile. Covey knew that she was taking a chance, striking up a
friendship with someone from the same island and agreeing to move
into lodgings with women who all knew one another. Still, by the time
Elly said, "Why don't you come live with us?" it seemed like the most
natural thing to do.

It was only then, in the cottony air of Elly's laughter, in the pots of
stew peas and rice on the kitchen table, in the novelty of walking down
the street together, that Covey realized just how bad she'd been feeling
until then. She hadn't been part of any kind of group since the swim
club. She hadn't had anything like a real friend since Bunny.

"Shhh," one of the other girls said through the door of their room
one night, rapping lightly on the partition wall. She and Elly had been
chatting too loudly, as usual. There were rules about such things. Better to have their housemates warn them than the landlady herself. They
should have been in bed but instead, they were both sitting on the floor
between their respective cots, peering at the map that Elly had smoothed
out over the rug.

"So this is where we are," Elly said. "See, here? The rocks in this
part of England are some of the youngest. Mostly covered by clay and
other soils left behind by glaciers."

"Glaciers," repeated Covey. The idea of a force of nature so vast and slow and cold, shaping the world, intrigued her. It made her think of the sea, of how they'd been taught as children that the world was land surrounded by sea when in fact, it was the other way around.

"This piece of land, here," Elly went on, shifting her finger along the waxy surface of the map, "was pushed into existence by violent processes and rose up to become what it is today." She raised her eyebrows. "Not so different from what happened to our own island, see?"

Covey nodded. She tried not to smile. In that moment, Elly's expression made her look more like a middle-aged schoolteacher than someone hardly older than Covey.

"Everything is connected to everything else, if you only go far enough back in time."

Covey thought of the ocean that stretched from where they were now to the faraway place where they'd both grown up. And without intending to, Covey found herself talking about her life before. "I used to swim," Covey said. "I used to swim in the sea. For miles and miles."

"Did you really?" Elly said. "How exciting!"

Covey revealed that she really was from the north coast of the island and not the south, as she'd told everyone who'd asked. "We had the most beautiful bay."

Until then, Covey had stuck to the invented story about her past. She had never told Elly or anyone else about the forced marriage to Little Man or his murder or even Gibbs, though she'd told Elly that she'd left home because of an unhappy family situation. She willed herself, now, to say no more.

"Have you tried to swim here?" Elly asked.

Covey scrunched up her face. "I tried but I couldn't. Too cold. Not for me."

"I've never learned to swim," Elly said. "I've only been to the beach once."

Covey's mouth softened into an *oh*. It was something she couldn't imagine, especially not on a small island like theirs.

Elly told Covey then that she'd grown up in the interior, high above the sea where cockle shells had been left in the ground by a prehistoric ocean. She reached into the pocket of her cardigan then, eyes gleaming.

"Look." Elly opened her palm to reveal three pink-and-white shells. "This," Elly said, leaning closer to Covey, "is what I'm going to do. This is what I'm going to do after nursing school."

"Collect shells?" Covey said.

"No," Elly said, laughing. "Study them. Geology. Everything about the Earth. The oceans and volcanoes and glaciers," Elly said. "Only I'll need to get a recommendation first, to convince a university to let me study there. They've had some women, but . . ." She stopped short, breathed out sharply. Covey nodded. Elly didn't need to say it. By now, she knew what was often left out of their conversations. The way people saw them and how it determined the roles that they were expected to play in life.

In lowered voices, they shared their dismay at some of the name-calling and other forms of prejudice they had faced in the mother country. Because that was what Great Britain meant to them, the mother country, even five years after the island's independence. They had spent their childhoods under British rule and had received a British education.

Covey and Elly agreed that they belonged, first, to the hills and caverns and shores of the island where they had grown up, but they also felt that they were part of the culture that had influenced so many aspects of their daily lives. Moving to Great Britain was supposed to be like coming to stay in a relative's home. A safe harbor for two young people who had lost everything else.

Of course, it wasn't quite that way once they'd crossed the Atlantic. In London, Elly said, she had discovered herself to be a dual entity, a sort of hybrid, someone who was both at home and foreign, someone who was both welcome and not. At the end of the sixties, postwar relief and optimism were beginning to wear thin. People were worried over limited resources. This added fuel to ongoing bigotry, despite repeated reports of labor shortages, which the government had called on immigrants to help fill.

"Don't worry, Elly," Covey told her. "You'll find a way."

"I know," Elly said, folding the map now. "I will. But what about you?"

"Me?" Covey breathed in slowly, deeply. *Say nothing, Covey. Say nothing.* "Well, the nursing is a fine opportunity for me."

"But with the certificate that you're getting, you won't get the better wages and you won't get the promotions. You know they won't let many of us island girls go for the higher-level certificates."

Covey looked down at her hands, dry and cracked where her fingers met her palms. She seemed to be spending more time cleaning bedpans and commodes than treating patients. Was Elly right?

"It's fine for me, for now," Covey said. She kept looking down. "I'm not sure what I would do otherwise." Which was the truth.

But Coventina wasn't cut out to be a nurse, Elly could see that. Just as Elly was not. For Elly, the nursing was a means to an end and she was already planning her next steps. She had never shared her ambitions with anyone until the night she told Covey about her plans to study geology. She'd never even told Sister Mary.

When the time came, Elly approached her advisor about helping her to enroll in a university course in geology. True, her science background was limited to mostly biology and chemistry, she said, but she had done quite a bit of reading in geology on her own. She was convinced that she could qualify for the course of study that she wanted.

Elly fingered a shell in her jacket pocket as she laid out her argument. She had realized that it would take some convincing, but she hadn't expected to fail. The same woman who'd told her what a fine mind she had for the sciences was now refusing to give her a recommendation. Elly squeezed the shell so hard between her fingers that it snapped.

Her advisor reminded her that the national healthcare system offered ample opportunities to promising young islanders with her training. Perhaps, her advisor said, she could recommend Elly for an advanced nursing course? But Elly was already walking out of the matron's office. Elly had a dream to realize.

Walking home that evening, Elly told Covey about her plan.

"I need to go where they won't force me to remain a nurse. I need to go back across the Atlantic, Covey. They'd take me in Canada."

"Canada?" Covey said. "But how?"

"Maybe I don't even need Canada. But I do need to leave here, if they won't help me, and I need to find better wages or pay less money for lodgings. I need to save money and figure out how to get into another university."

"But you're supposed to stay. It's part of our training agreement."

"Yes. Which is why we need to get far away from here, and as quickly as possible."

"We?"

"Yes, Coventina. We." Elly stopped walking, blocked Covey's path. "What are you doing here? Half the time, you don't even sleep at night. You think I haven't noticed? Why would you stay? We could change cities. It could be nice."

There was a train they could take to another city, another cold city, yes, but on the sea, and Elly knew someone who knew someone else who could get them both clerical positions in a wealthy trading company.

"They trade with the islands," Elly said. "There are people from the Caribbean there." Her eyes were gleaming now. "You might meet a nice lad," she said.

Covey was tired. She felt as though she'd had enough change for a while. But Elly was ready to go and where would Covey be without her? Elly was Covey's friend. And because Elly was determined to take her true place in the world, Covey let herself be caught up in her dream. The two of them packed their bags and set out for Edinburgh. The train sped through an impossibly green countryside that lightened Covey's mood. Covey told herself that it was the way to survive, to keep putting distance between her and her life before. To stop looking back, to think about Gibbs a little less every day.

Becoming Elly

———

AT FIRST, COVEY REMEMBERED VERY LITTLE. THE BLARE OF a horn, the cry of metal wheels against the tracks, the tumbling, tumbling, tumbling.

When she came to, she grabbed the strap of her friend's handbag, the first thing she was able to recognize through the cloud of dust and smoke. Much later, she would remember the screams, the smells, her body hurting everywhere, the burn of hot metal against her knees as she crawled, calling for Elly. Covey caught a glimpse of Elly's arm and the watch that she had proudly purchased at the emporium. She grabbed hold of her friend's arm. *Elly, Elly!* she cried. Then she saw the rest of Elly and the sight of her friend caused Covey to faint.

When Covey woke up, she was in the hospital with a tube in her arm and a pounding in her head. She could smell her own hair on the pillow, burnt oil and smoke mingling with the scents of cotton sheets and rubbing alcohol and the faint whiff of a bedpan. She saw Elly's handbag, sitting on the chair near her hospital bed. Where was her own purse? Where was her hat?

She looked under her blanket. She was wearing a cotton gown. Where were her clothes? She had been carrying her mother's wooden box in her jacket. She had stuffed it with pound notes and pushed it into a pocket that she'd sewn onto the lining of the jacket for the trip, touching the area around her waist periodically to feel for the bulk of the box. Covey swiveled her head further, despite the pain. There it was.

The jacket was gone but someone had removed the box and placed it on a wheeled tray. She stretched out her hands, trying to reach it.

A nurse, seeing what she was doing, picked up the box and handed it to her. Covey put the box on her stomach and held it there, arms trembling.

"How are you doing there, Eleanor?" a nurse said.

"Covey," said Covey.

The nurse frowned. "Pardon me?"

"Coventina," Covey said. The nurse hurried away, then came back with a second woman.

"Coventina Brown?" they asked. Covey nodded. "Was Coventina your friend?" Covey opened her mouth to speak. "We're so sorry, Eleanor." They were shaking their heads. "Coventina didn't make it. She didn't survive the accident." They meant Elly, didn't they? Covey closed her mouth, its parched corners stung by the salt of her tears. She thought of her friend's limp hand. Poor Elly. She felt a wave of nausea and leaned toward the edge of the bed.

One of the nurses coaxed Covey back toward her pillow and patted her wet face with a towel. Covey turned her head away and tried to shift her body but cried out at the pain in one leg.

"Careful, now, Eleanor," the nurse said. "You'll be all right but you're rather badly banged up there."

"Covey," Covey said.

"I know, Eleanor, we're so sorry. It's a terrible thing."

Covey was sobbing openly now. She replayed the last moments she could remember from after the crash. Elly was still alive when Covey found her, she was sure of it. Elly had made a kind of mewing sound as Covey tried to pull her up, as she tried to pull her out from under something heavy. If Covey hadn't blacked out, could she have saved her friend? Then she remembered what Elly had looked like under all that metal. Probably not. Elly really was gone, wasn't she?

Elly had always filled a room with light. How could that light be gone for good?

Covey drifted in and out of sleep, waking sometimes to find the room dark and filled with the snuffling and wheezing of other women on the ward. How many days had gone by?

"Is there anyone we can contact for you?" the nurse asked one morning. "Do you have any kin? Any friends?"

"Elly."

"Elly? Is that a relative?"

"Eleanor."

"Oh, Elly for Eleanor," the nurse said. "Of course. Is that what you prefer? Shall we call you Elly, then?"

Covey was too tired to argue, but her head was beginning to clear. Next of kin? She couldn't afford to have next of kin or friends notified, and Elly had no family. Covey thought that maybe some of their mates at the boardinghouse would have wanted to know, or maybe even that nun back on the island that Elly liked to talk about. But what about Covey? Would there be announcements in the papers? Would she be named as one of the survivors?

What if someone from the island found out that she was still alive and came looking for her? And if they found her, would they figure out Pearl's role in her escape? Or Bunny's? And what about the family she'd traveled with? Their children were still small but Covey knew this would make little difference to Little Man's family if they decided to seek retribution. No, even now, she still owed it to everyone who had helped her to stay hidden.

Early the next morning, when the others were still asleep, Covey reached for Elly's purse, rested it on the bed beside her, and pushed a hand inside, pulling out its contents, one at a time. Lip rouge. Pound notes. Train ticket. Passport. Tucked into the passport was a photograph showing a row of smiling young women, Covey and Elly included. Covey smiled, even as a tear rolled over her mouth. People used to ask Covey and Elly if they were sisters and they would laugh. But looking at this photograph now, Covey sees, in their smiles, in the tone of their skin, in the way they both tipped back their chins, why people might say that.

Elly.

Covey reached further into Elly's purse and pulled out a small sack with Elly's shells and coins and tortoiseshell hair comb. Elly's bag of treasures. Covey put one of the shells up to her nose, searching for the smell of the earth. Elly had never let anyone convince her to give up her dreams. They had been on that train to Edinburgh because of Elly's determination. Now that Elly was gone, Covey was back to being a person without a plan. Without a friend. What would become of her?

Covey wished she could have talked to Elly about Gibbs and the plans they'd made. She wished she could have explained how she was trying to let go of that dream and what it was doing to her.

Later, Covey took Elly's purse again and fished for the photograph of the women. She lay there looking at it for a long time, running a finger over the tiny, smiling faces, held the photograph to her chest for a moment, then tore it into bits and pushed the pieces down into a corner of the purse. Her hand found an air mail envelope, flattened against the bottom of the bag. Inside was a letter from Sister Mary. Covey read through the letter twice, then ripped the soft blue paper into strips and stuffed the pieces back into the purse with the remains of the photograph.

"Eleanor Douglas," she mumbled to herself. "Eleanor Douglas." She said the name over and over again. Elly had been her friend, but there was nothing that she could do for Elly now. For the second time in two years, Covey had nearly died. For the second time in two years, she'd been given a second chance. For the second time in two years, she was going to seize the opportunity.

The evening nurse walked over to her bed. "How are you doing, there, Elly?" she asked.

Covey said nothing, just nodded.

Elly, Elly

—

SOMEONE IS CALLING FOR ELLY BUT SHE IS VERY TIRED. SHE slips into a dream. She is digging cockle shells in the garden. A swallowtail dips low and flutters past her face. It is a land of miracles. There is no smell of burned metal in this garden, there is no pain, only someone who is calling *Elly, Elly*, holding her hand, pulling, pulling. Someone who has come to take Elly back home.

Eleanor Douglas

———

I N THE SUMMER OF 1967, THE NEWSPAPERS REPORTED THAT AN express train traveling at high speed through the north of England had plowed into a derailed freight car. One of those killed was a young West Indian woman identified through documents found at the scene as Coventina Brown, nearly twenty years of age. Miss Brown had been on her way to Edinburgh to assume clerical duties at a company there.

The trading company didn't hesitate to confirm its original offer of employment to one of the survivors of that crash, Eleanor Douglas, aged twenty-two, when Miss Douglas showed up alone at their offices several weeks later. At first, the young woman seemed a bit disoriented, wouldn't always answer when called, but she was courteous and caught on quickly. She turned out to be very good with numbers, though she never used the office calculating machine, and at first, her supervisor was quite satisfied that he had made the right decision.

Loss

—

BYRON AND BENNY HEAR THEIR MOTHER ASKING MR. MITCH, once again, to stop recording.

"Your mother was very upset at this point," says Mr. Mitch. "Losing her friend Elly was devastating, and taking on her identity felt like the point of no return."

Byron and Benny are both staring down at their hands.

"Should I go on?"

Byron and Benny nod. Neither of them can speak.

This is the thing about people, Benny thinks. You can look at a person and truly have no idea what they are holding inside. She wonders, did their father know any of this? Ma had lied to her and Byron about so many things that Benny can't even begin to guess how her mother's story is going to bring them to the sister they never knew about, much less the life they have now. Has Benny told that many lies about her own life? No, not like these. Not even close.

Benny realizes now that she had known that her mother was being deceptive about at least one thing. Those headaches she would get from time to time. Headaches so bad that she would lie in bed all weekend. Even then, Benny sensed that they weren't so much physical aches as something that was making her mother feel low. Very low.

Her ma had always been the exuberant one in the family, the most persistent one, the one who once waited and waited with Benny in the water until Benny learned to catch the swell of a wave and stand up on a surfboard for the first time.

"Don't rush it, Benny," her ma would say. "Pay attention, you'll know when."

Benny never was much of a surfer but the feeling of having timed it right, of having gotten up on the board that first time, was something that had stayed with her, that had left Benny feeling, even in her own low moments, that sooner or later life would lift her up again. Until she finally admitted that she might need a little help.

When Benny's therapist asked her last year if she had a history of depression in the family, Benny thought of her mother and said, *Maybe.* Because she could remember those times when Ma would grow very quiet at the dinner table, or skip dinner altogether, telling the rest of them that she had a headache and needed to lie down.

On some mornings, when she was little, Dad would shoo Benny out of her parents' bedroom and say, "Your ma needs to sleep in," only Ma would stay in bed all day. Once, Benny's father had left the bedroom door slightly ajar and Benny had peered through the opening to see her mother lying awake, staring at the ceiling.

Benny wonders now if it had been her mother's physiology alone to trigger those low periods or if they might have been brought on by everything she had lived through. Surely her mother must have felt, sometimes, that her past, and the effort it was taking to conceal it, had been too much to bear. How much, exactly, had she hidden? And how much more was left for her mother to reveal?

Mrs. Bennett

—

The second time I died, it was easier. I was devastated by Elly's death, but a door had opened up and I walked through it. I had all the papers I needed in Elly's purse. Remember, B and B, Elly had been an orphan and the people who had jobs waiting for the two of us in Scotland didn't know either of us personally, they only knew that one of us had been killed and the other still needed a job.

My colleagues and neighbors in Edinburgh were friendly enough and I was learning to relax. Two years had passed since my disappearance from the island and I was growing used to the idea that no one would be coming to look for me. Eleanor Douglas was an orphan from a remote part of the island and, whether you knew me as Coventina Brown or Coventina Lyncook, I was, now, officially dead. There was no one to ask if things were going all right for me. There was no one who cared enough to ask the right questions when I disappeared for the third time. Because, yes, B and B, there would be a third time.

Driftwood

—

JOHNNY "LIN" LYNCOOK LOOKED OUT ONTO THE BAY WHERE his daughter had disappeared two years earlier and asked himself what he could have done differently. Lodged in the sand next to him was a piece of driftwood so large that no one had ever tried to move it from the beach. Over the years, it grew roots into the hearts of the islanders who lived on the bay, who strolled by it daily, who embraced in its shadow, who could see it from way out on the water. Once in a while, a small piece of it would disappear overnight and show up in someone's garden or on their veranda or on a glass-topped table. The beauty of a thing justified its plunder.

The monster driftwood still retained the shape of the tree base that it had been years before, only it had been washed and polished by the sea and beaten by storms and slow-cooked in the sun. It was already there when Lin arrived on the island with his parents and it was still there on the day that his daughter disappeared just shy of her eighteenth birthday. Lin's daughter had been the color of that driftwood, her limbs strong like those of a tree, her face the kind that Little Man Henry had wanted to own.

The beauty of a thing justified its plunder.

Lin stood beside the driftwood now, his head clearer than it had been in years. He pulled off his sandals and walked to the water's edge. He had never been the kind of man to doubt himself but now, that was all he did. He'd thought the passing of time would have helped, but still, he kept asking himself, what if he had done things differently? First, his girl's mother had left him, and now his only child was dead. She had run off into the sea and drowned hardly four hours after being married to Little Man.

Everyone had seen how suddenly Little Man Henry began to wheeze and stagger before dropping his champagne flute and falling, facedown, onto the splintered glass, a line of froth issuing from his mouth. If he hadn't been such a hateful man, people might have believed that he'd died of heart trouble at a precocious age, but no one doubted that Little Man had been murdered. So many people had wished so fervently for it. Lin wasn't sorry to see Little Man go, but he didn't want to believe that his daughter was responsible.

And yet Covey had fled the wedding hall as soon as her new husband had fallen to the ground. This, Lin recognized, seemed as good an admission of guilt as any. Two years had passed since Covey's wedding dress had been found abandoned on the beach. In the first few days, the lack of a body had given Lin hope. Covey could have washed up unconscious on another shore, could have been trapped in an air pocket in a cave until low tide. But at this point, even Lin had to accept that he would never see his daughter again.

For all Lin knew it might only be a matter of time before Little Man Henry's brother had him killed, but for now, he seemed to be more useful to the Henry family alive. Lin still owed money to them and he was still the best person to handle the shops, which now belonged to them. Lin had lost his businesses and his daughter and this suffering of his must have brought some measure of satisfaction to the Henrys.

Like it or not, many people believed that Covey had poisoned Little Man, and most people still avoided being too friendly with Lin. Only Pearl seemed not to worry how Little Man's family would react. She still came to the house on Sunday afternoons and cooked for Lin, even though she had a job at the villa up on the hill.

Pearl barely spoke to Lin when she came to the house, but she'd walk into the kitchen as if nothing had changed. She always left him with oxtail stew or a pot of rice and peas and a bit of fried plantain, maybe callaloo, something that would last for a couple of days, since he never ate much. Lin realized that he'd known Pearl for as long as he'd known his own daughter, and while he knew little about her personal life, her absence from his daily routine deepened his sense of loss over Covey, if such a thing was possible.

If Lin had been a better man, he would have refused to let Covey marry Clarence Henry. But at what price, he wondered. He suspected that Little Man would have taken Covey anyway, and that would have been worse. His only child, defiled and left without a penny to her name. Maybe she was better off dead, after all. Maybe Lin, too, was better off dead. The sad truth was, if Lin had been a better man, he wouldn't have been in this situation to begin with.

Lin took a deep breath and walked into the sea. He would go the way his daughter had gone. And if there was anything on the other side of this life, as so many people believed, Lin might even find his daughter there. He felt the sand under his feet, tasted the salt in his mouth. He tried to hold on to the image of his daughter as she might have been on one of her best days, so happy to be in the water that she would have done anything to get there. He tried to make this his last thought before he died.

Later, Lin would not be able to recall the exact moment at which he was grabbed by the collar. Things had gone gray. He remembered two malnourished boys standing over him on the sand, their bellies sticking out like brown gourds over pinlike legs. They were probably from one of those families that lived in the wooden shacks just inland from there. He used to sell things to some of those families on credit until Little Man's brother put a stop to it.

The boys had managed to drag Lin all the way up to the dry part of the sand. He lay there, spent and ashamed. He hadn't even been able to kill himself properly. Soon after he got home, Pearl came running toward the house, wagging her arms in front of her, oblivious to what he had just gone through.

What was she saying? She was blabbing on about a local fellow, the one they called Short Shirt. Did the woman not see that Lin was soaking wet?

"He used to work for Little Man, remember?" Pearl was saying. The young man, she said, had been caught trying to poison Little Man's brother by putting something in his drink, and police now were accusing him of murdering Little Man two years earlier. Didn't Mister Lin see? Covey was no longer the main suspect.

So that was that. With any luck, this would mean no more threats from Clarence Henry's family, no more wondering if someone might hit Lin over the head and drop him downriver where the crocodiles liked to feed. But all of this had come too late to save his daughter. And Lin would still be forced to work like a coolie in his own shops.

A more honorable man might have headed back to the shore for another attempt at killing himself. But Lin was, fundamentally, a cowardly man. He was also a gambling man. He couldn't help but think that one day, he would find a way to win back everything. Everything, that is, except his daughter, Covey.

Short Shirt

—

M OST PEOPLE AROUND TOWN KNEW SHORT SHIRT HIGGINS, but until that moment, Pearl would never have thought him relevant to Covey Lyncook's story. Short Shirt was as skinny as a shadow but tall, and that was how he got his nickname. The shirts that his sister had sewn for him when he was still in eighth form continued to fit his slender body as he grew into manhood, the hems inching *up, up, up,* until you could see the brown of his stomach.

For a poor *yout* like Short Shirt, there were few options available but to work for Little Man Henry. Eventually, Short Shirt earned enough to buy himself two shirts that covered his torso, and trousers that reached all the way down to his shoes. But the nickname stuck.

By the time Short Shirt turned twenty-five, no one called him by his given name, except his parents and sister. His sister, though, hardly talked anymore. Earlier that year, she'd been beaten and left for dead under an oleander bush. The police said no one knew who had done this, but Short Shirt knew, and he was going to make the man pay.

Short Shirt's sister had complained, more than once, about the persistent advances of Little Man's brother, Percival. But what was Short Shirt to do, being in their family's employ? At the hospital, his sis clutched his hand and whispered her attacker's name before falling unconscious. After she left the hospital, she was shaky and slow-talking and given to occasional seizures, having taken the bulk of Percival Henry's beating about the head.

Short Shirt's mother had unwittingly supplied him with the solution. His mother had grown up among the ancient, forested hills and limestone caverns in the center of the island. She had taught her children to avoid plants like scratch bush, maiden plum, and burn wood. She had made them memorize the looks of things that they were never to put into their mouths.

One afternoon in 1967, Short Shirt was caught dripping water off the leaf of a poisonous plant into a drink that had been prepared for Percival Henry. *Short Shirt, of all people!* He didn't seem the type. But this was what could happen to the heart of a young man whose sister had been treated like she was rubbish when, in fact, she was a princess.

No one liked the Henry brothers and their ways, but everyone agreed you couldn't go around poisoning people unless you made sure you could get away with it. After his arrest, Short Shirt confessed and explained his motives, but he consistently denied his involvement in the murder of Little Man two years earlier. He hadn't even been in town that day. Eventually, Short Shirt went to jail for trying to poison Percival Henry but was never taken to court for Clarence Henry's murder.

Pearl knew that Short Shirt couldn't have killed Little Man, but for Pearl, the most important thing was that his case had raised too many questions about the unsolved murder for Covey to remain the obvious suspect. The gossip around town was that perhaps Coventina Lyncook had merely taken advantage of the fatal collapse of her husband and run off without looking back. And who, they admitted, wouldn't have done the same? Maybe one day, Pearl thought, Covey would be able to return home.

Pearl tried to get word to Covey about what had happened with Short Shirt, but her connections in Britain hadn't heard from Covey for some time. *Please try and get in contact with her,* Pearl asked. Eventually, Pearl received word from them of Covey's fate. There had been a terrible accident. Why had this happened to a child who had been through so much, a child who surely had merited a little bit of happiness? Pearl raised her arms in the air and railed at the God in which she had been taught to trust.

Bunny

—

UNTIL WORD ARRIVED THAT COVENTINA LYNCOOK, TRAVEL-
ing under the name of Coventina Brown, had been killed in a train accident in England, most people in her hometown hadn't realized that
she'd been alive to begin with. Those who had grieved Covey's loss
since her wedding-day disappearance into the sea were now doubly
heartbroken, including Covey's father and Gibbs Grant. Gibbs had
been studying in England at the time of the rail crash and realized, only
then, how close he had been to Covey all that time.

When Pearl told her about the rail accident, Bunny ran down to the
beach, looking up and down the cove, wishing for magic, thinking that
she might find Covey lying there, now, barely conscious but still alive,
just as she'd found her on the night of Covey's wedding ceremony. She
should have gone with Covey to Britain, Bunny thought, or followed
her soon after. Or maybe, it had all been a mistake, helping her to escape in the first place.

Bunny walked into the sea, still in her street clothes, and swam
straight for the horizon, *pull, pull, pull*. She imagined Covey just ahead
of her, told herself that nothing had changed, but after two hours, she
was forced to come back to shore and face the truth. She ran all the way
home, weeping, her wet clothes clinging to her like long strands of
seaweed, and climbed into bed.

The following year, Bunny was sitting on a bench at the swim club,
wrapped in a terry-cloth robe, scrunching and stretching her toes in

her rubber sandals and waiting for the coach. She moved her head to a rocksteady hit by Johnny Nash that was coming out of a radio on the coach's table. After a year of grieving for Covey, Bunny had come to understand that she needed to go on without her friend, and if she truly wished to honor her memory, she had to walk through the door that Covey had pried open for her. Bunny had a gift for swimming in the sea, her coach told her. One day, she could be famous, he said.

Another woman, a few years older than Bunny, walked into the pool area. It was that police girl the newspaper had been talking about, the first in their town. Patsy *something*. She'd been down at the beach with Covey's father on the day that Covey disappeared. Bunny's brother, who was also on the police force, said this Patsy girl was all right. The police girl looked at Bunny and nodded. Bunny nodded in return and the warmth spreading up the back of her neck made her think of Covey.

Bunny would continue to think of Covey every time she pulled her goggles over her face and set out on a swim. Bunny belonged in the sea, where Covey had first led her. In the sea, despite her fears. Her swim coach had found her a second instructor for the distance swimming and it had been a revelation. Bunny understood, now, what she might be able to accomplish.

In the worst hours, she would draw courage from imagining her friend just ahead of her in the water and in time, it would no longer bother her so much that Covey had looked happiest not when she was with Bunny but when she was with Gibbs Grant. In time, it would comfort her, simply, to remember that Covey had once been happy.

Bunny herself had struggled after Covey's departure. Only the swimming had helped. The swimming and Jimmy, who had been fixing local boats alongside his father since his primary school days.

Later, it would be awkward to explain to Patsy how she could let a man kiss her and make love to her. Hers was not a case, as with so many women, of being coerced into her first time. No, Jimmy had been a cheerful, joking kind of man, a good worker, and a good friend. He had always encouraged Bunny's swimming. He had never suggested, as some people had, that a woman who took to the open seas the way Bunny did was an *abomination to the Lord*.

"That boy has a crush on yoooouuu," Covey teased Bunny once, when Jimmy agreed to use his motorized canoe as a safety boat for one of their swims. Bunny had cut her eyes at Covey but she'd known it was true.

Jimmy had never questioned Bunny's dreams, and since it was the normal thing to do, Bunny didn't resist when Jimmy wanted to court her, wanted to hold her in that way. The heat of adolescence made it easier for Bunny to behave like other women, and Bunny felt comforted with Jimmy's arms around her. She assumed that it was only the absence of Covey, the loss of Covey, that made all sentiment, all desire, pale in comparison. It was only when she met Patsy that she realized she'd been wrong. And Jimmy realized it, too.

They had just stopped seeing each other when Jimmy was killed in a country bus accident. Jimmy and some other lads had been clinging to the outside of the bus as it drove off. As the vehicle barreled along a pocked and dusty road flanked by sugar cane fields, Jimmy lost his grip and fell. Bunny understood then that she had felt a kind of love for Jimmy, even though she could never have been his wife. There were different ways to love a person, and losing someone you cared for still hurt. That hurt made her more certain of how she needed to live.

By the time Bunny realized that the problem with her thickening middle was not the food she was eating but an advancing pregnancy, she and Patsy were preparing to leave for England together and arranging for Patsy's brother, still a young child, to join them when the time came. Patsy had made it clear from the start that she had promised her pops, the only parent left, that she would take care of him, and Patsy's loyalty had drawn Bunny even closer.

Back then, it was normal for two single women to live together. Back then, it was even expected. Back then, it was easy to let neighborly gossip spread the word that your new baby's father had died back in the islands. And here you were now, faced with navigating a new life abroad on your own. And wasn't it fortunate that you, at least, had a roommate from the same country to keep an eye on you?

"You what?" Bunny's new coach said, when she told him. He had been the one to arrange her move to England.

"How do you think you're going to manage to train, between a child and a job?" Coach said. His face softened now. "You're not going to let me down, are you, Bunny?" He was staking his reputation on this young talent he'd brought over.

"No, sir," Bunny said.

"And pick up your head, young lady. What kind of champion lets her head hang down like a piece of fruit?"

Bunny laughed.

"That's more like it." Coach stepped in closer so that Bunny, tall as she was, had to tilt her face down again to look him in the eyes.

"There are a lot of people counting on you, Bunny, you hear? But the only thing that really matters is you, and whether you can count on yourself when you're out there. This is no joke. That Channel will shred you to pieces if you don't treat it with respect."

"Yes, sir."

There were others waiting to put their support behind Bunny, people who were charmed by the distance swimmer from the islands, despite the times, despite the rising tensions between residents and immigrants over housing and other privileges. Despite her dark skin. Because they saw that Bunny's freakish talent and stunning smile would surely add luster to the image of the Commonwealth.

But first, there would be those iron-colored waves to conquer, colder than anything that Bunny had ever experienced, that anomalous drift that kept pulling her off course, the nausea, plenty of nausea, and the deep despair that struck Bunny at times, when she wasn't sure if she could manage the Channel crossing, all the while knowing that she was not fit to live any other life.

Bright
Future

———

THE NEW ELEANOR DOUGLAS HAD FINALLY STOPPED LOOKING over her shoulder wherever she went, afraid of being recognized by someone. Her new job was near the port in Edinburgh and her room in a bedsit was not far from the water. She was still walking with a limp when she arrived and she felt that the sea air did her good, even though the water there was so cold, she doubted she could ever swim in it.

Her supervisor at the trading company had been quite supportive. He'd given her a day to settle into her lodgings and learn the bus route. The other clerical workers looked at her shyly, spoke softly, at first. They would have heard her story, she imagined. How she had survived a train crash. How she had lost a friend in the same accident.

This new city was, like London, a jumble of traffic with oversized buses and gray streets and mostly pink-faced people, but it was different, too. There were bursts of color among the buildings. There was that broad, low hill that looked like a huge, green wad of discarded bread. There was that big castle up on a rise, what a place! But there was also a yawning sense of loss, the absence of everyone and everything that had been cut out of her life. She tried not to think of Gibbs and when she did, she whimpered herself to sleep.

Eleanor's new supervisor told her that she was off to a good start. He said that she was a capable woman, not to mention a very beautiful one. He stayed late at the office to show her the bookkeeping routine. He told her that this would allow her to advance in her position. He told her that she had a bright future ahead of her. And after a while, Eleanor allowed herself to believe it.

Until her supervisor stood too close.

Until he tried to kiss her.

Until he put his hands there.

Until what happened next stunned Eleanor into silence.

Unthinkable

—

Benny stands up, shaking her head from side to side. "No, I can't," she says, walking out of the room.

Byron leans forward and puts a hand against his forehead. He looks as though he could weep.

Mr. Mitch bows his head. If only Eleanor had been able to tell her family about this before. For as long as people have been mistreating other people, women have been subject to this kind of violence. It's high time they stop having to feel ashamed about it.

Benny walks down the hallway to her parents' room. She picks up a small framed photograph that sits on the nightstand by her mother's side of the bed, a Polaroid that was taken of her mother and father outside a government office on the day of their wedding. She uses her thumb to wipe a bit of dust off the glass. It could have been a photo of any special occasion. Two smiling faces, a pale shift dress, a brown suit, a small bouquet of peonies.

Benny studies her mother's face. At some point, her mother met her father. At some point, she fell in love again. At some point, Ma was happy, wasn't she? A person can still be happy after everything that her mother went through, can't they? Benny needs to believe that they can. No, she needs to know for sure. Benny puts the frame back on the nightstand, walks back down the hallway, and goes back into the living room. Without looking at Byron or Mr. Mitch, Benny sits down and pulls a cushion to her middle.

Mrs.
Bennett

—

B *and B, I'm so sorry that you have to hear this but you need to under-*
stand everything that has happened. The position at the trading company
near Edinburgh had provided me with a refuge, a place where I could rest
and begin to dream again. So, you can imagine how I must have felt the
following year, when I found myself in an impossible situation. When I
found myself forced to run away again.

You grow up thinking that when someone does something terrible to you,
you will react, you will fight back, you will run away. I had already proven
myself capable of doing this. But this time, it was as if everything had been
frozen inside. I truly did not know what to do. And I had no one I could trust
enough to turn to.

I went to work the next day thinking that I should say something or do
something, but my supervisor acted as though nothing at all had happened.
Except that I knew that it had, because he suddenly spent most of his time
in his office, almost never in the main room, no longer kept me late to go over
the books, never again spoke directly to me, addressed the clerical workers as
a group. I should have felt shocked that he could erase everything like that
but, the truth is, I was relieved. And I, too, tried to cancel out what had hap-
pened. I continued to work, go home, push the chest of drawers in front of my
door at night, and lie awake for most of the hours until morning.

One day, while collecting my wages, I told my employer that I would be
moving back to England. He immediately promised me a solid reference. Of
course, he didn't ask me to stay. And he didn't ask me why I was leaving.

Because he knew what he had done. He didn't look up at me as he spoke. He kept his eyes focused on his fingers as he picked through the stack of paychecks on his desk and handed me my envelope.

"Next," he said, then beckoned to the office girl behind me.

Even as he let me walk out of there, I still could not give a name to what I was feeling. Something that was not quite anger, not quite fear, but a yawning kind of grief. It was only when I felt my baby jabbing and shifting inside me that I was able to focus on my affliction. When I felt that stirring in my womb, I understood two things. First, that my child would be born a girl and, second, that she must never know how she had been conceived.

Separation

—

IN 1970, ELEANOR WAS BACK IN LONDON, DOWN TO HER LAST few shillings and clutching a flyer someone had just shoved into her hand. In large print, the piece of paper read *You are not alone.* At first, she thought it was talking about God. There were churches, in those days, that advertised themselves like department stores. Then she realized the paper wasn't talking about worship, it was talking about women like her. Unwed and pregnant. Nowhere did the blue ink of the ditto machine say it outright, but the words *young women in need* jumped out at her like a secret code.

This, after all, was what she really needed, this kind of help. Eleanor had earned enough money at the trading company to get herself back to London, trembling through the entire train journey, trying to shut out the memories of that not-too-distant accident.

Elly.

She had returned to London because she hadn't known where else to go. But on arrival, she realized that she couldn't go back to anything or anyone she had known here. She couldn't afford to run into anyone who had known her or the original Eleanor. And there would be no place for her to stay once the swell of her stomach under her A-line dress became obvious to others.

But it must have been obvious already, because a middle-aged woman had thrust this piece of paper at her as she stood at a bus stop. She took a bus to the address listed on the sheet of paper and found herself standing in front of a low brick building in a part of the city that she'd never seen before. Once there, she was given food and a place to sleep and told that she was doing the right thing. What a relief, to be surrounded by other women, even though they slept dormitory-style in a large room, with no choice but to hear one another's sighs and snores and sobs.

The nuns told her that she couldn't expect her child to have a decent future with a mother like her. But she'd done nothing wrong, she told them. She'd been forced. It didn't matter, they said. What mattered was the kind of future she wanted for her child. What mattered was the work that Eleanor would not be able to find or the kinds of things that she would be compelled to do to survive. The labels that her child would have to live with. What mattered was that her child deserved better.

What the sisters meant was, her child deserved something better than Eleanor. Her child deserved something that Eleanor was not.

Eleanor wanted to keep her baby, but she saw that who you knew yourself to be on the inside was not the same as how others saw you. Who you knew yourself to be wasn't always enough to help you make it in this world. The fact was, Eleanor could not guarantee that she and her baby would be all right.

"So that you will have a better future," Eleanor said to the swell of her middle. So that her baby would never know the shame, she swore to herself.

Her baby. It all happened so quickly. The pain, the wet, the screams. And then it was done and Eleanor had given birth to a long-fingered creature with a sweet wail, a small birthmark at the top of her pale forehead and a damp head of black hair. Until that moment, she had not known it was possible to love another person that way.

She gave her daughter her mother's name and nursed her for six weeks, her breasts aching at the sight of her child until the pink barnacle of her baby's mouth latched on to her nipple. When she wasn't nursing, she was down on her knees scrubbing floors or doing the washing, lifting the hem of her skirt to wipe the sweat from under her chin.

One day, one of the nuns told Eleanor to put on her good dress. They put her baby in a pram, then in a taxi, and took her into an office with yellow walls and wooden filing cabinets and posters for infant-care products. A woman there had Eleanor sign a piece of paper and took the baby out of her arms.

"No, wait," Eleanor said. "Could I just . . ." The baby's snuffling erupted into a full wail as the woman carried her away down a hallway and Eleanor, too, started to cry.

"Shush, now," the nun said on the way out. "Hold yourself like a lady."

Eleanor left the hostel for unwed mothers determined to find her baby one day, to find a way to take her back. Everything she did from then on, she did with the thought of being able to take care of a child on her own. Finding a boardinghouse, finding a secretarial position, walking to work to save money on bus fares, walking the long way around to avoid those streets where the windows, despite the laws, still bore signs that read *No Blacks, No Dogs, No Irish.*

Eleanor lived off tinned fish and fruit, and managed to save a few pounds. After several months, she tried to locate the adoption office that had taken her baby, but it was no longer there. She went back to the hostel and begged the sisters to tell her where her daughter had ended up, but they threatened to call the police, to claim that she was mentally unstable.

After that, none of the good that came Eleanor's way, not the love of a man, not the joy of giving birth again, not a plunge into the sea, would ever fully calm the undertow that had formed inside Eleanor and kept pulling her down.

On the worst nights, Eleanor dreamed of the empty pram and how, as she returned to the entrance of the home for unwed mothers, she leaned forward to see if, by some miracle, her baby had reappeared.

Mrs.
Bennett

—

Years later, I would learn that there had been other young women like me in various parts of the country, women who had felt coerced into giving up their babies, but at that time, no one knew any of this. I certainly didn't know, not for many years, until the news reports started coming out.

I can still remember those days after she'd been taken away and how, wherever I walked, I would move slowly, looking at every mother with a pram, straining to see if my baby girl was in there, stopping to compliment and coo, just to get a look at the infant. The curling fingers, the tiny mouth, always searching, always hungry. And me, alone, always searching, always hungry.

Reunion

—

ELEANOR HAD TAKEN TO TELLING HERSELF THAT HER LIFE WAS like one long swim. *Breathe deep and wide, take it one stroke at a time.* When you were several miles into a swim, the world could feel like an endless place. But when you were trying to stay invisible in a city where people once knew you, the streets and high-rises and bus lines and shops could squeeze in on you like a tightening net, until the inevitable—inevitably—happened.

"Well, I just didn't know what to say," she heard a familiar voice saying. Eleanor was standing in a queue to pay at the grocer's near her office. She looked over at two women in another queue, who had their heads bent together now, laughing, and saw a face she knew. It was Edwina from the boardinghouse where she and Elly used to live. Edwina, from the days when Eleanor was still Covey.

Edwina was wearing her nurse's cap and she looked so well. Eleanor had to fight the urge to cry out, to run up to Edwina, to hug her. She and Elly had spent some good times with Edwina and the other girls. But all that had to remain in the past. At any moment now, Edwina might look around and see Eleanor. Turning her face away, Eleanor set her basket of groceries on the ground and walked quickly in the opposite direction.

That was when she began to consider leaving Britain altogether. Canada and the United States were still open to immigration of educated young women from the West Indies. Eleanor had Elly's nursing degree and North America, after all, had been part of Elly's plan. But Eleanor's baby girl was somewhere in this country. And so was Gibbs. How could she bring herself to go so far away?

As the months passed, Eleanor admitted to herself that even if she could find her daughter, there was a difference between what she would be able to do for her child and the life that someone else might be able to give her. A difference as wide and deep as a canyon. She began to steel herself to accept a bitter reality, the likelihood that the path chosen for her baby, though it was killing Eleanor, might indeed have been the best for her child.

Eleanor opened her umbrella and ducked out into the rain, dragging her feet through the punishing, gray day. Closer to home, she heard a buzz of Caribbean accents, looked up, and saw a small crew of lads across the street. They were standing under the eaves of a building, apparently waiting for the rain to abate. *Good luck,* she muttered under her breath. Then she stopped and looked again.

One of the men looked back across the street at her. There was no mistaking it. She knew that man. That man was Gibbs and in a moment, she was Covey all over again. Here was the boy she'd been forced to give up when her father had married her off to Little Man. Here was the love she was meant to marry. Here was the man she had feared she might never see again.

"Gibbs!" Covey tried to shout but her voice wouldn't come out. She stepped off the curb to cross the street but her legs wouldn't hold her.

∴

GIBBS HAD BEEN THROUGH THIS BEFORE. CERTAIN HE'D SEEN COVEY when he knew that she was dead. It would happen every once in a while. He would see her on a bus, on a bridge, in a store. Missing someone could have that kind of power over you.

After Gibbs learned that Covey had disappeared off the coast back home, he felt like giving up. He didn't know anymore what he was doing all the way over here. He hadn't found the mother country as welcoming as he'd expected, nor all his professors as supportive as he'd hoped. It was only his determination to prove them wrong in their doubt of him that kept him going. What would he do if he went back, anyway, knowing that he wouldn't find Covey there? His parents were already gone. Gibbs's mother had been ill for a while and soon after she'd passed on, so had his father. Dead of a broken heart, his uncle said.

And then Bunny called. She reached him by long-distance operator to tell him the whole story. How Covey had survived, how Covey had escaped to England and why Bunny and Pearl hadn't told him. So close, she had been so close, but this time, she really was gone. Covey had been killed in that terrible rail accident up north, and this time they had the documents to prove it, the authorities had her photo.

Gibbs hadn't known until that moment that he'd had any heart left to break. First, his parents, and now this. How did a man survive something like this? He went to bed and stayed there for weeks until one of his professors, one of the kind ones, offered to help him pull his studies back together. Gibbs was exceptional, his professor said, he could do it, and Gibbs let himself be pulled along.

When Gibbs saw Covey standing on the far side of a London street this time, he assumed that it was just another one of his daydreams. He still thought about the plans that he and Covey had made together, to pursue their studies, to raise a family. He still thought of the swim club where he'd first met her, of the cove where they had first kissed. Five long years had passed. But he could see that this wasn't an illusion. He could see that the young woman across the street knew him. She was mouthing his name, reaching an arm out toward him. It was a wonder that Gibbs didn't faint, too, when he realized that Covey was still alive.

Gibbs ran across the road and caught Covey before her face could hit the ground. When Covey came to, Gibbs was holding her in his arms and he never did let go again until the day he died, four decades later. Covey and Gibbs had found each other again.

Back Then

———

ACK THEN, IT WAS EASIER TO DISAPPEAR. BACK THEN, YOU could open a new bank account or get a driver's license with just part of your birth name and maybe even your nickname. They didn't finger-print and face-recognition everyone and digitize your orthotic model and send your blood-test results by email. They didn't save your shop-ping preferences and the birthdays of everyone who'd ever received a chocolate-and-cheese gift package from you. They didn't make money by posting your age and address and so-called *facts* about you on the Web to lure other people into paying for somewhat-true-but-mostly-imprecise information.

Back then, it was easier for a young man, an only son whose parents had already died, to shorten his name and turn himself from Gilbert Bennett Grant into Bert Bennett, slowly change his documents to match, and cut all ties with his past to be with the woman he loved. It was easier then for a young woman to believe that you could build a family of your own in a vacuum because love and loyalty were the only true things in this world. So this is what Bert and Eleanor did.

Now

Benny

So her father, too, had lied about his past. Benny doesn't feel angry so much as sad. The more Benny learns about her mother, in particular, the more she sees that Benny wasn't the only one in her family who had paid a price for going against other people's rules.

True, Eleanor Bennett had, in the end, been much more fortunate in her life than many people. She had been reunited with her first love and they had gone on to have two children together. But Benny's mother would continue to mourn a series of losses so great that not even Benny can begin to imagine. Her first family. Her identity. Her first child.

Benny used to think she'd been a brave soul, insisting on being herself despite the bullying, despite the alienation from her family, despite the loneliness. She was proud that she hadn't run back home with her tail between her legs just because things hadn't worked out with Joanie, or with Steve, or with her plans. But lately, Benny has felt a bit ashamed of not having more to show for it all. Her mother, at least, had something to show for what she'd been through.

After all that she had experienced in her early years, why couldn't Ma imagine what was happening with Benny? Why didn't she give her advice? Why didn't Ma do more to hold on to her? And what is Benny supposed to do with these feelings, now that Ma is no longer around?

Byron

—

H AD BYRON'S PARENTS EVER TOLD THE TRUTH ABOUT ANY-
thing?

Had they been that good about covering things up? Or had Byron
just not wanted to see? The more Byron learns, the more some things
begin to make sense. A year ago, his confident, go-get-'em ma had become quieter, even clingy. More touchy-feely than usual, more distracted. He could sense that she was undergoing some kind of internal
shift. He could sense that it went beyond losing his dad, or missing
Benny. But he didn't want to go there.

Byron didn't want to think that whatever was ailing his mother
wouldn't go away on its own, the way it used to when he was a kid and
she was feeling down. Byron himself was feeling increasingly restless.
Disappointed with the way things had gone at the office. Surprised that
they still bothered him as much as they did. Frustrated that Lynette,
who was still living with him then, was demanding more of his private
time, just as he was trying to get as much mileage as possible out of his
public life.

Byron was being selfish, he can see that now. He needed his mother
to remain the clear-eyed, positive thinker who had always been there
for him, who had always told him to find his center and hold on to it
and, *You'll see, Byron,* things would work out all right. After all, he
thought back then, things had worked out all right for his folks, hadn't
they?

PART THREE

One Year Earlier

Etta Pringle

ETTA PRINGLE KICKED OFF HER SANDALS AND STEPPED ONTO a wooden platform set in the sand, waving to the crowd as she walked. The applause gave way to the sounds of her childhood. The sea, the palm fronds in the breeze, the memory of her mother's voice, admonishing her. *A young lady never removes her shoes in public!* her mother would have said. Etta smiled at the thought, then braced herself for the deep tug of nostalgia. At least her mother had lived long enough to see what Etta had accomplished. To see her grandchildren growing up. To believe that all was well with her only daughter.

Etta lifted her face to breathe in the sun and opened her arms. The crowd cheered. Just twenty-four more hours and she'd be on a plane out of here. With her mother gone and her brother in England, Etta had no reason to linger, even though she was the one who had wanted the ceremony to take place here, in her hometown, in this cove where it had all begun. And where so much had gone wrong.

"Etta Pringle isn't just a local girl who's made good," the prime minister was saying. "Etta Pringle is a woman who has conquered the world, one swim at a time, starting with this bay right here." Someone shouts her childhood nickname and Etta laughs and gives a thumbs-up.

"And now," the prime minister said, "this homegrown champion rightly nags politicians like me to do more to safeguard the environment, because no sea, not even ours, the most beautiful in the world, is immune to runoff, to the plastics, to the rising water levels, to increasingly severe weather."

More applause, then a medal, then the naming of this stretch of beach after Etta Pringle. Etta looks out past the waves frothing against the rocks. This was the bay where a much faster, bolder swimmer had led Etta past the seven-mile mark for the first time and made her realize who she was destined to become.

Etta had swum across the Strait of Magellan in Chile, circled New York's island of Manhattan, crossed the English Channel, and survived the icy waters off the Siberian coast, the first black woman in the world to have made all of these crossings. She had raised two children with another woman at a time when such things were not mentioned. She had spoken to entire stadiums full of people about overcoming obstacles. But there was one obstacle in her own life that Etta had never been able to overcome.

Etta scanned the crowd. There they were. A couple of the Henry boys. There was always someone from the Henry family hanging about, waiting for someone to slip up, waiting to offer their unique brand of assistance at terms that could never be repaid. There was a whole new generation of Henrys now, people who lived to exploit other people. People who enjoyed holding a grudge. Which was why Etta needed to get away from this island.

There Was
a Place

———

WHILE ETTA PRINGLE WAS BEING HONORED ON THE ISLAND, Eleanor Bennett was at home in California, nearly three thousand miles away, looking at her laptop. She noted with satisfaction that Pringle was trending on social media. Eleanor's husband Bert, rest his soul, would have gotten a kick out of that. He and Eleanor had been proud to see a woman from the islands, a black distance swimmer, become so famous. But in the five years since Bert's passing, Pringle had become even more popular, known to the younger generations for her motivational speaking.

And now, Etta Pringle had a beach named after her. *Imagine that, Bert,* Eleanor thought. Seeing the video of the dedication ceremony on the Internet brought the sting of salt water to Eleanor's eyes. It left Eleanor with a longing to be surrounded by folks from the islands, a need to remember what she used to be like before she and Bert started going out of their way to stay away from other West Indians, trying to avoid people who might know people who might remember them. *Caribbeans,* her son kept reminding her to say. It was more politically correct to say that. Wasn't that funny, how her child was telling her what to call her own home?

Even after all these years, it wasn't so common to hear a voice from the islands in Eleanor's neighborhood, so she got into her car and drove north to Los Angeles, the sudden change of plans being one of the perks of retirement. There was a place in the Crenshaw district where

Eleanor would go to pick up some of her favorite island foods. A bunch of plantains, a can of ackee, a jar of smoked herring paste, a bottle of hot pepper sauce. A place where she could also find Chinese egg noodles and a head of baby bok choy and didn't have to explain to anyone what *suey mein* was. Didn't have to explain that it wasn't so much Chinese food as island food.

A little over an hour later, Eleanor was walking along the aisles of the store, running her fingertips along the jars and burlap sacks, watching mostly brown faces leaning in to read the labels, listening to chatter in different accents and languages. Near the baking supplies, a soft-armed saleswoman in a purple skirt and yellow top was giving an in-store demonstration.

"When it comes to black cake," the woman was telling a small group, "a base of marzipan, or almond paste, is essential to successful icing." As she spoke, she dusted a cloth-covered board in front of her with confectioner's sugar.

"Once you have the cake ready, you want to cover it in a layer of marzipan before applying the icing. Otherwise, all that rum and other good stuff that makes your cake so special will cause the icing to go runny." She nodded and pointed. "Has that happened to you? Yes?"

The saleswoman dumped a wad of almond paste onto the sugar-dusted surface while people asked questions. Then she patted it down and picked up a rolling pin.

"Any of you here ever watch that English woman on YouTube? The one who's always talking about different ethnic foods? You know the one I mean, right? She does some interesting shows on local traditions around the world. *She* claims that black cake is not an authentic Caribbean recipe."

She tips her head to the side and raises an eyebrow. Laughter bubbles up from the crowd.

"She says we wouldn't have black cake without the Europeans dem coming over to this part of the world and bringing certain foods over here. She says the recipe comes from a mixing of different cultures. Different cultures? Well, what does she think the Caribbean is, anyhow?" Someone kissed their teeth and a buzz of comments went around the group of onlookers.

Eleanor breathed in the almond smell, remembering the kitchen in her childhood home, the marzipan spread out on the kitchen table, Mummy and Pearl gossiping and tittering. Eleanor tried not to think back to those days too often, to the days when she was still Covey, to the days before her mother went away. But on this day, she let herself imagine what it might be like to go back to the island today.

What if she could wander through her hometown unseen, past the old school grounds, past the swim club, toward the house where she grew up, with its white cement walls and corrugated tin roof and red hibiscus blooming at the corner? What if she could stop to pluck a naseberry from a neighbor's yard, stop to snap and strip a frond from a dwarf coconut tree? What if she could step into the backyard where her father used to play dominoes with the men and stand just behind him, and simply be his daughter again, before his weaknesses had gotten the best of him?

What if her mummy were still there?

What if Eleanor could return without having to explain where she had been all these years? Then, yes, she would go back, she would gather tamarind pods from the floor of the backyard and sit on the concrete steps of the veranda near the orange spikes of the bird of paradise. She would show her children how to crack open the pods, pull off the strings, and roll the pulp in a bowl of sugar. She would take them down to the cove to swim in the sea.

But you didn't just disappear for five decades and then go back as if nothing had happened. She wouldn't try to go back, anyway, if she couldn't take all three of her children with her. And after fifty years, Eleanor still had no idea where one of them was.

Decency

—

WHAT WOULD BYRON THINK OF HER IF HE KNEW THE WHOLE story?

Eleanor hugged her son before he walked down the driveway toward the car. She looked at him, bright-eyed and straight-backed like his father, and knew that nothing else she did would ever be as important as this, this raising up of a decent young person and sending them into the world. Because the world needed *decent*, even more than it needed *brilliant*, which her son also happened to be.

But this beautiful man had a weakness. He could be obstinate. With Benny, for example. He'd had an attachment so great to his baby sister that he had never really seen Benny for the young woman that she had turned out to be. Benny had grown up and asserted herself and Byron had resisted her evolution, just as, admittedly, Eleanor and Bert had. He had grown cooler to Benny over the years, though Benny had continued to follow him around the room with that puppy-dog look. Byron was like his father in that way. When he couldn't control or understand something, he would distance himself from it.

Would Eleanor lose her son's esteem if she told him the truth?

Eleanor's husband had always known part of the truth, but not all of it. Bert had covered for Eleanor for years because he believed that he was protecting their family, because he understood that the woman he loved had been robbed of her destiny. But he never did learn how much she had lost. He never knew about her first child. Eleanor had lied to her husband for all those years because she understood that if you wanted someone to keep loving you, you couldn't ask them to bear all of your burdens, couldn't risk letting them see all of who you were. No one really wanted to know another person that well.

Unless, of course, a person could say, *See? Here she is, my long-lost baby girl. I've found her. I've made everything all right.*

While her arms were wrapped around her son's rib cage, Eleanor felt his heartbeat *tap-tap-tapping* at her through the weave of his shirt. She felt this life-of-her-life in her arms and thought of her first child, a pale, wailing baby calmed by her breast, then pulled out of her arms at six weeks. Eleanor now felt that other child's heartbeat murmuring under her skin, rapping at the inside of her head.

Byron made a U-turn in the cul-de-sac and was waving slowly, one muscular, brown arm held out the window. *Look at that smile!* Eleanor wanted to run after the car, shout to Byron, call him back, explain to him that no, raising him and his baby sister was not the most important thing that she had ever done. What defined Eleanor most was not what, or whom, she had held close but what she had allowed herself to let go of.

Why hadn't she torn up the paper they'd made her sign the day they took her baby girl away? Why hadn't she bolted from the taxi while she still had the baby in her arms? Why hadn't she pounded on doors, robbed a bank, sold herself, done anything to keep her child? Had her daughter, in all these years, ever lain awake at night wondering, like Eleanor, about the mother who had left her behind? Had the questions burrowed into her bones like a woodworm, the way they did every time Eleanor thought about her own mummy?

In fifty years, times had changed. The forced adoptions had been in the news. Graying women like Eleanor were shown embracing their biological children, faces shiny with tears. The government was being asked to apologize. Someone had even made a movie. Elly had thought of renewing her search for her daughter, of asking the authorities for help. But each time, she'd hesitated. Her baby girl, now a middle-aged woman, would want to know about her father. And Eleanor's other children would want to know, too.

She tried to imagine what her daughter would prefer. Eleanor thought of her own mother, who had gone away and never come back for her. What would Eleanor really want to know about her mother's reasons? What if knowing the truth were to hurt more than the longing? Eleanor could tell her firstborn child that she'd met a handsome boy all those years ago and had yielded to temptation. People talked about these things nowadays. But she was afraid that her daughter would look her in the eye and know that she was lying.

Would her daughter hate her more, then, for having given her up or for having failed to stay out of her life?

And then there was that other matter, which was no small matter. If Eleanor Douglas were to resurface in England today, someone might note her connection to one Coventina Brown, born Coventina Lyncook, who had been reported killed in a train accident in 1967, who had suddenly disappeared from another country while under suspicion of having committed murder. A murder that remained unsolved.

The false narrative that Eleanor had woven for the benefit of her loved ones had become a net that had trapped her. And as if that weren't enough, Eleanor had also let go of her youngest daughter. She had allowed Benny to walk away from her and Bert when, perhaps, she'd needed them most. Only Eleanor hadn't seen it that way at the time.

Eleanor loved her children more than anything, but Bert had given up so much for her. He had risked his career by concealing the truth. She owed her loyalty to the man who had loved and protected her and their children all these years. When Bert had been stubborn, Eleanor had stuck by his side. You couldn't explain something like this to your child. You couldn't be honest with her about the way things were, not when it meant having to reveal that your life was resting on a web of lies. Eleanor's husband had been gone five years, but Benny still hadn't come back home.

The world couldn't be an easy place for a girl like Benny. So every once in a while, Eleanor would reach out to her younger daughter. She would leave phone messages. She wanted Benny to know that her mother still thought of her, still cared for her, despite the misunderstandings. But Benny hadn't called, hadn't come to see her.

Apparently, Benedetta had decided to keep living her life without Eleanor. And where did that leave Eleanor? Who was she now, without her girls, and without her husband, the only person who, all her life, had truly known her for who she was? It was as if she had never existed.

After Byron drove off, Eleanor stepped inside her home of forty-five years, the house that her husband had bought just in time for little Byron's birth. She was feeling tired. Tired of everything. She closed the front door, leaned her back against it, and made a decision.

The Accident

—

FIVE YEARS AFTER HER HUSBAND DIED, ELEANOR BENNETT went into the garage, pulled out her longboard, and drove south along the coast, looking for the right kind of wave and hoping for an accident. Her widowed friends had warned her it might be this way. They'd told her to just ride out the feelings and keep on going and she had. She'd even started to date again. But a huge part of her had crumbled. Bert was gone, which meant that Gibbs was gone. And if Gibbs was gone, then so was Covey.

Eleanor had always taken pride in being a survivor. She'd been raised to be strong. She'd been strong enough to run, strong enough to give up her past, strong enough to raise her head and move forward. And for years, so much of what she had received in return, her family, her home, her days of laughter, had felt like an affirmation. Very often, in her life, Eleanor had thought that what she'd gone through had been worth it. But not everything. Not the most important thing. She'd always hoped that things would work out in the end, that she'd find her first daughter, that she'd explain everything to her other children, that she wouldn't feel the way she does now.

No longer hopeful.

Enough, enough, enough. The conditions were right, a good southern swell. When the authorities spoke to her children, perhaps they would be kind, perhaps they would say that Eleanor's last breaths had been filled with sun and salt air, that she had been living life to the fullest in the moments before the end.

The thing is, a busty, sixty-something black woman on a surfboard in winter, without a wetsuit, no less, simply could not go unnoticed in Southern California. The lifeguard on duty had been keeping an eye on Eleanor and raised the alarm. By the time he and his colleague got to her, she was in pretty bad shape. The board had flown up and hit her in the head before she slammed into the ground and cracked her shin bone. Later, she would not remember being pulled out of the water.

Eleanor ended up in the hospital with pins in her leg and cracked ribs and a nasty-looking head wound, but otherwise fine. After her son had gone home for the evening, she lay drugged but awake, staring at the glow of the television and hoping that the sedatives would continue to mask the full depth of her sorrow. She wasn't sure which made her feel worse, knowing that she'd survived or knowing that she'd gone out there in the first place.

Byron

—

Byron's friend Cable was nicknamed Cable because, when he and Byron were kids, he used to love the pay-TV station with all the old classic films from when their parents were children. He knew all the ones where the black folks had good roles, though he loved all the classics, really, as long as the black maids or porters weren't portrayed in that bug-eyed fashion that could get a person riled up. And even then, he might still watch. He and Byron had gotten into their worst arguments over that.

Cable loved the old movies because they tended to have a clear attitude about life. The good guys made out good in the end. Or else they died heroes. Cable believed in the goodness of people, believed in making sacrifices for others, believed in redemption. He believed that things could work out decently, even in the worst of times. Cable was the kind of friend that every man needed in his life.

Cable called about meeting up for a beer but Byron begged off, told him his mother was in the hospital.

"A surfing accident? Mrs. Bennett? And you didn't tell me?"

"Sorry, man, it just happened yesterday morning," Byron said. "Banged up her forehead. Smashed up her leg pretty bad. They had to operate. But she'll be okay."

Cable was at the hospital twenty minutes later. "Surfing, huh?" he said, sipping from a cup of cafeteria coffee. "Where did this happen?"

"Balboa," Byron said.

"Newport Beach?"

Byron nodded.

"The Wedge?"

Byron nodded again. They sat for a while, silently, while Byron listened to the click of Cable's brain. Byron knew what Cable was thinking. Byron was thinking it, too. He had managed to surf the Wedge, but his mother had only watched from the shore and cheered him on. It was a haven for boarders and bodysurfers, but with the biggest swell in Southern California, it could also be a dangerous place.

"What was she doing over there?" Cable asked.

Byron turned his head slowly from side to side.

"You sure your mom hasn't got some kind of death wish, Byron? My mom did, after Dad died."

"Your mother? But she seems fine."

"She's better now. But you need to keep an eye on that old girl, Byron. Your mom is a good surfer, good enough to know that she's not *that* good."

Byron took off his glasses and stared hard at his childhood friend.

"I hear you, Cable. But it's been five years since my dad died. I think my mother's been a little bored, I'll give you that. So, she thought she could give it a try, and she made a bad call."

Cable said nothing, raised his eyebrows, took another sip of coffee. Byron looked away and sighed.

"Shhhi-it," he said.

"Either way, we need to do something. We need to find her a man, Byron. I mean, no disrespect to Mr. Bennett, you know I loved that man like an uncle but no, this is not good. We need to find her a man, someone who can keep up with her. He's got to be at least fifteen years younger. At least."

Byron shook his head and laughed.

"Why are you laughing? Don't laugh."

Everyone needed a friend like Cable. He could make Byron laugh in the worst of times. But later, Byron lay awake in the middle of the night, thinking about what Cable had said about his mother.

Death wish?

There was a feeling up under his rib cage, a kind of panic. He picked up his cellphone to call Benny, then put the phone back on the nightstand. He thought Benny should know, Benny should be here. Their mother needed to have her children with her. But his ma had to be the one to make that call. Either that, or Benny needed to get off her selfish rear end and get in touch. Of her own volition. Otherwise, they would just have to go on the way they had since before his dad died.

Without Benny.

With his sister's absence seeping into the cracks in their lives.

Much later, Byron would see that his mother's surfing incident was a turning point in their lives. After his ma left the hospital, Byron canceled a couple of work trips and went back to sleeping in his childhood home. His mother, still unable to drive or volunteer at the community garden, rented a wheelchair for a couple of weeks and planned some *playdates,* as she liked to call them. Byron drove her to one of the old film studios, to a museum, to a concert. Then he took her to see that famous black swimmer at the convention center. By then, she was fairly agile on the crutches and seemed happier than she'd been in months.

It was during that period that Byron first saw Mr. Mitch, the lawyer who apparently knew much more about Byron and Benny than they did about themselves. He should have guessed that his mother was up to something and that Mr. Mitch, like others before him, had already fallen under his mother's spell.

The Usual

—

THE WEATHER FOLKS SAID 2017 WAS TURNING OUT TO BE ONE of the hottest on record for California, and it didn't surprise Byron one bit. The whole year had been a bit *off,* as far as he was concerned. He didn't know yet that the coming year would be his mother's last. He only knew he was ready for it to end. All these brush fires. His mother's accident. Being turned down for that promotion. All the things that were not going well with Lynette. They were constantly arguing and half the time, he couldn't figure out about what, exactly.

"Ma?" he called, stamping his feet on the rug in the entryway. His boots released a chalky dust mixed with ash that had floated down from the brush fires up north.

"Hello, son," came his mother's voice from down the hallway. "How was your day?" His mother's mood seemed to be improving as her injuries healed.

"The usual," Byron said. The worst of the California brush fires had claimed lives and burned homes. All of them had stripped the hillsides of plant life, which would leave them more vulnerable to mudslides when it rained. Which would further erode the soil, pollute water sources, slow seedling growth, and, once again, destabilize hillsides. Each year, Byron was called on by local journalists to comment on stormwater flows into the ocean and polluted runoff, even though his work actually focused on other areas of research.

Byron was popular with the schools. It helped that he had a gargantuan social media following and was a brainy athlete. This last characteristic was especially appealing to educators, who invited Byron to their public schools to drive home the message that athletics and scholastic excellence could go together and that one should not be an excuse to eschew the other.

Byron was happy to be served up as a role model for students, especially those whose demographics continued to be underrepresented in science and tech careers. But in wanting students to break free of thinking that might keep them from going into certain careers, the schools were often guilty of reinforcing, rather than shattering, stereotypes.

The whole sports thing was an example. Everyone wanted Byron to highlight his track-and-field wins in college, everyone asked him if he'd ever played basketball. These were the sports he was expected to mention when talking with inner-city kids. No one had ever asked Byron about the sport that most clearly defined him as a California man: his surfing.

His mother had been the one to teach Byron how to surf. They had always gotten stares, the little black kid and his towering mother, leaning into their surfboards in an era when many Angelenos believed the sport had been invented by blond men. Sometimes she would bring him back to the sand and head out on her own with the board, drawing shouts of approval as she staggered back ashore.

"Some people think surfing is a relationship with the sea," his mother said one day, when Byron was struggling in the water, "but surfing is really a relationship between you and yourself. The sea is going to do whatever it wants." She winked.

"What you need to do, Byron, is know who you are, and where you are, at all times. This is about you, finding and keeping your center. This is how you take on a wave. Then you might find that you need to practice more, or there's a storm swell coming in, or the wave is simply too much for you. You might even decide that you're just not cut out for the surfing and that's all right, too. But you cannot know which of these is true unless you go out there with your head in the right place." This was true of surfing and it was true of life, his ma said.

Earlier today, as Byron got himself organized to visit two middle schools, he did something a little different. He placed his backpack and laptop on the passenger seat of his Jeep then turned back to grab one of his surfboards. Why hadn't he done this sooner, he thought, as he loaded the board into the back of the vehicle.

"How many of you have one of these?" Byron said, holding the longboard upright as he faced an assembly of students from several classrooms. Only two hands went up but Byron caught the wave, climbing through the connections between surfing and physics and his professional studies of the seafloor.

The idea to talk about surfing had come to Byron the evening before, as he sat in his car waiting for a highway cop to run a check on his driver's license. It was the fourth time this year that he'd been pulled over by police, and to keep his nerves under control, Byron had breathed deeply and slowly and imagined himself running toward the water with a board under his arm. That was when he decided to make a little change to his usual Career Day presentation.

"Like most of you, I was born right here in Southern California," Byron said as he faced a thousand students sitting on bleachers in the gym. "And I went to grade school, high school, and both of my universities in this state, always near the coast." He held the surfboard in place with one hand and tapped it three times with the other.

"As you know, California is famous for its surfing. And I like to surf, but in all my years growing up in Orange County, I rarely saw another black guy on a surfboard. Now, why do you think that is?"

One kid put up his hand. "Tradition?" he said.

"Tradition," Byron said. "I can see why you might think that. But whose tradition are we talking about?" He leans the board against the lectern and walks back to the kids.

"Black people surf in the Caribbean, where my parents were born. In fact, it was my mother who taught me how to surf. And folks surf in African countries, where more than a billion people live and where, as you know, most people happen to be black- or brown-skinned. And what about Asia? Long surfing history there. So why not here, in the surfing capital of the world?" Some of the kids were leaning forward now.

"Now, don't get me wrong," Byron said. "There's actually a whole group of black surfers farther up the coast. They even give lessons on weekends. But when I was growing up in my area, it just wasn't a thing. There are various reasons why surfing tended to be limited to only certain groups of people in California."

Byron loves this. A whole room full of adolescents, listening.

"But I'm not going to get into all of that here, that's a whole other story. What I want to say is this. The same thing is true for the work that I do. When I was still studying at university, I was the only black guy in my doctorate program."

Byron raised his hands. "Now, I know you think we're talking, like, the Neolithic Age."

Laughter.

"But it wasn't all that long ago. I'm happy to say that I finished my studies and I do useful work and I love my job. And now I see university students of different stripes getting into my line of research. Times have changed, it's true. But the numbers of students going for the sciences and following that all the way through to the doctorate level, or to jobs that offer real opportunities for promotion, have not been keeping up as they should. So, what's my point?"

Hands up, waving.

"Good, I want to hear your questions in just a minute, but let me just conclude by saying this: If you want to surf, don't wait to find someone out there who looks just like you before you go surfing. And if you're interested in my field, ocean sciences, remote sensing, or something like chemistry or biology or information technology, don't wait for someone to give you permission. Just go ahead and study and apply for programs everywhere you can, because we need more talented young people, of all kinds, and you can't win if you don't play."

Byron looked back at the kid who said tradition. "So, tradition. Yeah, tradition has sometimes told us that only certain kinds of people should study certain subjects, or engage in certain sports, or play in an orchestra, or what have you, but tradition is only about what people have or have not done; it's not about what they are capable of doing. And it's not about what they will be doing in the future."

A stand-alone blackboard had been set up in the gym. Byron walked over to it, picked up a piece of chalk, and started writing.

"I'm honored that the principal has invited me here to speak to you all today, as a kind of role model. But let me repeat myself. If you don't see someone out there who looks like you, you need to go for it, anyway." He turned to face the students again.

"Are you going to let someone else's view of who you are and what you should do hold you back?" He smiled, thinking of what his mother used to say to him when he was still in school.

"Now, I'm not going to get all Pollyanna on you here and say that there aren't genuine obstacles to confront, including financial barriers and stereotyping. Those of us who are a generation ahead of you are supposed to be working on these things and a lot of us are trying. But do yourselves a favor and think about it first before you *don't* think about it, okay?"

Applause.

Byron stepped aside to call attention to what he had written on the chalkboard: *RIDE THE WAVE.*

"This is what I would like to be able to say to you folks, that in life, you should just catch the wave and ride it. But what if you don't see any good waves coming your way? You need to go looking. Don't stop looking, all right? And one of the ways to do that *looking* is to keep studying. Do not underestimate the value of applying yourselves in school. Because you cannot win . . . ," Byron said, cupping both ears with his hands.

". . . if you don't play," the audience responded.

At the end of the Q&A session, some of the kids came up to him to ask about science programs and internships and the like, but he could see that a couple of them were just angling to get a closer look at the surfboard. That was all right, Byron thought, as he posed for selfies with the students. It was a start. But he knew that even if all of these kids were to take his advice, it wouldn't be enough. That was why he was going to start his own scholarship program someday.

"So you had a good day, son?" his mother was asking him now.

"Yeah, Ma, the usual. How's your leg?"

"Doing better, Byron. Better every day."

His mother was still using a cane after her surfing accident. She should have known better than to take on that wave. All of her talk about knowing who you were and where you were at all times hadn't kept his mother from acting like a daredevil and nearly breaking her neck in the process. Unless, as Cable suggested, his ma had known exactly what she was doing.

More than anyone, even more than his father, Byron's mother had taught him the value of strategic thinking, of calculated action. He used to think that he was most like his ma but lately, his mother had revealed herself to have a kind of reckless streak that eluded his own logic and left him feeling nervous.

Kind of like Benny.

My Name
Is Benny

—

THE YEAR BEFORE HER MOTHER DIED, BENEDETTA BENNETT found herself standing at a lectern in a Midtown Manhattan meeting hall saying, "Hello, my name is Benny." As soon as the words came out, she knew that she had made a colossal mistake. Benny stood there trembling, the electronic fizz of the microphone teasing the pause. A dampness spread across the small of her back. Her waistband itched. She looked up again at her audience, cringing at their open faces.

Thirty pairs of eyes. In those soft, warm seconds of brotherly love, they had no idea, did they? Those eyes would soon will her out of the room as she hurried down the aisle toward the door. They couldn't know what a state she was in. They couldn't know that half an hour earlier, she had nearly dropped to the icy sidewalk next to the doggy base of a tree, overwhelmed by despair.

Benny had gotten off the bus from one of her jobs and had been walking, walking, walking. Unable to shake off the leaden feeling inside, she felt her knees willing her to the ground. Just then, a man walked by and she caught the look in his eyes as he headed up a set of stairs to the entrance of a building. His forty-something face, though framed in a movie-star haircut and buffered about the chin by a cashmere scarf, seemed to mirror Benny's own bruised interior, only with something else, a look that bordered on relief. The man pulled open a huge door, paused, and looked back at Benny. The door was forest green, and forest green was Benny's favorite color. So she followed the man inside.

Benny passed through a dimly lit foyer smelling of dusty paper and school days and entered a large, warm room with rows of fold-up chairs and a table covered with snacks and flyers. She nodded her thanks when someone handed her a paper cup of coffee and a gluten-free cookie. She basked in the murmured welcomes, the sanctuary of unknown faces, the heat of the cup on her fingers. She was already feeling better. She could have stopped herself right there, but she didn't. Instead, she took a seat between a young man in a pilly blue sweater and a woman in a scarlet skirt and allowed the tide of goodwill and the need for catharsis to pull her up to the head of the room.

Until then, no one had wanted to know who she was, where she had come from, or why she was there, because, after all, everyone was there for the same basic reason and the *why, exactly?* of their presence on that particular evening, and the *who, exactly?* they had been, or hoped to be, would not require elaboration unless and until they took the floor. And now, she was holding on to the edge of the lectern with one hand and clasping a half-eaten cookie with the other.

"My name is Benny and I'm an alcoholic."

With those few words, Benny had officially crashed a meeting for recovering alcoholics for want of a place where people would say *Come in,* no matter what. Where they would support her even when she told them that she hadn't attended her own father's funeral service. Where they would listen without a trace of shock in their faces when she told them why. Where she could say, to people who might not understand but who would listen to her, anyway, that she was tired of having her authenticity as a person called into question simply because she did not fit the roles that others wanted her to play, or because she wanted to play roles that others seemed to feel were beyond her.

Benny knew that she should run out of the room without saying another word, but the cookie was homemade and she could taste a hint of ginger. And for the first time in a long time, someone was listening. So she spoke. She told them everything. Once she had finished talking about her father's rejection, about her mother's disappointment, about the brother who wouldn't talk to her, about the lover who had hurt her, she came right out and admitted that she'd attended the meeting under false pretenses because she hadn't known what else to do. She hadn't meant any disrespect, she said, she was going to be leaving right then. She stepped away from the microphone and headed straight for the exit, shaking her head and muttering, "I'm so sorry. . . ."

As she rushed past the chairs, a woman raised her voice and said, "There are support groups for that sort of thing, you know?" and a second person said, "At least you were honest," while Mister Movie-Hair, who had unwittingly led Benny there to begin with, said, "Good luck to you." Benny's face was burning but she had the feeling that somehow, her first and only AA meeting had been of some help to her after all.

Benny walked down the steps of the building and kept going for forty minutes until she reached her apartment. She sank into the couch and pulled a blanket around her, grateful for the warmth and the smell of last night's garlic still clinging to its fibers. *Enough, enough, enough.* Benny turned on her cellphone and called home but there was no answer. Later she would do the math, and she would figure out that her mother had been in the hospital after her surfing accident and that Byron hadn't bothered to call Benny to let her know. This was the kind of thing that could happen when you'd stayed away for too long.

Cake

—

BENNY LAY AWAKE FOR HOURS, THINKING OF WHAT SHE MIGHT have said, had her mother picked up the phone. At four in the morning, she got out of bed and wiped down the kitchen counter. She emptied the oven of the pots and pans that she kept stored there, took some eggs out of the refrigerator, and reached into a lower cupboard for the most important ingredient, the jar of dried fruits that had been soaking in rum and port. She poured the mixture into a bowl and added dates and maraschino cherries. No citron, though. She had never liked citron. Nor had her mother.

Benny had just enough time to go through the whole routine and set two black cakes on top of the stove to cool before getting ready for her morning job. She still felt the need to talk to her ma but she didn't have the courage to try calling her again. This would have to be her message, the cakes. She had taken some photos of the preparation. She would send them to her mother along with a letter.

Benny would let her mother see what she had learned from her, how closely she had been paying attention, how well she had improved her technique. Because baking a black cake was like handling a relationship. The recipe, on paper, was simple enough. Its success depended on the quality of the ingredients, but mostly on how well you handled them, on the timing of the various processes, on how you responded to variables like the humidity in the air or the functioning of the oven thermostat.

Benny hadn't been very good at relationships but she knew how to make a cake work.

Photo number one: the jar of fruits sitting next to a group of eggs. One day, Benny would develop an eggless version of this recipe, because times had changed and food was going to have to change with them, but that would take some experimentation and, probably, leave her mother appalled.

Snap.

Photo number two: the blacking of the sugar. Smoke rising gently out of the pot, the fire turned off just in time, the wooden spoon sticking out of the saucepan. *Snap.*

Photo number three: two cake tins filled with batter, each tin sitting in a pan of water in the oven. *Snap.*

"This is the only thing that I had left when I lost my family," Benny's mother once told her, tapping a finger on the side of her head. "I carried it all in here. The black cake recipe, my schooling, my pride."

Photo number four: a closeup of one black cake cooling on the counter. The color of moist earth, the smell of heaven. *Snap.*

Preparing the icing would take another full day's work, after which Benny would take a photo of her signature decoration, the one large hibiscus flower, orangey red and couched in deep green leaves on a simple white base. She was willing to bet her ma had never seen anything like that. She'd be proud of Benny. On those rare occasions when her mother telephoned Benny, there was usually a specific reason, like a birthday, but one day, Ma simply called and talked into Benny's voicemail.

"Remember our baking?" her mother said. "Used to drive your father and Byron mad whenever we blocked off the kitchen." Benny could hear her ma smiling. Then her mother fell silent for a moment before saying that Byron was doing well, often traveling, always on TV. Her mother left these messages on Benny's mobile phone in the middle of the night, East Coast time, when she must have known that Benny would have had the phone turned off. It's as if her mother had wanted to reach out, only not all the way.

Her ma always called from home. Benny assumed her mother had some kind of cellphone by now, but Benny had no idea what the number was.

In her most recent message, her ma said, "I've been doing some reading and thinking. About people like you. People with complicated relationships." Benny's mother still couldn't bring herself to name Benny's differences, but she was trying. She suspected that her ma would have come around long before, if it hadn't been for her father's resistance. Her ma had always done things her way. Except when it came to Benny's dad.

And this was something that Ma had passed down to Byron, that unquestioning loyalty to Bert Bennett. Benny had loved her father and admired him and she, too, had been loyal to him, until the day that he stopped being loyal to her. He was the one who had drawn the line in the sand.

Wasn't he?

Ma was right about one thing. It was true that Benny's relationships had been complicated. People had a tendency to relate to only one thing or another, not to people like her, not to in-betweeners, not to *neither-nors*. This had been true in politics, it had been true in religion, it had been true in culture, and it sure as hell was true when it came to the laws of attraction.

Benny had to watch herself, she was overmixing the batter. She was getting agitated. She was thinking of how she had been called a flake, called confused, called insincere. In trying to live with an open heart, Benny had set herself up to be perpetually mistrusted. Thank goodness times had changed since her difficult college days. But there was still a lot of misunderstanding to go around.

And when people didn't understand something, they often felt threatened.

And when people felt threatened, they often turned to violence.

Benny Writes

———

THE CAKE-BAKING PHOTOS WERE READY AND TUCKED INTO A padded envelope. Benny pulled a stool over to the kitchen counter and picked up a pen.

Dear Ma, Benny began.

Benny's first mistake was to write the note by hand. She'd always been a slow writer. Her second mistake was to think that she could explain herself in a handwritten note, not only because there was so much to say, but also because some things were too ugly to be written down. Still, she wanted to try, even though five years had gone by since her father's death.

I know it's been a long time since we've talked. I heard your messages. I just wanted you to know that I appreciated them and I think about you all the time. I'm really sorry about Dad's funeral. I'm sorry I wasn't there. Actually, I was there that day, I just didn't let you know it. I saw you in that peach-colored dress that Dad always loved and I am so glad you wore that instead of the conventional black. I could just imagine a couple of those ladies (you know who I mean) seeing the widow of the esteemed Bert Bennett wearing such a bright dress at her husband's funeral! Daddy would have found that funny.

There's a reason why I didn't go up to you and Byron. I know this is a long time coming but I want to explain. . . .

Benny wrote about Steve, about college, about the things she'd been trying to accomplish, about her disappointments. She was sorry, she said, that so much time had gone by but she would not apologize for being who she was, even if being who she was hadn't brought her a whole lot of comfort of late. Benny finished the letter and sealed it but it would be a while before she could bring herself to slip it into a mail-box. By the time she did, it was already autumn 2018, and Benny sees now that her mother had run out of time.

Now

—

Mrs.
Bennett

—

B *and B, I know your father could be strict with you children. He had such high expectations for you two. We both did. And I see, now, that this put a lot of pressure on you. But your father was my love and he gave me a beautiful boy and girl and he loved you two more than you will ever know. Maybe one day, you'll have children of your own and then you'll see.*

Benedetta, I'm thinking of you right now. Surely, you must know that your father cared for you deeply. You were his baby girl. But you had grown up to become such a different kind of woman from what we had expected. This does not mean that we didn't love you. And it does not mean that we didn't believe in you. But, yes, we had our own views and we expected you to hear us out. We were worried about how you were going to make your way in the world.

I realize that times have changed. It used to be that a solid education could make a difference in this country, especially for people like us, with all the prejudices that could get in the way. No one seems to know anymore what it takes for a young person to make a career or to have a stable home life. You young people have so much more freedom now, even in terms of who to love. But it also seems as though you have less guidance, despite all those how-to lists on the Internet. It's as if there are so many choices that it's no longer possible to know which path is right for you. And the prejudices are still there. Less formal, in some cases, but still present.

In any case, we felt that a college degree couldn't hurt, not to mention one from a prestigious university. When you dropped out of college and refused to go back, it just felt like the beginning of an unraveling of something that we had worked so hard to create for you, a kind of safety net that we thought you could carry with you for the rest of your life. And I hate to admit it, but we were a little offended, too, after everything that we had done for you.

I don't think you realize, Benny, how lucky you were to do so well in school. How could you? Except for that one dip in your grades in high school, all you had to do was show up and you were at the top of your class. It became evident that you had some kind of a gift, Benny, and we felt like you were throwing it away.

About that Thanksgiving Day. I know, your father and I had always taught you that love and loyalty counted for more than anything else. But what happens when love and loyalty are in conflict with each other? I love you children more than anything, but my loyalty to your father was the bedrock of our family. I needed to be there for your dad, just as he had always been there for me. For us. Without him, none of us would have made it this far. Your dad needed a little time to get his head around what you were trying to tell us about your social life. But then you walked out and his pride got in the way. Yours, too, I suspect.

I didn't think we'd end up going eight years without seeing each other. First, you ran off and never called again. Then your father became sick. And I figured I'd let you know once he was better, tell you to come back home to see us, but before we knew it, he was gone. And then we didn't see you at the funeral and that was just too much, even for me. It's true, I didn't feel like talking to you after that. I felt I needed to keep my distance to stay healthy in the head. What a fool I was, Benny. Once again, I had wasted time that was never mine to squander.

Once in a while, I'd leave a voice message on your cellphone but you never responded. But now I have your letter, the one with the photos of the cake. The photos you said you meant to mail to me months before. I called *you when I saw them. I left you a message. I love those pictures! And now I know. About your reasons for leaving college. About Steve. Why didn't you tell me any of this before? Why didn't you ask for help? Why do we women let shame get in the way of our well-being? I thought that times had changed since I was a girl, but apparently, not enough.*

Betrayed

Betrayed.

That's how Byron feels, hearing his mother's words. He doesn't even know what she's talking about. He doesn't understand what's happened with Benny. And who is this Steve person, anyway? All Byron knows is, he's been left out. He, who did everything for his mother while Benny was off who knows where.

How many times had Byron wanted to see Benny but had stopped short of calling her out of loyalty to his ma? How many times had he cursed his sister for not bridging the gap, for not reaching out? How many times had he asked around, trying to keep track of his sister without calling her directly? Now he finds out that his mother and sister were in contact and neither of them even bothered to tell him.

For a while, Byron had been so angry with Benny after her no-show at their father's funeral that he hadn't even wanted to talk to her. It had been the latest in a series of steps that had served only to agitate their mother. Dropping out of college. Moving from one city to another. Cooking in Italy, art in Arizona. Sharing less and less with them about her life. It seemed to Byron that his once openhearted baby sister had morphed into a self-absorbed bitch. *Don't use that kind of language about a woman,* his mother would have said, but that was exactly what was going through Byron's mind. And wasn't it true?

After his mother nearly broke her neck surfing last year, Byron had wanted to pick up the phone and call Benny and say *Benedetta, please come home,* because the idea that his stubborn, eccentric mother might want to do anything but live her life, even after their father's death, had shaken Byron's sense of security. But then he got to thinking, why should he have to call his sister? When was the last time that she had called Byron?

Although Byron had lived much of his adult life fully aware of the tenuousness of his existence as an African American man—the vulnerability of his job, his popularity, his physical safety, always, his physical safety—he had felt himself to be on solid ground once he'd stepped into his childhood home. The virtual disappearance of his sister and then the loss of his father had caused the foundation of his life to tremble, but it was his mother's so-called accident, and the state of mind that it seemed to imply, that had threatened to fully dislodge the cornerstone.

Byron also came close to calling Benny the last time he was pulled over by a cop. He was overcome, afterward, by the need to talk to her, to hear her voice, to hear her say his name, to tell Benny what had happened, to know that Benny, at least, was safe, even if Byron might not be. Might not ever be. He could not talk to his mother about such things. You could not talk to your parents about their worst nightmare. He picked up his cellphone and scrolled down to Benny's name but just sat there in his car, looking at the screen, his hands still shaking.

At least Byron knows now that his mother didn't go to her deathbed without hearing from Benny. That's a good thing, right? Still, he feels betrayed. He knows that he and Benny are going to need to have a real talk, soon. He just doesn't know how to begin that kind of conversation.

"Oh, wait," Byron says. "What was that?" He asks Mr. Mitch to stop the recording. He realizes he's just missed part of what his mother was saying. Mr. Mitch presses pause and reaches for a tissue box on the coffee table. Byron sees that Mr. Mitch's nose is bright red. *What's with this guy? He's not crying, is he?*

"Sorry, the allergies are killing me," Mr. Mitch says.

Right, Byron thinks, allergies at this time of year.

"Would you like a cup of tea or something, Mr. Mitch?" Benny asks.

"No, I'm fine, thanks. But, please, just call me Mitch, no Mister. Or Charles. That's what your mother called me. Charles." And the way he says *your mother* sets off a ding in Byron's head. Of course. Why didn't he pick up on that? There was something going on between Charles Mitch and Ma, wasn't there? Charles Mitch is in mourning, too.

"Okay," Benny says. She's hugging that cushion again, the way she used to when she was a little girl, just like that, over her middle. Maybe not the same cushion, a different color. His mother would have given the old one to a shelter years ago. She was always taking little pieces of their lives and giving them to families who had less. Their old toys, their old books, their old blankets. *These things aren't you,* she'd say, *these things are just things.* Right. Unless you were talking about that awful sofa of hers. How many times had Byron tried to convince her to part ways with it? Who invented crushed velvet, anyway?

Byron misses his baby sister. But this person sitting across from him, this is not really his Benny. This is a woman who has lived her life without him for the past eight years and keeps looking at him like she expects him to forget all of that. It's like, she's here now, so nothing else matters? Well, what about all the hurt? Hurt matters. Tomorrow they'll have a service for their mother and then what? Will it all be over? Will he and Benny just go their separate ways? Will there be nothing left of the life he used to know?

Mr. Mitch

—

THE THING ABOUT IDENTITY. THERE'S YOUR FAMILY HISTORY, there's how you see yourself, and then there's what others see in you. All these elements factor into your identity, like it or not. Charles Mitch is a proud member of the state association of black lawyers, but he suspects that part of his success over the years has been owed to the fact that many people haven't actually noticed his African heritage.

People have trouble seeing past Charles's skin. This, despite his history in the civil rights movement (and that photo of him as a student). This, despite his volunteer work with young offenders of color (though he's helped other kids, too). This, despite the appearance of his children (who've taken after their beautiful mother, may she rest in peace).

The thing about having a white man's nose. When your heart is breaking, everyone can see it because the nose turns red, along with the rims of your eyes. No wonder so many men in America try to hide from their feelings. Yes, Charles Mitch's heart is breaking. Charles's wife was the love of his life. And then he fell in love again, this time with Eleanor Bennett, the widow of a fellow attorney and a woman who would eventually reveal to Charles that she was a ghost.

Charles Mitch

———

CHARLES HAS KNOWN FOR ABOUT A YEAR NOW THAT ELEANOR wasn't really Eleanor. They'd been dating for a while but she didn't reveal this to him until he went to see her at the hospital after the surfing incident. It took him a while to understand what she was telling him. The accident hadn't been an accident, she told him, except for the part where she'd actually survived.

"Only my husband really knew who I was," Eleanor told Charles that day. "I feel like there's no one who recognizes me anymore."

And me? Charles wanted to say, but he didn't.

"That's normal," Charles said. "You lived with Bert for more than forty years. You raised a family with him. When my wife died, I felt like I had disappeared with her. I only hung on at first because the kids were so young."

"But this is different," she said. And it was then that Eleanor told him what she and Bert had done. How they'd come to California, in part to move far away from the East Coast's other British-Caribbeans.

"I see what you mean," Charles said. But what he was really thinking was *I still know who you are. Or do I?*

Charles and Eleanor first met years before at a mutual acquaintance's house, someone who, together with Charles and Bert Bennett, had volunteered his time providing free legal assistance mostly to black families who couldn't afford it otherwise. Sometime after the death of his own wife, when Charles began to adjust to the idea of being with someone again, he came to understand that it was best to keep his distance from Eleanor. She had a certain effect on him, left a kind of buoyancy in his heart, but she was married to someone else and Charles Mitch was not the type to go poaching the woman of another man.

He recalled that Bert didn't like to talk about his upbringing in the islands. Bert told Charles that both he and Eleanor had been orphans. Charles also recalled the way Bert and his wife looked at each other when they talked about their kids. No, Charles would never have succeeded in poaching that man's wife, even if he'd tried.

Charles was truly sorry to see Bert go the way he did, a fairly quick decline but long enough, and it pained him to see Eleanor's face as she stood by her husband's grave. She would look down at his coffin, then out in the distance as if expecting Bert to come walking out from somewhere among the trees. Only much later did he realize that she was looking for Benny.

After Bert's death, Eleanor went to consult Charles as an attorney, and their acquaintance gave way to something more personal. In time, some of the cracks in Charles's heart began to heal.

That night in the hospital, the nurses let Charles stay in Eleanor's room until late. He leaned forward and rested his elbow on the pillow next to her face while she talked. The next time he saw her, she smiled at him and Charles felt as though they'd both backed away from a ledge. Once Eleanor had healed enough for her son to go back to his own house, she and Charles started getting out together again. Eleanor was planning to organize a lunch for him to get acquainted with Byron when some follow-up medical tests showed that she had a problem.

In early 2018, a few months after the surfing accident, Eleanor's clinical chart indicated that she was almost seventy-three years old when, unbeknownst to the doctors, Mrs. Bennett, born Coventina Lyncook, had just turned seventy. The rest, though, was true. Blood type, O-negative. Disease, advanced. Chances of survival past the next year, roughly fifteen percent.

Eleanor Douglas Bennett, born Coventina Lyncook, took the news in her stride. She was the daughter of a gambling man. She had already died and come back twice. She had always gone against the odds. But what if she didn't make it this time, she asked Charles. She couldn't leave her kids like this. There was something she needed to tell him.

The Rest of
the Story

—

CHARLES IS ONLY HERE TODAY, GOING THROUGH THE EX-
cruciating process of hearing Eleanor tell her story again, because he
made a promise to her, as her attorney and as her friend. He promised
Eleanor that he would help her children get through this. It would be a
lot for them to take in. But who is helping Charles?

In 1970, there were fewer than four thousand black students en-
rolled in law schools throughout the United States. One of them was
Charles Garvey Mitch. In the nearly forty years that followed until his
semiretirement, Charles had seen or heard a bit of everything, both
professionally and personally. So he wouldn't say that he was shocked
when Eleanor Bennett, still using a cane after the surfing incident, came
zigzagging into his office and said that she needed to tell Charles the
rest of her story, the part involving a baby. In his experience, most people never told you the whole truth the first time around, anyhow. Especially not your lover.

To this day, Charles hasn't decided if Eleanor had been extremely
unfortunate in her life or far luckier than most people, having survived
the particular twists of fate that she described to him that day. She'd
come to his office, she said, because this needed to be a strictly professional visit and things had already become intimate between them. She
had come to his office, she said, because she was going to need his help.
That was when she told him about her daughter. Not the one she hadn't
been talking to. Another one.

Charles agreed to help Eleanor, and he went on to conduct his research and offer his professional advice to her as an attorney. But it wouldn't be easy to play this dual role. Charles had seen his share of difficult situations. He'd grown up a pale black kid in the fifties and sixties. He had lost his wife way too young, to a fast-moving disease that he cursed to this day. He had raised two African American boys and he'd lost some sleep wondering how to protect them from the world. He had learned to control his emotions. But that didn't mean that he didn't have feelings.

After his wife died, Charles had dated some. But with Eleanor, it was different. This was love. He couldn't help but suffer when Eleanor finally told him what she had gone through as a young woman. No man should ever have to hear these things. No woman should have to live them. Charles went home alone after their meeting, stumbled over the threshold of his townhome, shut the front door, and leaned his forehead against it until he turned and slid down to the floor.

ᛋHEN

—

Bert

—

I N THE EARLY 1970S, BERT AND ELEANOR BENNETT MOVED INTO
a pastel-colored, bungalow-style home in a small city near Anaheim
where real estate agents had agreed to show properties to black families. Orange County had Disneyland and Marine bases and beaches,
and Los Angeles to the north. There were aerospace, auto, and rubber
plants within commuting distance. There were plenty of jobs, even for
a black couple. Southern California became the answer to the young
pair's search for a place to build a new life together. It was as far as they
could get from other Caribbeans in New York, from the risk of being
recognized, without leaving the States.

Bert found employment at a rubber plant and Eleanor found an ad-
ministrative post with the government. Eleanor's bosses quickly recognized her eye for detail and facility with numbers and promoted her
over the years, paying for her classes in accounting. By the time Benny
started school, Los Angeles had elected its first black mayor and Bert
had become an attorney, his prior legal studies having made it easier for
him to face the daunting law school admissions process in the States
and squeeze through the invisible gates that had kept so many black
and Latino Americans from being accepted into law schools.

On the night of the day that their grown son finally began his doctoral program down in San Diego, Bert and Eleanor leaned back on

their pillows, clinked their wedding rings together as if in a toast, and held hands. They breathed in their good fortune, having seen worse, and told each other that they and their children would continue to see better. And better. And better.

·•·

IN ALL THOSE YEARS, BERT AND ELEANOR COULDN'T GO BACK TO the island, but Eleanor wanted to hand some kind of family tradition down to the kids. Like the black cake. That cake was all she had from her childhood, she kept saying, and she insisted it take its rightful place in their children's lives, too. This boiled down to her cordoning off the kitchen like a military zone for a couple of weekends every winter, with her and Benny on the inside and Bert and Byron hovering outside, just when they wanted to wallow in the slovenly feel of a morning about the house.

Eleanor hadn't meant to set up a male-female divide, she said. It was just that Benny was the only other person in that household who had shown any real interest in baking for Christmas. They'd raised a daughter who looked just like Bert but who had that same gleam in her eye as her mother did whenever she stood in the kitchen with an apron wrapped around her torso and a cracked eggshell in her hand. They loved working together, the two of them, handling those mysterious ingredients that could rise and take on a life of their own.

Which, predictably, led to the same exchange every year.

"Ma-aw," Bert's son would say, the complaint in his voice one hundred percent American, with no trace of his parents' accents.

"No!" would come Eleanor's reply, from behind the screens.

"Caw-fee."

"No, sir."

"Just a cup of coffee, is all I'm asking."

One of Eleanor's eyes would usually appear between a screen and the wall. "You know the rules. I do this one month a year and you know the rules."

"And, now, I'm only home on occasional weekends and you can't let me get a single cup of coffee?"

Eleanor had always wanted a kitchen with a door that could close off the whole space. In Britain, she had seen her first *shuttable* kitchens, as she called them, and had periodically talked to Bert about redoing their cooking area once the kids were fully out of the house.

Whenever Bert took Eleanor to a restaurant, she would cast a wistful eye in the direction of the swing doors that led to the cooking area. "Like that," she would say. "Even a door like that."

When they first moved to California, no one was selling houses with closed-off kitchens. And Bert and Eleanor didn't know if they'd be staying here for long, anyway. But sure enough, here they were, years later, still living in a single-story, single-family home on the Pacific coast with an open-plan kitchen, and a man-sized cactus outside their bedroom window, and a Californian boy and girl who had learned to ride ocean waves that dwarfed anything Bert and Eleanor had ever seen growing up.

By the time she turned fifteen, Benny was almost as tall as Bert but she'd still fling her arms around his neck and say *Daaaddy* in that drawn-out way that made him chuckle. Then she began to change. She was given to moodiness and her school grades tended to go up and down in sync with her humor. Which was particularly disturbing because, generally speaking, all Benny had to do was walk into a schoolroom and sit down to be at the top of her class.

Eleanor said it was just adolescence, but Bert's baby girl was beginning to worry him.

Thanksgiving Day,
2010

—

BERT DIDN'T UNDERSTAND WHAT BENNY WAS SAYING. OR MAYBE he did, but he didn't understand how it could be true of his daughter. It was bad enough that Benny hadn't gone back to college, bad enough that she couldn't focus on getting herself into a profession and gaining economic stability. What kind of rubbish was this *concept café* business, anyway? But it wasn't the café that was getting Bert agitated, not this time.

In recent years, he and Eleanor had encouraged Benny to bring someone home for Thanksgiving Day, but she'd never done so. Benny lived a day's drive away in Arizona and they wanted to know more about her friends, wanted to remain part of her life. Finally, Benny was saying that she might bring someone for Christmas, but first she needed to explain something to Bert and Eleanor.

Lord have mercy. Did she really have to tell them all this? What did she expect them to say? Was this why she had left school? Was this why she wanted to lock herself up in some little *concept* hole? To keep herself from having to function in the real world with real relationships? How was she supposed to live a decent life with this kind of confusion?

Bert, who had begun his law studies all over again in the United States under his new name. Bert, who had cut himself off from his life back in the islands and Britain to protect his wife and children. Bert, who had taught his little girl how to ride a bicycle, how to save money from her allowance, how to write a successful term paper, now felt betrayed. What had he been working for all these years? Who was this woman standing before him now, with her face twisted up in that way and shouting at him?

This was not the daughter he'd raised. This was a person who had walked away from the educational opportunities he'd worked so hard to provide for her. Who kept changing her mind about what she wanted to do and who now was flip-flopping her views on what kind of person she wanted to date. Benny kept complicating her life when he had tried so hard to make things simpler for her. The girl he had raised should have been more grateful. The daughter he had raised should have said *Sorry, Daddy* and run into his arms.

Bert turned and walked out of the room. His wife came running behind him soon after, her eyes wet. Eleanor put her arms around his middle from behind and placed her head against his back.

"Bert," she said, but he couldn't bring himself to speak.

Then Eleanor did what Eleanor did best in their relationship. She just stayed there, without moving, without speaking, letting him know that she was there, that's all. Once, a long time ago, they had nearly lost each other for good. They had nearly lost their chance to have this beautiful family they had made together. After that, she had never left his side.

"Just give me a moment, okay?" he said. "Just a moment. Then I'll go back and talk to her." But when Bert and Eleanor went back to the living room, Benny was gone and the first Thanksgiving guests were already coming in through the kitchen door. And Bert never did understand much about that day.

If Only

—

IF ONLY BERT HAD KNOWN THAT HE WOULD BE GONE IN SIX MONTHS, he would have stepped out of the car. He would have crossed the street, he would have rapped on the plate-glass window, he would have smiled. Instead, he remained in the back of a taxi outside the restaurant in New York where Benny was working, watching his daughter through the glass. He wanted to talk to her, but to say what? A year had passed and he still didn't feel comfortable with this life of hers. If it had been anyone else, anyone but his own child, he would have let them be. Would have said, to each his own, love is what counts. But this was his baby girl.

Young people had always wanted to do things their own way, and Bert had been no different. Only nowadays, there seemed to be this compulsion to eat up everything that was available to you and to let everybody know about it in real time, without figuring out things for yourself first. No, love was not the only thing that counted. What people could say or do to hurt you also mattered. This, perhaps, was what he would say to Benny if he could bring himself to do so: *What are you willing to do? And is it worth it?*

What was Benny doing all the way out here on the East Coast, anyway? Did she even have any friends in New York? Did she understand friendship the way he and Benny's mother did? And what about loyalty? The girl had moved here without even sending them her new address, just because Bert and Eleanor hadn't been able to pretend that everything was all right with them. She had let go of them that easily. Did she have any idea what it had taken for them to build a life for her and her brother?

It took work to keep tabs on Benny. For the second time in a row, Bert had told his wife he was going to a meeting out of state, but how many work commitments could a lawyer licensed only in the state of California claim to have outside of California in the space of a year? Their state had been the first to develop proper anti-stalking laws. If he weren't Benny's father, he'd accuse his own self of stalking his daughter. But Bert had needed to see Benny with his own two eyes. And he didn't want to say anything to Eleanor about this until he could figure out what to say to Benny.

He watched as Benny helped an elderly woman on with her coat. Look at how gentle she was. His daughter still had a good dose of respect in her. She had always been a bighearted child. But something had changed. After they'd argued that Thanksgiving, Bert was surprised to come back into the living room to find that Benny had left the house, dismayed when she didn't come back for dinner, with all those people coming over, no less, and later, angry that she didn't even call to apologize. It just wasn't Benny's way. Never used to be, at any rate.

That day, Benny had accused Bert of not being open-minded, but Benny was the one who had grown more closed, less patient in recent years, less willing to face the questions of others. She had run off because she couldn't face Bert and her mother, couldn't accept that they had their doubts. And when had anyone in their family ever worried about whether other people approved?

Where would they be today if Bert had been afraid to go to law classes at night, the only black man and the oldest student in the group? Where would he be today if he'd been afraid to move to a state with all those waxy-looking plants and rattlesnakes and earthquakes and chirpy-talking people? Where would he be today if he had been afraid to raise a family with a woman who could not permit herself to have a past? Who could not permit Bert to have a past? He wondered, sometimes, about his uncle and cousins back on the island. Wished he could pick up the phone and find out how they were doing. But a move like that could ruin his life.

Bert shifted in his seat and poked at the spot where he'd been having that pain. As he watched his daughter now, as she nodded and smiled at the woman, he found himself nodding along. He was worrying too much, wasn't he? She was still his Benny, just look at her. She was still young. She would find her way, she would get her life back on track. She would come back to him and her mother, someday, his beautiful baby girl.

My Baby
Girl

—

ON THE DAY THAT BERT BENNETT WAS LAID TO REST, BENNY'S left arm was in a sling against her bruised ribs and one of her eyes was swollen shut. A bandage covered half of her face. *Bicycle accident,* she'd told the driver who picked her up at the airport the day before. *Ah,* he said in that way that service professionals do.

The same driver picked her up at the hotel before the funeral. He took the seatbelt and helped Benny pull it into position. It was already heating up outside but Benny rolled down the window, breathing in the smell of sun-baked sidewalks and jasmine flowers and tilled soil and a whiff of salt on the breeze coming in from the west. The smell of home.

The cemetery went back to the time when Los Angeles had fewer than thirty thousand people and the county was more farmland than not. It had been SoCal's first such facility, with broad, grassy lawns that called to mind the kind of place where you might have laid out a picnic blanket. It made Benny think of those barbecues her parents used to organize in the park near the house. She would help her dad attach balloons to the trees with pieces of paper that read *Bennett Bash* and they'd be out there with a bunch of other families until the sun went down.

Benny could imagine slipping off her shoes now and strolling barefoot across the grass until she found her father's burial site. But she would not be getting out of the car today. She touched her hand to the wound on her cheek.

She asked the driver to follow the road through the grounds until she saw the crowd of bowed heads, all shades of skin, all sizes of black and navy suits and dresses. Her father had been a popular man, a successful man, a pillar of the black community. He'd been known as a bridge builder, a man of tolerance, but the last time Benny saw him, two years earlier, her father had refused to listen.

Her parents had always taught her that the greater your capacity to love, the better you could be as a person. But when Benny tried to remind them of this principle, her father put up a wall, stood up, and walked out on her. That quickly, her daddy had turned his back on her. And Benny never did see her father again.

Benny caught sight of her brother as the crowd began to break up. He was walking toward a line of parked cars, his arm around their mother, his head lowered toward hers. Ma was wearing a sunny, fluttery dress, her father's favorite. The color made Benny smile, even as the tears slid down her face.

Benny watched her brother open a car door for their mother, watched him keep his hand on her arm until she had settled onto the seat. Byron used to be that protective of Benny, too.

"That's fine," Benny told the driver. "We can leave now." As the car skirted the cemetery plot, Benny consoled herself with the thought that her father never would have wanted to see her in this state. They hadn't spoken for two years, and yet she was certain that if she'd told her dad what had happened to her just a few days before, he would have folded his arms around Benny the way he used to when she was little, he would have rested his chin against her hair and murmured, *My baby girl.*

Etta Pringle

—

ETTA PRINGLE LOOKED DOWN AT THE PROGRAM IN HER HAND. *Meet Etta Pringle, Endurance Swimmer and Motivational Speaker.* She was traveling so much right now, she made sure to double-check the date and location before speaking into a microphone. *February 27, 2018, Anaheim, California.*

Etta smiled as the emcee introduced her as a small-island girl who had grown up to conquer the world. He spoke of how she had swum Catalina and the English Channel and circled the island of Manhattan. Of how she had braved some of the colder swims on the planet.

Etta always spoke openly to her audiences about the challenges she had faced, but there was one thing that she could never tell them, that wherever she went, Etta "Bunny" Pringle still thought of her dear friend Covey Lyncook. And sometimes she thought she saw her.

Losing someone could have that kind of power over you.

After Covey's death, Bunny had been lucky to fall in love again, this time with someone who felt the same way. She and Patsy had raised her son and Patsy's baby brother in the UK and watched them grow up to become scholars and parents. Patsy had become one of the first black women to join Scotland Yard. And through it all, the seas that had tested Bunny's resolve each year had, ultimately, been good to her. Now, at seventy, Bunny had spent more years of her life swimming without Covey than with her, but she still couldn't face the waves, or her fears, without imagining her friend a few strokes ahead of her.

And now, Bunny saw someone who made her think of Covey. When Bunny was done speaking and the lights had come up for audience questions, she took a good look at a woman sitting on the aisle, gazing up at her as Covey might have done. Bunny looked away, then back in that direction and narrowed her eyes. Bunny, who had put her body through punishing routines for six decades, who was stronger than most people half her age, didn't think her legs could support the shock of what she thought she was seeing, but they did.

When you'd done as much public speaking as Bunny had, you learned to keep going despite the distractions. People coming and going to the bathroom. Someone talking into their cellphone. A fly buzzing around your face. But this, nothing had prepared her for. Bunny slipped her bare feet back into her shoes and took the steps that led down from the side of the stage. Her foot caught on the nub of the carpet. *Concentrate, Bunny!*

She answered one final question as she walked along the central aisle. Audiences loved that kind of close-up thing. People liked to see that a woman who could navigate the strong currents of the Molokai Channel was flesh and blood, too. They liked to see that she walked with a slight limp, had a mole on the side of her face, and was wearing a perfume that some of them, too, might have purchased.

Bunny went down the aisle and back up twice, buoyed by the certainty that this time, she was not hallucinating, not living out some fantasy fed by grief. She stopped. There was no doubt. That short-haired woman sitting in the audience was Covey. How was this possible? Bunny wanted to lean over and pull Covey out of her seat right then but she knew she couldn't. There were video cameras everywhere. At the end of her event, Bunny waited for the crowd to dissipate, then scurried over to Covey.

"Bunny," Covey said as she leaned on one of her crutches and embraced her. But then Covey squeezed her forearm and whispered urgently in one ear. Bunny stood up straight and stepped back but held Covey's right hand in both of hers.

Bunny put on her best greet-the-public voice. "I am so happy that you came to hear me speak," she said. "What did you say your name was, again?"

"My name is Eleanor Bennett," Covey said, leaning back on her crutches. "I saw that you were coming to speak near my home and I wouldn't have missed it for anything, even though I'm still on these," she said, wobbling on one of the crutches.

"How did you . . . ?"

"Broke my leg surfing."

"Surfing!" Bunny said. Covey nodded. They both laughed.

"Well, I certainly hope to see you again soon," Bunny said, pressing a business card into Covey's hand. Covey had white hair at the sides of her face. Covey was beautiful. *Covey was alive!*

A young woman in blond braids and a black pantsuit came toward them and beckoned Bunny toward a side exit. A clutch of television cameras followed them, eclipsing Bunny's view of her childhood friend. Still, the room felt filled with a kind of light that would continue to follow Bunny for a long time. Bunny had indeed lived a good life and now she knew that it would be even better.

Back at the hotel, Bunny had barely enough time to close up her bags before leaving for the airport. She was laughing out loud when her assistant rapped on the door.

"Etta," her assistant called.

"Just ten minutes more," Bunny called through the door. "I'll see you in the lobby." Bunny sat down on the edge of the bed and let herself fall back, arms splayed, legs bent over the edge of the mattress, staring at the ceiling.

Floating.

She had to talk to Covey right away. Bunny picked up her mobile phone to call but realized she didn't have Covey's number. Eleanor, she'd said her name was. Eleanor Bennett. But where exactly did she live? And how would she find a person with such a common name? Etta would try to find her but she might have to wait for her to get in touch. Either way, Bunny felt certain that it would be soon.

Eleanor

—

S HE HAD SPOKEN TO BUNNY FOR BARELY A MINUTE BUT IT HAD lifted her up. Seeing Bunny that way at the convention center, wrapping her arms around her friend after all these years, set all sorts of things right in Eleanor's mind. For the first time, she felt truly at peace with being Eleanor Bennett. For the first time in a long while, she felt that she was still Covey, too.

If this were only about her, at this age, Eleanor would be willing to shed a lifetime of pretense, talk openly to people about being Covey, go back to the island even, aware of the risks. But the fact was, when you lived a life, under any name, that life became entwined with others'. You left a trail of potential consequences. You were never just you, and you owed it to the people you cared about to remember that.

Because the people you loved were part of your identity, too. Perhaps the biggest part.

PART
FOUR

..

2017

—

Marble

—

As many times as Marble Martin had appeared on live television, it still surprised her, all the activity that went on around the host and guests right up to the last second before they were live on the air. This time, another guest, the coffee tycoon with the blue sweater, was adding to the fuss by giving Marble an earful during the commercial break.

"I think you're saying these things because you're trying to sell your book," he said.

"Wait, wait," said the host, "let's save this for the show." A woman with turquoise-painted fingernails was using hand signals to count them down to the start of the next segment. The host took a piece of gum out of her mouth, folded it into a piece of tissue paper, and held it out for a studio attendant to grab it. A second later, a signal light went on and she was leaning toward the camera as if confiding in a friend.

"Marble Martin," said the host, "ethno-food guru and author of the bestselling book on traditional foods *Something True,* says there's no such thing as Italian coffee. But the head of Caffè Top, Renzo Barale, doesn't like what he's hearing. What do you say to that, Marble?"

"I'm not saying there's no such thing as an Italian coffee *culture,*" said Marble. "Italy is famous for its blending of coffee beans and its brewing techniques. I, myself, adore a shot of Neapolitan espresso. I'm just saying that in many cases, we cannot ignore the agricultural and historical contributions of other countries and lay one hundred percent claim to a culinary tradition."

"We are not trying to *ignore,* as you say, the contribution of other countries," Coffee Man said. "Our highest-grade coffee is blended from beans that come from a dozen different nations and we appreciate their origins. But *we* are the ones who choose the beans that go into our blends, and *we* are the ones who invented the coffee-brewing techniques that make Italian coffee the best in the world." Coffee Man's sweater, Marble noticed, was the color of the Atlantic Ocean.

"What I'm saying," Marble said, "is that some foods are born, bred, and developed within a particular geographic area or food culture. Others are imported, and yes, they find their places in new cultures over time, but they wouldn't be there in the first place without long-distance travel, without commercial exchanges and, in many cases, a history of exploitation."

"We do not exploit coffee growers in other countries," Coffee Man said. "We purchase our beans through fair-trade agreements."

"I wasn't suggesting that your company exploits coffee growers, I was merely referring to the fact that some foods that are taken for granted in many products and recipes in Europe, for example, are produced in other countries, where in past centuries, their trade depended on forced labor or very low-cost labor. Cane sugar, for example." Marble could see that the coffee guru was finally listening.

"Which brings me to another example. What about the classic Christmastime fruit cake? In Britain, it's often made with cane sugar from the tropics. In the Caribbean, it's made with raisins and currants imported from colder countries. My grandmother, who was English but spent years living in Trinidad with her missionary parents, makes a divine rum cake, Caribbean style. She calls it black cake. But is it really Caribbean? Cane sugar didn't even originate in that part of the world. It arrived from Africa, which in turn got it from Asia. So, you tell me, whose cake is it?"

Marble chuckled at her own logic. "We cannot always say at which point one culture ends and another begins," she said, "especially in the kitchen. My book looks at family traditions that are indigenous to one geographic area and culture or which, at the very least, have been tied to local agriculture and customs for so long that if these recipes have roots elsewhere, we would need to go back more than a thousand years to take a closer look."

Marble reached for a copy of her new book and held it up where she knew the camera could focus on the front cover.

"So I might consider something like French honey in a French recipe, for example, or Welsh salt in a Welsh stew. To me, these are different from the rum cake I mentioned, which might use sugar and rum from Jamaica, port from Portugal, currants and raisins from North America or Europe, dates from Tunisia, and spices from Indonesia."

"So you're a culinary purist," said the host.

"No, not at all," said Marble. "The diaspora of food, just like the diaspora of people, has helped to shape many cultural traditions. But I am, indeed, fascinated by indigenous crops and highly localized culinary traditions, and that's what I've written about in this book."

"And what about your own food culture, Marble Martin?" said the host. "Which culinary culture is *true* to you?"

Marble sat back and smiled. "My tastes reflect who I am and, like many people, I'm an in-betweener. I was born and bred in London to a father from the north and a mother whose own mother grew up as a missionary kid in the West Indies. I grew up eating different things, and my favorite comfort food comes from the Caribbean."

"Meaning?"

"On cold mornings, my mother used to make cornmeal porridge, just like her mother before her, with a touch of vanilla and nutmeg." To Marble, cornmeal porridge was *this* close to heaven. As the hot porridge cooled, the top formed a thick film and when you broke the surface with a spoon, up came a wisp of steam with the spicy, milky aroma.

"But that porridge didn't come from my grammy's tradition," Marble said. "Her family adopted the habit while living in the Caribbean, then carried it back home to the UK. And the spices, originally, were imports from Asia. So, I guess that makes me a product of the food diaspora."

Marble smiled and leaned toward the coffee CEO. She could smell the bergamot in his cologne.

"The Italians make something thicker than corn porridge, a polenta, which they serve with salty meats and sauces. But that didn't begin until Christopher Columbus brought corn over to Europe from the New World. What you will find in my book, instead, is an ancient polenta made with fava beans and spelt that more closely resembles what the ancient Romans would have been eating long before that. There's also another one made from chestnuts."

Coffee Man was nodding. After the show, he asked for Marble's business card and pressed his own card into her hand and invited her to visit his company headquarters the next time she found herself in his city. She might just do that, she told him. His hands were manicured but calloused. The next time she saw him, he would explain to her that he liked to do his own gardening and that he also played the guitar. He wanted to see her again, he would say, he wanted to get to know her.

And Marble would tell him that she liked that idea, even if she was feeling increasingly unsure of who she was, exactly, this person that the coffee guru claimed he wanted to get to know. Until a few years ago, Marble would have described herself in an elevator pitch as a London-born art-history-scholar-turned-food-expert. She would have added that she was a mum. Nowadays, she simply said, *I write about foods with a strong sense of place.* Because it was a catchy line, though imprecise, and because that was all she wanted to say of what her life had become.

Recipe
for Love

—

MARBLE'S RESIDENCE IN ITALY WAS THE RESULT OF A PREDICT-able story. She had arrived from the UK for her art history studies and she had stayed for the love of a man. But in the beginning, it was just the art. And the food, of course. One day, she was looking at an ancient Roman mosaic of a bowl of mushrooms when she came up with the idea for a book on stories surrounding traditional recipes.

The book started out as a hobby, a labor of love. Later, when Marble started getting requests to do TV shows and conferences she thought, *Why not?* Weren't people always reinventing themselves? Marble's formula was simple. She would research one traditional recipe, then seek out an anecdote from a modern-day family or community or restaurant that used it.

Terrain and climate aside, food was often about who had colonized whom, who had been based where during wartime, who had been forced to feed what to their children when there was nothing else left. And, of course, it was about geography, too, so Marble decided to narrow her focus to traditional foods made with indigenous ingredients or foods that had been produced locally for more than a millennium.

One of the more perverse facts of life is that making a living examining art and archaeology would have been an enormous, if not impossible, challenge for Marble, while it was quite possible to make fabulous sums of money by talking about eating. She'd seen the reality TV shows, she'd seen the book titles on the Internet. So Marble came up with a plan. She would say that she was talking about recipes when she was really talking about history and culture and everything else.

The first step of Marble's plan had been to change her name. She undertook a carefully orchestrated campaign to be sure that all social media conversations referenced her preferred name, Marble, not Mabel. Then she applied for a grant to support her research into the stories behind the recipes. Ancient foods as characters in cultural narratives and family histories.

And that was how she met her husband. She was invited to speak to moneyed tourists about farro grown in Umbria, and there he was, on a weekend break from Rome, taking the class to practice his English.

There he was.

Chemistry is a funny thing. Much later, Marble would be able to list a number of things that had helped to create a bond between her and the man she would eventually marry but, the truth is, the chemistry was there from the start, like a breeze that slips through an olive grove, causing a universe of tiny leaves to flash silver in the sunlight. Not only sex. Chemistry. The latter wasn't only about the former.

From the moment she met him, she could imagine being in bed with him but, also, simply linking her arm in his and strolling, slowly, across a bridge, talking about food, arguing about politics, chatting about nothing in particular. She could not, back then, imagine what love could be like when it grew, despite the cultural and personality differences that came up, despite the arguments and disappointments. She did not know that after just a few years, another person could become part of your DNA.

When your lover was that wealthy, it was possible to embark on a marriage that easily. Here they were, a young Englishwoman with a middle-aged Italian man in the 1990s, commuting between cities. Of course, Marble knew what people thought. Wealthy businessman, female gold digger, probably headed for a rough end. When the end of the marriage did come, it wasn't in the way that most people would have expected.

Marble went to bed one Saturday night, slightly tipsy from the party they'd attended, and woke up the next morning a widow. Her husband had died in his sleep, quite peacefully, come to think of it, only it had happened at least forty years too soon.

For years to come, Marble would keep listening for the thud of her husband's briefcase against the front door as he put his key in the lock. She would keep undoing his side of the bed as she used to when she expected him to come home late. She would imagine saying to her young son, *There's your dad, love, he's come home.* Only her husband had died so soon that he never knew his own child.

Sugar

—

IT WAS THE SUGAR EPISODE THAT GOT MARBLE CALLED INTO THE CEO's office. She hadn't been up to George's suite in months, since before she'd started dating the coffee guy. There was no need. They saw each other often enough in all those ways that the head of a media production company and one of his star presenters tended to see each other. Whenever she got back to London, she usually ended up getting lunch with him, anyway.

Sometimes, George's wife Jenny would join them. Marble liked seeing them together. The teasing, the mock protests, the touch of a hand. George was one of the good guys, and Marble was sorry to see him feeling so uncomfortable. A *viewer of influence* had telephoned him about the sugar episode. In George parlance, that meant a big-money advertiser had dialed his personal line to complain about the show, bypassing the editorial group in the process.

"Was it the S-word?" Marble asked.

"I do believe it was the S-word," George said.

Marble had simply reminded viewers of a few things that everyone already knew, and only then because someone had written in to the live program to ask why Marble didn't profile more desserts made with cane sugar.

As many of my viewers know, I focus mostly on traditional, local foods. Many longtime recipes heralded as local traditions use cane sugar, but I prefer to talk only about recipes made with foods of local origin, indigenous foods or foods under local production for at least one thousand years. This is why I tend to stay away from recipes that use cane sugar, unless they come from Asia, where, as far as we know, it originated.

Sugar cane has traveled far from its indigenous territories, having been taken from Asia to Africa and other areas of the world, including the Americas. By the 1600s, sugar cane and the sweet liquid pressed from its stalks had taken hold in the Caribbean, turning some men into kings of commerce and others into slaves.

Marble was proud of that episode.

"Now, don't get annoyed, Marble," George was saying. "I'm just letting you know, okay? It's just that you already had that argument with the Italian coffee tycoon about the exploitation of producers. And now you say that anything made in Europe with sugar can't be considered traditional."

"Cane sugar."

"Huh?"

"Cane sugar. Not beet sugar."

"Right."

"And not just traditional."

"Eh?"

"Local. Traditional foods of local origin."

"Right."

"Plus, we didn't have an argument, the coffee guy and I, we had a difference of perspective. In the end, he came to understand what I was really saying."

There had, in fact, been only those few moments of tension between Marble and the coffee man until they'd talked it out on the show, until they'd gone to dinner together the following month, until they'd stayed out late, talking, until they'd met the following weekend in Milan, until they'd kissed a long, tender goodbye before taking trains back to their respective cities. But she wasn't going to tell George any of that. She didn't want to get him thinking about the fact that her late husband had also been Italian. She didn't want him feeling sorry for her.

"It's just that you're supposed to be a food guru, not a political commentator."

"What are you saying, George? That I should just share recipes and not tell people anything about food, about where it comes from? That's not what I do, I'm not a chef. My specialty is where food comes from, you know that. And if you talk about the way in which food moves around the world, you can't help but mention the social, economic, and political facts behind it. It doesn't mean I'm *engaging in* political commentary."

George stood up and walked around to the front of his desk and sat down in the chair next to Marble.

"Marble, I am your biggest fan, and you know that. I just loved that okra episode."

"You are a fan of the money I make," Marble said, raising an eyebrow.

"Money that allows you to do the shows that you want," George said.

"Oh, now you're just being mean."

"And you are just being a diva."

They both laughed. "No, George, really, I'm not sure what you expect me to do. Are you censoring me?"

"Oh, I don't even know what I expect you to do. No, I don't want to censor you, but perhaps you could think about the wording a bit more next time? Sure, we need to take a hard look at history, but we don't want to have our viewers feel sheepish about using a spoonful of sugar."

"Ah," Marble said, nodding slowly.

"You know we're aiming to sell distribution rights to international markets."

"Mmm-hmm," Marble said. She stood up, leaned over, and pecked George on the cheek.

"How's Jenny?"

"She's good. Misses the kids. Why don't you come around sometime? It's easier for her at the end of the day. Lunch is always a stretch."

"I'll do that. I'll call her." Marble wasn't angry at George, but she was irritated about that phone call. She went back to her desk and clicked on a web link to the sugar episode.

I don't believe that we can fully lay claim to a tradition if we are not willing to recognize what we have taken from other cultures over time, for better or worse.

Sitting there, watching herself on the screen, Marble realized what the subject of her next book was going to be. She would take a 180-degree turn. She picked up a pencil and wrote *SUGAR*.

Wanda

—

S HE HAD ALWAYS BEEN A LOVELY CHILD, STUDIOUS AND charming, just mischievous enough to be entertaining, never getting herself into any real trouble. But later, Wanda Martin's daughter was dealt a rough hand. She struggled to bring her pregnancy to term after her husband's sudden death. Wanda and her husband pleaded with Mabel to stay in London full time, but Mabel insisted on going back to Italy with the baby. And she was still there, sixteen years later, even though their grandson spent much of the year in a boarding school here in the UK.

Thank goodness Mabel's work brought her home from time to time. Wanda was happiest when she had her daughter nearby. She loved how ordinary this felt, being able to ride her bicycle over to her daughter's flat, being able to sit down with her for a cup of tea, being able to add a few drops of water to Mabel's orchids while Mabel squinted at her laptop. Just a few more minutes and Wanda would be on her way home, but first she leaned her hip against her daughter's back and read a few lines on the computer screen.

"No, Mummy," Mabel said, putting her hands up in front of the screen. Wanda loved it that her daughter, almost fifty years old now, still called her *Mummy*. She leaned in again to peek.

Sugar cane. A grass with stalks as thick as bamboo, squeezed to produce a sweet liquid that, ultimately, changed the world.

"I really don't want anyone reading this right now, Mummy."

"What's it for, dear?"

Without looking up, her daughter said, "I'm thinking of writing another book. These are just notes I'm making for when I get back home."

Did Mabel say *home*? Or did she say *to Rome*? No, she didn't say *home*. Because *this* was her home, near them, here in London. This was the center of everything that their daughter and grandson needed in life, wasn't it? Wanda and her husband had dedicated their lives to making it so. Because, more than anything, this was who they were. They were Mabel's mum and dad.

THEN

—

Because Money Talks

—

B ECAUSE MONEY TALKS, A SALLOW INFANT GIRL BORN IN
the winter of 1969 to an unwed secretary from the West Indies was not
given up for adoption through the official channels but was transferred
instead directly into the hands of a well-off London couple who had
paid the home for unwed mothers handsomely for the privilege. Wanda
and Ronald Martin did not think of it as buying a baby. They thought
of it as speeding up the process. They had filled in the applications.
They had done the interviews. They had waited and waited. They had
held out hope. They had nearly lost hope.

By the time the girl reached adolescence her adoptive parents, who
were both white, could see that their daughter was likely what some
would call a child of mixed race, but they pretended not to notice.
Wasn't race an outdated concept, anyway? But it was true that their
daughter looked very different from them. Darker, taller, thickset.
They told her she resembled one of her grandfather's people. They
told themselves that she had always been theirs. They told themselves
that she was their baby girl and that nothing and no one would ever
change that.

Height

—

I T WAS ONLY WHEN MABEL MARTIN'S BODY HAD FULLY BLOOMED into adolescence that she had begun to worry about the fact that she did not resemble her parents. It was sometime after that gamey-smelling American boy at school had groped her and called her *brown sugar* but before her growing discomfort with her bust and height had evolved into a more specific agitation over the fact that she was taller than the Randall boy, who lived two houses down and with whom she had fallen, suddenly and desperately, in love.

By age seventeen, Mabel was also taller and softer than both of her parents. Her mother pointed out that she had gotten her heft and nose from her maternal grandfather, whom she had never known and who could only be seen in a pockmarked, browned portrait on her mother's dresser drawer. *See?* Mabel's mother said, smiling. No, Mabel did not see, but she, too, smiled and nodded.

Nearly thirty-five years later, Mabel, now Marble, would feel her phone buzz as she sat under the helmet dryer at a beauty shop in Rome. She would see the words *Estate of* pop up on her screen and understand, instantly, that the email from an American legal firm, whose name she had never seen before, had something to do with the fact that she was six feet tall and had none of the pinkish tone about her face that both of her parents did. Marble would realize then that she had been waiting for this message for most of her life.

By then, she would be old enough to understand that if her mum and dad had lied to her about her origins all these years, it was out of either love or fear, or both, because, in that moment, these were the very feelings that washed over Marble and drenched the soft folds of her waist. A love of her parents, a fear of what she might learn, a fear of what she might feel. Yes, mostly fear.

Because no matter how much her parents had loved her and coddled her and invested in the dreams of her youth, their presence in her life could not extricate the tiny burr that had lodged itself somewhere under her rib cage and, bit by bit, had expanded over the years, poking at her from the inside. A feeling that someone else, a long time ago, may have decided that Baby Mabel hadn't been worth loving and coddling and investing in.

Her doubts about her family tree had ballooned when her son was born and his doughy, newborn face began to take shape. His ruddy, veiny skin gradually took on a more even, deep-olive tone, and his hair grew into a soft, brushy silhouette.

"Your grandson doesn't look a thing like you, does he, Mum?" Marble blurted out one day, when she was feeling catty.

"No, he doesn't, dear," her mother said. "You've got a little Italian boy on your hands there, is what you have." Which might have been a reasonable argument had Marble's husband not been a blond man born to pale-skinned parents. As her son Giò blossomed into adolescence, all he had to show for his father's side of the family was his freckled nose.

After Marble sent Giò to boarding school back in the UK, she continued to live most of the year abroad. She suspected that if she were to spend too much time around her mother and father, they would pick up on the growing doubt in her eyes. She had hinted around the subject enough times to see that her parents were not going to let her discuss the possibility that she might have been born to anyone but them.

On some days, Marble felt deeply resentful. On others, she looked at her mum and dad, thinning around the shoulders with age, and felt guilty. Her own son was the most beautiful thing in her life. Did her parents feel the same way about her? They might worry that they could lose her. As if such a thing were even possible.

Or was it?

Now

—

Mrs. Bennett

—

B and B, after fifty years, you'd think it was time for me to accept that I would never find my firstborn child, but I couldn't do it. Or, what I mean is, I couldn't live with that, not on top of the sense of isolation that had come over me after your father's death. As you know, I was feeling so low about it that I took that surfboard out to the peninsula and nearly broke my neck. A foolish thing, I realize that, but I can't say that I am completely sorry I went out there because, strangely, that is what led me to your sister.

If I hadn't ended up in the hospital and needed those follow-up tests afterward, I might not have found out so soon that I was sick. I was feeling fine at the time of the diagnosis. So if they hadn't started the chemo, if I hadn't been sitting at home one day with two bottles of pills in front of me, too tired to do much else but watch videos on the computer, I might not be here today, telling you the whole story.

B and B, you know that I'm making this recording because I don't think I'm going to live much longer. I won't lie to you, I'm sorry to go so soon. But in this short period of time, since that day when I came up with that stupid idea to kill myself, I have lived a lifetime's worth of happiness. And now, I get to share it with you.

Chayote

—

ELEANOR BENNETT HAD JUST FINISHED REPLENISHING HER seven-day pill organizer and was sitting at her laptop looking up the nutritional values of various foods, having decided that the only way to slow the progress of her disease, if at all, was through diet. She could feel the medication leaching the *good* right out of her seventy-year-old bones. As she read through an online article, one of those annoying onscreen ads popped up with an image of a chayote. The sight of the chayote's spiny, green skin took her back to her early years on the island.

In the years that followed her mother's disappearance, Pearl's maternal presence, with her daily, talcum-dusted hug, would be a source of great comfort to her. Except on Mondays, because Monday night was soup night. Not bouillabaisse night, not pepper-pot night, but beef-and-vegetable night, which involved the dreaded chocho.

In California, she had learned to call the vegetable *chayote*. She had discovered that *chocho*, the local word for the *Sechium edule*, sounded like the term some Spanish-speaking people used for a woman's nether regions. It was an association that, after all those years of resistance to the bulbous, lizard-green, dishwater-flavored squash, had brought her a perverse sense of satisfaction. She liked to believe that the chocho, were it a person, might be made to feel a bit awkward. She could never have imagined that one day it might deliver the surprise of her life.

Just the sight of the chayote on her computer screen was enough to make Eleanor's mouth turn down at the sides, but she clicked on the video box anyway. A narrator explained that the chayote had been spotted at a rural market in Italy.

"Not in the Caribbean," the speaker said, "not in Asia, but right here in southern Europe." She knew this narrator. There was something familiar about the woman's voice. Just then, the camera moved up from the chayote and past the presenter's fleshy throat and Mrs. Bennett found herself looking into the eyes of a middle-aged woman who looked just like her, only with lighter skin and darker hair, and whose voice, Eleanor now realized, was a close variation of her own.

It was there, right in front of her eyes, but Eleanor kept telling herself that it wasn't possible. It wasn't possible that Eleanor had searched for her daughter in vain, only to have her appear, just like that, on her computer screen. Her baby, Mathilda. It wasn't possible. Or was it? There was a name written on the video. Eleanor opened a search window on the Internet and typed it in. *Marble Martin.* There was her photo. And there was her bio. She'd been born in London in 1969. This woman was Eleanor's baby Mathilda, she knew it, now, from the way she felt her heart swell inside her to fill the hole that had always been there.

Despite her shock, Eleanor was able to register the irony of the moment. On the worst nights of the past fifty years, as she lay limp from the sorrow of having had her firstborn taken away, as she searched in vain for her daughter, as she closeted her anguish from her husband and other children, she would reach way back to the Monday evenings of her childhood, when shunning the chayote had been her chief concern, when she still believed that her mother would be coming back home, and before she learned that you could love a child even when it had been forced into your womb.

And it would be the memory of being pestered to eat that steaming bowl of soup, then being wrapped in the quilt of Pearl's embrace, that would turn out to be her greatest source of comfort.

Prognosis

—

*P*rognosis. *Prognosis. Prognosis.*

All these years, Eleanor had only wanted to find her firstborn daughter. Now that she knew who she was and how to contact her, she realized that she couldn't do it. It was too late. It wouldn't be right, not with this prognosis, for her, essentially a stranger, to walk unbidden into her daughter's life, only to tell her that her birth mother was about to die.

"I think she'd want to hear from you, anyway," Charles said. "I think she'd appreciate being given the chance to hear you say that you have always wanted to find her, that you never really wanted to give her up. Imagine what a gift that could be."

Charles was good. He had this way of convincing a person. But by the next morning, Eleanor had already changed her mind.

"Things are moving too fast," Eleanor told Charles. "My other children need to know first. Then we can call her."

Eleanor took Charles's hand. "I'm sorry things have turned out this way for us," she said. "This stupid illness." Charles leaned over and kissed her on the forehead, then on the cheek, then in the crook of her neck, pushing his nose into her skin until she laughed.

Her Baby Girl

——

She called her once but didn't have the courage to speak.

Eleanor had a UK mobile number for Marble Martin. It didn't seem possible, but that was what investigators were for, Charles had said. From what she'd read in the pile of papers that Charles had given her, Marble was a long-distance commuter, living between London and Rome. Eleanor read that Marble was a sort of stage name and that she'd actually been christened Mabel Mathilda. Her heart did a thump when she first read her daughter's middle name. Mathilda, her own mother's name. The people who'd adopted Eleanor's baby had kept the name that she had given her.

Eleanor could call back another time, when she felt ready. She didn't want to frighten the child, to shock her, to betray the people who had spent fifty years of their lives raising her and loving her. This needed to be handled with tact. Plus, her daughter might not want to talk to her. Eleanor had to be prepared for that, too.

For now, it was enough to have heard her daughter saying *Hello? Hello-o?* What a thing that was, to hear her own voice coming back at her. It was confirmation that after all these years of separation, Eleanor's baby girl was still part of her, had taken something with her when she was pulled away from her mother's nipple for the last time.

Iguana

—

WHEN THE PHONE RANG, MARBLE HAD BEEN LYING ON HER back watching an iguana. She was thinking that she'd been right all along to come to this beach so far away from everything. As much as she had tried, she hadn't been able to make peace with her doubts about her parents and her origins. She needed to think. She needed to be in a place where no one had any expectations of her. And this was the place. She knew it the minute she saw that gleaming black eye fixed on her from above. As she watched, the iguana did its thing on the sand right near her face, but Marble didn't mind the poop.

It was a work of art, the stillness of this creature, its spidery digits clinging to the tree limb, the fringy ridge along its back. Marble shifted her eyes to the turquoise waves crawling up shell-white sands, breathed in the nutty scent of her own skin warming in the sun, then checked the news headlines on her tablet.

There'd been a fire at a nuclear power plant in France, another massive earthquake in Italy, more refugees drowning in the Mediterranean. And fighting, just about everywhere else. People had troubles, big troubles, but for these few days, Marble wanted to focus only on her own, far from the photo shoots and microphones and meeting rooms, where she could let her feelings float up and hover, unabashed, above her body, and do nothing but gaze up at a mottled lizard as big as her dog. She thought of her dog at home and hoped the neighbor boy wasn't giving him too much to eat.

How are you, Puppy-Man? the boy always asked her dog, and Bobby always answered the boy with a little leap. That boy, now almost a man, used to go to school with her son, used to clamber up trees with her son, kept coming back to see her son when he was home on holiday from school. When Giò first left for boarding school, the neighbor boy would sit on the front steps of Marble's building, running a stick along the ground until Marble would open the door. Over the years, she struggled to look at his broadening shoulders, at his downy, new mustache, at this child who kept on growing right before her eyes while her son was so far away. But this kid had known her son since the two of them were in diapers, so finally one day she said to him, *Want to watch the dog for me?*

The iguana shifted its neck, then settled back into its gray-and-white stillness. Marble closed her eyes and imagined herself as the lizard, morphing into a lichen-covered mass of stone, sleeping through the long, chilly hours of the night and coming to life only in the warmth of the sun. She was holding on to this thought when her mobile phone started to vibrate.

An unlisted number.

"Hello?" Marble answered. No one spoke but she heard an intake of breath.

"Hello-o?"

Nothing. The signal was gone.

She waited for a while before putting her phone away. She knew that if it was important, whoever had called her would call again.

But they didn't.

Now
Inheritance

BENNY IS IN THE BATHROOM, WASHING HER HANDS AND LOOK-
ing at herself in the mirror. She has only ever seen her father's features
in her face, plus her mother's lopsided smile. Now she knows what else
she's inherited from her mother's side of the family. Her skin, for one.
Benny is so pale in comparison to her brother and parents that if she
didn't look so much like her brother, she might have doubted her origins. This must have come from her mother's father.

It has never really bothered her before, not knowing everything
about her family. Benny and Byron were raised to believe that their
parents were both orphans. Unanswered questions came with the
territory. This is who they have always been, an African American
family of Caribbean origin, a clan of untold stories and half-charted
cultures.

Now Benny finds herself wondering more specifically about the
generations that came before her parents, the arrivals from distant regions, the lives they lived, the different cultural influences. Benny is
thinking, too, about another kind of inheritance, a spirit of defiance that
she sees, now, comes from her mother. Her mother, too, struggled to
find her way despite other people's expectations, other people's defini-
tions of the kind of woman she was supposed to be. Her mother, too,
kept closing doors and moving on.

If only she had said something sooner.

In her recording, Eleanor says that Benny's dad really did lose both of his parents, though by then he was already a young adult. After Gibbs Grant moved to Britain to study and then dropped off the radar, folks back home must have assumed that Gibbs, like others before him, had simply drifted away on the current of his new, immigrant life. His mother's relatives might have tried to find him, but surely they could not have imagined that he would be hiding in plain sight under an altered name with a woman who was believed to be dead.

Benny's mother talks about feeling like a ghost after the death of Benny's father, feeling like there was no one around anymore to recognize her for who she really was. The reality of her mother's situation is beginning to sink in. Over time, Eleanor Bennett had given up parts of herself until most of who she had been was gone. Family, country, name, even a child. And she hadn't felt free to name her losses. Benny and Byron would never have been enough to fill the gaps that remained, would they?

Benny and Byron had never been enough.

Benny pulls a towel off a rack, sits down on the toilet lid, and buries her face in the mound of terry cloth, taking care not to let her brother and Mr. Mitch hear her crying.

. .

DOWN THE HALL, BYRON IS IN THE KITCHEN GRINDING MORE coffee, looking down at his hands. He and Benny look so much alike, they could be twins, were it not for the nine years and several shades of color between them. Apparently, Benny takes after their mother's father, that Lyncook guy, the man whose mistakes drove their mother away from the island.

Being the children of people from the Caribbean, Byron and Benny have always taken for granted that they might have ancestors from various backgrounds. But in his heart, Byron is a California kid and a black man first. This is his identity. Of course, in the minds of others, he is a black man, first, second, and always, which would be fine if it weren't to the exclusion of everything else.

If Byron ever has any doubt about the weight of color in his world, he only has to look at Benny. His sister was always a sloppy driver, capable of putting the fear of God in you on the freeway, but Benedetta Bennett, with her sand-colored skin, has never been pulled over by the police, while Byron averages three or four times a year.

It's getting to the point where Byron is afraid to drive at night. It's getting to the point where he's declined to visit certain friends in certain neighborhoods after a certain hour, not out of a fear of crime but out of fear of being stopped by police. It has gotten to the point where the last time he needed a new car, he bought a less sleek model, one that wouldn't catch the eye of someone who didn't think a black man should own a certain kind of vehicle. Because there's that, too. But he would never admit this to anyone, except Cable.

What does his British sister look like? he wonders. How does she navigate her world? Byron can't resist. He gets online and searches Marble Martin on his phone. Apparently, she has a huge following in the UK. He swipes and clicks until he finds a photo. He is stunned. Does this Marble person know, Byron wonders, how much she looks like their mother? The woman is as pale as Benny is, but there is no mistaking those eyes and that nose and that mouth. Those are his mother's eyes and nose and mouth, the sight of which fills Byron with a longing that he can only describe as a kind of homesickness.

Byron opens the freezer to put the remaining coffee beans inside and sees a disk-like form wrapped in tin foil. There it is. The black cake. He reaches out and touches it. *I want you to sit down together and share the cake when the time is right,* his mother wrote in her note. *You'll know when,* she said. Now he understands the *when*.

Anonymity

—

B ENNY OPENS HER SUITCASE AND PULLS OUT HER SILVER-
gray sweater. She refuses to wear all black to her mother's funeral tomorrow. She flaps open the sweater and hangs it over her old desk
chair. She hadn't planned on being here in her old bedroom. She's
never slept in her childhood home without her parents.

Benny had thought that staying in a neutral place tonight would
have been easier. She has always found comfort in the anonymity of
travel, in the no-man's-land of vast airport lounges, the plastic smell of
rental cars, the hotel key cards that wiped your identity clean on checkout. All those spaces free of emotional weight. But this time, it was
different.

Benny had booked a hotel for her stay here in Orange County, but
when she found herself lying in a standard-double room so close to her
childhood home, it filled her with a sadness that went beyond the death
of her mother, a downward draft that pulled at her when she touched
the brushed chrome faucets in the bathroom, the dimmers in the bedroom, the tiny tubes of fake cream beside the coffee machine.

The room was spacious and clean and carpet-quiet, just the way
she needed it to be after a cross-country flight, but it was only three
miles from the house. When Byron told her to stay over, Benny didn't
think she would. Byron wasn't even talking to her, except for covering
the obligatory comments. Keys, coffee, cremation. But after listening

to the first part of her mother's recording, after saying good night to Mr. Mitch, she looked at her father's armchair and knew that she couldn't bear to go back to the hotel. Of course, she must have known it would be this way. She had, after all, brought her suitcase to the house with her.

Depth

—

BYRON'S PHONE IS VIBRATING AGAINST THE KITCHEN COUNTER. He's forgotten about this morning's appointment at the hair stylist's. Haircut, no color. He doesn't mind that bit of gray at his temples, but his hair guy warns him he might want to consider keeping it to a minimum, for a while yet. Byron cancels the appointment, there isn't enough time, though he knows his mother wouldn't have skipped it. His ma would not have gone to a funeral without having her hair done first.

His mother would have said it was a sign of respect to do her hair, to check the condition of her clothes, to see if she needed to buy a new shirt. She really was quite conventional in some ways, though, as Byron has come to see, in fewer ways than he'd imagined. But one of his mother's mantras when he and Benny were kids was *Dress with respect!* That had never changed.

When Byron first got into his profession, he couldn't have imagined seeing his male colleagues with manicured eyebrows and the women with hair extensions. Times change, and people should feel free to primp and tweak with the trends. He just never thought it would become a professional necessity for geologists, engineers, and mathematicians to be Instagram-ready on any given day of the week. This was more than respect, this was showmanship.

Byron supposes he should be grateful for the social media, the signs that so many people are into the work that he does. He certainly continues to be intrigued by his own profession. With the sonar technology they have now, his team can amass thousands of square kilometers' worth of high-resolution maps from just one deep-sea expedition. On some days, Byron just laughs out loud at the beauty of it all.

Byron believes that a lot of the people who follow him online really do *get* how important underwater mapping is, that it isn't just about technology and being able to see the shape of the land below the seas. It's about weather patterns, tsunamis, territorial defenses, fisheries, Internet cabling, tracking pollution, and so much more. It's about how we will live in the future. And, of course, it's about money. Always, the money.

Byron lies in bed some mornings staring at the ceiling for a long while, wondering how much of his work is doing good and how much is only opening the gates to profit seekers who will use the information to do things like mine previously uncharted areas of the seabed for precious metals, rare elements, oil, and other riches. Much of which, he knows, benefits his own lifestyle.

People talk about responsible management of natural resources, they talk about sustainability and moderation, but Byron hasn't seen a whole lot of these things in the twenty-something years of his career. He thought that by doing his work well, engaging the public, aiming for the director's position, he would have done some good. But now that both of his parents are gone, he doesn't know anymore if his life has really made that much of a difference to anyone or anything.

His parents sacrificed so much to give Benny and him a good life. Is he doing right by them? Is he doing enough?

Byron doesn't know anymore if his parents gave him a gift or did him a disservice to make him think all these years that he was someone special. He hopes, at least, that being seen in this profession ultimately will count for something, for all those kids out there who look like him and who might want to follow in his footsteps, or for those who might just need to see their own faces coming back at them, smiling, looking good, being treated with respect.

Listening

—

IN 1978, NASA LAUNCHED THE FIRST EARTH-ORBITING SATELLITE designed for remote sensing of the planet's oceans. Forty years later, whenever Byron visited students in local schools, he liked to let them know about the black woman who'd been a project manager on the Seasat program. But the students were always more interested to learn that the same woman had been instrumental in developing early GPS technology. *Slick!* someone would always exclaim, or whatever the word of the day was.

Like a lot of people, Byron wasn't aware of any of this when he was in school, but he was already being pulled in that direction. The twenty-minute drive from the beach. The surfing. Learning how to react in the event of an earthquake. Byron grew up understanding that Earth and its oceans were in a constant state of agitation, and by the time he reached college, he knew that he wanted to spend most of his time listening to the seas.

Byron hears the rustle and clink of Benny in her room, getting ready for their mother's funeral. It has been Byron's observation that remote sensing, obtaining information about locations without physically being there, is a heck of a lot simpler than gaining understanding of another human being, even when they are right there in the same room with you. He has no idea anymore how to read Benny, how to talk to his sister. There are no machines to help you figure out that sort of thing.

Farewells

—

I T'S NOT REALLY A FUNERAL. THEIR MOTHER'S BODY ISN'T HERE. Eleanor Bennett's ashes will be delivered to Benny and Byron in the coming days in a container made for such things. But the pastor says that Eleanor Bennett is here in spirit, in this church where she used to volunteer, where she had so many friends.

Benny links her arm in Byron's and, thankfully, he doesn't pull away. She feels as though the crook of Byron's elbow is the only solid thing in her life right now. Benny tries not to think about all the secrets surrounding her mother's life. She and Byron still don't know the full story. They still have to finish listening to their mother's recording, they still have to meet the sister they didn't know about until yesterday. They still need to learn how much is left of the mother they remember.

The pastor wanted Benny to say something but she just couldn't. Byron went up front and thanked everyone for coming, said their ma would have appreciated it, then came back to his seat. Thank goodness for Mr. Mitch. At least he got up there and said something more on behalf of the family. Or Benny thinks he did. She stopped listening after "Each one of us knew a different side of Eleanor Bennett. Mother, friend, volunteer . . ." At some point, he left the lectern with tears in his eyes. That much Benny recalls. Charles Mitch, slipping back into the pew next to Byron, his eyes and nose as pink as peonies.

People are still going up to speak. This whole thing is becoming unbearable. Benny leans against Byron's arm. Byron puts his hand over hers and the touch of his palm, warm and dry, clears all sorts of dust out of her heart.

．．

SOMEONE IS PATTING BENNY'S FACE NOW, PULLING HER INTO A soft, wool-scented hug, invoking the name of her mother in warm tones. Benny is already looking for a way out. She scans the crowd in the living room, searching for Byron, and sees him heading through a clutch of people toward the kitchen. She follows her brother and for just one moment, she expects to see Ma in there at the sink with him, laughing, teasing.

Her ma.

If only Benny had known about her mother's past before now. A runaway bride, forced to move over and over again, struggling to find her center again each time she'd suffered a loss. If Benny had known all of this, she might have told her parents about her own troubles in college. It might have prevented the slow buildup of misunderstanding between them. Benny doubts her father would have been any more comfortable with her dropping out of school or with her love life but, being Bert Bennett, his anger over the way in which his daughter had been mistreated might have eclipsed all other concerns.

Instead, Benny had stayed away. Worse, after all that, she'd gotten into the habit of trying to keep her head down, trying to get along, trying not to rankle people, trying not to get hurt. What, then, had been the point of it all?

The truth is, Benny had wanted to go to that university almost as much as her parents had wanted her to be there. But just when she'd thought that her world was expanding beyond the suffocation of adolescence and into a new environment, she found that the boxes into which she was expected to fit—whether for race, sexual orientation, or politics—seemed to be making her world narrower.

Mostly, all it took was a look to let her know that she had strayed outside her designated box. Like the look she got from a white girl she'd been friendly with when she saw Benny coming out of a hairdresser's for black women. Or the look she'd gotten one afternoon from one of her black dorm mates when she'd walked into the common room, giggling with a couple of white girls. Or, being looked at repeatedly, but not spoken to, at the pride meetings. But looks were slippery things that you couldn't pin down easily. A kick in the face was more concrete.

The woman who pushed her and kicked her that time at college had been bugging her for weeks. *You think you're better than the rest of us?* she said to Benny that night. But no, Benny didn't think she was better than anyone. She just didn't see why she was any worse.

Then she saw the disappointment in her parents' eyes and the confusion in Byron's. So she went to Europe to get away and study cooking.

In Italy, Benny fell in love with a new city, a new woman, and a vision of the kind of person that she could be. She thought that the answer to what her Italian lover called her *disagio* might be to stay there, overseas, so that her distance from her hometown would camouflage the canyon that was being carved between her and her family. But Benny's discomfort had followed her.

There was a dinner. An international group of English speakers, all acquaintances of acquaintances. They commenced their happy, noisy settling-in at the table, sniffing at the aromas that drifted out of the kitchen, trading descriptions from the menu, when someone said, "And where are you from?"

"Me?" Benny said. "I'm from California." Even though Benny had already moved out of the state before going to Italy, she remained a California girl in her heart, first and always. She would have carried a Californian passport, had there been such a thing. Correction: Southern Californian. Because there was a difference.

But before she could go on to talk about her parents, someone else jumped in and said, "Benny is from the West Indies." Why were other people always answering this kind of question for her? For Benny, who had never even been to Florida, much less the islands. Plus, who says *West Indies* in this day and age?

"And you?" Benny asked another dinner companion, not wanting to get into it. Wanting to shift the focus away from herself. The woman who had answered on Benny's behalf laughed at Benny's question.

"She's American! Can't you tell? Look at all that blond hair." Without thinking, Benny touched her own hair, felt the soft, dark ridges above her temple. Three weeks later, after Benny had a falling-out with the Italian lover, she reasoned that she might as well go back home once she'd finished her course. Things didn't seem so different here, after all.

Of course, Benny had already begun to forget what had led her to Europe in the first place. Not cooking school so much as the need for distance from her family. Because it was easy to forget these things when you were homesick. Looking back now, it seems to Benny that she has spent most of her adult life yearning to return home, only now that she's finally back here, she feels that nothing was ever the way she thought it was.

Benny's mother is gone for good, in more ways than one, and the only thing left of her mother, a voice in an audio file, keeps driving home that message.

Mrs. Bennett

—

*B*enedetta, in that letter you sent me, you said that you thought I wouldn't understand why you'd kept quiet about your troubles, but of course I understand. More people's lives have been shaped by violence than we like to think. And more people's lives have been shaped by silence than we think. When I ended up pregnant with your sister, it was all against my will and no one close to me ever knew about it, until now. And I had to keep her from knowing. That was part of why I let them talk me into giving her up.

And I was ashamed, too. What happened to me had come as a complete surprise. I'd thought I was in a good place with a generous employer. I'd thought that I was safe. Afterward, I kept thinking, what did I do wrong? What did I do to bring that on myself? But these questions had no relevance. Such questions never have any relevance when someone else decides to hurt us. But we ask them, all the same, and they weigh us down. They can crush us. Fortunately, I realized that I simply had to get away from that office.

Benny, this is what I wanted to say to you in person, only I can't afford to wait anymore. When your father and I hesitated to embrace you as you were, to show you immediate acceptance, you ran. Of course, I wish that you had been more patient with us, but you were hurt and you were willing to walk away in order to protect yourself. I was deeply disappointed but over time, I realized that I could identify with what you'd done. I hope that you won't be afraid to make the same kind of choice again, if you feel that this is what you need to do to survive. Question yourself, yes, but don't doubt yourself. There's a difference.

Just don't go thinking that this is all there is to succeeding in life, this picking up and walking away from people. It should never be an easy answer to your troubles. I have lived long enough to see that my life has been determined not only by the meanness of others but also by the kindness of others, and their willingness to listen. And this is where your father and I failed you. You didn't find enough reassurance of that, in our own home, to dare to stick around.

Benny and
Steve

——

EACH TIME THERE HAS COME A MOMENT WHEN, AGAINST HER better judgment, Benny has answered Steve's phone calls, when he has made her laugh, when she has agreed to meet him. But this time, as Benny feels her phone buzzing inside her handbag, as she looks down to see that it's Steve calling again, she decides that she won't answer. Not this time. Or the next.

"I think that's your phone," Byron says.

"Yes, it is," Benny says. She taps on the screen to end the call and looks at the time. Mr. Mitch is talking to someone on his laptop, out on the patio. Benny still has time to speak to Byron. She turns to face him.

"Byron, there's something I need to tell you," she says.

Benny talks. She tells Byron about being bullied in college. She tells him about Steve. How Steve was good with everything, at first, until they ran into a former girlfriend of Benny's.

"But we've already talked about this, Steve," Benny said, as they argued afterward.

"I'm sorry," Steve said. "But I just can't get used to this." *This*, apparently, being Benny, the way Benny was. *Confused* is what Steve called her, but Benny couldn't recall the last time she'd felt particularly confused. She could only remember feeling rejected.

They argued. Benny yelled. Steve hit her. Said he was sorry, begged her not to leave.

"We kept trying," Benny says, now. "I kept seeing Steve, on and off," Benny says. "But it wasn't working. And Steve was getting more aggressive." She bows her head, puts a hand on her forehead. "Byron, Steve was the reason why you didn't see me at Daddy's funeral." She feels Byron take her hand and exhale slowly as she tells him about that night, six years ago.

What Steve said to her that night, before he pushed her against the pine table, was an ugly thing. What he said—before she grabbed at the tablecloth, dragging dishes and silverware and glasses and candles to the ground, before he shoved her face against the floor and into a shard of blue pottery, before she heard the snap of her left arm—was a word she never thought she'd hear from a man who had made love to her.

Because it was love they had made, she was sure of it, and Leonard Cohen was singing on the speakers as she tried to get up from the floor, and they both loved Leonard Cohen and Mary J. Blige and René Pape at the opera, they were both eclectic with music that way, and even though she had explained herself to Steve, over and over again, how she was with him because she wanted to be with him, simple as that, he still *freaked*, because, once again, they had run into Joanie. What was Benny supposed to do, she asked Steve, if Joanie happened to live in the same neighborhood?

At first, Steve was just irritable. He wouldn't finish the dinner that Benny had chopped and sautéed for him, he wouldn't even taste the sweet potato pie. It was her new recipe, she told him. He was supposed to be her taste tester, she said, forcing a smile. But then Steve raised his voice and said that word, and Benny was still trying to recover from the sound of it in his throat when he yanked her by the hair until the clip in her braids popped out.

Then the table.

Then the floor.

Then the blood.

And that was it. Benny decided to end the relationship then and there, only she needed an ambulance to do it. She had just gotten back from spending the night in the ER when Byron called to tell her that their father had died.

"The worst part is," she tells Byron, "I swore that it would be the last time I'd see Steve, only it wasn't. I kept thinking, he'll come around, he just needs time, he'll accept me for who I am."

Byron is shaking his head.

"I know, Byron, I know. I should have known better. It was never about me, not really. I *did* know better, but when you're in the middle of something, you don't see it that way, you know? You don't see what's obvious to other people."

Byron is nodding.

"And now, I'm thinking about Ma and everything she went through and how she used to say, *What are you willing to do?* Remember that, Byron? And what she said in her recording. That sometimes it's all right to walk away. Maybe I shouldn't have been so quick to walk away from you all, but I should have closed the door to Steve long before this."

Byron looks at Benny, nearly six feet tall and thirty-six years old, and sees, in the curve of her mouth and the slope of her shoulders, the little girl who used to follow him everywhere. He wants to lean over and put his arms around her, but something in the tilt of her chin, in the glint of the small scar on her cheek, stops him. Instead, he stands up and reaches out one hand to pull her to her feet.

"Benny, I'm sorry," he says.

Benny nods, mouth tight.

"I mean it, I'm really sorry, I've been a bit of a shit."

She nods again. She is still holding his hand.

"Me, too," Benny says.

"Yeah," Byron says, raising his eyebrows.

And they start to laugh.

Beautiful Girl

—

BENNY IS SIX YEARS OLD AND ZIGZAGGING DOWN THE supermarket aisle while her mother squints at the food cans. She runs into a nice lady who tells her how cute she is, how sweet she is. And how old is she? And what's her name? Look at all that beautiful hair, says the lady, patting her curls. Benny feels fuzzy and happy. Until her big brother comes along to get her, saying, there you are, let's go back to Ma, and the nice lady gives Byron a good, long look up and down his tall, dark frame, and looks back at Benny and makes a flat kind of mouth before turning away. Benny feels the fuzziness going away, that lady doesn't like her anymore, but no matter, Benny's brother is holding her hand tight, her small, pale fingers nestled in his long, brown ones, and Benny knows that as long as she's with Byron, she will always be safe and happy.

Benny

—

B

ENNY IS SITTING ON HER MOTHER'S BED. HER PARENTS' BED.
She should have understood this thing about her parents, her high-
achieving, picture-perfect mother and father, who had demanded excellence from their children to the point that it had nearly crushed
Benny. She should have realized earlier that their demands and their
resistance to her orientation might have been born, in part, out of fear.

Benny is leafing through a *National Geographic* issue she's found on
her mother's nightstand. There's an article on a guy who climbed El
Capitan without a rope. *Jeez*. Her ma was really into that kind of stuff.
The folks who climbed mountains, who trekked the Antarctic, who
sailed the oceans solo, who swam the most notorious crossings. Benny,
who only wanted to find warmth and comfort in this world, had been
birthed by a closet adventure freak.

No, not so *closet*. Sometimes, after bringing her and Byron in from
the water, their ma would go back out there on her own. She was always taking the surfboard farther out than before, always taking on
waves that were just beyond her competence. Sometimes, on the way
in, her mother would wipe out pretty badly and stagger ashore like a
toddler. When Benny was small, those moments when her mother disappeared inside a wave would terrify her. But her father never seemed
concerned, he would only laugh and lean back against his towel. And
her mother, too, would laugh as she trudged across the sand.

Her parents had always behaved as if nothing could happen that could really shake them, as if they'd seen it all. Benny had seen her parents angry, she'd seen them worried, but she'd never seen them truly afraid, not until the day she sat them down to tell them about herself, about the kind of life she thought she'd be living, and saw that new look in their eyes. She should have realized then that it wasn't as simple as disapproval. Eleanor and Bert Bennett were afraid that their children might not manage to live as easily in the world as they had hoped, after everything they had done to make it so. And so, they became part of the problem.

Benny picks up the envelope that Mr. Mitch has given to her. Inside, there are receipts that her mother had saved from her father's files. Airlines, hotels, restaurants, plus a page torn from his calendar from 2011. Benny looks again at the locations and dates, each one like a dab of salve on a wound. Her father had been to New York more than once. He'd scribbled various addresses on the calendar page. Benny's apartment, the restaurant where she'd been working, the studio where she'd taken art classes on Saturday afternoons.

After that miserable Thanksgiving Day in 2010, Benny and her father never did speak again, but now she knows he never let her out of his sight.

Mrs. Bennett

———

*B*yron, my son. On the day that you were born, your father took your tiny foot in his hand and closed his fingers around it and just looked at me. There are no words for that kind of feeling. Then you came along, Benny, smiling from day one, and thanks to you children and your father, I had love in my life again. But not a day went by when I didn't think about your sister. It was like a huge hole in my life, like the death of someone I loved, over and over again. But I was not the first person to go through the world living two separate lives, one out in the open and the other locked up inside a box.

In all those years, your father never knew about the baby that had been given up for adoption. I never did tell him what had happened to me at the trading company. I couldn't. I was so ashamed. He only knew that the supervisor had been making unwanted advances and that I'd decided it was time to move on. Nothing unusual about that. Women have always had to do that sort of thing. Move on, under that kind of pressure. Act like it was nothing, their lives turned upside down.

I kept telling myself that if I could find a way to track down my daughter, I would tell Bert about her and he would understand, he would accept her, he would forgive me for not telling him right away. But I couldn't find her, and I kept my secret. As the years went by, I felt I could no longer tell your father.

I knew that Bert wouldn't blame me for what my employer had done to me, but what about the rest? He might wonder about everything that I'd done which had led me to that point. How I'd gone to Scotland alone, even *after Elly had died. How I'd stayed on the island with my father, four years earlier, instead of leaving right away when your dad had begged me to go. How, in the end, I hadn't been able to stop that agency from taking away my baby. I worried that he would think these things because I had, too.*

Once your dad died, I didn't have to worry anymore about what he would think, but I did have to face myself in the mirror every morning and acknowledge my own doubts. A part of me felt that I had brought it all on myself by wanting to do things my way, for refusing to accept the life that others had expected me to live. It took me a long time to get past some of those feelings.

Which brings me to you, Benedetta. I see, now, that your father and I may have made you feel that way, too, made you feel that you had to choose between being yourself and having our support. And you, Byron? Did we make you feel that the only way to have our approval was to do things our way, even if it meant leaving your sister out there on her own? This was never our intention. We loved you both so much and held you both in such high regard that it never occurred to us that you might truly doubt it.

Fish Story

—

BYRON IS CHUCKLING. HE FEELS STRANGELY LIGHT, NOW THAT their mother's memorial service is behind them. After yesterday's full house, he and Benny are finally alone in the kitchen, and he feels that he can slip from sorrow to laughter and back without embarrassment.

"What?" says Benny. "What?"

Byron lifts a casserole dish out of the sink, the one with the fish design on the bottom. After listening to the rest of their mother's recording, Byron and Benny have prepared a late breakfast for Mr. Mitch, spooning a few leftovers into the one dish. Mr. Mitch is now in the living room, laying out papers for the next phase of their discussion. He says he's already sent an email to their sister.

They need to learn to say it out loud. *Our sister.*

"The fish," Byron says. He can barely spit out the words through his laughter. He turns the inside of the stoneware dish so that Benny can see it. It has the design of a fish painted on the bottom. "The fish, remember?"

"The fish," Benny says, and doubles over.

Castaic Lake. Benny was eight, Byron seventeen. They, children of the Pacific shoreline, had been taken inland to fish at an artificial lake. Their mother had called the plan *ridiculous* but they'd ended up loving it. The shrubby hills all around, the water so calm. They hadn't known until that day that water could be so easy.

They had two lines in the water when their father started shouting,

"I got him, I got him!" and yanked upward. A largemouth bass came flying out of the water, catching the sunlight on its flank and slamming right into their mother's face.

"Eeeuw!" Eleanor Bennett squealed, waving her hands and pushing her husband away.

"Oh! You afraid of a little fish?" Bert Bennett said. He pulled the fish off the hook and put it in a bucket. He was laughing. "Come on, now, lovey, don't be mad."

No, not *lovey*.

Covey.

Byron's dad said Covey that day, he's sure of it now, but it's only thirty years later that the word makes sense. Until two days ago, Byron didn't know that Covey was the name of a person, let alone his own mother. He'd just assumed it was a flub of the tongue. He still remembers because it was funny, how the word came out. *Come on now, Covey, don't be mad.*

His ma gave their father a cloudy look, grabbed the bucket where the fish lay struggling against the air, and turned it over, dropping the fish back into the water.

"Oh!" their father yelled. "That was my fish!"

"Not anymore," their mother said. Byron and Benny laughed until their eyes were wet.

"You two be quiet," their mother said, and they laughed even harder. The next Christmas, their father gave the fish dish to their mother as a joke. That dish turned out to be one of her favorites. She used it to make casseroles, scalloped potatoes, sometimes even coffee cake, but never fish.

Byron and Benny are still chuckling now, wiping their eyes. Benny reaches out her hand, Byron gives her the dish, and she wipes it dry with a towel. She looks up at him with those eyes, same as his eyes, and he smiles at her, then puts an arm around her when she starts to cry.

Recipe

—

BENNY WAITS UNTIL SHE'S ALONE IN THE KITCHEN TO look through the junk drawer. She has to jiggle the kitchen drawer at the end of the counter while pulling at the same time. It's the only way to get the thing to open, one thing that hasn't changed around here.

This is where her mother kept dented pencils, ink-clotted ballpoint pens, freebie notepads from the pharmacy and the drain-cleaning service, confetti-colored paper clips and tiny plastic devices whose original purposes most people had long forgotten but which Benny could always figure out.

Ma would hand something to her from the junk drawer and say, *What's this?* And Benny would squint at a pointed or twisted or curled-up object, turning it over in her hand, holding it close to her face and picturing its intended life. Benny runs her fingers now along the side of the drawer. There it is, where it has always been, a piece of folded, lined notepaper where her mother had scribbled down the recipe for her black cake.

Benny unfolds the paper and runs her finger down the list of ingredients. *Rum, sugar, vanilla*. And the occasional verb. *Cream, rub, mix*. It is only now that Benny realizes that the recipe has no numbers, no quantities at all. Wait, was it always this way? It's the same one from her childhood, she's sure of it. Benny sees, now, that her mother's recipe was never so much a list of firm quantities and instructions as a series of hints for how to proceed.

What Benny learned from her mother had been handed down through demonstration, conversation, and proximity. What Benny learned from her mother was to rely on her own instincts and go on from there.

Byron

—

BYRON'S PHONE IS RINGING. IT'S LYNETTE. SHE DIDN'T COME to his mother's memorial service after all. He wonders. He thinks of what happened to Benny all those years ago, about her reasons for not being at their dad's funeral. He can't get over the fact that he and his mother had no clue. You never really know what a person could be going through.

When Byron answers, Lynette is sobbing. He can hardly understand her.

"A what?" he asks.

"A busted taillight, Byron," Lynette says. "Jackson was just trying to get his wallet, get his ID, and the officer pulled a gun on us. I thought we were going to die."

"Jackson? Jesus, is he all right?" Jackson, Lynette's nephew. Great guy. It's made Byron proud to see Jackson make his way into the professional world. A young scientist growing his confidence, a young black man opening doors.

"He was just trying to get me to the doctor, you know?"

"Doctor? What, are you sick? What happened?"

"No, Byron, I'm not sick. I just, I wasn't feeling well. I'll explain later. We still were hoping to get to your ma's funeral but then they took Jackson into custody."

"What?"

"I'm serious. They put handcuffs on him, Byron. And for what? We don't know because they eventually released him. No charges or anything, but it was terrible. There we were, sitting in the car, and it was like everything just stopped, you know? It's like, there was this one, long second where I just . . ."

Byron hears a sharp breath on the other end of the line. He thinks of Lynette, sitting there, right next to Jackson. Anything could have happened. He tries not to think about it, everything that might have gone wrong. But trying to undo the worry is like trying to undo his blackness.

"I know, Lynette. I know. Are you going to be okay?"

"I think so, thanks, Byron," Lynette says, but he hears her voice breaking again.

"I'm coming over," he says. "Can I come over?"

"Mmm-hmm," she says. She's crying again.

After he hangs up with Lynette, Byron checks the news on his laptop. Jackson has gone viral. There's a video online.

What was the kid supposed to do if he was asked to show his driver's license?

How is a person supposed to reach for their wallet?

Are black people in America not allowed to have hands?

Byron wants to believe that this epidemic of mistreatment, this bullying of unarmed black men is just that, an outbreak, though prolonged, that can be brought under control. He wants to keep believing in law enforcement officers, to respect the risky work that they do, knowing that every day they step into unknown territory. He wants to know that he can still pick up the phone and call the cops if he ever needs to. There's a lot of anger out there. A lot of hurt. Where are they all gonna end up—black, white, whoever—if things don't get any better? What would his father say, if he knew that things were still this way in America in 2018? He has a fleeting thought, a blasphemous thought, that maybe it's just as well his dad isn't around anymore to see the way things are.

Byron turns to Mr. Mitch and Benny.

"Look," he says, holding out his cellphone for them to see the images. "That's my . . . ," Byron says. He doesn't want to say *girlfriend* but he doesn't want to say *ex,* either. "That's my friend's nephew in the car."

Benny takes his phone, looks at it for a moment, then starts swiping away at her own phone.

"I'm sorry, I have to go," Byron says. "I have to go right now."

Protest

—

MOST PEOPLE AROUND BYRON ARE HOLDING THEIR SMARTphones above their heads, one arm stretched high and waving softly, as if in worship. Others have small candle holders in their hands, the light glowing under their chins, the cloying smell of melting wax turning Byron's stomach. Byron is just standing there in the crowd, hands at his sides. Byron doesn't do street protests and Lynette knows this.

Byron believes the best path to activism is to gain status, accumulate wealth, exert your influence in the centers of power. But Lynette says this is not so much a protest as a vigil, for all those people who weren't as fortunate as Jackson. For all those people who didn't survive a traffic stop gone wrong. For all those people who are still in mourning. *Including us*, Lynette says. *We need to allow ourselves to grieve, clear our heads*, she says, *so that we can go back into the city halls and courtrooms and boardrooms and classrooms and work for change.*

Jackson is up in front with his attorney and parents. Mr. Mitch is up there too. He knows the organizers of the vigil. Mr. Mitch seems to know everyone, like Byron's dad did. There are people speaking into the microphone, politicians and activists and even that famous actor. Finally, a group walks up front to sing. Lynette says Jackson didn't want all this attention, but he does want police to set the record straight, he wants the police to acknowledge that he was wronged. Byron looks over at Benny. Her eyes are closed and she's singing with the crowd.

Byron is trying to think about Jackson but he keeps looking down at Lynette's stomach, pushing out against her coat. Lynette hasn't said anything to him but it's evident she's pregnant and she's been that way for a good while now. She hasn't mentioned another man. There hasn't been time to talk about anything but what happened to Jackson. What happened to Lynette, too. Lynette was still shaking when Byron got to her house, hours after the police incident.

I need to talk to you about something, Lynette said on the phone before his mother's memorial service. Was this what she wanted to talk about? So much else is happening right now, Byron will have to wait to find out.

All he can do, for now, is try his best not to stare.

Expecting

———

THEY ARE SITTING ACROSS FROM EACH OTHER IN A BACK ROOM at Lynette's house as Lynette tells Byron about her pregnancy. Lynette says she's due in three months. She says Byron can ask for a DNA test if he wants, but she has no doubt the baby is his. Still, she insists, the baby will always be hers first. Byron needn't feel obligated. She says they can meet again to talk, if he's really and truly interested in being part of the boy's life.

He needn't feel obligated? What kind of comment is that?

Byron doesn't mean to leave things the way he does. He doesn't intend to raise his voice at Lynette that way. He doesn't mean to slam the door on the way out of her house. But why is she treating him this way? The baby is hers? More than his? She was the one who left Byron. She was the one who didn't tell him about the pregnancy back then. She was the one who didn't give him a chance to participate from the get-go.

If Byron's mother were here right now, she'd probably say Lynette is right, she's the one giving birth to the baby. Byron's father, on the other hand, would surely agree with Byron, would say that Lynette should have told Byron that she was pregnant. But this doesn't change the fact that Byron is standing alone at his kitchen counter, tonight, wondering if the boy that Lynette is expecting will look anything like him. Wondering at what moment, exactly, Lynette decided that she could live her life without Byron. Wishing he could go back to that moment and somehow change it.

Byron is still standing at the counter when the night sky gives way to a morning gray. There's no time to sleep. Charles Mitch is due back at the house in two hours to finish playing his mother's recording. But first, Byron needs to talk to Lynette. Though he isn't sure what to say. How does he get her to understand how much he wants to see her again? How much he wants to watch this child of his grow up, to keep him safe in these times. How he needs her to spell it out for him, tell him what to do, tell him what she really wants.

How he realizes he's been getting it wrong for years, not quite knowing how to be there for the people he loves.

Once he's cleaned and dressed, Byron dials Lynette's number. Her phone rings and rings. He calls again but she still doesn't answer. Heart hammering, Byron grabs his car keys and pulls open the back door, but Mr. Mitch is already here, coming up the driveway.

Who I Am

—

B and B, I don't know how you will feel after hearing everything that I've had to say. I ran away, I changed my name, I invented a past. Until now, you children didn't really know where I had come from or how I had lived before coming to the United States. You had no idea that you had an older sister. You may be upset about this, I can see that. You may be asking yourself if you can ever really know who I am, if you can believe anything that I say. When your father died, I, too, had my moments where I thought, who am I? What's left of me? But then I came to realize that the answer had been there all along, right in front of me. And this is what I need you two to understand: You have always known who I am. Who I am is your mother. This is the truest part of me.

Marble

—

WHEN MARBLE GETS THE MESSAGE FROM ELEANOR BENNETT'S lawyer, she is leaning her head back under a stream of warm water while the hairdresser rinses fake-pineapple suds from her hair. She's in one of those salons that specializes in hair extensions for African women in Rome, the term *africana,* in this case, not referring to the continent but a wide range of clients from any number of countries in Africa, Europe, and the Americas.

Marble isn't the only non-*africana* who comes to this shop. There are always a couple of women who know they can get a good deal on quality hair extensions, or people who, like Marble, are relieved to have found a *parrucchiere* who actually knows how to work with their thick, springy hair. Marble loves her slovenly hours at the beauty shop, chair-dancing to the music on the audio system and trading quips with the chatty mix of black and brown and parchment-colored women who form this small, multilingual community.

Marble feels the buzz of her mobile phone through her purse. Once her hair is wrapped in a towel, she reaches into the mouth of her hand-bag and taps the screen of the phone. She reads the email a couple of times. The subject heading is *Estate of Eleanor Bennett.* The lawyer would like to schedule a telephone call to speak with her about a confidential matter of relevance to Marble regarding this Bennett woman. From the wording of the email, Marble might not have guessed right away. Had she been petite and blond, like her mummy, she might not have guessed right away. Had she not been living with a growing sense of unease about her identity, she might not have guessed right away.

She sets up a call with the American lawyer for the next day, and afterward she just sits there, trembling. She must fight the urge to call her mother in London. Her mum is the first person Marble thinks of whenever she needs to talk. It has always been this way, even when her husband was still alive. But this is not the kind of news that a daughter can share with her mother by telephone. This is not the kind of anger a daughter should express by telephone. She swipes at the phone's screen and starts looking up flights. She needs to go to London tonight.

Wanda

——

WANDA AND RONALD MARTIN ARE JUST SITTING DOWN TO supper in their London townhouse when they hear someone wiping their shoes on the doormat outside. It's Marble. They recognize the weight and drag of those feet. They recognize the way she presses her finger against the doorbell.

"I didn't know she was in London."

"Nor did I."

"Why doesn't she let herself in?"

"Maybe she left her keys in Rome."

Wanda pulls open the front door, her chest swelling with the feeling that the arrival of her daughter always brings, but when she sees Marble's face, everything falls inward. She knows, instantly, why her daughter is here unannounced.

Fifty years.

Their daughter is almost fifty years old.

Wanda had hoped that after five decades, they'd be safe.

Wanda had hoped that she and Ronald would never need to have this conversation with Marble, this talk about another woman, a young, unwed mother from the Caribbean. Their daughter's birth mother. Wanda's true life began when she took little Mabel into her arms all those years ago. Now, looking at her daughter's face, Wanda fears that the charmed life that she and Ronald and their child have lived all these years is about to crumble.

Benny

—

What a strange feeling. Benny is about to meet her long-lost sister for the first time. Marble Martin is coming to the United States and, after several weeks in New York, Benny is on her way back to California to join Byron. When Benny first heard the name *Marble* in her mother's recording, it had seemed familiar to her, but it had taken a while for her to place it.

Back in the fall, a friend had told Benny about an expert she'd seen in the UK who was doing shows about indigenous foods. Benny had written down the name in her agenda, but she had never looked it up. She'd had a lot on her mind. Making a living, trying to get a business loan, going to therapy. Then Benny's mother died and she had gone back to New York weighed down by everything that she had just learned about her family.

Marble Martin.

Benny has decided she doesn't want to look her up at all. Byron says Marble Martin looks like their mother. Benny doesn't want to see that. She'll wait to meet her.

Benny is hunched over her sketch pad in an airport lounge when a woman in an emerald-green jacket stops next to her.

"That's pretty," the woman says. She must be as tall as Benny. And beautiful. "A hair comb?" she asks.

"Yes, a peineta," Benny says, holding up her sketch pad so that the other woman can take a better look.

"Oh, yes, one of those things those Spanish ladies wore to hold up their mantillas," the woman says, lifting her right arm into the air with a flourish that calls to mind the flamenco. The broad sleeve of her jacket falls back to reveal a wrist the color of copper and a bracelet with a stone like the iris of someone's eye.

"Exactly," Benny says, chuckling.

"This one looks really special."

"It is. It's my mother's. *Was* my mother's. Tortoiseshell."

"Or an imitation. You're not allowed to make things out of tortoiseshell anymore."

"I know, but this one's really old."

"Is it?" the woman says, nodding. Lingering. Benny runs a finger along the side of the design.

"So, my idea is to do a cake decoration topped by something like this. My hairdresser in New York is getting married."

"What a great idea! You make cakes?"

"I do."

"And you're an artist?"

"Well, I did go to art school," Benny says, "but I also took pastry classes."

"Do you take commissions?"

"For cakes? Or drawings?"

The other woman laughs. She hands Benny a business card. "I'd like to see the drawing of that comb when it's finished." She points at the business card. "Could you send that to me? We're always on the lookout for a good illustrator. You never know."

Benny looks at the business card. An art director at a home brand company. High-end. Is this woman really asking to see more of Benny's artwork? As the woman walks away, Benny puts the card to her nose. Sandalwood with hints of vanilla and cacao. Benny smiles to herself.

Marble

—

SOMEONE SHOULD HAVE TOLD MARBLE ABOUT THIS LONG AGO. Someone should have prepared her for this moment. They should have let her know about this single-family, bungalow-style home in Orange County, California, not far from the Pacific shore, with the smell of jasmine in its backyard, and a living room filled with photos of a brown-skinned woman who looks just like her.

It seems the emails and phone calls from the lawyer were not enough to prepare her. It seems the transatlantic flight was not enough, nor soaking in the hotel tub this morning. Marble tries to do now what she does when she is standing in front of a television camera, when she pays only minimal attention to all the signals around her, the director and crew moving and gesturing from the side and beyond the camera, and thinks only of one thing, thinks only of the person on the other side of the camera, just that one person, with whom she needs to communicate.

She tries to do that now, she tries to focus on these two strangers who have summoned her here and are watching her every move, she tries to mind her manners, tries to smile warmly but not too broadly, she follows them to the dining nook where they have laid a sunny-looking table with toast, jam, eggs, coffee, and an inferior brand of tea, but rather promising-looking scones. She tells herself to focus only on them, but this house is filled with distractions, with the sofa and drapes and coffeepot that her birth mother must have been using until just weeks ago.

Someone could have warned Marble of this new mix of emotions she's experiencing. Someone could have told her that having breakfast with her brother and sister would feel like being on a blind date, with everyone dressed to impress and making small talk and casting shy glances in one another's directions. And with Marble wondering why in the world she's agreed to do this, why she is allowing her sense of who she is to be stripped away. These people, this place, that coffeepot, all tell her that she is not who she thought she was.

She doesn't have to be here, does she? She could just stand up right now and walk out of this house. She could dodge those noisy crows loitering at the end of the driveway and that silly cactus in the backyard and fly back to her mum and dad. It's just that Byron and Benny are so tall and thick-boned, just like Marble, and there is something about their bulk that is difficult for her to resist. Plus, all those photographs of Eleanor Bennett, Marble's own face, staring back at her.

She'll feel better, perhaps, after she's had a bit of a rest. Marble is tired from yesterday's long flight over and annoyed at having to change rooms this morning. The first room they gave her at the hotel late last night was decorated in lilac *everything* and Marble just had to get out of there. Where in the world, Marble wonders, does one manage to find a lilac lamp?

Marble looks at Byron and Benny. *My brother and sister,* she thinks. She calls on all her professional skills now, trying to convey curiosity and friendliness and none of this undercurrent of agitation that she is feeling. She talks around the elephant in the room. She talks about her mum and dad, she talks about her late husband and her son's schooling, she talks about her plans to go back to the UK full time.

One thing Marble doesn't say is how hard it will be to leave Italy, to leave the everyday memories of her husband behind, even after more than fifteen years. Even after the occasional lover. Even after a man like Coffee Man. She suspects he would fly to England to see her, if it came to that. And it will have to come to that. She knows it's time to make the move. She's been feeling this for a while now, ever since she sent her son back to the UK for prep school.

How to begin again? Marble has clothes in the closets, food in the pantry, plants to think of. She has Bobby the dog. The thought of putting poor Bobby in a crate and carting him over to London, the thought of emptying out her husband's home, is weighing on her. But this is too personal, this isn't any of Byron and Benny's business.

Looking at Byron and Benny, now, Marble is aware that she is feeling resentful. She knows these two have nothing to do with Marble being abandoned as a baby, but the fact is, Byron and Benny are the ones who grew up with Eleanor Bennett, while Marble is the one who was left behind. Byron and Benny might not have been born yet but their mother, in effect, chose them over Marble.

Marble knows that she should ask herself, what would a woman have to go through to make the kind of choice that Eleanor Bennett had? It was fifty years ago. A woman like Marble, a person with financial and social resources, cannot presume to judge a woman who came of age in another time, or under different circumstances.

And yet.

Marble will find out more tomorrow how all of this happened. Her birth mother's lawyer says Eleanor Bennett left a letter and recording for her before she died. Maybe she should have gone to the lawyer's office first, but the thought of it had made her throat unbearably dry. Ease into it, she'd thought, but now the questions are driving her mad. What will Eleanor Bennett have to say? Will it be enough to cancel out what Marble is thinking?

She didn't want me enough.

All this thinking about her birth mother makes Marble miss her son terribly. Her Giovanni, her boy Giò. She wants to tell Byron and Benny that she, Marble, never had any doubts about wanting to be his mother, not even when she found herself widowed and pregnant at a young age and without warning, with all her visions of the future dashed. She wants someone to ask her, right now, *What is he like?* so that she can take out her mobile phone and show them the photos of her son.

Marble wants to say that she would trade being here with Byron and Benny, trade the chance to learn anything about her biological mother, for knowing that her son would be back in his own room when she returned home, and not tucked away in a boarding school. Giò is her real family, not these two people sitting at this table with her.

Byron is a funny sort. The man looks like a movie star but he is gaping at Marble as though she's stolen his favorite teddy bear. She doesn't think he likes her very much. Benny is sweet, but a bit needy. Marble notices that Benny is shifting her seat closer to her. Inching, inching. Marble is not sure what to make of this.

"About your son," Benny says.

Marble takes a breath.

"So, he goes to school in England?"

Marble nods.

"But you live in Italy."

"I go back and forth. I started Giò in the Italian schools but then I wanted him to get exposure to the UK system. After this, he'll be able to live and work wherever he wishes."

"So your son won't really be Italian and he won't really be British?"

"He'll be both, I suppose. Like many people, he isn't any one thing." Though right now, Marble is feeling that she is indeed one thing, more than any other. She is Giovanni's mum, and she has been letting her son grow up out of her sight. What in the world was she thinking?

Five years have passed and Marble has mourned every single month that her son has lived away from her, gone to school with kids she doesn't know, rested his head at night in a room under a different roof, come back home for the holidays looking and sounding different from the child she sent away. She doesn't understand how so many other parents like her have done the same thing, generation after generation, sent their eleven-year-olds away to school because they could afford to do it, because they'd convinced themselves that this was the way to guarantee their children the best future possible.

At one point, Marble thought of taking her son out of the boarding school, but he seemed to have adjusted so well. Now it's too late. Exams to finish, university to plan for. What Marble doesn't understand is how all this time, not a single boarding school mum has ever taken her aside at a dinner, at the supermarket, in a doctor's office, to say *I hate this, I want my child back home.* Surely she is not the only one who feels this way.

"Do you have pictures?" Benny asks. Marble feels her neck relax. She picks up her mobile phone and swipes through to the photo gallery and hands the phone to Benny.

"Oh, look at him, he's gorgeous!"

Marble nods.

"And he's doing well in school?"

Again, Marble nods. She cannot speak. She has a lump in her throat. Benny places a hand on Marble's arm.

Byron

—

Byron's hands are still shaking. He is still trying to get used to this ghost of a woman who is walking through the rooms of the house where he grew up, this British-talking, beechwood-colored version of his mother. When she walked into the arrivals area, Mitch and Byron shook Marble Martin's hand but Benny embraced her. On the way to the airport, Benny looked happy.

Byron is opening and closing kitchen cupboards when he sees a large glass jar tucked into a back corner of a lower cupboard behind the rice and sugar. The fruits. He'd forgotten about the fruits for the black cake. What to do? Before hearing his mother's recording, he might have gotten up the courage to wash the mixture down the garbage disposal, perhaps once his ma's clothes and books and furniture had been cleared out and the stake of the *For Sale* sign had been driven into the front lawn of their childhood home.

He puts the jar on the counter and keeps a hand on either side, as if steadying an infant. *This is your heritage,* his mother had told him many times, but he'd never appreciated that. Now he sees. When she fled the island, his mother lost everything but she carried this recipe in her head wherever she went. That, and the stories she'd spent a lifetime concealing from her children, the untold narrative of their family. Every time his mother made a black cake, it must have been like reciting an incantation, calling up a line from her true past, taking herself back to the island.

Five years ago, Byron was staying over with his mother while she recovered from a routine operation that nevertheless had left her in some pain. Byron had just finished washing the supper dishes when he heard it, that certain kind of creak in the house frame, then a rattling of something brittle, probably the glass in his mother's small china cabinet, the one she'd received as a belated wedding gift from their father four decades earlier, and which had signaled the arrival of every earthquake since.

Most of the tremors in Southern California were just that, tremors, followed by speculation among neighbors, office mates, and shoppers at the supermarket checkout about *when* and *how* the Big One would hit, followed by discussion of the efficacy of building codes or the threat of dormant spores released by the shaking of dry hillsides.

These conversations typically led down a slippery slope toward accounts of other natural threats, of soil erosion, winter flooding, and the relationship between these happenings and human activity. The stripping of land for housing, for agriculture, for oil and gas drilling. A psychotherapist with a pallet of bottled water in her shopping cart once told him her clients, all children, were starting to display anxiety over the environment. She was writing an article about it. She said it was becoming a thing, though Byron wondered if it was a real thing or just a marketing thing.

But this tremor felt different. Ended with a good jolt. Could be a sign of a biggie on the way. Byron opened the front door wide and left it open, pulling the emergency bag out of the hallway closet, the wheeled suitcase already stuffed with a change of clothes and medicines and water and copies of documents. He could hear voices down the road, neighbors trying to decide what to do next. He turned back to get his ma but she was already coming down the hallway, though slowly. She had managed to put on her street shoes.

By the time the next quake arrived and hit the house with a *huh* sound, Byron and his ma had already gone back indoors and started settling into bed. A couple of car alarms went off.

"Here we go again," Byron called. Down the hallway, his mother was hoisting herself off the mattress. He grabbed the handle of the emergency bag and took his mother's hand as they walked down the driveway toward the street. He raised his hand in salute to a couple of the neighbors, then ran back inside the house, grabbed his mother's purse and an extra blanket for sleeping in the car, and pulled hard at the front door, which was sticking more than usual.

"No, Byron, no!" his mother called. She was leaning against the side of the car, her hand pressed over her wound.

Byron stopped and frowned at his mother. "What? What's wrong?"

"The fruits, Byron, the fruits!"

The fruits? She wasn't serious, was she? Byron looked at his mother for a good long second. Oh, she was serious, all right. Goddamned fruits, a reminder to Byron that he was not only a California man but also a Caribbean American and would be plagued for the rest of his life by his mother's inordinate attachment to black cake. But this was going too far. Now his mother was expecting her only son to risk his life by going back into their kitchen to pull a two-liter glass jar, sixty-eight ounces of ebony-colored slosh, out from behind the dried beans and rice and sugar and peppercorns, while a seismic event was in process, no less. Surely no good could come of this.

Byron is smiling now at the memory. He is still standing there with the jar of fruit and rum when Benny and Marble walk into the kitchen. One sister looks like their father, the other is the spitting image of their mother, but the expressions on their faces are identical as their eyes rest on the jar. The two half sisters turn their heads toward each other and when they turn back to look at Byron, their mouths are open in twin smiles. And he starts to talk about Ma.

Later, Byron will find the women with the jar open and a tablespoon of the mixture poured into a saucer. They will be taking turns scribbling on the same piece of paper. When Byron walks over to them, they will not look up at him, they will not seem to notice him standing there until he puts an arm around Benny's shoulders.

Another Message

—

M R. MITCH HAS MADE AN APPOINTMENT WITH MARBLE FOR the next day, and Byron and Benny have agreed to meet up with Marble afterward for lunch. But when they show up at Mr. Mitch's office to pick her up, she is no longer there and she doesn't answer their phone calls or text messages.

"I think the meeting was a bit rough on her," is all Mr. Mitch will say.

"What did the message from our mother say?"

"You know I'm not at liberty to give you details," Mr. Mitch says, "but there wasn't really anything that you don't already know. Just give her a little time."

Byron and Benny nod. They have privately agreed that they cannot bring themselves to call Mr. Mitch *Charles*. Maybe one day. Or maybe they'll call him *Mitch* without the *Mister* but, for now, they prefer to think of him as their mother's lawyer, not her boyfriend.

They agree to give Marble some space but after two days, they begin to worry. They go to the hotel and find that Marble has checked out. When they finally receive an email at the end of the week, Marble confirms that she is back in the UK.

"I believe I need some time to process this," Marble writes. "Thank you for everything. All best."

All best? Byron and Benny go out to a restaurant and drink two beers each but never get around to touching their food. *All best?* And what about the black cake their mother left them?

"Okay, enough of this, it's time," Byron says. "Ma wanted us to share the black cake with Marble? Well, she had her chance and she's not here. Let's just do it."

"I don't know," Benny says.

Back at the house, they walk into the kitchen together, open the freezer door, and stare at the foil-covered cake. After about ten seconds, they look at each other, then close the door again. Benny leans against the counter, running her hand along the avocado green surface. It's so seventies, so *Ma*.

After a week, Benny goes back to New York and Byron goes to a conference. They plan to meet up again soon to start clearing out their mother's house, but there's still no word from Marble. Byron says they've lived their entire lives without Marble and they may just have to keep on doing so. But just in case, they'll leave the cake where it is for now.

Cake

———

BACK IN NEW YORK, BENNY HAS MADE HER BEST BLACK CAKE yet. She has poured and folded and stirred and channeled the memories of being with Ma in the kitchen. She has worked out her frustration over Marble's continued silence. She has told herself that for a couple of hours there, back in California, she and Marble really did make a connection. If they hadn't, she wouldn't be doing this right now.

Benny and Marble chuckled over their shared interest in food that day in Ma's kitchen. *What a coincidence,* Marble said, and Benny said, *It's no coincidence, it's in our blood.* What if Benny had actually seen a video or photo of Marble before knowing about her mother's hidden past? It would have been a shock. It was a shock as it was, to see a white woman with her mother's face, with her mother's voice, walking into her childhood home, standing in her mother's kitchen.

As it turns out, Benny and Marble don't really look at culinary tradition in the same way, but when they spent that hour or so chatting in Ma's kitchen, Marble offered Benny some excellent advice for her next visit to the bank.

So here she is. Benny wraps the black cake now in wax paper, closes it in a tin, and takes it to the bank. Benny tells the bank guy that she knows the city doesn't need another coffee shop, per se, but it needs a place like hers. She tells him that her concept café will highlight the diaspora of food, the migration of cultures to this country through recipes, the mix of traditions that feeds into contemporary America. It will be a place to learn and reflect. It will be a place for people to be together.

Benny explains that she is working on a lesson plan for children with local educators. She won't share the black cake with the children because of the alcohol content, but she will take a sample for them to see and smell and she will tell them about the flawed narratives that have always aimed to draw clear boundaries around cultures and people's identities.

There are Italian restaurants and Chinese restaurants and Ethiopian restaurants and Polish delis and what-have-you, but her menu will feature recipes from different cultures that could only have come about through a mixing of traditions, a mixing of fates, a mixing of stories. Plus, her mother has left her enough money to help fund daily operations for two years, after which she expects to be able to make a profit, so, given her changed circumstances, would the bank reconsider her previous application for a business loan?

About Love

—

HOW IT BEGINS: IN A PARKING LOT AT THE SHOPPING CENTER in the suburbs.

"I don't get it, what are you?" says a man, who is taking a pamphlet from Benny.

"I'm Manny the Meerkat," says Benny, lowering her voice into character. Manny the Meerkat is one of her weekend gigs, one of the assortment of jobs she will continue to juggle until she has confirmation of financing for her café.

"Meerkat?"

"Meerkat."

Benny straightens her back and head and lifts her chin, peering off into the distance through the tiny holes behind the eyes in her costume, her stance inspired by the calendar on her kitchen wall where a clan of meerkats stand in a cluster, scanning the horizon for threats. Each slender creature would be an easy mouthful for a predator but they know that their strength lies in banding together.

When the manager at Manny's Electronics first saw her, he said he'd never hired her type to do the job before, meaning, presumably, female or *of color* or both, but he said that Benny was getting the job because of her height and heft, and she has tried to make that work for her. No matter that she is cloaked in twenty-five pounds of velvet-covered foam rubber for the precise purpose of hawking electronics, even after the fuss over the printer at the call center. Anyway, it's not that Benny doesn't appreciate electronics, it's just that she feels they should last much longer.

"On the lookout for bargain prices, you know?" Benny-as-Manny says to the man who has taken a pamphlet.

"Uh, okay," the man says, and walks away, leaving a slightly woody scent in his wake. Then he stops and turns back and Benny is hopeful that he will ask more about the forty-percent-off electronics sale. She wants him to put off heading for his car, put off pressing the little button on his key that will make his car blink and chirp like a small animal, put off going home with the one small plastic bag that he is holding in his other hand. A small bag, not sacks full of groceries. Probably not a family man, Benny thinks. Possibly single.

Benny hopes the man will end up inside the store, waving the discount-price flyer, evidence that Benny, as Manny the Meerkat, has been doing a good job of luring shoppers, even though there's talk of another recession on the way. Instead, the man frowns and says, "Shouldn't there be, like, a bunch of you? Don't meerkats do that thing where they all kinda huddle together?" He flexes the meat of his arms and shoulders in a way that calls to mind the curved backs of a football team, rather than the straight-necked crowding together of small, shiny-eyed animals.

Benny is beginning to feel sweaty inside the meerkat costume and she can feel her period coming on, that slight achy-flu-ey feeling. And still two hours to go. She reminds herself that each hour brings her closer to paying the month's expenses. The money her mother left Benny in her will must go toward her business plan and nothing else.

"Oh, look, it's Sid from *Ice Age*," Benny hears a little boy say. She can feel a small hand pulling on the flank of her costume.

"That's not Sid," the child's mother says. "Sid is a sloth, not a chipmunk." The child backs away now where Benny can see him. Benny sees that the woman is more likely to be the child's nanny than his mother. The child's hair is so blond it's almost white and the nanny has Byron's complexion. Benny notices the woman has a Caribbean accent of some kind, and she is dressed flawlessly, like a plainclothes cop or one of those religious people who stand on street corners handing out booklets.

There's a good likelihood this woman is the employee of a well-heeled television executive or lawyer or financial analyst, something like that. Someone who wires part of her earnings back to the island. After which, she still might have more money left over at the end of the month than the extra bit of cash Benny earns by doing things like dressing up like a meerkat, taking other people's dogs for walks, and making the occasional one-of-a-kind, decorated cakes for clients who are wealthy enough and busy enough to appreciate that sort of thing.

One of Benny's sketches might earn her more than some people get in a month, but art does not guarantee an income, while taking someone else's dog out to pee does.

"He's not a chipmunk," says the man. Benny is surprised to see he's still hanging around. "He's a meerkat." Benny notes the man has a lot of hair on his forearms. Practically a carpet of the stuff. Blondish-reddish. It isn't so common these days to see that, what with everyone running off to get waxed here and there. He is as tall as she is, this red bear of a man.

"You saw meerkats at the zoo, remember?" the nanny says, touching the boy lightly on his shoulder.

"Oh, I know those," the kid says. "They stand around in little gangs and look like this," the boy says, doing an impressive imitation of a meerkat on the lookout. That child should have Benny's job. The woman smiles and tousles his hair. Benny as Manny continues to extend her arm here and there, handing flyers to people who pass by and take them without looking at her.

The man steps closer to Benny now, and she feels a buzz run up both sides of her face. His cologne is a smoky kind of thing that triggers a slight churning below her navel. Benny has never understood what draws her to a person. She only knows it when an individual who crosses her radar sets off a ping.

Ping.

"You *are* a girl, right?" the man asks.

"Woman."

"Oh, right, sorry."

Inside her costume, Benny smiles.

"Did you know," Benny says, "that a gang of meerkats is led by an alpha pair, and that the dominant member of that pair is the female?"

He is peering at her through the costume's eye holes. A smile crinkles the skin around his eyes.

"Do meerkats drink coffee?" he says.

The head of Benny's costume tips to the side. This man has never seen Benny. He does not even know the shape of her. And yet he is interested.

Ping.

How it will end: Benny doesn't know yet, but already this is a gift, this openness to try love again.

More Than Life

———

THE SOUND OF METAL CLICKING OVER METAL PULLS MARBLE out of her stupor. She is sitting alone in the half light, holding a cold cup of tea in her lap. She hasn't told her parents she's back in the UK, that she's been sitting alone in the apartment here for two days. They've already had that long, painful conversation with her about her adoption, their voices muddied with tears, and they have been largely silent since then, getting in touch only to be sure that she'd arrived safely in California, and that she'd flown back to Italy all right. They didn't ask how things went. She knew they wouldn't. They would be waiting for her to say something first.

Marble's attitude toward her parents has already softened since then. She has learned from Eleanor Bennett's message that her parents kept the name that had been chosen by her birth mother. Baby Mathilda became Mabel Mathilda and, even when she changed her first name to Marble, her longtime nickname, she unwittingly held on to the name of her biological grandmother. Her parents may not have wanted to admit that she was adopted but they hadn't erased every trace of her birth mother, either.

When Marble hears the key turning in the lock, she worries about a break-in, but then she remembers the orchids. Her mother always comes to water the plants, which Marble insists on keeping, despite the fact that she spends most of her time elsewhere. Her mum is perennially worried about opening the door and finding the orchids dead, but

Marble reminds her that orchids are hardy creatures, that orchids grow naturally on every continent, that there is an orchid in someone's garden in Singapore that has been blooming for well over a century.

"Marble!" her mother says.

Marble doesn't get up, doesn't feel she can. She looks at this petite woman standing before her. Her mum's hair, originally a dark blond, has taken on brilliant streaks in recent years, the hairdresser's artistry mixing in with her natural white. She gives Marble one long look, walks over to the sofa, takes the cup and saucer from her, and places it on the coffee table. Then she sits down next to her and takes one of Marble's hands in hers.

Marble plays the recording for her mother. She waits until her mother has finished shedding tears. Later, they will share it with Marble's father. They will let him listen to the voice of this woman who sounds so much like his own daughter. They will let him hear the part where Eleanor Bennett says what a beautiful, accomplished woman Baby Mathilda has turned out to be and that it is all to their credit.

They will let Marble's father read the letter where Eleanor says she is forever grateful to him and his wife for giving her baby a safe and loving home and, if they have felt for Marble even a fraction of what she felt the first time she nursed her baby, then she knows that they must love her more than anything in the world, they must love her more than life itself.

Reunion

—

A COOL VAPOR RISES FROM THE ALUMINUM FOIL AS BENNY pulls the black cake out of the freezer. This is what Eleanor Bennett wanted, all three of her children together. Marble has come back. It took her a full month since her last message to get in touch but here they are again, in the kitchen where Benny used to spend entire days baking with her mother, at the table where Benny and Byron ate most of their meals growing up. In the house where their mother nursed a yearning for her firstborn daughter who was lost but who finally has been found.

Byron and Benny take some solace in knowing that their mother didn't die before learning where her eldest daughter was and who she had become. Their mother left this world believing that one day all three of her children would be here in this room together to fulfill her dying request. When Marble ran back to England after hearing their mother's private message for her, Byron thought they might never see her again, but Benny never doubted that they would. Nor did Mr. Mitch, who continued to make arrangements according to their mother's wishes. There are trips to be made, he tells them, people their mother wanted them to see.

But first, this.

Their mother wanted her children to sit down together and share the black cake she'd made for them. *You will know when,* she wrote in her note to Byron and Benny. And this is the *when*. Benny picks up a knife and gestures to Marble.

"You're the firstborn," Benny says.

"No, you do it," Marble says.

Benny looks at Byron. They hold the knife together, as their parents used to do, and they sink it into the cake. *We never did have a wedding cake* is what their mother told them toward the end of her recording. *There wasn't time. And who would have been there to celebrate with us?* But once her parents had moved from London to New York to California, once they felt they were settling into their new lives, Ma filled a jar with fruits and made the first in a series of anniversary cakes.

"Oh!" Benny says. The knife hits something hard. They cut open the cake to find a small glass jar inside, wide and squat. Their mother had cut the cake on the horizontal and dug out the middle to fit the jar in there.

Benny wipes off the jar and taps the side of the lid on the table to unseal it. The first thing they fish out is a piece of paper, folded and cracked. It is a black-and-white photograph of three young swimmers standing on the sand, the sea at their backs. Byron and Benny recognize the teenaged faces of their parents. The third person still has her swim cap on and is clasping Covey's hand in a kind of silent cheer. They've never met her but she's easy to recognize because she is famous, the only black woman in the world to have done exactly what she has done. The distance swimmer Etta Pringle.

Byron turns the photo over and on the back, they find three names written out in their father's handwriting.

"Gilbert Grant," he reads, "Coventina Lyncook, Benedetta Pringle." He looks at Benny.

"Benedetta?" he says.

"Etta was short for Benedetta!" Benny says. Benny must have been named after her mother's childhood friend. The one who helped their mother escape from the beach on the night that she was believed drowned. The three of them sit there silently for a moment, thinking of small but profound inheritances. Of how untold stories shape people's lives, both when they are withheld and when they are revealed.

In the bottom of the jar they find their parents' wedding rings, both with the same inscription inside, *C and G*. Benny remembers seeing the inscription once and asking her mother about it. Her mother told her the letters stood for *comprehension* and *generosity*, two qualities that she said were essential in a good marriage. Now she knows that they are the initials of her parents' original names. Coventina and Gilbert, Covey and Gibbs. All this time, their parents' true identities have been hidden right here in this house, in these rings, in this photograph.

Finally, they turn the jar over and let the rest of its contents fall onto the kitchen table. Three cockle shells, whitish on the outside, pinkish beige on the inside. Their mother must have found these in the purse that belonged to Elly, the original Eleanor Douglas, the girl who befriended their mother and who, unwittingly, gave her a chance at a whole new life.

Byron feels a hum of excitement. He's past some of the shock now, he's ready to learn more. He wants to go to the island. He wants to see where his parents grew up. He wants to see the part of himself that he never knew. He has to. How will he manage this, otherwise? This disappearing of the life he once thought he had.

There is one more thing, jammed against the curve of the jar. A narrow slip of paper that says *THE BOX*. Byron and Benny look at each other and nod. They have already found the wooden box, the hinged ebony container that once belonged to their mother's mother, Mathilda. Their ma kept it on a shelf in her closet. Inside are four medallions, yellow-gold disks stamped with crosses that they both used to play with, and the old hair comb that their mother let Benny wear one Halloween, wedged into her braids and covered with an old veil like a Spanish lady.

They know these items by heart. As children, they both ran their hands over the fine curves etched into the surface of the comb, over the browns and golds and grays of the tortoiseshell, over the cross on the face of each coin. Benny goes to her parents' bedroom and comes back with the wooden box, hugging it to her middle.

Benny and Byron have already talked about the box. Their mother wanted them to give it to Marble, to give her a chance to fiddle with its contents, just as they had in their younger years. They will give Baby Mathilda a piece of the childhood that she might have experienced had she grown up in their family. They will give Marble the only objects left from their mother's former life.

"Our ma's box of trinkets," Benny says. "She always said the box belonged to her own mother but that she'd found the comb and medallions in the backyard at the orphanage. We think they must have belonged to Elly, the original Eleanor." Benny hands the box to Marble.

"We used to play with these all the time, Marble. Now it's your turn."

Marble smiles at the box and smooths her hand along its silky surface, puts it up to her face and sniffs at the wood, then lifts the lid. Her mouth drops open when she sees what's inside. She puts on her glasses.

"Oh, my," Marble says, smoothing her finger over one of the disks. "These aren't trinkets. This is gold. From a very long time ago. These probably belong in a museum." Marble sits up straighter and reminds them that before she wrote about food, she studied art history. She pulls her tablet out of her purse and searches the Internet for a news story about divers who recently salvaged gold coins from the site of an ancient shipwreck. She shows Byron and Benny a closeup of the coins. They are identical to her mother's medallions.

"This comb, too, has to be about three hundred years old. Could be from the same ship."

"Dude, you're kidding me," Byron says.

At the word *dude*, Marble gives Byron a look that he can only think of as being extremely British.

"But if we go public with these," Benny says, "won't we have to explain where they came from? We might have to say something about our parents. Our parents invented a narrative for a reason, to hide their true identities."

"But they're not around anymore," Byron says.

"No, they're not," Benny says. "But some of the people they knew are still around. Where does that leave us? What happens if we alter even one part of that story? What about the murder?"

"What about the murder?" Byron says.

"We still don't know who killed Little Man, do we?"

"Exactly," Marble says. "Do you think it was your mother? I mean, you know. Our . . ."

Byron and Benny cast her the same, big-eyed look. Marble has to get used to saying *our mother*. Or does she? She's glad she finally knows about her birth mother, but her mum, Wanda, will always be her mum.

"I've thought about it and thought about it, but I really don't know," Byron says. "A year ago I would have said there's no way my mother would have killed a man, but there's a lot we didn't know then. In her recording, our mother never actually denies killing Little Man."

"I wouldn't blame her if she had," Benny says. "The point is, our parents told us a lot of lies over the years. We might never know how much of the truth our ma has told us."

"Maybe when we go to the island, we'll find out."

"We can't go to the island, Byron. We don't really know what we're getting into. There are people who helped our mother escape. We don't want to cause them any trouble, do we? Not after everything they did for her. What do you think, Marble?"

Marble says nothing. She picks up the coins and comb from the table, puts them back into the wooden box, and closes the lid.

Shipwreck

———

IN 1715, A HURRICANE PLOWING THROUGH THE CARIBBEAN SANK two Spanish ships and smashed eight others into the shallows off the coast of Florida. Later that year, a pair of pirate ships set out from the island and returned home loaded with treasures, most of which the Spanish had already pulled up from the shipwrecks. Back in Port Royal, the raiders unloaded bullion, dyestuffs, tobacco, and other valuable items, some of which were not listed anywhere on the manifests of the ruined fleet and which promised to fetch a good sum on the black market.

Twenty years later, a runaway slave emerged from the bush in the interior of the island and sneaked onto the plantation from which he had fled four months earlier. Under the cover of night, he ran off with his woman, whose stomach had grown thick with child. She left with only the clothes on her back, two guavas in her apron pocket, and a large hair comb belonging to the mistress of the house. The mistress, on the occasion of her marriage to the master of the estate years before, had received the comb along with a case of gold medallions and other gifts from a high official who, it was said, had sent his men to Florida to loot goods recovered from the shipwrecked Spanish fleet. It was an assertion that he had always denied.

The enslaved woman had been waiting to reclaim her freedom. She had been listening for a signal every night for four moons but, as in all such things, she repeatedly steeled herself for disappointment. She knew that her man might never make it back. When the time finally came, she had only minutes to escape. She was already running across a rain-soaked field, holding fast to her man's hand, when she realized that the comb was still wedged into the waist of her skirt. She would have washed the comb and put it on the mistress's dressing table that evening, had she had the time, had she not been slipping in the mud and stumbling over tree roots in her quest for freedom.

The mistress had usually treated her kindly. For a slave. The master, not so kindly. More than once, in fact, he had treated the young woman *not so kindly*. But the child inside her would be hers, not his. This child would grow up free in the hills with the others who had escaped and who were teaching their children the old ways. She threw the comb into the field as she ran. It sank into the mud, where it would be washed clear to the bottom of the garden by a heavy rain, then tucked farther into the earth by one of the men's shovels. She thought of the coins that she had taken from the master's house, one at a time, and buried in the dirt down the way. There was no time to retrieve them. There was only time to survive.

More than two hundred years would pass before an orphan girl named Elly, raised at a children's home on the site of the former sugar cane plantation, found a dirt-encrusted hair comb in the garden, along with cockle shells from a prehistoric era and one well-fed garden snake, the latter of which she quickly tossed aside. She washed the comb in the tub where she was given her afternoon bath and later squirreled it away in her personal tin of treasures. Inside the tin were four gold coins which she'd found near the potato plants the year before.

Mapping
the Ocean

—

SCIENTISTS HAVE COME UP WITH NEW WAYS TO MAP THE deepest parts of the ocean. At one time, many imagined that the seafloor was a dark, sandy plain dotted with unseeing fish or cartilaginous giants and, perhaps, a few clumps of coral that could survive without light. But technology has come to confirm what Etta Pringle had always sensed, that the seafloor is a universe of underwater crests and valleys and rivers, of mineral deposits and jewels, of entire continents of life. The blues, the greens, the yellows, the blacks.

When Etta learned that the most remote corners of the seafloor were going to be unveiled, she had confirmation of why she had been put on this earth to swim. She was meant to spend the rest of her life doing her part to remind people that Earth was not so much land as water, that this planet was a living thing to be cared for and protected and used with care, not to be drained and littered to the point of extinction.

Machines are sophisticated but they cannot read love. They cannot tell researchers what it feels like to be part of the sea, to be a blip of arms and legs, a small cavern of a mouth, skimming the briny surfaces of the world. Some people wonder what it would be like to fly. Etta already knows. So she keeps flying through the water and she will keep on fighting to protect it.

Etta travels around the world to speak in public and meet with politicians and plead the case of the world's oceans and seas, the last remaining barrier between life on Earth and oblivion. She reminds intergovernmental assemblies that even creatures from ten thousand meters below the marine surface have been found with plastic fibers in their insides. What, she asks, does that tell us about what can happen to our own children?

And now this mapping business.

Etta knows that only a small fraction of the seafloor has been mapped. She knows that this can be dangerous. Look at the submarine that ran into an underwater mountain some years back. She knows that people need more information and more resources. But not only. People have always wanted more, period. This is one of the laws of human nature. What's to stop those maps from becoming a mere tool for exploitation?

And so, Etta fights then swims then grieves then trudges back onshore to fight. She speaks out for the seas that grew her, that gave her friendship, that taught her to love. She doesn't do the distances she used to, but she still holds a couple of world records. People come to see her presentations, they want autographs, they want selfies, but she wonders, how many of them are listening to what she has to say? Some people call her ugly names in public, rather than engage in real dialogue. This, too, is one of the laws of human nature. If you are visible, you become a target.

Though, mostly, Etta feels the love.

One day, when Etta is all talked out and wondering how she can sneak out in advance of the reception that's been organized just for her, she looks up to find herself face-to-face with a younger man, maybe forty, forty-five, who looks very familiar. He looks like someone she hasn't seen in decades.

He looks like Gibbs Grant.

The man is talking to her. He works on seafloor mapping. He says they should talk about that sometime. But Etta is distracted by those eyes and by something else, his smile, a grin that pulls sharply to the left. There's no mistaking it, that is Covey's mouth. The man puts out his hand to shake hers and Etta is pulled back into the sea of her girlhood.

Trembling, she takes the man's hand in both of hers. Then two women step out of the dispersing crowd and stand on either side of the man, both of them the color of straw. One of them looks like a pale photocopy of her long-lost friend, Covey.

Benedetta "Bunny" Pringle takes a step back. She looks around, her chest filling with anticipation. Covey. Where is she? They had made a plan to meet here in Los Angeles tonight, just outside the auditorium.

The last time she saw Covey, Covey had whispered hurriedly in her ear. "I found him, Bunny. I found Gibbs. We changed our names. We had children. We live here." There was no time for anything else. Etta gave Covey her business card and thought she'd hear from her again, but she didn't, so Etta asked one of her assistants to locate a Mrs. Eleanor Bennett somewhere in the Anaheim area. In the fall of 2018, she called the number she'd been given.

"This is Etta Pringle," Etta had said, taking care to keep her tone steady and professional. "I am looking for Mrs. Eleanor Bennett."

"Oh, Bunny," the woman on the other end of the line said, and she knew it was Covey.

"Mrs. Bennett, I have another date coming up at the convention center where we met."

"Eleanor. Please call me Eleanor."

"Eleanor, do you think you could make it? We could work out a way to meet after that for a proper chat. I could leave you two passes, for you and your husband, or more, if you'd like." It was then that Covey told her that Gibbs had died. They were both quiet for a while, then ended the call agreeing to meet on this date. There was no need to say *no more phone calls, no emails, no letters*. They had found each other again. But they would have to be discreet.

Bunny stands before Covey's children now, turning this way and that, looking for Covey. The young woman who looks just like Gibbs shakes her head.

"Our ma," she says. "She got sick." Her eyes start to tear up.

Bunny looks at the other woman for a moment until what she is telling her finally registers.

Covey is gone.

She covers her mouth with one hand. Then she spreads her arms and embraces all three of her friend's children.

The Letter

───

Byron has the same face, the same deep tone, same broad shoulders as his father, only he is thicker than Gibbs Grant was, at least the last time Etta saw Gibbs. He was barely twenty years old when he left the island and Etta never did see him again. Though not for lack of trying. She tried to contact Gibbs sometime after she and Patsy had moved to London, after the birth of her baby, but Gibbs seemed to have disappeared. Now Etta knows why.

Gibbs and Covey's son, now well into his forties, hands Etta an envelope. Etta tears it at one end and pulls out a sheet of paper. She feels her face grow warm at the sight of her old friend's handwriting.

My dearest Bunny,

I am writing to you now because I don't think I will be able to see you again. I'm so sorry. We had a plan, I know, but my health is failing me. I didn't want to upset you by telling you. I thought I'd be well enough to make our little rendezvous. I can't tell you how wonderful it was to lay eyes on you again at the convention center, after so many years. I have always followed you in the news, Bunny, every single one of your swims, and I am so proud of what you have accomplished. You don't know how many times I wanted to get in touch before this year but, well, we both knew the situation. Finally, I took a risk and went to see you that day and I am so glad.

Bunny, you have been a true friend. You did more for me than I could ever repay. So please forgive me for asking you to do me this favor. It's about my children. This won't be easy for them. Can you help them? Charles

Mitch, my lawyer and close friend, will tell you more about what I am asking you to do. He will tell you more about what has been happening in our lives.

There's so much I wanted to tell you in person but I'm afraid that, unless there is some kind of miracle, I will have to say my farewells here. But only farewell, Bunny, not goodbye. I won't go far, I promise. I'll be there in the water with you, every single time. I always have been.

Take care, dear friend, and watch out for those naughty jellies.

Yours always,

C.

Etta holds the letter against her chest, stands there for a while, eyes closed. Then she folds the paper back into the envelope, tucks it into her jacket pocket, and nods at Eleanor's children.

"Okay," says Etta, "I need to see Charles Mitch. Can you take me to see him?"

Pearl

—

THE THING ABOUT THE ISLAND WHERE PEARL GREW UP IS, A LOT of people end up leaving. They may go looking for work, or follow their grown children overseas, as did Pearl. Either way, many of them carry something from the island deep inside, a story or memory that, for one reason or another, they never share with others. The same is true for Pearl. That's why it always does her a world of good when Bunny Pringle comes to town.

Bunny knows more about Pearl than most. Bunny understands that Covey's mother wasn't just her employer. Mathilda had become her friend and Pearl tried to take care of Covey after her mother left but it wasn't enough. She watched Covey grow from a bighearted little rascal to a tough and driven young woman, knowing that underneath the girl's bravado was a well of dejection as deep as the sea.

Bunny comes to visit whenever she passes through this part of Florida. Bunny is a grandmother now. Hard to believe it, even though Pearl herself is a great-grandmother. It's just that the children will always be children, no matter how old they get. Bunny must be seventy-three years old, now, maybe seventy-four, and she's still doing her crazy swimming. All those years ago, her coach told people Bunny would be a champion someday and, sure enough, look at her now.

Over the years, Pearl has seen Bunny on the television and even on her cellphone. She remembers watching on the television when they named a cove back home after Bunny. Seeing the pictures of Bunny's seaside ceremony on the Internet left Pearl feeling proud of Bunny and sad at the same time. Covey should have been alive to see that, too.

There's Bunny now, getting out of a car at the bottom of Pearl's driveway. Three other people are getting out of the car with her, a man and two women. Pearl nearly has a heart attack when she gets a good look at them. She only needs ten more seconds to be certain of what she is seeing, to understand that something impossible has happened, something marvelous, praise God. Bunny told her she'd be bringing some people with her but Pearl would never have guessed. What a story Bunny is telling her now. What a story.

Pearl is standing in her backyard, flanked by Covey's children, and trying to act normal-like. She stands at the edge of the canal, pointing out the mangrove and the birds and fish. Why is it, Pearl jokes, that the only fish you can ever see in there, the ones who jump all the way out of the brackish water and flip themselves back in, are the homely-looking ones, so quick to show themselves off?

Covey's children all laugh, low, bubbly laughs, just like Mister Lin. Imagine that.

Covey's son and one of the daughters look like Gibbs, though the girl has Mister Lin's complexion. But it is the other child, the oldest, that Pearl can't stop looking at. This white woman is Covey through and through, down to the way she shows all her teeth when she tips her head back and smiles. To think that all these years, Covey was alive and raising a family with Gibbs.

After Gibbs Grant went to England and never came back, people took to saying that maybe he'd become too big for his britches, couldn't be bothered to stay in touch with his own uncle. Or maybe something had happened to him, Pearl thought. But, no, all this time, Gibbs was with Covey in California. The Lord works in strange ways, indeed.

If only, Pearl thinks. If only Mathilda could see this. Her daughter's children. Which makes Pearl wonder for the millionth time, whatever happened to Mathilda? Another person who had simply disappeared. That, too, is part of Pearl's untold story, how Mathilda managed to run away from home. She used part of the black cake money she'd saved up, and left the rest of her share to Pearl for Covey. Mister Lin had no idea how much a woman could make baking a proper cake for a wedding. He never did take women's kitchen work too seriously. Which was a good thing. Otherwise, he might have found the money and gambled it all away.

Lin

—

BY THE TIME HE REACHED RETIREMENT AGE, JOHNNY "LIN" Lyncook was a wealthy man. He had moved to a suburb of Miami where he knew folks from the island, earned a chunk of cash on the black market, invested his profits in stocks and bonds, and liquidated his gains before the 2008 crisis. He learned to stay away from everything else. No casinos, no poker, no cockfights, no sports. The betting had already cost him too much. Two wives and his only daughter, his one true regret.

Lin's newfound wealth proved very useful. He acquired a third wife and her two young children, produced with other men but welcomed into his home. He sent the boys to pricey universities and watched with satisfaction as his investment paid off. The boys have their own homes and families now, and their children call him Papa Lin, to distinguish him from Papa Shaw, their mother's dad.

Lin was also in the position to pay a private investigator to locate his daughter Covey, who was reported to have been killed in a train accident in England years before but who, Lin learned, was actually alive and living in California. There was a photograph. It showed Lin's daughter with Gilbert Grant who, like Covey, had changed his name and left his past behind.

The idea to search for his daughter after so many years had come to Lin after he'd watched a video online with some kind of food expert, a white woman who looked so much like his daughter that he nearly slid right off the couch. Then Lin sat down with the investigator and told him everything he could think of about Covey, including Gibbs and his own departure from the island.

Lin hadn't tried to contact his daughter. If she'd wanted to get in touch, he was certain she could have found a way. It wouldn't have been hard to find him. As it was, half the island was now living up in Miami. But Covey has never sent word. Whenever it has hurt Lin to think about such things, he's reasoned that Covey had little choice. It was likely best for Coventina Lyncook to remain dead to everyone who once knew her, even fifty years after her disappearance. True, any young woman in her situation might have fled the day of Little Man's murder, guilty or not. But, still.

So much time has passed since then and Lin is getting up there in years. Not long ago, he was thinking he should just go ahead and get in touch with Covey after all, forget his pride, when an email arrived from Bunny Pringle. Bunny was writing to say that she had important news and would be calling him. On the telephone, she told Lin that she was calling about their *mutual acquaintance, Miss C.* Bunny confirmed that Covey had been alive all these years but that now she really was gone, she'd gotten sick.

Coventina. That fool-headed child.

Bunny says Covey was survived by three children. *Three* children? The investigator only mentioned two. At any rate, Bunny tells Lin they want to meet him, which surprises Lin, considering what happened to their mother. But here he is, now, sitting in his sunroom, waiting for them to arrive.

Lin hasn't seen Bunny in years, except in the news. She's famous now, for all that swimming of hers. She was always *different,* that Pringle girl, but she was a good child at heart and she was a loyal friend to his daughter. Bunny always defended Covey's name. She never, ever cast doubt on his daughter's innocence, not even when Lin himself did.

Perhaps it is this last thought that finally does it, that lifts the fog in his mind surrounding the day of Covey's disappearance. The thought of Bunny and Covey, as close as twins, cheek-to-cheek in their shiny dresses. Lin was already fairly drunk when it happened, when Little Man dropped dead in front of him. Still, he was close enough to have seen something, that's what he realizes now. Had he really forgotten, boozed up as he was that day? Or had he, like most men at critical moments in their lives, merely refused to accept something because he did not want to?

The doorbell rings. When Covey's children finally walk into Lin's house, the shock of seeing that woman in person, the one who looks just like his daughter, eclipses all other thoughts. Only later, when Bunny stumbles over a coffee table, *Still clumsy, that girl,* will Lin take a good, long look at his daughter's best friend and think back, once again, to that day in 1965.

Meeting Lin

—

THEY ARE ROUNDING THE CORNER PAST A HOUSE WITH A BURST of yellow-and-orange crotons and a lanai enclosed with mosquito screening. As they park the car in the driveway and walk to the nearest door, Byron sees a small swimming pool under the lanai. The border of the pool is tiled with a dolphin motif. The door to the house has a dolphin-shaped wind chime and a dolphin-shaped *Welcome* sign. *Very Florida,* Byron thinks, as he wipes the sweat from his temples, as he pulls his shirt away from his damp torso, as he longs for the cool morning air of the Pacific coast.

A small, fleshy woman answers the door. She has toothpaste-ad teeth and a Cuban accent.

"Come in, Mister Lin is in the back," she says, leading them across a broad room with cream-colored flooring.

Byron shakes his head as he walks. *Why are they even here?* Do they really have to meet this man? The nervousness he's been feeling on the ride over from the hotel is morphing into a kind of irritation, compounded by Marble's presence. Sure, Johnny Lyncook is her grandfather, too, but it's different for her. Her whole relationship with their mother and this family is different.

By the time he gets to the next room he's decided he's going to have it out with this man. This man, who is supposed to be his grandfather. This man, whose irresponsible behavior and betrayal drove Byron's mother away, nearly killed her, caused her to lose everything and everyone she knew. And sent her, ultimately, into circumstances that no young woman should have to face.

Byron sees an old Chinese guy with hair as black as coal, sitting on a wicker sofa. Next to him is a cane and a glass-topped table packed with photo frames. He bows his head as he uses the cane to push himself up from the seat. He's a tall man, this Johnny Lyncook. But he's a wispy-looking character, except for the hair, monochromatic and thick as a wig. The side table has photos of children. This man probably has other grandchildren. This man, who does not deserve to be called *grandfather.*

Always respect your elders, Byron's mother used to say. What his ma really meant was, always be polite, always be considerate. But no, Byron thinks. If we really mean to respect people in their maturity, then we must acknowledge them as fully formed individuals with long histories; we must be prepared to see them as they are, to recognize that a shit is a shit, young or old. Like this man, who ruined his mother's life. This man does not deserve Byron's courtesy.

Johnny Lyncook does not say hello, does not shake their hands, does not invite them to sit. He merely opens his mouth and stares at Marble. Then he pokes Benny on the arm and wags a finger back and forth between her and Byron.

"You two. Just like your father," Johnny Lyncook says, nodding. "Just like Gilbert Grant." Now he's back to staring at Marble. He turns to the side table full of photo frames, leans down to pull one out of the bunch, and presses it into Marble's hands. Byron sees that it's a black-and-white photo of a teenaged girl in a school uniform, a plaid tunic over a white shirt. There is no mistaking who that girl is. She looks just like Marble, only much darker. Benny takes the frame from Marble.

"Our ma!" Benny says. Byron feels his throat go tight.

Byron looks at this old guy. Who does he think he is, keeping a photograph of Ma in his living room? Byron doesn't even feel connected to this man. But then Johnny Lyncook smiles a lopsided grin. It's his ma's smile. *Jeez,* it's Byron's own smile. Which makes Byron want to grab hold of the man and shake him until he crumples to the floor.

Johnny Lyncook turns back to the sofa and eases himself onto the seat. Etta Pringle trips over something as she maneuvers around the coffee table between them.

"Bunny Pringle," he says, in a tone that Byron can't decipher. Almost like an adult who's fixing to reproach a child. No, it's something else. Something sharper. It's because she knew, isn't it? She knew that Covey had survived that plunge into the sea, all those years ago, and she never told him.

"Mister Lin," she says, sitting down at the other end of the sofa, without looking at Johnny Lyncook.

Byron, Benny, and Marble follow Etta's lead. They each sit in a chair facing the sofa.

"Marisol!" Johnny Lyncook calls. The woman who opened the front door earlier comes into the room, wheeling a serving cart of drinks and peanuts. "Lime water," he says, and waves a hand toward the cart. There are slices of lime and a maraschino cherry floating in each drink. Marisol places a glass in front of each of them.

"You remember lime water, don't you, Bunny?" he says to Etta. "You and Covey used to love this stuff. You loved all the same things, didn't you? Always did everything together, just like sisters."

Etta shifts in her seat. "Sure, I'll try one of these," she says, reaching for her drink without looking up at him. Byron watches Etta over the rim of his glass. The charismatic woman who threw her arms around Byron when she first met him is turning into something still and cold, right before his eyes. A person capable of keeping lifelong secrets. A person harboring a well of anger. She hasn't gotten over her resentment of Johnny Lyncook, has she? Well, that makes two of them.

Etta Pringle is here because their mother asked her to take them to meet their grandfather. So here they are. But Etta is looking tight-mouthed and Byron is beginning to feel ill to his stomach. Benny and Marble, on the other hand, seem fascinated by this encounter with their mother's father. They are leaning forward as Johnny Lyncook explains who the people in the other photos are.

As if they should care.

And now, Johnny Lyncook is saying something about the olden days but Byron isn't really focusing on that. Byron has come to a decision. He's going to get up and walk out of this room. He knows he shouldn't punch out a ninety-year-old guy but he's thinking that if he stays in this room, that's exactly what he's going to do.

"You want the bathroom?" Lyncook says, when Byron stands up. "Marisol, show Byron where the bathroom is." Byron nods. He might as well make a pit stop before leaving. As he follows Marisol back across the broad marbled floor, he hears Lyncook saying, "I was big into the gambling, you know?"

Byron stops and looks back. His mother's father is leaning forward on his cane, leaning toward Benny and Marble.

"I liked to gamble and I liked to drink. That's how I lost my daughter."

Byron turns back. "Lost your daughter?" He is aware that he is raising his voice as he crosses the floor. "Did you say you lost your daughter?" He is standing over Lyncook now. "You didn't *lose* her, you threw her away. You *sold* her to a criminal."

"That is not true. It wasn't that simple," Johnny Lyncook says. "I had no choice."

"No choice!"

Byron grabs the cane from the old man's hand and flings it to the ground.

"Byron!" Benny says.

"Do you have any idea what you put your daughter through?" Byron says. "Do you know how our mother had to struggle to survive?" He turns to point at Marble. "This woman," he says, "was your daughter's first child. Do you know how your daughter ended up pregnant with her?"

"Enough, Byron," Benny says.

"Do you know what happened to her?"

"By-RON!" Benny says, raising her voice, using a tone that she has never used toward her big brother. Byron looks at Benny now, and then at Marble, who is looking at him with her brows pulled together,

her lips twisted apart. He wipes the perspiration from his nose. He shouldn't have said that, not that way. Not in front of Marble. He wants to take back what he said. He wants to take back the whole day but he can't do that, so he walks out of the room, heads straight for the front door.

Fifteen minutes later, Byron is halfway across the causeway when it occurs to him that Etta, Benny, and Marble have no car and he has all their luggage.

Shit.

Byron turns back at the end of the crossing. When he gets back to Johnny Lyncook's house, the three women are standing at the edge of the driveway like travelers waiting at the end of a dock for a ferry boat. Benny and Etta each have an arm wrapped around Marble's waist. Marisol stands at the door, watching, until they get into the car and slam the doors shut.

Unthinkable

—

BECAUSE SOME THINGS ARE UNTHINKABLE, LIN'S BRAIN WILL do what it must. It will fire a signal to block the flow of oxygen that carries unthinkable thoughts. It will flood its own backyard with blood and short-circuit the idea that is trying to push its way across Lin's cortex. It will leave Lin with only this: the memory of Covey at age ten, scrambling out of the back of his station wagon with Bunny and the neighbor kids, squealing as she rushes toward the waterfall, whooping as she crashes through the curtain of water, the sound of her laughter, and *Look at me, Pa!* mixing with the boom of the cascade and echoing off the grotto behind her.

Look at me, Pa!

When Marisol walks back into the house where she has been employed for the past ten years, she will find Lin's head tilted at a forty-five-degree angle against the hibiscus-patterned cushion on the wicker couch, one side of his face in a droop. She will check his pulse then pick up the phone and dial 911 and, as she speaks to the dispatcher on the other end of the line, she will sit down next to Lin and pat his arm.

"Hang on, Mister Lin," she will say, "they're coming to help." Then she'll lift her hands to his head, shift his hairpiece back into place, and smooth it behind his ears.

Plunder

—

LIN HAD PAID A PRIVATE INVESTIGATOR. HE HAD LEARNED almost everything about his daughter's life over the years. But until Byron's outburst in his living room, Lin did not know what had happened to Covey in Britain. He still didn't know, exactly, but he could make a fairly good guess.

The beauty of a thing justified its plunder.

And nothing was more beautiful than a girl who was fearless.

Byron

—

THEY DON'T TELL YOU HOW TO LIVE WITH THIS KIND OF ANGER, this prickly feeling under your skin. That's the thing about false narratives that ultimately define your life. When you finally learn that you've been lied to for years by the people you've trusted the most, even when you can see why they might have done it, that awareness contaminates every other relationship you have.

You begin to revisit all those actions and comments you never fully understood, the things people never said, the times you were sure that someone acted a certain way for a certain reason, only you couldn't prove it. And then you get to thinking about all the lies you've been telling yourself over the years. About how good everything's been, about how much you've been appreciated, about how much people have cared. About being friends, about being one big team, about how certain things were *just business, Byron, nothing personal at all.*

Then everything shifts.

And you can't push it back.

One day, you wake up and you find yourself standing at the mouth of something wide and howling, like the open door of an airplane, the kind you jump out of with a parachute for fun, only it's not any fun, you can't see the ground, you don't know what you're doing, but you know you're going to have to fling yourself out there and you don't know exactly where Out There is, you only know that it's where your life is going to be from now on.

Byron fishes his phone out of his jeans pocket and dials Lynette's number for the umpteenth time. This time, Lynette answers.

Consultation

—

BYRON NEEDS THE NAME OF A LAWYER, HE TELLS MR. MITCH.
A good lawyer, someone who understands workplace discrimination issues. Someone who understands issues of persistent, ingrained, institutional barriers, racial or gender or otherwise. Byron needs someone who believes that such issues should be resolved, ideally, through open dialogue but who, if absolutely necessary, is capable of landing a well-placed, legal kick in the butt.

"I need someone like you," he tells Mr. Mitch. "I need someone like my dad."

He tells Mr. Mitch how he's just been passed over for the director's position a second time. How even Marc, the colleague who's gotten the job, said Byron was the better man, hands down. Mr. Mitch listens for a long time without saying anything. Byron has noticed he's good at that.

"I'm not your man but I know someone," Mr. Mitch says, finally. "You might be able to win this. But Byron, do you really want that job?"

Byron tips his head. "I deserve that job."

Mr. Mitch nods. "You know, your colleagues are going to give you hell."

"No, they're not," Byron says. "We have our disagreements but we're a community. We're scientists. We mostly love the same things. And every scientist knows that every once in a while, if an experiment or calculation isn't giving you the result it should, you need to be willing to adjust the process, you have to be willing to take a step back and correct your mistakes." Byron puts on his best TV smile, confident with a tinge of coy. He straightens his shoulders as he leaves Mr. Mitch's office. Later, he will practice that stance in front of the mirror to convince himself.

Surf

—

THIS ONE'S A BIGGIE, THE WEATHER GAL SAYS. *STAY OFF THE ROADS if you can help it.* Byron looks out at the driveway. The trees are bending in the wind. The rain is coming down in leaden sheets. He nods at the window.

Perfect.

Byron grabs a shortboard and his helmet and plunks them into the back of his Jeep, turns on a Black Eyed Peas album and heads for Cable's house. They sit at the end of Cable's driveway discussing the pros and cons. It's a nasty storm, all right, but they've seen worse. They are, after all, SoCal guys. Byron shifts the car into drive and they head for the shore.

Byron swerves as the frond of a palm tree breaks off and flies across his windshield.

"Whoa, Byron, good save!" Cable says.

When he gets to the beach, they're all there, all the regulars, wetsuited and shiny and yelping like a pod of sea lions. One of the middle-aged guys throws a shaka at Byron and Cable, shaking his hand in the air, thumb and pinkie extended. When they were kids, it wasn't this easy to be around the others. They would get ignored. They would get threatened. Unless, of course, Byron's bombshell mother was there with them, in which case, the guys were mostly focused on her, only pretending they weren't. But time passes. And that can be a good thing.

"Oh, no, Byron," Cable says. "Not the helmet."

"Rather have fun than be toast, my man," Byron says, pulling the straps of the helmet into place. He stretches, takes a couple of deep breaths, and runs until he hits the water. He and Cable are laughing as they run, but inside, Byron is burning up. He doesn't know what else to do with all of this anger. It's as if everything that has been bugging him for years has been piling up inside like tinder, and his mother's death, and everything else that's happened in the past couple of months, has just struck a match.

It's a little dicey out here but he'll work with the waves until he begins to feel more like his old self again. Because this is who he is. He was born to surf the waves. He was born to listen to the ocean. This, more than anything, is what he has inherited from his mother, this visceral connection to the sea.

There it is, he's in the zone. Back to the top of the wave and then down. Back and then down. Byron slips into a long, still moment in his head where he sees that whoever else his mother was in her lifetime, no matter her name or address, she has always been part of this world and always will be. And this is the one place where he knows he can always come to find her.

Director

___

Byron raps on the open door of the new director's office. The two of them have been colleagues for fifteen years now. Of the two, Byron has the higher qualifications by far, a sounder track record and better people skills, but Marc is very good at political maneuvering, which Byron admits is a necessary skill in this job.

"I need to let you know something, for the record," Byron begins.

"If you're here about the failure-to-promote claim," Marc says, "I already know that you went to see a lawyer." He jabs a finger at Byron. "What the fuck do you think you're doing, Byron?"

"Hey, Marc, it's nothing personal."

"Nothing personal?" Marc walks out from behind his desk and comes up to Byron. "Nothing personal? You don't get to go after a job that I've been given and say it's not personal."

"I'm sorry you feel this way, Marcus. In fact, I wanted to acknowledge what was happening, out of professional respect, out of appreciation for our years of work together. Why don't we just carry on, business as usual, and let the bureaucratic process play itself out. Then we'll see what happens."

"Fuck you, Byron," Marc says.

"Whoa! Hold on, there."

Marc lunges for Byron but someone is rapping on the door. He straightens up and pulls the door open. Byron's assistant is holding his cellphone in her hand. He must have left it on his desk.

"Sorry, Byron, but someone keeps calling and calling," she says.

It's Lynette's sister, Jackson's mother.

"Hurry, Byron," she says. "It's Lynette. We're at the hospital."

Baby

T
HE SOUND OF THE BABY'S WAIL CUTS THROUGH THE MURMURS
in the hospital room. A nurse wheels the infant into the room.

Lynette reaches out her arms. "There you are, little one," she says.

The baby is still easing out of his peevishness, his mouth turned
down in a way that reminds Byron of Benny when she was a newborn.
The first time he held his little sister, she twitched and snuffled and
latched on to one of his knuckles with her mouth. Then, at the sound
of his voice, her mouth pulled to the side in that way that both she and
Byron had inherited from their mother.

Byron watches the boy now, his face half-hidden under Lynette's
smock as he feeds.

"Who's my little one?" Lynette says, nuzzling her face against his
head. "Who's my Baby By?" She says she's decided to name the baby
after Byron. Byron isn't sure how things will work out between Lynette and him, but when she told him about the baby's name, Byron felt
a click, the unlatching of something small inside, the swinging open of
a door.

He watches Lynette and thinks of his ma, of the last words on her
recording.

Who I am is your mother. This is the truest part of me.

Byron and Lynette will have to talk some more. Then they'll see.
Lynette calls Byron over and holds the baby up to him. Nothing in his

life has quite prepared him for this kind of feeling, not even holding little Benny in his arms when he was nine years old.

"Hey, you," Byron says. He lifts the baby up to his face and puts his lips against his forehead. His son releases a hiccuppy sound filled with milk. *His son!* Then Baby By follows his voice with his head, eyes scrunched shut, and a tiny, lopsided mouth, the sight of which causes Byron to catch his breath.

Benny

—

THE BAD NEWS IS, BENNY HAS BEEN TURNED DOWN, AGAIN, FOR a bank loan. She won't risk opening a café without the financing. But she won't give up, she'll try another bank. The good news is, she keeps getting commissions for her artwork, and the one she did of Etta Pringle has gone viral. It shows Etta swimming through boiling seas dotted with plastic parts. Not the cheeriest of material, but that was what Etta wanted. And her online followers love it. Well, some of them hate it, actually, but Etta says that's a good thing, too. Benny's not really into social media, but Etta says that'll have to change.

Benny is perplexed by this turn of events in her life.

Nothing is going quite the way she expected.

But she doesn't mind all that much.

Marble

———

Giò WANTS TO SPEND HIS LAST SUMMER BEFORE UNIVER-
sity with Marble.

"Let's go to California," her son says. "Didn't you promise to take
me to meet my secret aunt and uncle?" Because this is what he has
called Byron and Benny, ever since Marble sat Giò down to tell him
about her birth mother and the siblings she has never known.

It really is like a scene from one of those films. Marble's mobile
phone rings before she and Giò even get off the plane from London.
Byron and Benny are that impatient to see them. And there they are,
standing outside the Arrivals exit. Benny is holding a piece of cardboard with the words *WELCOME, GIOVANNI!* written across it and
she is bouncing up and down like a schoolgirl.

Marble already knows that later that summer, after she and Giò get
back to Italy, she will let the dog out and follow him down to the next
giardinetto and bang on the door of the neighbor boy who watches him
for her. And she will finally be able to say his name, which is the same
as her son's. And he will kiss her son on both cheeks and say, "*Ciao,
Giò,*" and her son will say, "*Ehi,*" and they will stand there, saying
nothing, really, in that wonderful way that teenagers have of not making conversation.

Answers

—

CHARLES MITCH OPENS THE REPORT AND READS IT. THANKS to new information provided by Pearl, Charles has been able to look into the whereabouts of Eleanor's mother, Mathilda Brown.

Covey's *Mummy*.

Pearl insists that Mathilda had always intended to go back for her daughter. She says something must have gone wrong. And now Charles is pretty sure he knows what happened.

Mathilda,
1961

—

I T WAS A BEAUTIFUL THING, DEEPER AND BROADER THAN ANY-thing Mathilda had ever seen. She stood at the edge of the thundering falls and breathed in the cool air, felt the light spray on her skin, drew courage from the power of this place. She had read that this waterfall was one of the wonders of the world. But nothing had prepared her for being here. Nothing had prepared her for the wide open spaces of North America. The bigness of it all.

Mathilda leaned over the railing, smelling the moist wood, the silty earth, the sun on her skin. She had made it this far. She would challenge Lin, she would find a way to get Covey from him and bring her daughter up here to live. She'd come over as a domestic worker, it was the only way, and the wages were low. But it was a start.

She needed to get a message to Pearl, let her know that things were going well, find out how Covey was doing. They couldn't afford to tell Covey that they were in contact. Covey was too young, she couldn't be expected to keep a secret like that to herself. *Give Covey a hug for me every day,* she'd said to Pearl the day before she left.

It would be a long time before they found Mathilda, years after she'd slipped and fallen. By then, her wallet would have been pulled from her purse by the currents under the rush of the falls. By then, her employer, unable to locate her, would have given her job to someone else. By then, the police would have filed away the case. A missing col-ored girl? They had more important things to deal with.

Back then, things were different. Less sophisticated tissue testing. No computerized searches. It was easy for the case of a Jane Doe skeleton, found in the mud near a bend in the river, to go unresolved until decades later, when a California lawyer renewed the search for a certain Mathilda Brown, a young immigrant from the islands last seen in an American city near the Canadian border in the spring of 1961.

Etta
Pringle

THE AUDIENCE APPLAUDS AS ETTA PRINGLE KICKS OFF HER SHOES
and strides across the stage. It's actually become a meme on the Internet, this trademark move of hers. She laughed the first time she saw
that snippet of video repeated over and over again, an image of her
feet, flinging off her shoes. The things people think of.

This is her last public appearance before the fundraising swim tomorrow. This one will be ten or so miles, depending on the currents,
not much of a distance for her, even at her age. Even with all that
medicine in her body. But it's a challenging crossing for other reasons.
Poisonous jellies, for starters.

The news reports and social media will talk about jellyfish, they will
mention her age, they will talk about the advantages that mature women
have in endurance sports. They will mention her color. They still do,
after all these years, even in 2019, and that's fine with Etta. Let them see
her. *Let them see her!* No one will talk about Etta's illness, they don't
know about that yet. With any luck, they won't, ever.

Etta will have to work to keep the focus on broader concerns. This
is why she is here tonight, to talk about the environment. She fears an
easy narrative, one in which the responsibility for environmental degradation is placed solely on the shoulders of private industry without
driving home the direct connection to consumer demand for minerals
and other resources. She will talk about sustainability. About the need

to hold on to some sort of balance in nature. She will urge people to insist on a more circular economy.

Byron Bennett is already on stage. As the head of a new consulting firm, Byron will talk about the importance of mapping the seafloor. He will explain how countries, industry, and international bodies work together to share information. He will talk about his own love of the sea and his childhood on the California coast. Byron will say that knowledge is power and Etta will say, "My point, exactly, but what kind of power?"

They will argue onstage and it will please Etta immensely to do so, to appear in public with the brilliant son of her childhood friend. She will feel proud, as if she had watched him grow up all these years when she was, instead, unaware of his existence, unaware that his mother was still alive and watching Etta's every move. Later, Byron will explain to Etta why he left the institute he used to work with, and how the out-of-court settlement helped him start a new venture of his own and seed a scholarship fund. And Etta will think, *Well done, Covey, look at your son.*

They won't mention Byron's mother, who helped to make Etta the champion that she is, who first introduced her to open-water swimming. He and his sisters have agreed that their public narratives must never connect them to Coventina Lyncook. Perhaps one day, when they are older, when their children are grown, they say, but Etta suspects that it is only a matter of time before someone who knew Gibbs or Covey recognizes something of them in the faces of Covey's children. Byron and Marble are all over the Internet now, and the Internet is what the street market back on the island used to be. Sooner or later, you run into everyone.

Etta looks offstage to where Byron's girlfriend is standing, their son snug in a carrier against her chest. She marvels that they have brought the child all the way to Polynesia from California at this tender age. Modern jet travel corrupts all reason. Etta has never been the image of prudence as an athlete but as a young mother, she was quite careful with the kids, always insisting on keeping them close to home until a certain age. Which suited Patsy just fine.

Etta is swimming for her children now, and for their children, too, not for the records. She uses every chance she can to talk about the health of the oceans. Seafloor damage, runoff, plastics, rising water temperatures, overfishing. She calls for the designation of additional protected zones. But she also takes the time to show the audience old photos of herself as a girl in a swim cap, plus her favorite snapshots of Patsy and the boys when they were little, poking around a tide pool in Wales, their shoes clumped with wet sand. She never forgets to show the joy, to show the love. Because, otherwise, what would be the point of anything?

Survival is not enough. Survival has never been enough.

Funny to think that after more than sixty years of distance swimming, Etta is still a bit nervous about what lies under the water, still hypervigilant of the symphony of life below. But this is what she is fighting for, for the preservation of life in all its vibrant and venomous and toothy mystery.

Her doctor grumbles. She says Etta can't afford to get stung or cut right now with her immune system being so low. But Etta isn't aiming to get hurt. She promises she'll do everything to avoid it, except stay out of the water, of course. This is who she is. This is how she lives.

Etta could say to herself that she has raised two kind and useful children, that she has already done the most important thing a person could do, but she knows that this is not enough for her. When she was just a girl, Etta used to think that she deserved all the good things that came her way. She didn't see why she should have to dream smaller dreams than other people, just because she was a girl from the islands. That hasn't changed but with every passing year, she realizes just how fortunate she's been. Things could have gone very differently for Etta Pringle, and she still has a debt to pay back to the world.

Lin

—

MARISOL BRINGS LIN A GLASS OF ICED TEA. LIN IS BACK TO drinking and eating on his own after his most recent stroke, and he can walk around using only the cane. He leans back against the sofa and watches Etta Pringle on the television news. Bunny Pringle. The girl must be more than seventy years old now, and she's still doing those harebrained swims.

Lin should have known it would come to this. He should have known the day he saw Bunny and Covey swimming in the midst of that tropical storm back in 1963. Should have realized that if you were capable of going that far, in that kind of water, if you would take that kind of risk, then maybe you weren't like other people. Probably, there was a lot that you would be willing to do to get what you wanted, that others wouldn't dare to try.

*T*HEN

—

*One
Summer
Night*

—

Ｏ NE SUMMER NIGHT IN 1965, BUNNY HEARD SOMEONE RAPPING at her bedroom window. Her parents were already asleep. She opened the louvers just enough to peer out and saw Covey standing there in the dark, her mouth wide open in a silent cry. Bunny ran outside.

"What?" Bunny whispered. "What?"

Covey wouldn't speak. She was trembling. Bunny had never seen her friend like this. This was Coventina Lyncook, after all. The one they'd nicknamed Dolphin. She had swum through squalls, jumped over vipers, ignored the gossip about her parents. Bunny knew that Covey could face anything. Only Covey had not yet told her about Little Man.

As Bunny hugged Covey, as Covey wept and started to talk, Bunny felt the full weight of their girlhood crashing down on them. Bunny and Covey had grown up believing that anything was possible, even for them. But when you were a girl, people could tell you how to walk, how to sit, how to talk, what to do, where to go, how to think, who to love.

And who to obey.

Pearl,
1965

———

On his daughter's wedding day, Mister Lin had gotten drunk even quicker than usual.

"You still in the kitchen, Pearl?" he said. He gestured vaguely toward the table in the reception hall where Pearl had been seated, on and off, unable to take more than the obligatory bite of food. "Come, sit down and have some cake with us. It's your cake."

"Just a moment, Mister Lin, I'll be right there," Pearl said, turning back to the kitchen. "There's something I need to take care of first." There was something that Pearl needed to find.

Glancing this way and that at the hotel staff, Pearl hurried toward the counter, where the cake had been resting before being wheeled into the reception hall. Nothing. She reached down to the shelf below where her apron lay and lifted to check underneath. Nothing. She crouched down to take a better look but still couldn't find what she was looking for, the small bottle she'd shoved behind a mixing bowl earlier that day. It needed to be kept far away from the food. This was not her kitchen, nor Mister Lin's, she was merely a guest here. Any number of people could have come along and moved things around.

The sound of a fork going *ting-ting-ting* against a glass and the clearing of a throat against a microphone brought Pearl back to her feet. She smoothed her dress and moved toward the reception hall with what she hoped would look like a confident stride. Someone must have found the container and moved it into a cupboard or locker, wherever they kept things like that. Things like laundry soap, bleach, rat poison. The container was clearly marked. Pearl told herself not to worry.

But, later, Pearl would indeed find herself worrying. For years, she would ask herself what had happened to that bottle of poison. Surely, someone there had seen it, someone had moved it. And, probably, someone had used it. But who? The police had found something in Little Man's champagne glass. Thank goodness they hadn't found anything in the cake or Pearl would have ended up in prison for something she hadn't even had the courage to do.

Pearl had thought so long and hard about harming Little Man that she would go on to spend the rest of her life feeling some measure of guilt about his death.

But never sorrow.

The
Moment

THE BIGGEST MOMENTS IN OUR LIVES ARE OFTEN JUST THAT, A matter of seconds when something shifts and we react and everything changes. Covey had been going through the wedding reception in a kind of stupor, but when she saw Little Man collapse on the floor of the reception hall on the day that she'd been made to marry him, her head began to clear. Covey looked up in four directions, and this became her decisive moment.

First, Covey looked for her father. There he was, just behind her, mouth open. Then she searched for Pearl, who was on the far side of the room, moving quickly toward the commotion. Now she looked at Bunny, who was only a few paces away. Of these three people, only one of them was looking back at Covey as Little Man took his final breaths. Only one of them held her gaze while everyone else focused on the dying man. And that was when Covey knew. Covey had seen what had happened, she just hadn't understood its significance. Now she turned in a fourth direction, toward the sliding glass door that opened out onto the back lawn of the hotel.

The door was just a few feet away. The lawn sloped off onto a path that led down to the shore, at one point running alongside a series of broad, stone steps where tadpoles were hatching and growing in pools of water that had gathered there. Covey's mummy used to stop at these steps to show her the tadpoles. They matured at different rates, so that some were still wriggling around like tiny fish, while others were already sprouting the first stubs of their little frog legs and taking on a boxy look about their bodies until, soon, they would be ready to leap into the bushes and lunge toward the rest of their lives.

As Covey ran through the door, as she stumbled and lost her shoes on the lawn, as she pulled her wedding dress away from her body and left it on the sand, she vowed that she would go to her grave without revealing what she had seen. As a child, she had been taught right from wrong, but even then, she had understood that you couldn't always separate the two.

Covey never did tell the truth, not in the letters and recordings she'd left for her children at the end of her life, not in her conversations with her lawyer and lover, not in the muggy comfort of her marital bed. Even when she'd dreamed of returning to the island to show her children where she had come from, she knew in her heart that she could never go back because she would never be able to clear her name.

Those four decades of marriage to a man whom she had loved and who had given her two of her children had been an enormous gift. If you had been blessed with such a life, if someone else had taken such a great risk to help you, what would you have been willing to do?

More than fifty years later, Covey's children will dare to ask the question outright. They will ask their mother's oldest friend if she thinks that Covey Lyncook killed Little Man Henry in 1965. They will be relieved to see Bunny Pringle shake her head, slowly and firmly. Relieved to hear Bunny say that there were any number of people who had wanted to see Little Man dead. They will realize, also, that Bunny's answer had not brought them any closer to the truth of what had happened on that day.

Back Then

———

Back THEN, THERE WERE NO VIDEO SURVEILLANCE CAMERAS. The wedding photographer was off in a corner changing his film. The music men were busy making music. The waiters were still delivering plates of cake to some of the tables. The father of the bride was finishing yet another drink. The bride was stabbing at her cake with a fork, trying not to cry. Everyone was busy looking somewhere else as one of the guests pulled a small bottle out of her purse.

Back then, everyone knew that champagne could go to a young lady's head. That she might wander from one table to another with a glass in her hand, that she might lean in between the newly married couple and deposit a kiss on her friend's cheek, that she might rest her glass on the table, that she might knock a plate of cake onto the bride's lap then accidentally pick up the bridegroom's flute instead of her own. No one would think anything of this because, out of the water, Bunny Pringle had always been a clumsy girl.

No one would even realize, at first, that it had been a glass of champagne to bring an end to Little Man's life. When a police officer finally sniffed at the broken flute and uttered the word *poison*, some of the wedding guests would think of their own secret wishes, their own deep resentment toward the dead man. Toward the kind of man who drew satisfaction from the coercion of others. They would hope that the person who had done this would never be caught. So many people had been in and out of the kitchen that day, it could have been any number of them.

Back then, it was easier to commit murder. You only had to concentrate, know where your loyalties lay, and not think of the consequences.

Now

—

Rest in Peace

—

"**I**SN'T THERE SOME KIND OF LAW AGAINST DIGGING UP bodies?"

"But it's our father."

"Would it be different because they're ashes?"

"Let's ask Charles. He'll know."

It has taken a while, but Byron and Benny have finally grown accustomed to calling Mr. Mitch by his first name. Charles is, after all, someone their mother cared for deeply. And he knows more about their lives than most people ever will. Plus, his nose turned pink the first time Benny called him Charles. That alone made it worth the switch, Byron said that day, laughing.

Yes, Charles tells them, they will need a license, but there are services that can help. They're not the first to make this kind of decision. Eventually, Byron and Benny get permission to exhume their father's remains.

One year after Eleanor Bennett's death, Marble and Etta fly in together from London. The next day, Benny and Marble chop scallion and garlic and stir coconut milk into a pot of rice and beans. Byron fires up the barbecue and Etta makes a sweet rum punch that goes down a bit too easily, while Lynette dances with their baby on the deck at their beachside place. It is the kind of lunch that gathers people as the hours go on, Charles and one of his daughters, Cable and his wife and kids, plus the neighbors from across the way.

The old house, the bungalow where Byron and Benny grew up, belongs to another family now, a young couple with small children who have put in new plumbing. It seems a fitting role for the old Bennett house, to grow a new family, and the thought makes Byron smile. Still, he tries not to drive down that street if he can help it.

When Etta is sufficiently tipsy, Eleanor's children extract a promise from her. Yes, she says, she will take them all to the island someday. They can work on a plan. They, their partners and children, even Charles, if he wants to. Surely, enough time has passed between *now* and *then*, they say, though none of them is certain.

But first, this.

Eleanor's children are taking her ashes, now mingled with those of Byron and Benny's father, out to sea. Etta swims out ahead of the boat, her neon-colored cap the same orange as the inflatable buoy strapped to her body. Once they've gone three miles off the coast, they drop the ladder and pull Etta out of the water, throwing a towel around her. They stand there for a moment, listening to the creak of the boat against the waves before they nod at one another and scatter the ashes overboard. Then Marble, Byron, and Benny take what's left of their mother's last black cake, crumble it, and let it fall into the water.

Author's Note

NOT EVERYONE SITS DOWN TO WRITE A BOOK BUT EVERYONE is a storyteller, in one form or other. As I wrote this novel, a lifetime of anecdotes and fleeting impressions shared by the Caribbean members of my multicultural family helped me to develop some of the fictional characters and scenarios from the 1950s and 1960s. The scenes from the unnamed island in the Caribbean reflect some of the geography and history of Jamaica, where my parents and other relatives lived before emigrating to the United Kingdom and the United States. The fictional town where members of the book's older generation grew up is inspired by the northeast coast of that island and uses a mix of actual and invented locations.

Most of the characters in *Black Cake* are people who do not quite fit into the boxes that others have set up for them. They struggle against stereotypes and the gulf between their interests and ambitions and the lives that other people expect them to lead, based on gender, culture, or class. Their difficulties are both universal and specific to the times and places in which they live.

In the process of writing, I read articles and historical accounts from journalists, scholars, and online archives such as those from the National Library of Jamaica and the National Archives and the British Library in the UK. I found interesting online posts by people who identify with Caribbean and British culture, and discussions of the Chinese diaspora by institutions like the Chinese American Museum in Los

Angeles. I have peered at countless photographs, videos, maps, and recipes.

The backdrop for the older generation in the story includes reference to inter-ethnic tensions involving Chinese immigrants and their families in Jamaica in the 1960s. It also takes into account some of the difficulties faced by Caribbean immigrants identified as black or "colored" in the UK during the same period. I found the research process eye-opening.

I was aware, for example, that many Chinese immigrants who came to the Caribbean as indentured servants from the mid-1800s to the early 1900s had faced harsh labor conditions and significant poverty before greatly improving their economic circumstances. I did not realize, however, that despite representing only a tiny fraction of the population in Jamaica in the mid-1960s, Chinese or Chinese-Jamaican businesspeople had come to own a majority of the shops and other businesses in that country. This relative prosperity burgeoned at a time of increasing disillusionment among other Jamaicans, most of whom were of African descent and many of whom were feeling the weight of job shortages, class distinctions, and colorism in their postcolonial society. The novel's depictions of violence and riots targeting Chinese-owned businesses were fictional but inspired by real-life conflict from that period.

I knew that immigrants from the Caribbean and other Commonwealth nations were actively recruited to study nursing and work in other sectors in the UK in the post–World War II years. But until I had read firsthand accounts of immigrants, I was unaware of the extent to which some Caribbean trainees and employees found themselves harassed, discriminated against, and limited in work opportunities within their professional fields.

It was my personal familiarity with a particular Caribbean food, black cake, that led obliquely to this book. It started me thinking about the emotional weight carried by recipes and other familial markers that are handed down from one generation to the next. Then it had me writing about characters who must hold fast to their sense of self when they learn that their lives have been built on a dubious narrative.

Despite the use of some historical and present-day context, this narrative focuses primarily on the emotional lives of the invented characters and is meant to be fable-like in its recounting of some of its main events. For fictional stories more deeply rooted in the political and social discourse of multicultural lives in various Caribbean countries and the Caribbean diaspora in the mid- to late twentieth century, I would like to remind readers that there are a number of wonderful authors to turn to, such as Edwidge Danticat, Marlon James, and Jamaica Kincaid.

I would like to recommend also a few books that I discovered while finalizing this book: The novel *Pao* by Kerry Young and the nonfiction account *Finding Samuel Lowe: China, Jamaica, Harlem* by Paula Williams Madison offer different but fascinating insights into the Chinese Caribbean experience. In a related note, I would like to mention Jamaican-born producer and director Jeanette Kong, who did a film based on Williams Madison's book and other documentaries on this aspect of Caribbean life.

The Lonely Londoners by Sam Selvon and, more recently, *Small Island* by Andrea Levy do a delightful job of bringing to life some of the nuances of ethnic relations in Jamaica and the Caribbean-UK immigrant experience in the post–World War II years. I also found *The Windrush Betrayal* by British journalist Amelia Gentleman to be useful in capturing the sense of dual identity that many Caribbean members of the Commonwealth felt as they settled into new lives in the UK. This is by no means an exhaustive list and I encourage readers to continue their own exploration of these topics.

Even when stories are made up, they typically contain emotional truths. It is my hope that the emotional notes in this story will resonate with people of various backgrounds who have thought about shifting concepts of home and family, about longing, loss, and second chances and, of course, love.

Acknowledgments

IF IT TAKES A VILLAGE TO RAISE A CHILD, THEN THE SAME MIGHT be said for this book. I am happily indebted to Madeleine Milburn who, together with her talented team of literary agents and assistants, opened a series of doors that ultimately led to publication. Many thanks to editors Jessica Leeke and Hilary Rubin Teeman for embracing this novel with open hearts, questioning minds, and discerning eyes, and to everyone at Penguin Michael Joseph and Ballantine who nurtured and nudged this project out into the world. A special thank-you to those who have encouraged me along the way: my family, GR, and my bookworm friends, some of whom took the time to read through the early pages of this novel. Finally, a shout-out to my fellow writers, including the brilliant ArmadillHers, who inspire me daily with their love of stories and life and their concern for our world.

BLACK CAKE

CHARMAINE WILKERSON

Random House Book Club

Because Stories Are Better Shared

™

A BOOK CLUB GUIDE

A Letter from the Author

Dear Reader,

Long before I started writing *Black Cake*, my mother sent me the recipe for her legendary fruitcake. I didn't know it at the time but that recipe, scribbled in pencil on lined notebook paper and mailed from New York to California, would later inspire the title of my first novel.

I hadn't looked at my mother's note for quite a while when a younger member of my family texted me on my smartphone to ask for the recipe. He was about to be married and had my mother still been alive, she surely would have made him a black cake for his wedding reception. It was a tradition in Jamaica, where my mother had grown up.

That episode started me thinking about the cultural markers that people inherit and how we choose to hold some symbols closer to our hearts than others, especially in a multicultural family like mine. Still, it was never my intention to write a book with a cake in it.

Initially, my thoughts about food, diaspora, and identity were just a few paragraphs in a personal journal. Then I found myself circling these ongoing thoughts in a series of fictional scenes which I kept writing and filing away in my laptop. At some point, I realized that the characters in these stories were connected to one another. The novel had begun to take shape. Then the black cake simply popped up one day in the narrative and insisted on having its own story.

By the time I finished the book, the cake had come to symbolize various things: family connections, sisterhood, diaspora, and nostalgia. It also represented the ways in which our identities can be shaped as much by untold stories as by the stories we choose to share. Like the hidden reasons behind the cake in Eleanor Bennett's freezer.

Charmaine Wilkerson

Questions and Topics for Discussion

1.   What was your favorite part of the story? Favorite location and time period? The character who interested you the most?

2.   Black cake was a Bennett family recipe, made for weddings, anniversaries, Christmas, and other special occasions. Do you have a traditional family recipe? What does it mean to you?

3.   In *Black Cake*, Eleanor Bennett leaves her children a voice recording, disclosing the story of her life. What was the most surprising part of her past for you? The saddest? The most interesting?

4.   Secrets are a huge part of the novel. Why do you think Eleanor kept her story from her children for so long and only shared it posthumously? Which do you think is more complicated: the secrets you keep or the secrets you share?

5.   Eleanor wanted Mr. Mitch, Benny, and Byron to listen together to the voice message she left behind. Why do you think she specifically made this request? What would have been different if Benny and Byron had each listened to everything separately?

6.   What are your thoughts on Benny and Byron's relationship? Why was it complicated? How did they grow apart after being so close? If you have siblings, did you understand the push and pull of their relationship?

7.   Why do you think Bert and Eleanor disagreed with Benny's life choices? Do you think they were wrong to be so hard on her? Why or why not?

8.   When Bert was too stubborn to apologize to Benny, Eleanor stayed by his side out of loyalty. Do you think she made the right decision? Why or why not?

9. While listening to the recording, Benny and Byron discover that Eleanor kept a secret from Bert for their entire life together. What do you think of Eleanor's choice to keep that secret? How do you think Bert would have responded if she had told him the truth?

10. Even though Lin had run a business and raised a family on the island, he was still seen as an outsider. Why do you think that is?

11. "The thing about identity. There's your family history, there's how you see yourself, and then there's what others see in you." How is this statement true for each of the characters in the novel?

12. Forgiveness is also a major theme in the novel. Eleanor struggles to forgive herself, Marble to forgive her parents, Benny to forgive her family, Byron to forgive Lin. Do you find any of the characters' actions to be unforgivable? Why or why not?

Eleanor's Black Cake Recipe

Quantities are approximate. Eleanor never did write them down.

INGREDIENTS:

- 12 ounces flour
- 4 ounces breadcrumbs
- 1 teaspoon baking powder
- ½ teaspoon baking soda
- 1 or ½ teaspoon salt
- 1 teaspoon mixed spice (cinnamon, nutmeg, cloves)
- 1 pound dark brown sugar (plus extra for the blacking)
- 2 teaspoons vanilla
- 1 pound butter (4 sticks), at room temperature
- 12 eggs
- 5 to 6 cups dried fruit (raisins, prunes, currants),
  soaked at least 4 months in white or dark rum and port to
  cover. If using, dates and maraschino cherries should only be
  added at mixing time.

INSTRUCTIONS:

Preheat the oven to 350°F.

Add all the dry ingredients to a bowl and blend. In a separate bowl, rub together the sugar and butter, or use a mixer on low, until smooth and fluffy. Add vanilla. Add 1 egg, mix 1-1 ½ minutes, add 1 ⅓ ounces flour-breadcrumbs mixture. Repeat until all eggs and flour are gone. Mix in the blacking. Make the blacking by melting brown sugar in a saucepan over low heat until it is caramelized. You will need more than you think! Puree half the fruits in a blender. Combine and add to the batter. Grease two cake tins. Cut wax paper circles to line the bottoms of the tins. Pour in the batter until the tins are three-quarters full.

To BAKE: Place the tins on the middle rack of the oven. Place a separate pan filled with tap water on the rack beneath. Bake for 1 to 2 hours, until the cake starts to pull away from the side of the pan and a knife inserted into the middle comes out dry. Depends on oven, tin size, and weather.

A Playlist Inspired by Black Cake

The text in the parentheses are the author's insights into the characters and why she chose these songs for them.

"Take Her to Jamaica"—Lord Messam (Mathilda and Pearl in the kitchen)

"Cheek to Cheek"—Ella Fitzgerald and Louis Armstrong (Mathilda dancing)

"Many Rivers to Cross"—Jimmy Cliff (Covey alone. Lin alone. Etta Pringle alone.)

"It's My Life"—Bon Jovi (Byron)

"It's My Life" (acoustic version)—Bon Jovi (Benny)

"Pump It"—Black Eyed Peas (Byron going surfing in the storm)

"Dance Me to the End of Love"—Leonard Cohen (Benny and Steve)

"Isis und Osiris" (from *The Magic Flute*)—René Pape (Benny and Steve)

"True Colors"—Cyndi Lauper (Benny and Joanie)

"Can't Stop"—Red Hot Chili Peppers (Byron and Eleanor surfing as adults. Etta in the water.)

"Calypso Queen"—Calypso Rose (Etta Pringle late in her career)

"The Greatest"—Sia (Benny in distress)

"I Want to Know What Love Is"—Mariah Carey (Benny thinking of her mother. Byron holding his son.)

"Good as Hell" (feat. Ariana Grande)—Lizzo (Benny)

"High Hopes"—Panic! At the Disco (Benny)

"Sweet and Dandy" (1968 Release)—The Maytals (Happier times)

"Hold Me Tight"—Johnny Nash (Bunny and Patsy)

"Family Affair"—Mary J. Blige (Byron's backyard gathering)

"Diamonds"—Rihanna (Etta Pringle swimming)

"Gli Ostacoli del Cuore" ("Obstacles of the Heart")—Elisa (with Ligabue) (Unrevealed secrets, relationships ". . . so many things you don't know about me . . . so many things to carry in this journey together. . . .")

CHARMAINE WILKERSON is an American writer who has lived in Jamaica and is based in Italy. A graduate of Barnard College and Stanford University, she is a former journalist whose award-winning short fiction has appeared in various magazines and anthologies. *Black Cake* is her first novel.

This book was set in Fournier, a typeface named for Pierre-Simon Fournier (1712–68), the youngest son of a French printing family. He started out engraving woodblocks and large capitals, then moved on to fonts of type. In 1736 he began his own foundry and made several important contributions in the field of type design; he is said to have cut 147 alphabets of his own creation. Fournier is probably best remembered as the designer of St. Augustine Ordinaire, a face that served as the model for the Monotype Corporation's Fournier, which was released in 1925.

RANDOM HOUSE BOOK CLUB

Because Stories Are Better Shared

Discover

Exciting new books that spark conversation every week.

Connect

With authors on tour—or in your living room. (Request an Author Chat for your book club!)

Discuss

Stories that move you with fellow book lovers on Facebook, on Goodreads, or at in-person meet-ups.

Enhance

Your reading experience with discussion prompts, digital book club kits, and more, available on our website.

Join our online book club community!

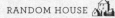 randomhousebookclub.com

Random House Book Club ™

Because Stories Are Better Shared

RANDOM HOUSE